A Specter Raps on My Windowpane:
A Noir Urban Fantasy Novel

This is a work of fiction. Names, characters, organizations, places, events, and incidents are either products of the author's imagination or are used fictitiously. Any resemblance to actual persons, living or dead, or actual events is purely coincidental.

Copyright © 2023 by Douglas Lumsden
All rights reserved.
ISBN: 9798874231231

No part of this book may be reproduced, or stored in a retrieval system, or transmitted in any form or by any means, electronic, mechanical, photocopying, recording, or otherwise, without express written permission of the publisher.

Cover design and art by Arash Jahani (www.arashjahani.com)

A Specter Raps on My Windowpane:
A Noir Urban Fantasy Novel

By

Douglas Lumsden

To Rita. Always.

Books in this Series

Alexander Southerland, P.I.

Book One: *A Troll Walks into a Bar*

Book Two: *A Witch Steps into My Office*

Book Three: *A Hag Rises from the Abyss*

Book Four: *A Night Owl Slips into a Diner*

(Standalone Novella): *The Demon's Dagger*

Book Five: *A Nymph Returns to the Sea*

Book Six: *The Blood Moon Feeds on My Dreams*

Book Seven: *A Specter Raps on My Windowpane*

Table of Contents

Chapter One 1
Chapter Two 13
Chapter Three 25
Chapter Four 33
Chapter Five 41
Chapter Six 51
Chapter Seven 61
Chapter Eight 67
Chapter Nine 75
Chapter Ten 83
Chapter Eleven 93
Chapter Twelve 105
Chapter Thirteen 113
Chapter Fourteen 123
Chapter Fifteen 133
Chapter Sixteen 143
Chapter Seventeen 151
Chapter Eighteen 161
Chapter Nineteen 171
Chapter Twenty 179
Chapter Twenty-One 187
Chapter Twenty-Two 195
Chapter Twenty-Three 207
Chapter Twenty-Four 215
Chapter Twenty-Five 225

Chapter Twenty-Six 233
Chapter Twenty-Seven 243
Chapter Twenty-Eight.. 253
Chapter Twenty-Nine 261
Chapter Thirty..271
Chapter Thirty-One.. 279
Chapter Thirty-Two 289
Chapter Thirty-Three... 301
Chapter Thirty-Four 309
Epilogue: Benedict Shade 319
Acknowledgements 325
About the Author 327

Chapter One

I woke with a smile on my face and the scent of Mrs. Shipper's perfume tickling my nose. The smile faded when I remembered she was dead. The scent, as real as a dream, lingered for another minute, tantalizing me with unlikely possibilities, until it too faded, swept away by slowly emerging rationality. Almost fully awake, I rolled out of bed with a groan and stumbled into a lukewarm shower.

When I'd discovered several weeks earlier that Cindy Shipper had married into the Hatfield family, I'd known right away that I'd have to investigate the cause of her death. Off the top of my head, I could think of a dozen reasons why I shouldn't, and why doing it anyway would make me a hundred different kinds of stupid. That was jake with me. I've always said that persistence takes you farther down life's highway than intelligence. And I was every kind of persistent.

I'd already made a few inquiries, but other priorities, such as earning enough dough for food and rent, insisted on stalling my efforts. It didn't help that I hadn't had a case in more than a month, and my client in that one had died before she could pay me. That case had come to me by way of my new website, but the site hadn't generated anything since. Nothing had come in over the phone, either, and hardly anyone ever walks in from the streets through a private dick's front door anymore. Word of mouth was failing me big time. Rob Lubank, the attorney who provided me with my most lucrative cases, told me he had nothing going on at the moment, and, anyway, anything he'd get for me would go toward paying off the debt I already owed him for representing me during my last case. My checking account was down to two figures, and I'd been running up a debt on my credit card. The end of the month was only days away, and my rent wouldn't pay itself. And, to top it off, I was down to my last six-pack of beer.

On the plus side of the ledger, I had a full jar of peanut butter, half a box of frozen waffles, enough coffee to last me for at least a week, three-quarters of a tank of gas in my car, and plenty of free time. With nothing standing in my way, I decided it was time to find out once and for all how the former Mrs. Shipper had died, and why. The one-man firm of Alexander Southerland, Private Investigator, had a hot new case, even if I didn't have a paying client. Oh well, it wouldn't be the first time.

I first met Cindy Shipper after the spectacular murder of her husband, Donald Shipper, a prominent mortgage banking executive. Something had sparked between us then, I think, but circumstances prevented us from fanning those flames. I still didn't know the degree to which she might have been involved in her husband's untimely demise, although I had my suspicions. I was convinced that she'd orchestrated the death of her stepson, too, although prosecutors hadn't been able to build a case with enough stick to impress a judge. In the end, not only had she evaded all charges, but she'd outmaneuvered her stepdaughter and walked away with most of her late husband's fortune. Clever dame. I hadn't run into her since the resolution of those cases. Not in the flesh, anyway.

The last time I'd seen Mrs. Shipper alive was when she'd given me a goodbye kiss as I was walking out her door. The next time I saw her was when she'd appeared to me as a horrifying spectral vision, her pretty face melting away in flames as she admonished me for failing to prevent her fiery death.

I'd been unaware that Mrs. Shipper had died, and I knew better than to trust a supernatural visitation without verification through more mundane channels. When I checked into it, however, I discovered that the opportunistic widow had indeed run out of luck.

My inquiries revealed that Cindy Shipper had married Alu "Al the Torch" Hatfield, the youngest son of "Old Man" Bowman Hatfield, the patriarch of Yerba City's preeminent crime family. The marriage had taken place the previous February, and the happy couple had been married for only two months when Cindy's charred remains were found among the rubble after a fire at one of the Hatfield Syndicate's warehouses. The Yerba City Daily Herald (a rag known locally as "All the News City Hall Allows Us To Print") buried the story deep inside its Saturday edition, and the former Mrs. Shipper hadn't even merited an obituary. Foul play was never alleged, and the Hatfield family lawyers had made sure it never would be.

Despite living a quiet life and ruling his family business from behind the scenes, Old Man Bowman was a Yerba City icon. Or maybe it was *because* he stayed out of the limelight that his legend had grown. Seldom seen in public, the Old Man was a shadowy figure, a giant spider in the center of a web of wealth, corruption, and iniquity, the reclusive king of Yerba City's underworld.

Bowman's eldest son, Terrell, known as "Terry the Tantrum," had died in his early twenties, bumped off by a rival family. The gang war that followed his murder solidified the Hatfield Syndicate's position as the chief provider of the city's illicit goods and services. While the Old Man pulled the strings from his family's private compound in the exclusive Galindo District on the west side of the city, his second son, "Fats" Ferrell, operated from the top floor of the family's downtown office park as the public face of the business. In contrast to his secluded father, the jovial Fats appeared at so many charity events and ribbon-cuttings that an article in City Magazine once referred to him as Yerba City's most photographed figure.

The youngest of the Hatfield sons was the most enigmatic. Old Man Bowman took pains to keep himself out of the limelight, but Al the Torch took isolation to an entirely different level. I spent much of an afternoon searching for the skinny on Bowman's third son, but managed to dig up only two photographs of the elusive Al. One was a picture of the young Alu, just a toddler, at a post-adoption ceremony. Bowman's wife, Velma, had brought the boy home with her after a cruise in the South Nihhonese, proving that anything, even family, could be bought with enough dough. The second photo showed a grown-up Al lurking in the background at his brother Fats's wedding. It was an interesting photo. Like his father and brother, he'd been dressed in a tux. Rather than a top hat, however, he'd worn a black balaclava that covered his entire head except for a narrow strip for his eyes. I searched in vain for a photo from his own more recent marriage to Cindy, but found nothing: not a story, not even a wedding announcement. I found only an official record of the wedding, which had been held in a government office rather than a public venue.

I hadn't known Mrs. Shipper for more than a few days, but she'd impressed herself on me in ways I couldn't explain. If she hadn't been married; if I hadn't had reason to believe she'd encouraged, at the very least, or even orchestrated the murders of her husband and stepson; if, once she was legally cleared, I'd sought her out, or taken a chance and made myself available, well, who knows what could have been. Or maybe I was kidding myself. Spark or no spark, Cindy gravitated toward money, and money avoided yours truly as if I had leprosy. Still, as long as she was alive and out there somewhere, I could entertain the fantasy of looking her up one day and finding out whether we had anything real to share. I was an investigator, after all. Finding people was something I did. She and I were both slightly over thirty, still young, or young enough, and even though I'd been living in the same apartment above my office and running my same P.I. racket for the past decade, neither of us were so settled we couldn't have accepted a few changes in our lives. But that was over and done. Cindy Shipper had married a Hatfield, and, within a couple of months, she'd died under violent and mysterious circumstances. Her death was something I needed to know more about, and, depending on what I discovered, do something about. I told myself I owed it to her memory, or maybe to the possibilities that could no longer be fulfilled.

I put on some work duds and climbed down the stairs to my office. After firing up the coffeemaker, I wandered down the hall to my laundry room to check on Chivo, my 'boarder.' Chivo was out, but Siphon was busy circulating fresh air into the room from the partially open window. Before Chivo, a mangy goatlike creature I'd caught rooting through my garbage, had taken over my laundry room, I'd been using the area as a makeshift gym. I'd kept some weights there, along with a homemade heavy bag, and I'd put it all to good use as often as I could find the time. The problem was that the only ventilation in the room was provided by a single small window that let in air from outside the front of the house. With Chivo adding his own cocktail of odors, the room had become all but uninhabitable.

Fortunately, I had a special talent: I was born with the rare ability to summon and command small air elementals, spirits of the winds. I'd summoned one, a two-foot funnel of whirling air, and given it the task of siphoning the bad air from the room and replacing it with fresh air from outside. Once I'd begun providing Chivo with a steady supply of food, he'd lost some of his rank gaminess. The atmosphere in the laundry room had become tolerable, at least to a bachelor like me, and I'd dismissed the elemental from its duties. The spirit, however, had decided to continue its task of circulating air through the room, declaring that the task "fit" its nature. That was jake with me: Chivo still smelled like a wild goat, and my own odor after working out hadn't improved any. I told the elemental it could stay as long as it wished and gave it a name: Siphon.

Over time, Siphon forged a bond with Chivo, and the elemental rarely left the goat-creature's side. Chivo—that is, the legendary Huay Chivo—had once been a sorcerer-king called Cadmael. As the ruler of an ancient kingdom in the Cutzyetelkeh Peninsula, King Cadmael had opposed and been cursed by Lord Ketz-Alkwat more than five centuries ago after the Dragon Lord had conquered the northern half of the Western Hemisphere and formed the Realm of Tolanica, which Lord Ketz still ruled. Stripped of most of his powers and transformed into an undying monster, the Huay Chivo had roamed the countryside, feeding on the blood of livestock and whatever else he could hunt down, including the occasional unlucky farmer. Recently, the Huay Chivo had been mostly cured of his curse, regaining his sentience and much of his magical talent. He could even "speak" to me, using our mutual telepathic link with Siphon as a go-between.

Finding Siphon at his task in the laundry room without Chivo present was odd. I got Siphon's attention and asked the elemental if it had seen Chivo lately.

A voice like a wind instrument emerged from the whirling funnel. "Lord Cadmael is away."

Lord Cadmael? This was new. "He's Lord Cadmael now? What happened to Chivo?"

"Lord Cadmael is away."

I rolled my eyes. Talking to elementals required a great deal of patience. "I can see that 'Lord Cadmael' is away, Siphon. Do you know where he went?"

"Lord Cadmael commandsss me to serve you until he returnsss."

"Oh? That's nice of him. Lord Cadmael commands you now?"

"Siphon servesss Lord Cadmael. Lord Cadmael wishes me to serve you until he returnsss."

It was true, then: the bond between the two was a formal one. I'd suspected that was the case, but Siphon had just confirmed it.

"Okay, Siphon. Tha— what?!"

At that moment, a much smaller air funnel, about two inches tall and the color of swirling smoke, zipped through the window and came to a stop in front of my face.

"Smokey?"

"Greetingsss, Aleksss," hissed the tiny elemental.

"What are you doing here? I didn't summon you." Smokey was my favorite and most well-trained air spirit, but I expected it to be flitting beneath the eaves of the Black Minotaur, where it spent nearly all its time happily soaking up cigarette fumes from the lounge and smoke from the kitchen grill when I wasn't calling it into my service.

"Lord Cadmael left you a messssage," Smokey hissed, sounding like a leaky radiator hose.

"A message? What message?"

"Lord Cadmael saysss to tell you... 'Beware the cold, and resissst the pull of death.'"

I stood, blinking. "That's the message? Beware the cold and resist death?"

"Beware the cold and resissst the *pull* of death," Smokey corrected.

I nodded. "Good advice. But are you serving Chivo, I mean, Lord Cadmael, now?"

It was silly, but I felt like my heart was breaking in two. Although elementals possessed only a limited degree of sentience, I knew they were more than mere tools, and Smokey had become something like a friend to me. Maybe even my best friend, considering how little time I spent socializing with fully sentient creatures.

The little whirling elemental floated to my shoulder. "Smokey servesss Alekssss."

I was almost ashamed to admit how much better those three words made me feel. "Thanks, buddy," I said, meaning it. "Chi... Lord Cadmael is using you to send me messages?"

"Lord Cadmael assssked. Smokey agreed."

"Where is he?"

"Lord Cadmael is far away."

Well, that narrowed it down. He might not even be in this realm of existence. "Great," I said. "He and I have a lot of talking to do when he comes back."

I sent Smokey back to the Minotaur and left Siphon to work his magic with the laundry room's musky air, shutting the door behind me as I stepped into the hallway.

Back in my office, I filled a king-sized mug with steaming hot brew (black, because I like my coffee to taste like coffee) and sat down at my computer to search for info on Cindy and Alu Hatfield. After a frustrating hour, I discovered nothing new except the extent to which the Hatfields had suppressed the story of Cindy's death. Even the archived story I'd seen in the City Herald when I'd first looked into the matter had been removed from view.

I was about to refill my coffee cup when a window appeared on my screen informing me that I'd received an email from the Province of Caychan Treasury Department. An unexpected tax refund? More likely an audit. I sighed and opened the email.

The subject line slapped me right across the chops and caused the blood to drain from my temples: "Notice of Suspension of License To Operate."

Lord's flaming balls! They were suspending my P.I. license? Why? I read the message.

Dear Alexander Southerland:
The Bureau of Licenses recently upgraded its data systems to improve the quality of its services. During the transfer of information, the photograph on your operating license was inadvertently deleted. As a result, your License To Operate as a Private Investigator has been suspended until such time as you can have your photograph retaken in our offices. Until this matter is resolved, you will be unable to operate as an authorized Private Investigator. Please click on the following link to schedule an appointment.

Son of a bitch! Could this be a scam? But, no, the address was legit. Their message somehow gave the impression that the whole mess was my fault. They're the ones who lost my photo, and then they turn around and make *me* suffer the consequences. Typical bureaucratic bullshit. I clicked on the link and discovered that the bureau had an appointment time available that morning at ten-twenty, and the next available time wasn't until the following Monday, six days away. I'd have to go downtown to the courthouse to get my picture taken. It was nine fifteen. I could make it, but I'd have to hustle. I scheduled the appointment and ran upstairs to get my hat and coat.

I made it to the courthouse with a couple of minutes to spare, so naturally I had to wait twenty minutes before the clerk was ready to see me. My P.I. license was good for ten years, and I'd received it nine years earlier. Because they'd lost my photo, I was required to fill out forms for a replacement license, which would still expire the following year, as scheduled. That meant I was going to have to come back in another few months and go through this all over again. Lord's balls!

That's when I received my next kick in the crotch.

The clerk, a bored-looking gnome with a blond wig and a romance novel spread face-down on her desk, informed me I'd be receiving my replacement license in the mail in eight weeks.

I was incredulous. "Did you say, 'eight weeks'? You've got to be joking."

The gnome lifted her glazed eyes to the level of my chin. "No, sir. Eight weeks. You may restart your operations when you've received your replacement license."

"I can't operate for eight weeks?"

"No, sir."

"Can't you issue me a temporary license until I get the permanent one?"

"No, sir. We can't do that, sir."

"Why not?"

The quickness with which she answered my question suggested she'd had this conversation many times in the past. "We don't have the facilities for issuing a temporary license, sir."

"You've got a computer and a printer—what more do you need?"

"We're not allowed to issue temporary licenses, sir. It's against provincial policy. We *can*, however, expedite the issuance of your permanent license."

"Expedite? How soon would I get it?"

The clerk smiled. "It would just take a few minutes."

"A few minutes?" I thought I knew where this was going and reached for my credit card. "What's it going to take to make that happen?"

The clerk's smile grew wider.

By eleven I was in the corridors of the courthouse, brand new operator's license in hand, my ugly scowling mug in the upper corner. As I was leaving, I spotted two familiar figures sitting on a bench outside one of the courtrooms.

Detective Laurel Kalama looked up at my approach. "Hello, gumshoe. What brings you here? You being arraigned for something?"

"Not today. Just had to take care of some clerical issues with my P.I. license."

Kalama's lips curled at the edges. "And how much did it cost you?"

I grimaced. "A little more than my monthly rent. I can continue to operate for another year, but I might have to move into my car if I don't get another case soon."

The detective snorted. "All hail the Realm of Tolanica. The best government money can buy."

"I don't know about 'best,' but then I don't have anything to compare it to. It's the only one we've had since the spirit of the Waning Blood Moon summoned Lord Ketz-Alkwat from Hell some five hundred years ago." I nodded at her with my chin. "What are *you* doing here?"

Kalama dug an elbow into the side of her partner sitting next to her, a blank expression on his bulldog face. "Blu has to testify today in a case he was involved in when he was in vice."

I smiled. "Blu has to talk? That should be fun."

Blu grunted without moving.

Kalama smiled. "I think you just heard his testimony in full."

"He looks eager," I said, returning her smile. "I'll bet he's been looking forward to this all morning."

"He's a little upset because they made him check his gun at the door. Now he'll have to answer the defense attorney's questions instead of just shooting him."

Blu's upper lip twitched, revealing a glimpse at the pug-like detective's clenched yellow teeth, and I was reminded that the laconic detective was a shapeshifter who could transform into four vicious bulldogs. Waiting for his imminent court appearance, Detective Blu seemed to be more dog than human.

"Let's hope he doesn't jump out of the witness stand and snap the DA's neck with his jaws," I said.

Kalama chuckled. "That would be fun. He'd be more likely to go after the defendant, though. Blu caught him handing out opioid gummies to a group of schoolgirls during recess."

Blu's upper lip lifted another notch, and a low growl emerged from behind his teeth.

I shook my head. "What's the world coming to? That slime-ball dealer's lucky he's still in one piece."

"They're claiming excessive force," Kalama said, throwing a glance at her partner. "Hard to imagine from this little sweetie." She turned back to me. "I just hope we're done before lunchtime. It's Taco Tuesday, and the truck will be outside our office at noon. We need to be out of here by eleven-thirty to beat the crowd. Sometimes they run out of limes."

I let out a chuckle. "I don't like your chances. Hey, do you remember Cindy Shipper?"

Kalama looked up at me, a quizzical expression on her face. "Sure. A real cutie. Too bad she was a homicidal maniac. You heard she died, right?"

"Yeah. After she married one of Old Man Bowman's sons."

"Right. Al the Torch."

"She died in a fire."

Kalama sighed. "And you want to look into it. Look, gumshoe. I know you had a thing for the woman. You slept with her, right?"

"It wasn't like that."

"So you say."

"We got drunk—really drunk—and wound up in my bed."

The detective snorted. "Right. While you were investigating her as a murder suspect." That elicited a snort from Blu, who otherwise appeared to be half asleep.

I lifted my arms from my sides, palms out. "Nothing happened. We both woke up fully clothed, and neither of us could even remember how we got there."

"I can't imagine how disappointed you must have been. It must have killed you when you heard she married a Hatfield. And now you want to find out if they had her done in. But there's nothing to see here. It was an accident. She was in the wrong place at the wrong time."

"Was it your case?"

Kalama hesitated. "Someone else had that one."

I tipped my hat back from my forehead an inch. "You didn't investigate it yourself?"

"We're a big department. A lot of people get murdered in this city. I don't get every case, which is good, because I've got plenty on my plate as it is."

"Who got it?"

"What do you care?"

I closed my eyes and squeezed the bridge of my nose. "Because you're the best homicide dick in the city, and everyone from your lieutenant to the mayor knows it. The death of the wife of one of Bowman's sons is a big deal, and if you didn't get the case, then maybe someone didn't want the facts to come out."

The detective rolled her eyes. "I appreciate the flattery, gumshoe, but this isn't the movies. We're a moderately well-funded big-city police department here with a lot of experienced professional people in it. The YCPD found no evidence of a homicide. An old warehouse burned down, most likely because of a fault in the wiring. It was an accident."

"An accident? Not arson? Maybe for the insurance?"

"Not as far as I know. I *do* know that no one ever put in an insurance claim. At least, not yet. And it's been several months."

"But still—"

Kalama cut me off. "Look! The case is closed, gumshoe. It was closed good and tight before the fire was even out. Get it?"

I got it. A warehouse owned by the Hatfields burned down. Bowman Hatfield's daughter-in-law died in the fire. I sighed. "So what you're saying is that no one will be seeing any forensic evidence from this fire anytime soon."

Kalama snorted. "What I'm saying is that the YCPD doesn't have any evidence of a crime. And that comes straight from the top."

"You mean from the police commissioner?"

"I mean from the mayor's office. And you won't find anything from the fire department, either. It was an accident. Period."

"And you're okay with that?"

The detective met my eyes. "It doesn't matter what I think. No one's asking me for my opinion." Her face broke into a smile. "No one important, anyway."

The door to the courtroom opened, interrupting our conversation, and a clerk poked her head through. "Detective Blu? They're ready for you."

The bench creaked as the two detectives stood. Kalama poked Blu with her elbow. "Get this over with quick. I don't want to miss the taco truck." She turned to me. "You want to investigate your late girlfriend's death? Knock yourself out. If you find anything worthwhile, let me know. But I've got nothing for you, so don't bother asking for any help. And watch out for the Hatfields. They aren't going to be thrilled about you poking your nose into their family business. Al the Torch might want to burn it right off your face." The two detectives disappeared into the courtroom.

Chapter Two

Taco Tuesday. The thought triggered a sudden craving for spiced beef, cilantro, onions, olives, sliced radishes, and red pepper sauce in a crispy corn shell. A taco stand called A Touch of Azteca was just four blocks down the street from my office. I tried to go there at least once a week, because the tacos were amazing and relatively inexpensive if you restrained yourself to no more than four. Telling myself I didn't really need more than three, I rushed out of the courthouse to get my car.

My phone buzzed when I was in the parking garage. When I saw who was calling, I stopped and connected the call.

"Southerland."

A sultry feminine voice hardened by decades of smoke from a million cigarettes purred in my ear. "Whatcha doin', handsome? You still in bed?"

"Nah, Gracie. I've been up for hours."

"Oooo, you don't say? You're going to make me blush, sugar."

I chuckled. "That'll be the day. I had to go to the courthouse, but I'm just leaving. Want me to come by your office and take you out for an early lunch?"

"Mmm, sounds fantastic, honey. But you need to go to a hotel."

"What, before eating? If you're looking for some afternoon delight, then I'm going to have to put some fuel in the tank first, baby."

"I like the way you think, sweetie. But I'm afraid my husband has something special in mind for you today."

Gracie, a voluptuous, if somewhat plumpish blonde bombshell, was a shameless flirt, but she was married to my attorney, Rob Lubank, and, in truth, the two were hopelessly devoted to each other. That didn't stop her from pressing my buttons every opportunity she had. I was pretty sure her teasing was all in fun, though sometimes I couldn't help but wonder. At the very least, she was a good actress. "Something special? In a hotel room?" I said, feigning shock. "I've told you before, Gracie: Robbie's not my type."

Gracie adopted a pouting tone. "Because he's a gnome? Don't knock it if you haven't tried it, honey."

"More because he's a man."

"Oh, honey," Gracie sounded disappointed. "Where's your sense of adventure?"

I sighed. "What's this about, Gracie? Does Rob have some work for me?"

"Maybe. He got a call from a very strange man who said you referred him to Robbie. He wouldn't leave his name, and he refuses to come to the office. He wants to meet Robbie—and you—at the Cotopaxi Hotel over by Pier Twenty-Seven."

"The Cotopaxi? That place is a dump."

"I know! I wouldn't be caught dead in that joint."

"I don't want to get caught dead there, either. He wants to meet both of us?"

"He insisted, sugar. Robbie's already left, and he wants you there pronto. Robbie will meet you in the parking lot and you'll go up together. Oh, and sugar?"

"Yeah?"

"Do you have a gun?"

"Not on me, no."

"That's okay, sugar. Robbie's got two."

***

The Cotopaxi was a gaudy tourist trap with a cartoonish Quscan theme. In a courtyard outside the main entrance stood a colorful fifteen-foot statue of a stereotypical mustachioed Quscan peasant standing next to a llama with an overstuffed burlap bag, presumably filled with coffee beans or coca leaves, strapped to its back. Given the goofy asymmetric smile on the peasant's florid face, my money was on coca leaves.

I wheeled my car, the beastmobile, into the double-decker parking garage and spotted Lubank inside his car on the upper level. He spotted me, too, and was there to greet me by the time I'd squeezed my monster-sized car into a parking space.

"Alkwat's balls!" he roared. "Took you long enough."

Rob Lubank, perhaps the most feared, and certainly the most corrupt, defense attorney in Yerba City, flipped a half-smoked cigarette to the floor and reached up to adjust his hairpiece, which was wedged between a pair of oversized rounded ears. Only as tall as a human child, the gnome managed to stand out in a crowd with his green suit and red tie. Not many men could have pulled it off, but Lubank had the swagger of a rock star, not to mention the upfront belligerence of a rabid raccoon.

"I'm not even sure why I'm here," I said. "What's up?"

Lubank waved me toward the elevators. "I don't know. This whole thing sounds fuckin' fishy, but in an intriguing sort of way. Oh, here...." Lubank handed me a pistol, a thirty-eight semi-automatic. "Take this. Gracie says you don't have a piece. This one's got nine in the magazine, one in the chamber."

"Do I need it?"

"Beats me. But better safe than sorry, I always say. This mug we're meeting's either in danger or he's got a screw loose. Either way, I want to be prepared."

The elevator door opened, and I pushed the button for the lobby, one floor down. "Tell me about this guy."

Lubank shrugged. "I don't know much. He called me in a panic, but he wouldn't give me his name. He didn't sound all that coherent. He told me that he checked into this place late last night and that he needed a lawyer right away. He said, and I quote, 'I know too much.' But what he thinks he knows is anyone's guess."

I stared down at the gnome. "He actually said, 'I know too much'?"

Lubank barked out a laugh. "Like a guy who's seen too many movies. He sounds like a fuckin' juicehead."

The elevator door opened, and we stepped into a lobby decorated with scenes of mountainsides and peasants harvesting crops with sickles, as if modern agricultural equipment hadn't been introduced to the heavily industrialized Quscan countryside more than two centuries before.

"Why did you agree to meet with this fruitcake in the first place? And why did you drag me along?"

Lubank glanced up at me as we crossed the floor of the lobby. "I agreed to meet him because he said the three magic words."

I peered down at him. "I love you?"

"Money's no object." A gleeful smile lit the gnome's face as he rubbed his hands together in anticipation.

"Ahh, *those* three magic words."

Lubank stopped at a sign on the wall directing us to the rooms. "And you're here because he says he got my name from you, and that you would vouch for him. He told me he wouldn't say another word unless you were with me." He gestured with his chin. "Come on. It's Room One Thirty-One. That's up to the end of this corridor and to the right."

When we reached Room One Thirty-One, Lubank knocked loudly. "Anyone in there? It's Robinson Lubank."

"Is Southerland with you?" The voice coming from the room was familiar, but I couldn't place it.

"Yeah, he's here. Open up."

I detected a faint rustling sound from the other side of the door. "I want to hear him," came the voice.

"It's me, Alex Southerland."

More rustling. "Anyone else with you?"

"No," Lubank said through clenched teeth. "Lord's balls—let us in already!"

"I want to hear Southerland say it!"

"It's just us," I said. "Lubank and me. There's no one else here, I promise."

After a pause, the voice said, "All right, I'm going to open the door. But keep your hands where I can see them. And no monkey business. I've got a gun, and I won't hesitate to shoot first and ask questions later."

Lubank and I looked at each other, and we both shrugged.

When the door opened, I went in first, slowly, arms away from my side. Lubank scurried in after me and pushed the door shut behind us.

"All right," Lubank said, turning to the man standing in the center of the room. "We're here. Now lose the fuckin' peashooter, or we turn right back around again. Got it?"

I stared openmouthed at the figure holding the gun, too stunned to speak. His arms, legs, and chest were wrapped in tinfoil, and he'd fashioned a tinfoil hood, which covered most of his head and was pulled down to his powder-blue eyes. His face was pale, the palest face I'd ever seen, and I recognized it immediately. "Corporal? What the hell!"

Former corporal Tom Kintay lowered his pistol and smiled. "Hello, sergeant. Long time, no see."

I held out a hand to indicate the foil wrapping. "What's with the tin suit, corporal?"

Kintay's eyes widened, and if his face could have blanched, it would have. "Protection, sergeant. They're after me."

"Who's after you?"

Kintay's eyes darted back and forth between Lubank and me. "Can we trust him?" he asked.

"Lubank? Are you kidding? No, you can't trust him—he's a fuckin' weasel! But he's on our side, as long as you can pay him."

Kintay stared at Lubank for a moment, considering, and nodded. "Okay. You two better sit down. Either of you want anything? Coffee? Water?"

Lubank shook his head. "We're good. Let's get on with it."

Kintay poured himself a glass of water and led us to a table. Once we were all seated, he leaned forward, as if he had a secret that he didn't want to fall into the wrong ears. "It's the aliens," he breathed in a hoarse whisper. "The aliens are after me."

Lubank, his head barely above the tabletop, threw up his hands. "Okay. Let's get out of here, Southerland." He moved to slide off his chair.

"No, don't go!" Kintay turned to me, his eyes pleading. "Make him stay, sergeant. He has to listen to me!"

I sighed. "Fine, corporal. Just rein it in a bit. Tell you what...." I held up a hand as if I were calming a wild beast. "Why don't you start from the beginning." I gave Lubank a quick glance before turning back to Kintay. "But please don't tell me that you've been sampling your product."

"No, no!" Kintay protested. "Well, I mean, sure. Some. But you know me—I know what I'm doing. Nobody mixes a batch like I do, and I wouldn't unleash a product on the market I haven't tested personally."

Lubank, half out of his seat, shot me a meaningful glare. "Wait a second.... Is this your buddy who makes designer drugs for the Hatfield Syndicate?"

The corners of Kintay's lips twitched out of control, and his arms flailed wildly as he spoke, causing the foil to flutter and rustle. "But I haven't engineered any new drugs for the Hatfields in months! They pulled me out of that a couple of years ago when they put me on their new project." He clamped his hands over his mouth and leaned back over the table. "Top secret!" he stage-whispered. "Shhh! No one can know about it. No one! Must not talk about it." He smoothed the foil over his arms to make sure it was secure.

The Corporal Tom Kintay I remembered had been a larcenous, but carefree sort of joe, and reasonably stable, with a passion for developing ever more exotic combinations of drugs designed for recreational use. I'd caught him boosting pharmaceuticals from a military medical facility when he was still in the service and I was an MP, and, for some reason, the career crook had decided anyone clever enough to nab him was worthy of being his friend. The Hatfield family had scooped Kintay out of a military prison to help them in 'product design,' and we'd both wound up in Yerba City, where we'd renewed our acquaintanceship. In my line of work, it pays to have some contacts on the other side of the law, and Kintay had always been happy to help me out when I needed advice on the underground drug trade or, occasionally, with inside dope about the inner workings of the Hatfield Syndicate. Three years earlier, he'd been instrumental in helping me deal with a mysterious container of stem cells that had fallen into my hands after it had been smuggled into Yerba City by a rogue police captain. *That* Tom Kintay had always had a smile on his face and was always game for a bit of mischief. I barely recognized the overwrought bundle of nervous tics seated in front of me now, with his darting eyes, flailing arms, and tinfoil armor.

"Corporal," I said in my MP's voice. "You're wasting our time. You've got a story for me? Then get on with it."

"Right, right, right. Okay. It was back when you brought me that box, remember?" He glanced meaningfully at Lubank.

"Talk, Corporal. Lubank knows about the stem cells."

"The *alien* stem cells," Kintay hissed.

I started to correct him, but decided there was no point. "Whatever you say. Go on."

"Right. Well, after that, the Hatfields put me on their new project. The secret one. But it didn't involve drugs. It involved those stem cells, or something a lot like them. They'd been altered and cloned, but I recognized the stuff as soon as they gave it to me to work on. It was the same basic shit but mutated in different ways. They had me experimenting with it and injecting it into rats with some really interesting results." Kintay's eyes looked like they wanted to pop out of his head. "This one rat, I swear to you, sergeant—it was buzzing around the lab like it wanted to fly! And this other one—"

I stopped him. "Enough! I got it. You've been working on a secret project for the Hatfields, and it's not recreational drugs."

Kintay turned on me with his wild eyes. "Not just the Hatfields. They're working for someone else—an alien!" Foil scraped and rustled as he pointed to the sky. "I'm tellin' you—that motherfucker came from outer space!"

"You've seen him?" I asked.

"Fuck *yes* I've seen him!" Kintay's lips were twitching out of control, and he raised his voice to power through his facial tics. "He only comes into the facility every once in a while, and he always comes in the back way and goes directly to the project manager's office. But he's come into the lab a few times. It's fuckin' weird, sergeant! He can be there one minute, and then he's gone! And it's like... like I've lost a couple of minutes from my life. Like time just stopped until he could get away. That's how I know he's an alien! He's got these super alien mind powers! I know it sounds crazy, but you've gotta believe me!" He stared at me with a pleading expression, like an innocent man with a bloody knife in his hand.

I knew, of course, that Kintay's "alien" was an elf who had taken the smuggled stem cells from me and was using them for his own purposes. The nameless elf had contacted me out of the blue one day and jammed a crystal shard into my forehead. Afterward, I could "see" without using my eyes, even in pitch darkness, and "hear" over long distances without using my ears. That was the least complicated way I knew of to describe what the elf had explained as "enhanced awareness." Another result of this new awareness was that my body was more attuned to its inner workings, which meant that my bodily functions were more efficient than normal, and I could heal myself at a rate doctors described as magical. I had to admit that was useful, and that my magical healing powers had saved my life on more than one occasion.

The elf was using the mysterious stem cells as a part of his plan to overthrow the Dragon Lords, who had emerged from an unearthly realm called Hell some six thousand years ago and wrested control of this earth from the elves in a war known as The Great Rebellion. At the conclusion of the war, the Dragon Lords used the trolls, dwarves, and gnomes who had followed them from Hell to hunt down and exterminate the remaining elves. According to the official accounts, the genocide had been successful, and elves were extinct. The official accounts, however, were self-serving and inaccurate. At least one elf that I knew of had survived, and he'd recruited me into his schemes to depose the autocratic immortal Dragon Lords. I didn't have any strong feelings about the Dragon Lords one way or the other, but the elf's gift had saved my life on more than one occasion, and I owed him. Besides, I'd recently become more sympathetic to his cause.

After receiving the stem cells, the elf had come to a collaborative agreement with The Hatfield Syndicate, which now provided him with facilities and security. I had no idea what the Hatfields were receiving from the elf—presumably a boatload of dough—nor did I know what the elf was actually doing with the cells. For all his larceny and his peculiar quirks, Kintay was a genius when it came to alchemy and biology, and I'd long suspected that the Hatfields had turned him over to the elf to help with the new project. Apparently, no one had let Kintay in on the secret: the head of the project was a legendary creature thought to be long extinct. So Kintay had come up with his own crazy theory about the mysterious figure in charge.

Lubank gave me a long sidelong glance, but I held Kintay's eyes. "Corporal, I once told you that those stem cells had originated from elves, and that I had met an elf. Do you remember that?"

Kintay smirked. "Sure, I remember. What I *can't* believe is that you're still peddling that bullshit." He snorted. "Elves. Lord's balls! I'm not crazy, you know. Elves only exist in horror movies. I should know. I've seen almost all of them." He stared down his nose at me, his foil-covered arms crossed over his puffed-out chest.

I sighed. "All right, forget I mentioned it. You think the top boss is a space alien? We'll go with that. But hurry up and get to your point. Why did you call Lubank? Why are we here?"

Kintay uncrossed his arms and leaned over the table. "Right, right, right. I'm getting to it. So, I'm working on this big project. A few other guys are, too: another alchemist, a couple of biologists, and some engineers. As brilliant a collection of nerds as you'll ever see outside a comic con. And none of us know what this project is all about. We've got these theories..., but, okay, you're not interested in that. All right, anyway, this guy, Petros Papadopouli.... He's a data processing engineer: a computer tech. A good-looking guy, but a real wonk. Big, thick glasses. Always carrying about a dozen pens in a fuckin' monogrammed pocket protector. You know what I'm saying? Been on the project from the beginning."

I frowned. "Papa....?"

"Papadopouli. A fuckin' genius—but weird!"

I took in Kintay's tinfoil suit and glanced at Lubank, who snickered. I shook my head and turned back to Kintay. "Go on. What about this guy?"

Kintay's eyes went so wide I thought they might fall out of his head. "He went missing!"

"What do you mean?"

"I mean he's gone! I think he might be dead! He came in one day, this was back in early April, and he says he found out all about the project we've been working on, and that it's—and these are his words—he says what we're doing is a 'fuckin' abomination'! That's what he says: a 'fuckin' abomination.' And I say, 'What are you talking about?' And he says he can't tell me, 'cause it's too big and that I'd never believe him. But he says he's going to get proof, and then everyone will see."

"Proof? What kind of proof?"

"I don't know, sergeant, but a week later he comes over to my workstation and he hands me this thumb drive, and he says the proof is on the thumb drive, and he's going to upload it online so that everyone can see it. But before he can do anything else, one of our security goons shows up and says that the boss wants to see him pronto."

Lubank frowned. "Boss? You mean the 'space alien'?"

Kintay squinted at Lubank. "No, no, no. Not the space alien. The project manager! A gnome called Coleridge. We call her "Cold Fish" because, well, I guess you can figure out why. She orders us around, but she doesn't want to know any of us. She almost never comes out of her office, which is fine with the rest of us. Nobody knows what she does behind those closed doors, or anything about her, but she's in charge of the operation, and she reports directly to the Hatfields. Hell, she might be a space alien, too, for all I know."

I let out a breath. "Focus, corporal. What about this proof?"

"Right, right, right. So Papadopouli goes off with the goon, but he leaves the thumb drive with me. And that's the last anyone has seen of him! He never came back to the lab after that. He just disappeared!"

Lubank was practically salivating. "So, you're saying you've got this thumb drive with proof about what the Hatfield's secret project is all about?"

Kintay's eyes narrowed. "It's in a safe place. I haven't been able to look at it. Motherfuckin' Papadopouli encrypted it, and I can't break the code."

Lubank rolled his eyes. "Then what good is it?"

Kintay shook his head. "You're missing the fuckin' point! I've got this data that might reveal something big. And Papadopouli has disappeared."

I glared at Kintay. "I still don't know why we're here."

Kintay stared back at me, fear in his eyes. "It's the alien! It's been hanging around the lab more than usual lately. The new lab, I mean. We had to move. Too bad. I liked the old lab. This new one is too antiseptic. And there's no place to run off to when I need a break to..., uh..., to get my head sorted, if you know what I mean."

"Kintay?" I prompted.

Kintay's upper lip twitched. "Right, right, right. Where was I? Oh yeah! That was four months ago, right? And I kind of forgot about the whole thing. But then about a week ago, I started getting this weird vibe from Cold Fish. Coleridge, I mean. I can't put my finger on it. I mean, usually she acts like I'm not even there. Like I'm just a working part in the machine. I mean, we're just cogs or tools as far as she's concerned. But a week ago, she starts, I don't know... *noticing* me. Looking at me, like she knows something. And then she spoke to me. She, like, asked me how I was doing. And if everything was all right. I mean, it was crazy! And then two days ago, the alien came into the lab. I hadn't seen him since before the fire. He comes in, and he looks right at me—right into my eyes—and I swear that... that *thing* was reading my mind!" Kintay reached across the table and grabbed my arm. "It knows, sergeant! They know I have the data! I think Papadopouli must have still been alive. I think he was hiding, and they found him. He must have talked. And now people are looking for me! I'm being followed! And someone's been in my place, too. I mean, they didn't take anything, and nothing seemed to be moved, but I can tell when something's off. And something's off! And... and... and...." Kintay's lip twitched out of control. "And that's why I'm wearing this tinfoil!" he sputtered at last. "Because it blocks out the alien's mindreading powers!"

Lubank gave me a long sidelong glance before turning back to Kintay. "Why don't you just give them back the thumb drive? Tell them your buddy left it on your desk, but it's encrypted, and you don't have any way to see the files. You're basically in the clear."

Kintay shook his head so hard it almost dislodged his foil cap. "No! I don't know what this alien is up to, but he made Papadopouli go missing. And now he's found him, and now he's probably dead again. I mean, now he's probably dead for real. Or he's disappeared for good. Or... I mean..." He threw his arms up in surrender. "I don't know what I mean. That's why I had to get out of there!" He straightened the foil cap and pulled it more securely over his brow. Leaning toward Lubank, he lowered his voice to a near whisper. "I decided to give the data to an attorney, and I remembered your name from when the sergeant here told me about you this one time. Don't you see? You can use the data to bargain with the alien. And you can keep me from disappearing, like Papadopouli!"

Lubank glanced at me, his lips curled into a half-smile, before turning back to Kintay. "And you've got money?" he asked.

Kintay brushed the question away. "Sure. Money's no problem."

Lubank nodded. "Okay. Then here's what we're gonna do...."

At that moment, I became aware of two figures, one large and one small, rushing up the hallway toward our room and not even trying to be quiet about it.

I rose to my feet, pulling my gun from my pocket. "We've got company!"

Lubank drew his weapon, and the two of us darted toward the door. Kintay jumped out of his chair and dove to hide behind the bed, foil sliding off his arms and legs. Lubank turned into the bathroom, and I took up a position against the wall to the side of the door.

The door burst from its hinges and fell into the room.

Chapter Three

Two men—a troll and a dwarf, each flashing iron—rushed into the room. I reached up and shoved the barrel of my rod into the troll's ear. "Drop it, partner. I can put five rounds into your earhole before you turn around."

The dwarf whirled toward me with his hand cannon, but froze when he spotted Lubank slipping out of the bathroom with his gat raised.

"Make a move, Short Stuff," Lubank growled. "I want you to."

My instincts, or maybe my enhanced senses, told me the troll was going to take a chance, so I stepped behind him and jammed the gun barrel into the base of his skull. "Don't do it. I've got enough here to take your head off."

The troll relaxed and held out his gun hand, letting his heater dangle from his fingers. Lubank, keeping the dwarf in his sights, snatched the troll's piece from his hand. The dwarf let out a breath and, with deliberate care, set his weapon down on the carpet.

Kintay chose that moment to jump up from behind the bed, his gat pointed in our general direction. "Don't move!" he shouted.

"It's okay, corporal," I said in what I hoped was a soothing voice. "They're disarmed. The situation is under control. Put that gun down before you shoot yourself."

The troll stared at Kintay, a confused look on his face. "Th'fuck you wearin'?" he asked.

Kintay's face twitched violently. He shook his head to stop the tics, and the foil hood slid from his head. He reached up to catch it, and the gun in his hand went off, sending a bullet over the troll's head and into the ceiling.

I was momentarily distracted, and the dwarf, acting fast, launched himself into my side, pushing my gun hand away from his partner. Gunfire echoed throughout the room, and I fell to the floor, buried under the weight of the troll and the dwarf. I struggled without success to regain my feet, pounded from all sides by knees, elbows, and flying feet. Without knowing how it happened, I found myself flat on my back, pressed down by enough weight to force the air from my lungs. The explosive cracks of gunshots ceased, but shouted curses filled the air to replace them. Glass shattered, and the weight holding me down lifted. I gasped for air and sat up, my eyes darting around the room.

Lubank squatted next to me. "Th'fuck, Southerland. I thought you were supposed to be some kind of ace streetfighter."

I groaned. "What happened?"

"Your buddy, the tin man, shot up the walls real good. I hope he doesn't think I'm going to pay for it. Technically, he's not my client. We never signed anything."

I glanced at the trail of tinfoil leading out to the hallway. "Did he hit the torpedoes?"

"That lunatic couldn't hit the broad side of a barn from ten paces, but he managed to put one in the troll's butt. Big target. Lucky shot."

"What about you?" I asked.

"I'm fine, and thanks for askin'."

"What I meant was, did you shoot anybody?"

Lubank adjusted his hairpiece. "Nah. Couldn't get a shot off. You were all tangled up in there with those two, and I didn't want to risk pumping you full of lead."

I stood and dusted myself off. "Did they get Kintay?"

Lubank grimaced. "Not yet. After he emptied his gun, he cracked the dwarf over the head with his glass of water and lammed it out the door. The two lugs went after him. Got to hand it to your buddy, he's quick on his feet. Especially for a lug wearing a tinfoil suit. I guess he had the advantage of running for his life. Fear gives you wings, they say. Besides, the troll's got a bullet in his ass, and there's a reason you don't see dwarfs running hundred-yard dashes."

I picked the thirty-eight Lubank had loaned me off the floor and handed it to him. "Thanks, but I guess I didn't need this after all."

Lubank put the gun in his pocket. "I don't know. I thought you sounded real tough when you threatened to blow that troll's head off. I think he might have blinked once just before the little fellow knocked you down like a bowling ball picking up the ten-pin for a spare."

"Fuck you. What were you doing while I was wrestling two hitmen to the floor?"

"Is that what you were doing? I was dodging the pills from your buddy's heater. He might shoot better if he tried it with his eyes open."

"Funny."

Lubank looked up at me. "Hey, peeper—you ever run into either of those two gunnies before?"

"Nope, don't think so. Not together, at least. I think I'd remember a troll-and-dwarf act."

Lubank scratched at his chin and wiped his nose. "Huh. I'll see if I can find out anything about them."

I took a last look at the holes decorating the walls of the hotel room. "Let's get out of here before we have to answer any questions. You hungry?"

Lubank waved me through the door. "No time, peeper. I've got to get back to the office and figure out who to bill this last hour to."

***

On the way home, I picked up some tacos at A Touch of Azteca and brought them back to my office. I ate them at my desk, taking the time to enjoy them, and pushed all thoughts of Tom Kintay, his tinfoil suit, and the odd pair of hitmen out of my mind as much as I could. My hunger satisfied, I poured myself a fresh cup of coffee, spiked it with a shot of hooch from the pint bottle I kept in my desk drawer, and opened the day's mail with a letter opener I'd picked up recently at an Army-Navy surplus store as I thought about how I was going to spend my afternoon. I took a minute to admire the letter opener. It was shaped like an ancient elven dagger, though it was made of brass, rather than bronze. A professionally etched inscription on the blade read "Congratulations on your promotion, Major" in flowing calligraphy. The words "KILL ALL OFFICERS" had been carved underneath the inscription in scrawling capital letters with the point of a knife. I didn't really need a tool to open envelopes, but I appreciated the story this one told about life in the Tolanican Army.

I considered trying to find out what happened to Kintay, but quickly dismissed the idea. Whatever mess that miscreant had got himself into was none of my concern, and I had a job to do. I'd hired myself to investigate Cindy Shipper's death, and, so far, I hadn't turned up much. The internet wasn't providing me with any useful information. Cindy had met her death in a fire at a warehouse belonging to the Hatfields, and the family was doing a bang-up job of keeping the details of the incident under wraps. I decided I needed to see a guy who might have some answers, provided he was willing to dish them out. I took out my phone and tapped in the number for Anton Benning.

My call was answered by a woman with a soothing professional voice who told me that I had reached the law office of Mr. Anton

Benning. I asked to speak to Mr. Benning, and she told me, with what sounded like genuine regret in her voice, that Mr. Benning was not currently at his desk. She asked if I would like to leave a message. I gave her my name and told the woman that Mr. Benning had my number. In a much brighter voice, she asked if I would like to state the nature of my call. I told her my call was regarding the former Mrs. Cindy Shipper, and that he could call me back at any time that suited him. She assured me with an air of confidence that she would see that Mr. Benning got my message. I thanked her and disconnected the call. She sounded like a swell dame. I wondered if she knew her boss was one of the most unscrupulous and dangerous motherfuckers in the city.

Benning called me at about four. I'd spent the afternoon treating myself to a shave and a trim at the neighborhood clip joint and following that up with a shower to wash the loose hairs off my neck and back. I felt like a new man afterward, hale and hearty and fit as a fisherman's cat, but just that much lighter in the wallet. I was four chapters into a sultry potboiler when my phone buzzed.

Benning's voice was smooth as a silk strangling cord. "Mr. Southerland. It's been ages since we last spoke. I'll have to have you over again soon for a drink."

Anyone hearing him speak would have thought we were old friends. "Sure," I said. "Just send a troll to pluck me off the street and stuff me into one of your black sedans, like you always do. You always seem to know where I am. Are you sure you aren't tracking me with a tiny air elemental?"

"Oh, hush, my dear boy. I'm a busy man, and I can't always dilly-dally about when I need to see someone in a hurry. Besides, haven't I always been a good host once you arrived? As for tracking you, I told you once that I don't need to employ an air elemental for that purpose. I have other, more reliable sources of information. But enough of that. My receptionist informed me that you called in regards to poor Cindy Hatfield. Such a tragic loss. Please, how may I be of assistance?"

Listening to the oily Benning speak always made me want to punch a hole through a wood-paneled door. The condescension in his voice whenever he referred to me as 'dear boy' made my skin crawl. But I couldn't let him shake me out of my game. I shut my eyes and focused on the matter at hand. "Right. I'm looking for information about Mrs. Shipper and the circumstances surrounding her death. It occurred to me that the chief counsel for the Hatfield Syndicate might be able to help me out."

"Of course, dear boy. But, officially, Cindy was Mrs. Hatfield when she died. You're aware that she married Bowman's son, Alu?"

"Yes, I found that out recently. It was quite a surprise to me. I knew she had a bit of a shady side to her, but I thought she had better sense than to marry into the biggest family of crooks and thugs in the city."

If I'd thought that referring to his people as 'crooks and thugs' would rattle an operator like Benning, I was mistaken. "How well did you know Mrs. Hatfield?" he asked me, his voice showing no hint of tension. "I'm aware that you investigated the death of her late husband, Donald Shipper."

It didn't surprise me that Benning knew about that. It's not that I was well known, but the spectacular nature of Shipper's death, combined with the involvement of Madame Cuapa, an enormously powerful witch known as the Barbary Coast Bruja, had brought the case to the top of the local news broadcasts and the front page of the Daily Herald. My name wasn't mentioned in any of the stories, but not much happened in Yerba City that Benning wasn't aware of. In addition to providing legal counsel for the Hatfield family, Benning was the head of security and chief fixer for Yerba City's mayor, Montavious Harvey, who owed his office to the Hatfields. Besides, Benning had taken an interest in me for various reasons and made it clear that he wanted me to work directly for the Hatfield Syndicate. I wanted no part of that, of course, but I knew that Benning was sitting on some information he could use against me if he wanted to. I was hoping it wouldn't come up, but I knew it was only a matter of time.

Sweat was beginning to roll down the side of my face, and I switched the phone from one ear to the other before answering Benning's question. "I didn't know Cindy—Mrs. Hatfield—well, or for long, and I'd lost track of her. But I'm not ashamed to admit that she made an impression on me."

"Yes, I can see where that might be the case," Benning drawled. "She was a lovely woman."

"When I discovered that she had died under mysterious circumstances in a Hatfield facility, well, let's just say that I grew curious."

Benning didn't respond right away, and the sound of ice cubes clinking against the side of a glass came through my speaker. My mouth watered at the memory of the taste of his smooth shawnee whiskey.

Benning waited until he'd finished savoring his drink before speaking. "I have to ask you, Mr. Southerland. Are you investigating Mrs. Hatfield's death in a professional capacity?"

"Professional ethics prevent me from answering that question," I said.

"I see. In that case, let me ask you this: what use do you—or your client—intend to make of any information you might gather regarding the demise of poor Mrs. Hatfield?"

"You want to know if I'm looking to blackmail anyone. I don't do that, Benning, and you know it."

Benning responded quickly. "You misunderstand me, Mr. Southerland. I had no wish to impugn your integrity. Or your professional ethics. It's just that Bowman was quite fond of Mrs. Hatfield, and he would be distressed to find that someone was looking into her unfortunate death for the purposes of besmirching the poor girl's reputation. He is quite keen to let his late daughter-in-law rest in peace."

"I'm sure he is."

Benning hesitated for an instant before speaking. "Mr. Southerland, I hope you aren't trying to imply that the circumstances of Mrs. Hatfield's death are in any way suspicious. I can assure you it was nothing more than a tragic accident."

"I'm sure you're right, Mr. Benning. The fact that she was married to a mobster known as 'The Torch' is entirely incidental to the fact that she was burned to death in a warehouse fire."

Benning chuckled without humor. "Ah, Mr. Southerland. You can see why Bowman would prove to be most unwelcoming of any further inquiries into the death of his son's wife. If even a man as intelligent and reasonable as yourself finds the circumstances suspicious, can you imagine what the press would do with this story if they were allowed to run with it? And yet there is no story here to be found. Cindy and Alu met, fell in love, and were most happily married with the full approval of the family for all too brief a time. They were barely back from their honeymoon and on their way to planning a bright future, when, in the most tragic and unfortunate of circumstances, the young woman found herself trapped in a building that was consumed by flames due to an electrical malfunction. The building was filled with flammable material, and it went up quite quickly. Any suffering on Mrs. Hatfield's part would have been intense, but soon over with. The entire family is most distraught, and remains so, Alu most of all. And I'm afraid that's all there is to it."

"I see. So what you're saying is that it was all just one tragic and unfortunate accident. Can I ask you one question? How did Cindy and The Torch meet?"

"Mr. Southerland, I'm afraid I've helped you all I can. Please accept my assurance that there is no reason for you to launch an investigation. Nor would it be in your best interests to do so."

I leaned back in my chair and lifted my feet to let them rest on the corner of my desktop. "To be clear, Mr. Benning, I didn't just hear you threaten me, did I? You're such a sweet talker that sometimes the subtle undertones of your discourse slide right past me."

"Oh, pish posh, my dear boy. I don't need to threaten you. You know full well that the release of certain video footage from a security camera at a certain property management company would be damaging to your reputation if it fell into the hands of law enforcement. Thus, I need not send any threats your way."

"Gosh, I can't tell you what a relief it is to hear that you aren't threatening me."

Benning chuckled again. "Like I said, there's no need. There is nothing to find, and you have no need to search. Take my advice and leave this alone, Mr. Southerland."

The phone beeped and the call dropped.

I set the phone down on my desk and stared up at the ceiling fan revolving slowly above the center of the room. I didn't know what disappointed me more: the fact that my call to Benning had yielded no useful information, or that the treacherous snake didn't think I was worth a plausible lie. The idea that an intelligent and sophisticated woman like Cindy Shipper had just happened to wander into a dirty Hatfield warehouse, for who knows what reason, just in time to be burned to death in a fire started by an 'electrical malfunction'.... It wasn't just hooey, it was the worst kind of hooey. It was hooey with no pretense at being anything other than hooey. For a professional man like Benning to sling that kind of bullshit at me? It was a show of deliberate disrespect.

A burning sensation rose from my gut to my head, and I knew there was only one answer to that kind of heat. I grabbed my hat and coat and headed out to get myself a drink.

Chapter Four

tap tap tap tap tap
I tossed in my bed, turning from one side to the other.
tap tap tap tap tap
The dream that had been disturbing my sleep dissipated like mist in a strong wind, despite my frustrated attempts to retain the particulars in my memory.
tap tap tap tap tap
I groaned and pulled the covers over my aching head, regretting that 'one for the road,' not to mention the three or four 'just one more shot's that had preceded it.
tap tap tap tap tap
My eyes popped open. That noise. Had it been part of my dream? But I was hearing it now with eyes wide open. Was I still dreaming?
tap tap tap tap tap tap tap tap tap...
"Okay already," I mumbled through a clogged throat and a mouth full of mud. I threw off the covers and sat up on the side of the bed, sniffling into my blanket and rubbing my eyes and nose.
tap tap tap
The incessant tapping was coming from my window, and, given that I was on the second floor, I assumed it must be a bird. I rose from the bed and slipped on a robe. I steadied myself after a brief bout of dizziness, crossed the room, and pulled up the blinds.
I didn't see anything at first, but then a single disembodied finger appeared on the other side of the glass. Tiny baby blue flowers were painted on the perfectly manicured fingernail. A ring with an impressive row of diamonds mounted on a white gold band circled the base of the slender and delicate finger. The finger curled, and the diamond ring rapped at the windowpane.
tap tap tap tap tap
The smell of perfume wafted into the room.
A chill ran up my spine. A scream filled my throat, and I swallowed it down. I took an involuntary step backwards and bumped into the side of the bed. The finger stopped rapping, and a face emerged at the window, a pretty face with light-brown eyes, a faint row of freckles

spread over her nose and cheeks, and soft lips spread into a cool smile, all framed by waves of strawberry-blond hair.

"Cindy?" I croaked, stepping toward the window.

The lips on the face moved. No sound disturbed the night, but I didn't have any trouble reading the words on those lips: "Help me."

"How?" I asked, my voice stronger. "What do you want me to do?"

Again the lips moved: "Help me, please."

I took a reluctant step toward the window, fighting down a sudden bout of nausea. "Cindy? Is that really you? What can I do?"

The specter in the window turned her head one way, then the other, a look of loss in her eyes. Cindy's lips moved again, and her voice rang in my head: "What happened to me? Why? Why am I here?"

Frost formed on the windowpane, obstructing my view. After a moment of hesitation, I slid the window open, and a moist breeze swept past me into the room. My thin robe was no match for the cold. A shiver swept over me, and my lips went numb.

Cindy's eyes found mine. "Alex? Is that you? How did I get here? I don't remember.... Alex? Help me, please!"

I forced words through unfeeling lips. "It's okay, Cindy. Were you looking for me? Did you come to see me?"

Cindy stared at me, confusion in her eyes. "I.... Yes! I wanted to find you." Certainty replaced the confusion. "I need you, Alex. I need you to help me."

"Why did you come here, Cindy? What do you want me to do?"

She opened her mouth, but the certainty left her expression. "What's happened to me? I don't know.... What's happened to me, Alex?"

"Cindy! I...." I wanted to help her, but I couldn't find the words that would provide her with any comfort. Finally, I blurted out, "Cindy, you're dead!" and I knew instantly I'd made a mistake I couldn't take back.

Cindy's face contorted, and her eyes widened until the irises were surrounded by white. Her mouth opened wide, and she emitted a scream I could feel in my bones but couldn't hear. With her face locked in an expression of fear, Cindy's hair burst into flames. Her skin darkened and split, and patches of blackened skin peeled off her face and vanished in the breeze until only a skull was left behind: a skull with Cindy's brown eyes still fixed on mine. As I stared back, openmouthed, a sludge of half-frozen blood pulsing through my temples, Cindy's eyes bulged and popped. My stomach lurched as oily black liquid poured from the bony sockets. The jawbone came unhinged, and, after hanging on for a moment, fell away. What remained of the skull exploded, and bone fragments disappeared into the night.

Pushing myself from the open window, I lowered myself to the side of the bed and breathed in the fragrance of Cindy Shipper's perfume, no longer sweet, but scorched and bitter in the frigid air, until the scent faded from the room.

***

I didn't know much about "ghosts," or whatever you want to call them. I'd recently learned that Islanders from the South Nihhonese believed that all people have two spirits, a spirit called a *qaitu* that stays with the body until it dies, and a spirit called a *hau* that can be enchanted away from the body while it is still alive. I'd seen examples of both in action. The *hau* was, more or less, a disembodied form of the physical person, with all of the memories, personality quirks, and mannerisms intact. The *qaitu* was something else again, much more akin to the ghosts in horror movies. This was the second time I'd seen Cindy Shipper's *qaitu*. Both encounters had ended with a vision of her fiery death.

It was time for a crash course on the subject of ghosts.

Going back to sleep was out of the question. After a stiff cup of coffee to chase away the worst of my hangover, I dragged a razor across the stubble on a craggy face that might have been cute when I was six. Turning away from the mirror, I rinsed off with a steaming hot shower. The thought of breakfast turned my stomach, but, knowing I needed all the fortification I could get, I smeared a blob of peanut butter on toasted waffle and forced it down with a second cup of coffee. I spotted my flask on the kitchen counter, but I decided to leave it behind. My head was muddled enough as it was, and, for the meeting I had in mind, I was going to need a reasonably clear head. I was counting on the morning sea-tinged air and my magical healing powers—and a third cup of joe—to give it to me.

The sun rose on a crisp morning with no fog, the slightest of breezes, and only a few low-lying clouds. The cool morning would turn into a warm afternoon, so I left my ties hanging in the closet and unclasped the top button of my shirt. Jamming my phone into my back pocket and my hat on my head, I headed out the door.

I walked up the block to pick up the beastmobile from Giovanni's Auto Repair. Gio was flipping the "closed" sign outside the door to his shop to "open" when I reached his lot. The stocky mechanic saw me coming and waved at me with a red rag, which he then used to wipe away the beads of perspiration already forming on the back of his neck. "You gonna make it to poker tomorrow night?" he asked.

"I'll try," I said. "I'm working a case, but I should be free as far as I know."

Gio unlocked the door to the shop and pulled it open. "I hope so. For some reason I always seem to do better when you're there. You're like a good luck charm or something."

I suppressed a chuckle. I was a semi-regular at Gio's Thursday night poker games, coming as often as I could and breaking even most of the time. The others all figured me as a safe, conservative player, too chickenshit to drop more dough into the pot than I could afford to lose. In truth, my enhanced awareness allowed me to read the faces of the other players like a book, giving me a distinctly unfair advantage if I chose to use it. But I was there for the comradery, not the money, and the only use I made of my gifts was to make sure Gio didn't get cleaned out. He was by far the worst poker player I'd ever seen, and I didn't know the other players nearly as well as I knew Gio, so I was happy to throw a few hands his way and make sure the others didn't take advantage of him.

Gio stood in the doorway. "I'm assuming you're coming for the beastmobile."

"Yep. Got an early call to make."

"I'm about to put on some coffee. Got time for a cup?"

"Sure thing. I only had three before leaving the house, and I could use another."

"Rough night?"

I groaned in reply and followed Gio into his shop and around the counter to his office.

As the coffee was brewing, Gio turned to me with a broad grin. "Hey, guess what? Antonio mailed off his application yesterday. He told me to thank you again for your letter of recommendation."

"Tell him it was no problem. I was happy to do it."

"The kid really wants to spend his mandatory fixing jet engines. I'm crossing my fingers. He'll be disappointed if he gets rejected."

"If he does, I'm sure they'll put him in a motor pool."

Gio grabbed a mug from a shelf and filled it with coffee. "That would be jake with me. Just as long as they don't hand him a rifle and send his ass off to combat. That would about kill Connie. She still wants her boy to be some kind of professional man, a fucking' doctor, or at least a dentist. I tell her, 'Leave the boy alone. He fixes things, like his ol' man does. And I was good enough for you, wasn't I?' But she wants 'more' for her only son."

Gio's son, Antonio, had started his senior year in high school, which meant he would be entering his mandatory three-year service to the Realm once the school year was over. A wizard with automobile engines after helping his old man in the repair shop for most of his adolescent life, he was hoping his government service would offer him a new challenge.

Gio pushed the mug my way and filled one of his own. "So where you off to so early this morning? Got a hot lead?"

"I'm working on something," I said, taking a sip of my fourth cup of the day. At least this one was free. I didn't want to think about how much dough I'd dropped at the Black Minotaur Lounge the previous evening. "I gotta go talk to someone about ghosts."

Gio's eyebrows shot up. "Ghosts? Alkwat's balls, Southerland. Do I even want to know about this?"

"Your daughter's a witch," I pointed out. "She probably deals with that kind of stuff all the time."

Gio held up a hand. "Gemma's *learning* to be a witch. She's only been studying for a year. She's still shuffling cards and mixing herbs. Lord's balls, the girl's only twelve—it's going to be a while before she's conjuring up spirits. A long, *long* while, I hope. Like when she's safely out of the house."

"Thirteen."

"What?" Gio stared at me in confusion.

"Gemma. She turned thirteen last spring."

Gio's eyes widened, and he slapped at the tabletop. "Son of a bitch! You're right. Lord's balls, where does the fuckin' time go? They grow up so fast—and she's my youngest! Sierra's already fifteen, and she's got a fuckin' boyfriend! At least I think she does. Her and Connie are being pretty coy. They think I'll blow my top and screw it up if I find out about it. Ha! Fact is, I don't want to know. If the little punk is anything like I was when I was his age...." He shivered and took a gulp from his mug.

I shook my head. "Parenthood. I'm glad I skipped it."

Gio shot me an amused glance. "It's not too late for you, you know. Fuckin' kids, man. Best thing I ever did in my life besides marrying Connie was raising them kids. But, damn, will I throw the biggest shindig you've ever seen when they're all safely out of the nest? You bet your fuckin' ass I will!"

I chuckled. "I don't know, man. What woman in her right mind would marry a lug who works when he feels like it, barely manages to scrape enough coins together to pay the rent every month, and spends his morning trying to find out everything he can about ghosts?"

Gio's eyes narrowed. "So, what's this all about with the ghosts?"

"I saw one last night. Well, early this morning. Outside my bedroom window."

A look of skepticism twisted Gio's round face. "Sure it wasn't some wayward chick giving you a booty call?"

"My apartment's on the second floor."

"Then you must have been dreaming."

"You don't believe in ghosts?" I asked.

"Oh, sure I do. I mean, I've never seen one, but Connie says she used to see the ghost of her dead sister from time to time, and who am I to say she didn't? She's a helluva lot smarter than I am."

I took another sip of coffee. "What does she say about it?"

Gio crossed his arms. "You know, the usual. Comes at night. Kind of shimmers. Oh, and everything around it gets real cold, you know? A cold you can feel in your bones."

An involuntary shiver ran up my spine as I remembered the frost and ice on my window. "Did it talk to her?"

"I mean, I guess so. She says it did. Nothing too, you know, coherent. Connie says it was mostly gibberish. But sometimes she would say something that let her know it was really her sister. You know, personal stuff. Pretty spooky, but, hey, why not?"

I finished my coffee and set the mug on the table. "This wasn't the first time I'd seen this ghost, if that's what it was. She wants me to investigate her death. Or at least I think she does. Why else would she come to me?"

"That's your case? Was she murdered?"

"I don't know," I said. "Maybe. She was involved with the Hatfields. She married Al the Torch a couple of months before she died."

"Oh, shit!" Gio set his mug down next to mine. "Why do you want to get yourself involved with *those* goons again?"

I shrugged. "Can't be helped."

Gio shook his head. "Lord's balls, Southerland. Ghosts and goons. Whatever you do, watch your damned ass. We got poker tomorrow night, and I don't want to lose my good luck charm!" He stood. "So where are you off to now?"

I stood, as well. "I'm headed for the adaro settlement," I said, taking a last swallow from my coffee mug and setting it back down on the table. "I need to speak to a dead woman."

Chapter Five

The settlement had changed since the last time I'd been there, when I'd smuggled a group of adaro women off the grounds and helped them escape into the ocean during the deluge the previous spring. It had become less a center for resettlement and more a compound for ethnic isolation. Visitors now had to enter the settlement through a checkpoint, where a navy security guard recorded names, makes of cars, and license plate numbers on a computer. I was forced to get out of the car and open the trunk of the beastmobile for a cursory inspection.

The guard took off his hat and wiped his brow as he stared at my car. "What do you got in there?" he asked, nodding toward the hood.

"Four hundred forty-two horses."

The guard whistled. "Sounds like they're all champing at the bit. You got a hood lock on that beast?"

"Got one installed a while back," I said. "It's got a spell on it that unleashes twenty-five thousand volts on any unauthorized joker who messes with it. My mechanic insisted."

The guard grunted. "Smart man. You'll need a good lock if you're going to leave your car unattended in this neighborhood."

They didn't find any weapons or other contraband inside, so they let me through. I'll say this for the naval security personnel: the whole process was efficient and surprisingly quick.

I was headed for the street market, but, on a whim, I took a detour to the site of The Dripping Bucket, the former headquarters for the Northsiders street gang. I'd heard that the bar had burned to the ground, and I wanted to take a look. When I got there, I found the bar's scorched remains on the empty lot. I parked the beastmobile and stepped into the ruins.

Nothing was left of the joint except a few charred beams, now lying broken on the blackened and discolored cement floor. If anything of value had been left behind after the fire, it had long been salvaged. I shook my head, wondering what I was looking for.

Something nagged at me. Before moving into The Dripping Bucket, the Northsiders had met at an old dive called Medusa's Tavern. It had also burned to the ground, and I had wandered its remains the same way I was now walking through what was left of the Bucket. I'd noticed something peculiar about the burn pattern at Medusa's: none of the damage had extended beyond the walls of the bar. The dried weeds outside the place had been untouched. It was as if the fire that had destroyed Medusa's had been painstakingly managed and controlled. Curious, I walked the length of the floor of The Dripping Bucket. The scorch marks stopped dead at the edge of the cement foundation, a perfect ninety-degree angle marking what had been the corner of the room. There was no evidence of fire beyond where the walls of the joint had stood. Like the fire at Medusa's, this one had been perfectly contained.

I considered how such control could be possible.

Back in the beastmobile, I pulled out of the lot and headed for the open-air market in the center of the settlement. I was relieved to find it still intact and reasonably active, although where once the marketplace had bustled with a teeming mix of sentient species, now the shoppers were almost exclusively adaros. After naval authorities cleared out the slums, only adaros and naval personnel were permitted to live in the settlement. Overnight guests were required to register, and, intimidated by the checkpoints and increased presence of the Tolanican Navy Master-at-Arms, humans, gnomes, dwarfs, and trolls no longer flocked to the settlement's marketplace for fresh-caught seafood and hard-to-find goods at bargain prices. No cars were allowed on the market grounds, but traffic in the settlement was light, and I found plenty of free parking spots near the entrance.

I wandered into the marketplace, bracing myself against the odor of rotting fish that hung over the grounds like a low fog and hoping to run into a familiar face. The last time I'd seen her, Sunny and her crew had been running a solicitation racket, hooking naïve human men with promises of exotic pleasures to a hut off the beaten path where thugs lay in wait to separate the hapless victims from their dough. I was fairly certain she was pursuing a more legitimate operation now, or at least I hoped she was.

I stopped at one of the larger booths, where an adaro woman was selling fresh tilapia—so fresh, in fact, that the fish were still swimming in a tank. She looked up when she heard me coming, and her face hardened when she laid eyes on me.

Like all adaro women, this one appeared to be no older than thirty, though she could have been twice that age. Her soft blue hair was tied behind her head, exposing the feathery gills on either side of her neck, and she glared at me with eyes the color of the sea under the noonday sun.

"You want tilapia?" she asked, her tone suggesting she'd be happy if I shopped elsewhere.

"Actually, I'm looking for someone, and I was hoping you could tell me where to find her."

"I don't know her," she said, turning away.

"I haven't told you who I'm looking for."

"I don't know her," she repeated. Raising her voice, she called out, "Next in line, please."

An adaro stepped up to the counter, easing me off to the side.

Was it something I said?

I moved to another booth, where a smiling adaro was offering kelp-based dessert snacks that spilled out of little paper containers. Her smile faded somewhat when she saw me, but she maintained a professional front. "Can I help you?"

"I hope so," I said, arranging my weatherworn face in a way I hoped was disarming. "I'm looking for a friend of mine. Sunny? Do you know her?"

Her expression never changed. "Sorry. I don't know anyone by that name."

I tried eight more booths, and each time I was met by faces that ranged from blank to suspicious to openly hostile. I wasn't sure why, but I had some ideas.

I was about to try another vendor, when I became aware of a different kind of presence approaching me from behind. I turned and waited for the uniformed Master-of-Arms to reach me.

"Sir?" he asked, his voice somewhere between firm and friendly. "Let's step away from the crowd, shall we?"

I took in the naval cop's baby face. He didn't look old enough to shave. Not a lifer, he was probably in the midst of his mandatory service. That made him, what, about twenty? Had I been this young during my year in the Military Police? I'd been nineteen when I became an MP and twenty when I was released from my service. That had been eleven years ago. I'd thought of myself as much older then. I was certainly a lot older now.

The MA interrupted my thoughts. "Sir? Step this way, please."

I held my ground. "Why?"

"I'm afraid you're creating a disturbance. Could you come with me, please?" The MA offered an arm in a way that told me he would drag me off the street if necessary.

I carried two hundred fifteen or twenty pounds on my six-foot-one frame. I could have dug in my heels and dared him to do something about it, but I didn't see the point. He was just a kid doing his job.

When he'd led me to a quiet spot away from the flow of shoppers, he stopped and faced me head on. "What are you doing here, sir? You aren't buying anything."

"I'm looking for a friend."

The navy cop looked me up and down. "Can I see some identification?"

"What for?"

The MA's only response was to hold out a waiting hand. With a sigh, I pulled my wallet from my pants pocket and removed my driver's license.

The MA plucked the license from my hand and studied it for a moment before looking up to compare my face to the picture. I removed my hat to make it easier for him.

He handed the license back to me. "It's a little early to be soliciting, sir. Why don't you hit up one of the brothels in the city later in the day? Or come back here after dark. Visitors are more welcome then, as long as you're gone by morning. And the navy turns a blind eye to a lot of what goes on here at night. Don't let anybody know I told you that, or I'll have to kill you." He smiled to let me know he was trying to be funny.

"I'm not here for that," I said, keeping my expression neutral. "Like I said, I'm looking for a friend."

"An adaro?"

"Yes."

"What's her name?"

"When I last saw her, she called herself Sunny. She wasn't legit then. She is now, though, so she might be going by a different name."

"Sunny?"

"That's right."

The navy cop's eyes narrowed. "The medium?"

"Medium? Is that what she's calling herself? All I know is that she's a channel for the late Leiti La'aka."

The baby-faced MA rolled his eyes. "So she claims," he muttered. He looked up. "What do you want with her?"

"I want to talk to the Leiti."

"It's a lot of hooey, you know. She was a grifter before, and this is just another grift."

"It's my money," I said. "Do you know where I can find her?"

He let out a resigned breath. "Yeah, sure. She's got an 'office,' if you want to call it that, just off the marketplace grounds. Go down to the end of the marketplace, take a right, and then your second right after that. Follow the street to a cul-de-sac. You'll see a sheet-metal shack that doesn't look like it would survive a stiff breeze. That's her place."

"Thanks." I started to walk away.

The MA put a hand on my arm. "Sir? You look like a decent enough joe. I don't know what you've heard about this Sunny character, or why you think you need to speak to a dead witch, but do yourself a favor. If you want to throw away your money, go home, wipe your ass with it, and flush it down the toilet. At least you'll be getting some use out of it." He sighed. "You look like a gent who's seen a little action in his day, but this neighborhood isn't healthy for men from the outside."

I stared at the MA's hand on my arm and looked up. "I'll be careful," I told him.

He removed his hand. "Don't say I didn't warn you. And don't come crawling to us when she's taken you for everything you've got."

"Don't worry," I said, brushing imaginary lint off my arm where he'd placed his hand. "She won't get nothing from me I'm not willing to give her."

I turned and headed off in the direction he'd pointed me.

***

Sunny's hut wasn't hard to find: it was the only structure in the cul-de-sac, and, as the MA had observed, it wasn't exactly the Huntinghouse Hotel. I stepped up to a door that was nothing more than a slab of plywood leaning against a windowless sheet-metal wall. Three plastic tarps laced together and nailed into the walls served as a roof. Forget about a stiff breeze—I could have taken the whole thing down with a well-placed kick.

Sensing life inside, I rapped my knuckles on the plywood.

A tired voice called, "Who is it?"

"A customer," I answered.

"You've got the wrong place."

"Is that you, Sunny? I'm here to talk to the Leiti."

After a few moments, a panel in the plywood slid to one side revealing a peephole with a blue eye staring through it at me. In the next moment, the plywood door was pushed open.

I stepped inside the hut, and Sunny used two handles attached to the inside of the door to put it back in place. I found myself surrounded by three young adaros in thin, loose-fitting robes, sleepy smiles on their faces, and a thick covering of blue stubble on their shaved heads.

Sunny was the first to speak. "Alex Southerland. It's been a while." She looked me up and down. "You haven't changed a bit. You still a dick?"

"A private investigator. Yes."

She raised an eyebrow. "You're here awful early. Too early for business. We weren't even up! You want some water? We keep some bottles of fresh water for human guests."

"You got any coffee?" I asked.

Sunny laughed, a pleasant sound. "Not for free, that's for sure. But Sandy can go out and get you some if you want it. You're buying."

"Water will be fine," I said, taking a look around at the inside of the hut. Three sleeping mats lay side by side at the far end of the room behind a circular wooden table with four wooden chairs. A counter holding various pots, pans, utensils, bottles, and jars, most filled with kelp or dried fish, stretched across one wall. A large spiral conch shell with a brilliant pink interior sat at the far end of the counter. Otherwise, the room was bare.

The air in the place was already hot and stifling, and it was only going to get worse as the summer day wore on. I wondered how Sunny and her crew could stand it. They must have spent most of their day outdoors, either in the streets or in the waters of the patrolled cove at the northern end of the settlement. I took off my hat and used a handkerchief to wipe away the sweat rolling into my eyes.

Sandy, the only one of the three wearing gloves to cover the registration number tattooed around her left wrist, crossed the room to the counter and poured water from a bottle into a jar.

"Sit over here," Sunny said, directing me to one of the chairs. Sunny sat in one across from me, and Coral, her sister, sat to my right. Sandy brought me the jar of water and took the seat to my left.

Sunny lifted both arms to indicate the entirety of the little room. "What do you think of our place? Pretty cool, huh?"

"All three of you live here?"

Sunny's lips curled into a sly smile. "Cozy, isn't it. It's all we need, at least for now." She leaned toward me over the table on her elbows, and her robe opened enough to expose a healthy bit of cleavage. "So... how've you been doing, honey?" On either side of her, the other two adaros watched me with amused expressions on their faces, their lips parted to expose the tips of their small, pointed teeth.

I leaned away from them and consciously slowed my breathing. In their natural habitats, adaro women outnumbered their men by about ten to one. It had been that way throughout the history of adaros as a sentient species. As a result, the women, through millions of years of evolution, had developed a unique set of survival traits. First, adaro women were naturally attractive to men, possessing those physical features that most men dreamed about. On top of that, the women emitted powerful pheromones that stimulated the desires of men. Women, too, for that matter, which was fortunate, since in the adaro communities fewer than one in ten adaro women mated with a man. Legally, at any rate.

The point is, I'd found myself in a small, enclosed space occupied by three alluring adaro women, each in their late teens, each dressed in robes thin enough to leave next to nothing to the imagination, and the atmosphere of the room was hot, steamy, and heavy with active pheromones. All three of them knew the score, and they were sweetly savage enough to enjoy watching me squirm.

I picked up the jar and poured the water over my head. The three adaros all broke into laughter.

When they'd settled a bit, Sunny said, "Maybe we'd better open the door and let in some air."

"I've got a better idea," I said. "Give me a minute."

I formed a sigil in my mind and sent out a command. Within seconds, two whirling funnels, each between two and three feet tall, swept into the room, pleasant breezes circulating in their wake. After a few minutes, the room had cooled a bit, the pheromones were less heavy, and I could breathe deeply without losing my train of thought.

Sunny sat back in her chair, a satisfied look on her face, but Coral stared at me, her lips twisted in disappointment. "Spoilsport," she said. "You're no fun at all."

Sunny dug both fists into her waist. "Coral! He's a guest. Be polite."

Keeping her eyes locked with mine, Coral crossed her arms in front of her chest and let out an exasperated sigh.

I held up the jar. "I could use more water."

Sandy took the jar from me. "I'll get you some. Are you going to drink it this time?"

"That's the plan. We'll see how it goes."

Sandy breathed in slowly. "Those elementals are bringing in plenty of salt air. I like it. Can we keep them?"

"Only if you can control them," I said.

"We only control *gruurbluurbls*."

My eyes darted involuntarily around the room, alert for puddles. I'd nearly drowned in a water elemental left as a trap for me by an adaro a few years earlier, and I'd never quite shaken off the experience.

Sunny caught my eye. "How'd you find us, mister dick?"

"I asked around about you in the market. Funny thing. No one wanted to give me the time of day."

Sunny scowled. "You're surprised? This past year has been rough on us. You humans have turned this place into a prison."

"You're still free to move about the city."

"Sure we are. All we have to do is ask permission from the bureau officials, sign some forms, get our picture taken for their files, let them know when we're going to be back, sign another form verifying our time of return, promise to behave, and wait for them to decide it's okay. Then we're tracked everywhere we go. And if we're not back when we said we'd be back, they alert the city cops, who drag us back in handcuffs. Other than that, we're free as the fish in the sea." She glared at me. "And you wonder why they don't like you? As far as they're concerned, you're just another jailor. It's a good thing they don't know who you are—you'd be lucky to get out of here with your skin!"

"What do you mean?"

"Don't be stupid. You're the reason they tightened things up around here."

I didn't argue. I might not have been the only reason, but I knew I was a big part of it. "Would you rather I'd have left well enough alone?"

Sunny sighed. "I don't know. That whole thing was weird. You helped a bunch of us return to the sea, but your whole city might have been destroyed if it hadn't been for what you did. Then *all* of us adaros would've been free."

"The settlement would have been destroyed along with the rest of the city. A lot of adaros would have been killed."

"Maybe. But the adaros around here resent you humans more than ever before."

I shrugged. "I don't blame you. The Dragon Lords tore apart your whole world. They separated you women from your men and forced you into these settlements. It's not right. I'd be pissed, too, if I were in your place."

"Oh, we're pissed all right. But don't you go around feeling sorry for us. We're gonna make you all pay someday." She smiled at me. "But you tried to help us, so I'll be sure to warn you when it happens."

Sunny got up and brought a bottle of salt water and three empty jars to the table. "You never answered my question," she said, pouring water from the bottle into a jar. "How'd you find us?"

"An MA gave me directions."

Sunny smiled. "Which one?"

"I didn't get his name. Young. Baby-faced. Friendly enough. He told me you were a grifter, and that you'd take everything I had if I wasn't careful."

Sunny's smile broadened. "That's Walt. Coral's in love with him."

Coral's eyes widened and she slapped her sister on the arm. "I am not! You're such a bitch!"

Sunny's eyes brightened. "You are, too. And he loves you."

"Stop it! He does not."

Sunny turned to me, still grinning. "He comes around here to 'check up on us,' but, really, he just wants to see Coral. He's actually kind of sweet. For a human. But he only wants one thing."

Sandy chimed in. "Yeah, and he wants it from Coral."

Coral reddened. "Stop it! I hate both of you!"

"You should marry him, Coral," Sandy said, a sly grin on her face. "Then you'd be free to leave the settlement."

Coral punched her on the arm, hard.

I took a drink of water. It was warm and tasted fishy, but it cooled my thirst by a degree.

Sunny glanced at me and pressed her lips together into a tight smile. "See what I put up with?"

I took another drink of water and said nothing.

Sunny sighed and folded her hands on the table. "All right, let's get to it. You said you came to talk to the Leiti?"

"That's right. I need to learn about ghosts."

Sunny flashed me a cheerful smile. "Then you came to the right place. Let's see if she's awake and ready to chat."

Chapter Six

Without a word, Sandy got up and brought a bottle of something brown to Sunny. I sniffed the bitter scent and recognized the drink as kava. Sandy returned to the counter and carefully lifted the conch shell. She brought it to the table and set it down next to Sunny, who was gulping the kava straight from the bottle. After a few sips, she sat upright and shut her eyes. Her breathing slowed and her face relaxed and went blank. Sandy and Coral sat quietly, hands folded in their laps, eyes on Sunny. A minute passed, and water poured from the conch shell, rolling over the edge of the table to the floor at Sunny's feet. Sunny's eyes opened and peered into mine.

"I remember you." The voice was Sunny's but the inflections belonged to someone else, someone older, someone with confident authority. "Mister... Southerland? Yes, Southerland. We stopped the storm." A smile came to Sunny's lips, but it wasn't Sunny's wide grin. It was smaller, less spontaneous and free, a practiced, professional smile.

"Did we do the right thing that night, Leiti?"

"We did what was necessary, Mr. Southerland. Many people, both adaro and human, would have lost their lives had we not acted. Havea Hikule'o is satisfied. And what was done is done. It cannot now be otherwise."

"And you?" I asked. "Are you satisfied?"

"Who am I that I can be either satisfied or dissatisfied?" came the response. "I am the *hau* of Leiti La'aka, whose *qaitu* is in Pulotu."

I leaned forward, curiosity getting the better of me. "Are you... alive?"

"I am neither alive nor dead. Those words have no meaning for me."

"Where are you, I mean, your *hau*, when you're not possessing Sunny's body?"

"Elsewhere. Nowhere. I am a thought in the mind of Havea Hikule'o. I am the Leiti and I am the spirit from whom Pulotu flows."

"Pulotu is what the Islanders call the land of the dead, right?"

"It is the eternal sanctuary for the followers of Havea Hikule'o when their *qaitus* depart their bodies."

"Can you tell me something, Leiti? I recently encountered a spirit called Cizin, who once ruled a place called Xibalba, also described as the land of the dead. And I once had a run-in with a dog spirit named Xolotl who brought me to the brink of yet another land of the dead, a realm called Mictlan. How many of these lands of the dead exist? And who goes where?"

Sunny's eyes seemed to catch a ray of light shining through a seam between the metal wall and the plastic roof. "There is one realm for the dead, a world beyond all other worlds and outside of time. But it is a different experience for everyone, just as the land of the living is a different experience for everyone. More than that, I cannot say."

I thought about that, nodding slightly. Somehow it made sense to me. Or at least enough sense for the moment. I remembered why I had come. "Leiti, I've had a recent experience with a ghost, or maybe it was a *qaitu*. I'm not sure if these are the same thing or different. It was the second time she's appeared to me. The first was on the night we stopped the storm. I know that a *qaitu* is one of the spirits of the living body, along with the *hau*. But being with you, your *hau*, is a lot different than being with a *qaitu*, or a ghost, or whatever it was. I'd like you to help me understand who, or what I met."

Sunny pushed non-existent hair from her face. "Ghost is a name. *Qaitu* is another name. What they signify is the same experience experienced by different people. I will tell you about *qaitus* and you will hear about ghosts. Is this satisfactory?"

"Sure," I said. "I'm willing to give it a shot."

Sunny, or the Leiti, took another sip of kava and set the bottle down with an ecstatic moan. Her smile broadened and her eyes softened. "How I miss kava. Odd, because I never thought much of the taste when I was alive. I enjoyed other sensory sensations more. But, somehow, of all my material pleasures, it's kava I remember most fondly."

She set the jar on the table. "The first thing you must realize is that the *qaitu* is not the same as the person it left behind. The *qaitu* is that person's memory of their life's experiences, and that memory is distorted. Your memory is not a camera, or a tape player, recording events with perfect clarity. You remember what your attention was drawn to during the moment, and your memory of events becomes distorted when it flows and mingles with other memories. When your *qaitu* separates from your body at the end of your life, it is the sum total of your distorted memories. In the realm of the dead, the *qaitu* loses these distorted memories of itself and becomes the composite of new experiences of a much different nature than those experienced during the person's life. With me so far?"

I nodded. "I think so. But do all *qaitus* move on? Why am I seeing them here in *this* world?"

"Death is not an easy transformation for most people. Life is not an easy thing to give up. People want to hold on to what they know, even if their lives have not been pleasant. The *qaitu* moves on, but it also holds back, and sometimes, especially if it has left an important part of its life unresolved, it holds back with great strength and resistance. These unresolved desires become anchors in this world. But the longer the *qaitu* resists the journey to the next realm, the more of itself it loses. Qaitus that refuse to step away from this world eventually lose all vestiges of their old experiences and memories, and become mindless spirits attached entirely to whatever it is that has kept them from cutting their anchor in this world and moving on. They become disembodied monsters of obsession."

I ran my hands through my wet hair. "These unresolved anchors to this world.... If, let's say, a person has been murdered? Would that be something that would create a hold?"

Sunny's head bobbed. "That's certainly something that can create a powerful resistance to the idea of moving on. But many desires and attachments can become anchors. A desire for revenge. A desire to relive an event that brought pleasure. A desire to alter a traumatic event that brought lasting pain. An attachment to a comfy chair. Or a relative or dear friend. The *qaitu* may maintain a foothold in this world, seeking resolution or satisfaction, even as it is moving into a different phase of experience. But there's more to it. When a *qaitu* manifests itself to someone, its... shape—its identity—is reshaped by that other person's memories of the departed person."

I shook my head. "I don't understand."

The Leiti peered at me through Sunny's eyes. "What is the name of the... ghost... that you met?"

"Cindy."

"Right. So when you met Cindy's ghost, you met her memories of herself and her life experiences. But those memories were modified by your own memories of Cindy. She became both what she thought about herself and what you thought of her, and what you continue to think about her. You mold her, to some extent, into the person you remember her being, or who you want her to be. And the more often you interact, the more of a mix of memories she becomes, modified still further by your direct contact. She becomes a product of your interactions. Does that make sense?"

"I think it does. Or, at least, I think I'll be able to figure it out if I think about it hard enough." I took a sip of water and discovered that my throat had gone dry. "These interactions. They aren't pleasant. The space we're in becomes cold. Icy cold. And, I don't know, there's more. I become disoriented, like my mind is floating."

Sunny's eyes narrowed. "Know this, Mr. Southerland. There is a danger in communicating with a *qaitu*. You speak with one at your peril. The *qaitu* of a body whose life has ended is drawn by strong spiritual forces to the world of the dead. When you are in the presence of a *qaitu*, especially if you speak with one, your own *qaitu* gets swept up in this pull. The pull is stronger if you were close to the person when they were alive. Remain in the presence of a *qaitu* of such a person long enough, and your spirit will be ripped from your flesh. Later if your will is strong, sooner if it's not. And then your body will die." Sunny's lips widened into a sly smile. "In short, Mr. Southerland, speaking with ghosts is a good way to become one."

That stopped me, and we all sat in silence for a bit as I chewed it over. Smokey's warning message from Chivo came to me then: "Beware the cold and resist the pull of death." I wiped sweat from my forehead with my shirtsleeve. Even with the elementals circulating the air, the room was heating up fast as the morning approached noon. Finally, I asked, "Is there a way to call a *qaitu* I wish to speak with and keep it away from me when I don't?"

Leiti La'aka's laugh came through Sunny's lips. "Any halfway talented witch can do it. But you can't. Not without the aid of artifacts."

"Artifacts? Like charms?"

"Maybe. Are you wishing to attract this ghost of yours or repel it?"

"Both. What can I use to bring her to me?"

A frown appeared on Sunny's brow. "You knew this Cindy in life, right? Did you share some material object that had common meaning for the two of you? A gift from one of you to the other, perhaps?"

I thought about that. "Possibly. We only knew each other for a few days. But, yes, there might be something."

Sunny's head nodded. "If you keep that object near you, it might bring her, if that's what you wish. Any object precious to her could work."

"And how can I send her away again, or keep her from bothering me in my sleep?"

Creases formed above the bridge of Sunny's nose in a way that reminded me strongly of Leiti La'aka in life. "That's a lot more difficult, especially if she is persistent. The best way to keep her away is to find out why she clings to this world in the first place. Once you know why your ghost chooses to haunt you, you might be able to figure out what you can do to persuade her to let you go and move on."

I'd been focusing intently on the Leiti's words, and I was a bit startled to hear Coral's voice break into our conversation. "Sunny is getting tired, Mr. Southerland. She can only keep this up for a few minutes."

I looked at Sunny and noticed that her eyes were beginning to droop.

"Coral's right," the Leiti confirmed. "It's tiring for me, too. I hope I've been able to help you."

"You've helped a lot. Thank you for your time."

"Take care, Mr. Southerland. I don't know this Cindy of yours or anything about her. But remember, her *qaitu* is not her. And it has no interests except its own. Don't forget that. It will seek to manipulate you in ways that the Cindy you once knew might not have when she was alive."

"I'll keep that in mind," I said, remembering how ready Cindy had been willing to use me for her own purposes in the short time we'd known each other. I couldn't imagine how her *qaitu* could be any worse.

***

I was hungry when I left Sunny's place, and on the way back to my car I called Walks in Cloud on my cell phone. Walks, a computer wizard with few, if any, peers, and a priestess of the Cloud Spirit, lived in a small apartment behind her workshop in the Nihhonese Heights District not far from the adaro settlement. She spent most of her life in her shop, designing and troubleshooting security software for major corporations and government agencies. She'd helped me out a year earlier by working with the Cloud Spirit to hide the formula for something called Reifying Agent Alpha, something that Lord Ketz-Alkwat himself had been searching for, although I'd since heard that the Dragon Lord no longer needed it. Walks was expensive, and I shouldn't have been able to afford her services, but she'd aided me for reasons of her own. The two of us had become friends, and a little more than friends when the occasion called for it.

"I'm in the adaro settlement," I told her after she'd connected. "Want me to pick you up some fish stew or something?"

"I'm a little busy, but, sure, why not. A girl's gotta eat, right? Anyway, I've been wanting to talk to you about something, so, sure, come on by."

"You all right? You sound a little ragged."

"Gee, thanks, Jack." I heard her take a puff from a cigarette. "I'm okay. I just need to put on a fresh pot of coffee. There might even be a little left for you if you don't take too long to get here."

Thirty minutes later, Walks and I were slurping down fish stew and black coffee at her worktable, where she'd shoved a pile of folders and an ashtray filled with old butts to one side to make room for the food.

Walks was making short work of her bowl of stew. "Mmm! Thanks, Jack. I guess I was hungrier than I thought. Whoops!" Some of the fish sauce had slipped from her spoon and dribbled down the front of the pink flannel robe that covered her shapeless body from her neck to her toes like a blanket. "Hand me a napkin, willya?" She pushed a long black braid off her broad lap and over her shoulder to hang down the back of her wheelchair.

"Been busy?" I asked, just to get her talking.

"Busy enough." She concentrated on rubbing at the stain on her robe and not meeting my eyes.

Walks spent most of her days working long hours alone with nothing but her computer, an endless supply of coffee and hand-rolled cigarettes, and the lurking Cloud Spirit, and that was the way she liked it. I'd become a frequent lunchtime visitor over the past year, and we were comfortable enough with each other that we didn't need to waste a lot of words in pointless small talk. But she'd told me on the phone that she wanted to talk, and I had a few things I wanted to share with her, too. Now that I was there, however, she seemed reluctant to get started.

I swallowed a spoonful of stew and watched her, aware of an odd tension growing between us.

"What have you—"

"I was wondering—"

"You go first," I said.

"No, you," she countered. She smiled, and her face relaxed. "What's new, Jack?"

"Not much. Oh, I was visited by a ghost this morning."

Walks rolled her eyes and started to scowl, but she must have seen something in my expression. "No shit? Really?"

"Yep. Did I ever tell you about Cindy Shipper?"

"I don't think so. If you did, I don't remember."

"I met her on a case a while back. Pretty. She might have arranged the murder of her husband and stepson."

"Sounds lovely." Walks scooped up more stew, taking care to keep it from spilling.

"We got along okay. Anyway, she married Old Man Hatfield's youngest son this past winter."

"Al the Torch?"

"Right. A couple of months after the wedding, she burned to death in a warehouse fire."

Walks's eyes widened. "I remember reading about that."

"She paid me a visit this morning. Outside my bedroom window on the second floor. It was the second time she's come to me. I think she wants me to help her."

Walks swallowed. "Help her? With what?"

"I'm not sure yet. I talked to another dead woman this morning in the settlement. She's a witch of sorts who I met when she was alive. An adaro I know channels her spirit now that she's not. This spirit thinks I need to find out what's holding Cindy to this world so that I can help her move on to the next."

Walks scooped another spoonful of stew. "Interesting. Are you going to do it?"

"That's the plan. The trick is not letting her drag me off with her in the process."

"Good trick. You should learn it."

"I'm working on it."

Walks frowned. "So, this chick was married to Al the Torch...."

"And she died in a fire," I finished.

Walks pressed her lips together to form an upside-down smile. "I'm no detective, but this doesn't sound like much of a mystery."

I chuckled. "They don't all have to be hard to solve. The problem is that it throws me up against the Hatfields. I had a little talk with Anton Benning yesterday. He's not happy about me bumping up against Hatfield business. According to him, Cindy's death was an unfortunate accident, and he told me to back off."

"Mm. The Hatfields...." Walks dabbed at her stew with her spoon, her mind suddenly elsewhere.

I waited a few beats before asking, "What about them?"

Walks returned from wherever she'd been. "Hm? What was that?"

"The Hatfields. You were about to say something about them before you drifted off."

She smiled. "Sorry about that, Jack. I was just thinking…. I know you've had run-ins with the Hatfields and that you don't like them much."

"The Hatfields? What's not to like? They're a swell bunch of pimps, extortionists, pushers, and killers."

Walks peered across her worktable at me. "And yet, this elf you work for. He made a deal with the Hatfields to help him with this secret project of his."

"I don't work for the elf. I'm self-employed, like you."

"You do jobs for him when he asks you to, and he doesn't pay you."

"I owe him."

"Right. My point is, you're helping him, and the Hatfields are helping him." She met my eyes. "Are you comfortable with that?"

My throat tightened. "Why not? It's not like I'm working for the Hatfields themselves."

"No, just with them. On the same project."

I shook my head. "It's not like that."

"It kind of is, Jack."

She was right, and it was something I'd thought a lot about. I let out a breath. "I owe the elf. This… thing he put in my forehead. I don't know how many times it's helped me heal from injuries that probably should have killed me."

Walks picked up her coffee cup and set it down without taking a drink from it. "You never asked for it, though."

"True," I admitted. "Still, though…." I let it hang.

Walks reached over the table to lay her hand on mine. "Have you ever thought about getting out of that arrangement? You can't be comfortable working with the Hatfields in any capacity, even if it's contributing to a common goal. You can't be feeling good about that. I get that you owe a debt to the elf, but can't you pay it off in some other way? Something that has nothing to do with a project he's working on with the Hatfields? Especially now that you might be running up against the Hatfields while you're helping this ghost friend of yours. They might have killed her."

Her hand felt cold on mine, but I didn't disturb it. "Believe me, all this has crossed my mind. No matter what Benning says, I'm going to find out how and why Cindy died, even if it means ruffling a few feathers."

She gave my hand a squeeze and pulled hers back. "Even if some of those feathers belong to the elf?"

"Let's hope that's not the case," I said, scooping up some stew. "But, yes, even if I wind up pissing off the elf a little. That's a risk I'll have to take."

Walks reached back and pulled her braid over her shoulder to her lap. Her eyes drifted toward some imaginary point over my head.

"Your turn," I said. "You said you had something you wanted to talk to me about?"

"Hm? Oh. No, that's okay. It's nothing."

Chapter Seven

Later that afternoon, I searched the closet in my laundry room for something I'd tossed in there a little more than a year earlier. I found it jammed into the back corner of the closet and carried it to my office, where I spread it out on the floor in the center of the room. The canvas, two feet tall and six feet wide, was slashed and wrinkled, and the wooden frame was broken into pieces, but I could still clearly make out the painting of a crow standing on a mesa and gazing out at the sunblasted desert panorama stretching into the distance. One long, jagged piece of the frame was missing. I'd had to destroy it before the police could find it and test the stain that had soaked into its pointy end.

I don't know if the painting had been valuable before it was damaged—what I know about art would fit in the bottom of a shot glass—but I'd been drawn to the painting from the moment I'd seen it mounted over the sofa in Cindy Shipper's living room. Later, it had been sent to my home with no return address. It was too large for my office, but I'd managed to squeeze it into the space above my filing cabinets where I could gaze at it and lose myself in its brown and red vistas whenever my mind needed a place to drift. It had been a casualty of an altercation in my office, one of the many times my place had been trashed. Chalk it up to the hazards of my profession. The painting was ruined, but I hadn't had the heart to throw it away. It reminded me of Cindy Shipper and a life that might have been if a million things had been different, a life that I knew in my heart of hearts would have been a nightmare for both of us.

I left the painting spread on my office floor and climbed the stairs behind my desk to my apartment.

After fortifying myself with a can of beef stew and a couple of glasses of cheap convenience store rye, I walked back down to my office, made myself comfortable in my desk chair, gazed at the painting, and recalled every moment I'd spent with Cindy Shipper.

I remembered how detached she'd seemed from her memories of her recently departed husband, and the contempt she'd felt for her admittedly contemptible stepchildren. I remembered having too many drinks with her at the Minotaur, where she told me that crows were watching her house, and she'd maneuvered me into inviting her to come to my place. We'd been rousted out of my bed (fully clothed—I'd told

Kalama the truth) the next morning by the police, and later it occurred to me how convenient it had been for Mrs. Shipper to have stayed with me that night. Lastly, I remembered Cindy pressing her body against mine and kissing me goodbye in her doorway after yet another visit by the police. I was convinced that little scene was just one more bit of manipulative theater, one that might have set me up to be murdered by a jealous would-be lover if I hadn't acted first. It had been the last time I'd seen Cindy, and I was left to conclude that she'd never viewed me as anything more than a useful tool. But then she sent me her painting. At least, I assumed she had been the one to send it. I spent a lot of lost time after that wondering if she'd felt any of the connection that I imagined I'd sensed between us. Or maybe she'd simply wanted to rid herself of any lingering links to her old life, and she'd noticed me examining the painting with appreciation.

I poured the last of the booze into a glass and held it up in a toast to the late Mrs. Hatfield. No, not Hatfield. The *qaitu* haunting me was shaped in part by my memory of her, and, for me, she'd always be Cindy Shipper no matter who she'd been married to at the time of her death.

It was too much to ask that Cindy's *qaitu* would pop into the room in the middle of the afternoon just because I'd rolled out an old painting she used to own, so I wasn't overwhelmed with disappointment when it didn't happen.

Lubank called me early that evening with information about the two gunmen who had come for Kintay. "They're a couple of out-of-town pros," Lubank told me. "The troll is called Breakspear, and the little guy is Tavish. As far as I can tell, they've never worked in Yerba City before. According to my sources, they've been holing up in Angel City, although they worked a job in New Helvetia not that long ago."

I set a half-empty cup of coffee on my desk and leaned back in my chair. "They're a team?"

"They seem to be. Freelancers, apparently. Mid-level gunnies, mostly working Central and Southern Caychan, with the occasional jaunt into Azteca."

I thought about that. "But never Yerba City?"

"Not before yesterday," Lubank said. "At least, that's what my sources say."

"How reliable are your sources?"

"Southerland, please. Are you doubting my connections?"

I snorted. "With all the crooks who owe you for getting them off on technicalities? Not a chance."

"Hey! Some of those crooks were innocent," Lubank protested.

"I'll bet none of the innocent ones have intel on hired guns."

"True, true."

"Got any background on these guys?" I asked.

"Yep. They're your kind of people."

"Huh?"

Lubank chuckled. "They used to be partners in a private investigation operation in Angel City. They even had legit licenses. They didn't exactly do divorce work, though. Word is they played rough. Real rough. Seems like the firm was just a cover for their actual racket, which was mainly button work. They aren't picky about who hires them, or what they gotta do for the dough." He let out a single sharp laugh. "Ha! I might hire them myself sometime. Their rates are pretty damned reasonable."

"They ever kill anyone notable?" I asked. "Or anyone we know?"

"Not really. If you want to bump off the governor of Caychan, you get someone else. An assassin. Like the Rakshasa."

"Who?"

"The Rakshasa! The head of the Varadkhar family."

"Oh, right. I've heard of him."

"Lord's balls, Southerland. I should think so! He's the most famous contract killer in the history of the world! He'll take out anyone you want, anywhere in the world, using nothing but a dagger. No target is safe from him. All you gotta do is pay him enough dough per kill to buy Yerba City."

"You sound envious. And here you are, just a crummy lawyer."

"Fuck you, Southerland! I'm a *great* lawyer. You oughta know: I've kept your ass out of stir more times than I can count."

"If you say so."

"Anyway. We aren't talking about elite assassins here. We're talking about your garden-variety journeyman professionals. Competent. Effective. But ordinary. You want to knock off your business partner, these might be the guys you call."

"How about a corrupt attorney with a bloated ego?"

"Forget it, pal. These mugs are reasonable, but you still couldn't afford them."

I sat up. "Anything else you can tell me about this pair?"

"Not much. They're supposed to be stand-up gees. They don't make a lot of noise: they fly in, do the job, and fly out."

I considered that. "Hmm.... If they were here to take out Kintay, then this job didn't go as planned."

"Unless they caught him."

"Yeah.... But if Kintay got away, then the goonie twins are probably still in town."

Lubank sighed. "Yeah, I was thinking that, too. We messed things up for them. They might come after us, next."

"You think so? I don't know. Loogans like that are strictly in it for the dough. Far as I know, no one is paying them to bump *us* off. If they caught up to Kintay, they're likely on a plane back to Angel City. If Kintay's still breathing, they're going to stick around until they correct their mistake. That means—"

Lubank cut me off. "Th'fuck, peeper. You aren't thinking of trying to stop them, are you? I know Kintay is an army buddy of yours, but the man is a nut job, not to mention a career criminal. Lord's flaming pecker, Southerland. What do you care if he gets popped?"

"He came to us for help."

"So fucking what?"

"So I think we should help him."

"Uh-uh, peeper. Ix-nay on that noise. I ain't getting in between that psycho and a couple of professional hitmen. Even ordinary ones. Lord's fucking balls!"

"He's a decent guy who got in over his head through no fault of his own."

"Not my problem."

"He and I go way back."

"That supposed to mean something to me?"

"He offered you money."

I sat through a long pause. Finally, Lubank broke the silence. "He did, didn't he. And right now I'm discussing him with a potential witness, which means I can bill this hour to him. And since you're also a professional consultant, I'm going to have to bill him extra for your time."

"Does that mean I'm getting a fee from you?"

"I'll tell Gracie to take it off what you owe me for the Clara Novita case. So what's your next move, peeper?"

I chuckled to myself. Lubank was my attorney, and I did investigative work for him. It was an exchange of professional services. But somehow when the debts were balanced against each other every month, I was always the one on the short end of the ledger. The way I figured it, he'd foreclose on my coffin when I was six feet under.

I took a sip of cold coffee. "My next move? I've either got to find Kintay, or I've got to find Breakspear and Tavish."

"Any idea where Kintay might be?"

"No. Not yet at least. But I'm guessing our hit team is staying in one of the hotels by the airport. People aren't likely to forget a troll and a dwarf hanging out together. They probably won't be hard to find."

"Hey—*hey*! You aren't going to try to tackle them alone, are you?"

"Are you kidding? I'm not going to try to tackle them at all."

"Then what's the plan?"

I leaned back in my chair. "My plan? Same as it always is. I'll snoop around a little and see what happens. Then I'll play it by ear."

"Lord's balls! You call that a plan?"

"Plans are for suckers. They always fall apart."

Chapter Eight

Yerba City International Airport was located on the east side of the peninsula just across the southern boundary of Yerba City proper, though legally speaking it was still considered city property. I considered taking a bus to the airport to save on gas money but decided against it. The beastmobile still had more than a quarter tank of gas in its belly, and I calculated that should be enough to get me there and back again if I didn't make any side trips. I strapped on a shoulder holster, complete with a loaded gat, and hit the streets.

The sun was beginning to set when I reached the hotel park outside Yerba City International. If the gunmen were high rollers, they'd be staying at the Aguilar or the Stanton. Lubank had described them as "mid-level," and I guessed that applied to their choice of accommodations, as well. That could mean the Galaxy or the Chumash, or possibly the Golden Gate if they were on a tighter budget. Of course, if they regarded comfort as an unnecessary luxury, they might gravitate to any number of motor hotels farther from the airport, in which case my chances of finding them before they flew out of town weren't great. And if they'd already finished their job, they wouldn't still be in the city at all. But that was useless negative thinking, and I shoved it aside. If worse came to worst and I drew a blank, I'd hit up the hotel bar at the Aguilar before heading home. The drinks were overpriced, but the ambience was worth it. Just one drink. I'd pay with my credit card and hope the Bureau of Licenses had left me with a little change after shaking me down for my expedited operator's permit.

I decided to start with the Galaxy and work down from there.

Neither the uniformed desk clerks nor the snooty concierge had seen a troll and dwarf check in at the same time, and if anyone working in the bar had seen a pair matching their description come into the establishment, they weren't talking. As for the hotel detective, he was more concerned with clearing me out of the lobby than giving out information on hotel guests. Apparently, I wasn't classy enough for the joint. I decided the Galaxy was a no go and moved on to the Chumash.

The Chumash was a wash-out, too, although the hotel dick was sympathetic. He told me that he'd seen a troll and a dwarf together in the lobby with a high-end adaro joy girl, but the detective had recognized the dwarf from his days as a vice cop for the YCPD.

"Hit man?" The detective sniffed. "The only kind of hits he supplies are the ones you snort up your nostrils and rub over your gums. Besides, he's been peddling his overpriced nose candy around here for years. No way he's a contract killer."

I left him one of my business cards, and he promised he'd call if he ran into my pair of loogans.

The Golden Gate was a step down from the Galaxy and the Chumash, but hardly a fleabag. Not a place the chairman of the board would check into, but his junior sales staff would be comfortable enough there. The lobby was smaller, the desk clerks wore standard business attire rather than uniforms, and the concierge doubled as the hotel dick. He proved to be talkative, too, once I bought him a drink from the flask I brought. It was convenience store hooch, but he took two big swallows and didn't care.

"Thanks for the pick-me-up, fella. You're a good man. Now, I don't know whether your guys have a room here, but they checked into the bar about a half hour ago. A troll and a dwarf, and both of them looking like they mean business. If they aren't the lugs you're looking for, they'll do until something better comes along."

I thanked him and made my way to the hotel bar.

I spotted them right away in a booth near the back of the room, Breakspear with his back to the wall, Tavish across the table from him, and a half-empty quart bottle of rye between them. The troll saw me as soon as I saw him and alerted his partner, who turned to watch me as I moved in their direction.

I grabbed an unoccupied chair and dragged it to the end of their table. "Evening, gents. Mind if I join you?" I sat without waiting for an answer.

The troll turned his burning red eyes on me, and his lips spread into a tight smile. "Evening, Mr. Southerland. Flag down a waitress and get yourself a glass."

"Thanks, Breakspear. I'll do that." I turned to the dwarf. "How y' doing, Tavish? How's Yerba City treating you?"

Tavish ran his fingers through his thick beard. "Nice town. I like it. Traffic's a bear, though."

"True," I acknowledged. "But it can't be worse than Angel City, can it?"

Tavish smiled. "Not much, but the streets are straighter there. These Yerba City streets wind all over the place."

"And everything's on a hill," Breakspear added. "Angel City is flat as a pancake, at least downtown. The hills and canyons are on the outskirts. It's a lot harder to get where you want to go here."

"This place can be hard to get used to, especially when the fog rolls in. You need someone local to show you how to get around." I caught the troll's eyes. "You wouldn't happen to know anyone, would you?"

Breakspear kept his face expressionless. "We've managed well enough on our own so far. The navigation app on our phone helps."

"It must help a lot. You found out where Kintay was staying pretty fast. He'd only checked in the night before. You even found out which room he was staying in. I kind of thought someone was feeding you good intel, and that he must be a local."

Breakspear gave me a blank look, and Tavish said, "Who's Kintay?"

"No one," I said. "Did you get him yet?"

Tavish dropped his eyes, and Breakspear sighed. "Nahhhh," he drawled. "He's a slippery little bastard."

"But we'll get him," Tavish added. "We always do."

A waitress came by our table with a glass, and Breakspear filled the bottom third of it from the bottle of rye. I held the glass up in a toast. "Thanks. You guys must be pretty good."

Tavish sipped from his glass. "You've done some homework on us, just like we've done some on you, Mr. Southerland. You already know we're reliable." He poured another splash of rye into my glass to replace the amount I'd put away with my first swallow. "It's a shame the mug we've got business with is a friend of yours. But it's nothing personal. We've got nothing against you."

I took another sip, smaller than the first. "It's good to know that I'm not included in your contract."

Breakspear's lip stretched into a half smile that produced a dimple in his hairless cheek. "Nah, you're clear. For now." He tossed back the remainder of his drink and poured himself another one. The bottle was well on its way to becoming a dead soldier.

Tavish stared at me. "Did you and that shitster go to the cops?"

"Not yet," I said.

"Why not?"

I shrugged. "What would they charge you with? Willful destruction of a hotel-room door? I don't have a stake in that tourist hole, so it's no skin off my nose. Now, if you had put a hurt on Kintay...." I locked my eyes on his.

Tavish smiled through his beard. "You wouldn't know where he is, would you?"

"Do I look like someone who would tell you if I did?"

Tavish indicated Breakspear with a glance and a nod. "My partner might have something to say about that."

I reached for the bottle and poured the remaining liquor in the troll's glass. "Can't tell you what I don't know," I said. "Shall I buy us another round?"

Breakspear held up his glass. "Nah, I think we're good. This stuff's weak as shit, anyway. What we need is some trollshine. Now that's a drink for a Hellborn warrior."

I put on a smile. "But not for a human. I'd rather live through the night."

Tavish let out a relaxed laugh. "I'm as Hellborn as he is, which is to say some distant ancestor of mine followed a Dragon Lord out of Hell, same as him. But no trollshine for me, thank you very much. That shit'll knock your hair off your chin." He finished the rye in his glass.

I looked from the troll to the dwarf. "Is there anything I could do to get you to nullify your contract on Kintay? He's crooked as fuck, but he's essentially harmless. Now that he knows what kind of mess he's in, he's going to be too shook up to do whatever your client thinks he might do."

Tavish and Breakspear looked at each other and turned back to me. Breakspear shook his head. "Sorry, man. You're a private dick, so you know what stiffing a client would do to our professional standing."

Tavish nodded. "We used to do what you do. We had a license and an office in Angel City. Did all right, too."

"What happened?"

Breakspear picked up the story. "A guy we were tailing pulled a gun on us, and we had to take him down. Got off on self-defense, but now we had a reputation."

Tavish continued the story. "After that, about the only jobs anyone offered us was hits. That turned out to be okay, though. Turns out that takedowns bring in a whole lot more dough than peeping through windows. We did a couple, and then that was the only kind of job we would take."

Breakspear grunted. "And we don't have to do that many, either. Three or four a year, and we make more than we ever did when we were straight."

"We have to travel more," Tavish added. "To tell you the truth, though, Angel City has become a little hot for us. We can't hardly work there anymore. What about you, Southerland? How did you get into the P.I. racket?"

"I was an MP down in the Borderland. Once my mandatory was done, I kicked around for a while until I wound up here in Yerba City. That was almost ten years ago. I came to pay a visit to the grandmother of one of my buddies who didn't make it out of the Borderland. She owned some properties here and asked me to do a background check on a potential tenant. She liked the job I did and helped me get a license. She even rented me one of her buildings, and I've been operating out of it ever since."

"It's working out for you okay?" Tavish asked.

"Some days are better than others," I said.

Tavish flashed a grin and nodded at the troll. "Don't I know it. I had to dig a bullet out of this big idiot's butt cheek today. Motherfucker doesn't know how to duck."

Breakspear grunted. "If my ass hadn't come between you and that lead pill, it would have taken your eye out. Besides, you loved it. My booty is fuckin' irresistible. I should've charged you for the peek."

Tavish grimaced. "Th'fuck! You ever smell a troll's ass up close? I don't recommend it."

A smile came unbidden to my lips. "I got as close as I needed to earlier today. I'm just glad the big lug rolled off me before I suffocated. My ribs are still sore."

The troll let out a laugh. "Serves you right for shoving a gun barrel in my ear. I can't believe I let you get the jump on me like that. I must be getting careless."

Tavish snorted. "Once again I had to save your bacon."

Breakspear's eyes widened. "What? How do you figure?"

Tavish glared at him. "I shoulder tackled this bum away from you. Are you telling me you missed that? It was a fuckin' smooth move." The dwarf nodded at me. "Tell him, Southerland."

I shrugged. "You caught me by surprise." I turned to Breakspear. "But you're lucky the impact didn't cause me to jerk the trigger. I'd've blown your head off."

Breakspear scowled. "So, what you're saying is this reckless little punk almost got me killed."

"Yeah, pretty much." I polished off the remainder of my drink.

Tavish rolled his eyes. "What does he need with that fuckin' head anyway. It's ugly and he never uses it."

Breakspear made a face at the dwarf and signaled for the waitress. "Yerba City seems like a swell town. I'll bet you know a few drinking holes that the tourists don't know about. Maybe you can show us around next time we're back."

Tavish grinned. "Yeah, and maybe you can teach us how to get around on the back roads and avoid the heavy traffic."

I looked from the dwarf to the troll. "You guys sure I can't buy you another bottle? The night's still young."

"Nah," Breakspear said, smiling at the waitress who'd come by with the check. "Big day ahead of us, and Tavish needs his beauty sleep, not that it will help him any. And I've got some trollshine waiting for me up in our room. I need a real drink after the way that little fucker butchered my butt today."

The dwarf snorted. "Next time I'll leave it in. I never want to see that wrinkly fart box of yours again for as long as I live."

Breakspear picked up the check and studied it for a moment. I offered to chip in a couple of bucks, but the troll wasn't having it. "You're an all right gee, Southerland," he said after writing in a tip and signing the check off to his room. "I hope we don't run into each other tomorrow."

I nodded. "Likewise."

After the two hitmen left the bar, the waitress came by and asked me if I'd like another drink. Deciding one more for the road wouldn't hurt me any, I ordered a glass of whiskey. I took my time with it, savoring the smooth single malt and considering the two surprisingly affable contract killers I'd been drinking with. I marveled at the vicissitudes of fortune that could turn two legitimate and respectable members of my own profession into cold-blooded executioners. These two murderers were intent on knocking off Tom Kintay—a career criminal, to be sure—but a man with whom I'd been on good terms for more than ten years. I didn't want to see Kintay killed, and yet I found it impossible to generate any animosity toward the men who'd been hired to kill him—men, I reminded myself, who would put me down for keeps without batting an eye if I got in their way. They were, after all, simply doing their jobs.

The hell of it was that I wouldn't hesitate to pull the trigger on my two newfound drinking buddies in order to save Kintay's life. Why? Could I even count Kintay as a friend? We'd had some amiable conversations, but he worked for a notorious underworld crime syndicate designing and producing narcotics that had undoubtedly done irreparable harm to an untold number of families. The first time I'd met Corporal Kintay was when I locked him up for stealing drugs. Why did I value Kintay's existence over Breakspear's and Tavish's? Because I'd known him longer? How did that make him a better person than a pair of professional gunmen? Maybe the answer was that Kintay had helped me out a couple of times, and that meant I owed him. That's what it came down to, I supposed. Maybe life was nothing but a series of transactions, and the best good people could do was honor their debts. I shrugged off the thought and handed my credit card to the waitress when she came by with the check.

Two minutes later, the waitress returned and told me that my card had been rejected, and, per my bank's policy, shredded. I had just enough cash to pay the bill and left without leaving a tip.

Chapter Nine

A crowd had gathered up the street from the Golden Gate Hotel. Spurred by curiosity and a need to clear my head before climbing behind the wheel of a moving vehicle, I wandered over to see what was up. A piercing voice cut through the buzz of the swarming onlookers, and, as I drew closer, I caught sight of the speaker, a young woman in a camo jacket with an olive-green cloth scarf over her long brown hair. She held a fist in the air as she railed against what she referred to as "the colonialist war of Tolanican expansion into the historically Quscan-owned territory of the so-called Borderland." I sighed and shook my head. Nothing good was going to come of this.

"Day after day, week after week, month after month," the speaker intoned, her voice filled with a passion that sounded genuine. "Year after year, and, yes, decade after decade. Our young men and women, children on the verge of adulthood, forced into the meatgrinder, nothing but grist for the mill, fuel for the Dragon Lord's hellish war machine. And for what? So that one Lord from Hell can prove to the other Lord from Hell that he has a bigger dick. These two foreign lords are bringing Hell to our world. If they love Hell so much, let them descend back down the hole they crawled up here from. You over there. Do you have children? Yes? Are you ready to send them off to die in this endless war fought to satisfy the egos of monsters? You there. How old are you? Sixteen! In two years, you start your mandatory government service for the Dragon Lord of Tolanica. Are you ready to spend it killing young men just like yourself? What will you get from it? A pat on the back, a ticket home, and a life filled with nightmares. A life filled with jumping in terror at every loud sound. A life of headaches, a life of drinking to forget and drugging to ease the pain. And that's if you're lucky. If you're not so lucky? A free ride home in a box."

People in the front of the crowd reacted to the agitator's speech in a variety of ways, some cheering and clapping, some whooping and laughing, some jeering and heckling. These antiwar rallies had become more and more common over the past several months, and they were starting to catch the attention of the mainstream media, which tended to dismiss the rallies as curious sideshows put on by drunken malcontents, attention-seeking narcissists, and self-entitled young adults who'd been coddled as children. Well known newscasters, established film actors, and popular musicians criticized this minority of ungrateful young troublemakers, as well as the overly permissive parents who lacked the will to properly discipline their children. Quscan agitators and agents were said to be behind the demonstrations.

Someone pushed against me from behind. Turning, I saw that the gathering had grown from a few dozen onlookers to nearly a hundred since I'd arrived, and the increasingly unruly crowd was now spilling into the street, interfering with the flow of traffic. The sounds of blaring horns and shouted curses threatened to drown the speaker's words out altogether. Not wanting to get caught in the press, I made my way to the outer fringes of the mob.

A new sound pierced the night: the shrill screech of police whistles. The mob scattered as a squad of uniformed cops charged in, swinging nightsticks and shoving bodies aside. The bulls surrounded the speaker and hoisted her from the wooden apple crate she'd been using as a makeshift stage. A handful of zealous onlookers came for the cops, who beat them to the ground with their sticks and kicked at their fallen bodies with heavy boots. The rest of the mob retreated, and the cops soon had the speaker in handcuffs. Her scarf had been ripped from her head, and blood flowed from her nose and over her lips.

I was about to walk away, when I saw a black van, gleaming in the light of the streetlamps, pull up and stop alongside the scattering crowd. It had the shape of a typical prisoner transport, but it was unmarked, lacking not only police insignia, but identifying features of any kind, including a license plate. The passenger door opened, and a strange, gray-suited man stepped out. I guessed he was human, but, if so, he was one of the oddest-looking humans I'd ever seen. His huge beak of a nose and bushy eyebrows that sat above his eyes like a pair of gerbils buried the rest of his face in shadow. Tall and thin as a drinking straw, the wraith-like figure floated toward the cops holding the rabblerousing speaker. One of the cops held up a hand to stop him, but something in the odd man's face caused him to quickly step away. When the thin man reached the bulls restraining the speaker, he reached into his pocket and pulled out a card. The bulls looked from the card to the man's face and released the agitator into his custody. The thin man escorted the young woman back to the van and locked her inside.

The crowd, cops included, disappeared in a hurry, but I stared after the van as it drove off. Even from twenty yards away I'd felt an aura of something unpleasant coming from the wraithlike figure, something that had left a sour lump in my stomach. Human? Probably. A witch? Maybe. Whatever he was, I was certain I knew who he worked for: the Lord's Investigation Agency. The LIA was Lord Ketz-Alkwat's own department of justice and the highest law enforcement agency in the realm. It was also the Dragon Lord's internal spy service, his personal police force. Leea, as it was sometimes known, had authority over every agency in Tolanica, and local cops deferred to them completely. Leea saw and heard everything, and when they wanted someone to disappear—someone like a dissident speaking out against the Dragon Lord's war policies, for example—that person would vanish from the face of the earth as if they had never existed. A wave of sympathy for the young woman I'd seen loaded into the van swept through me. By the end of the night her name would be scrubbed from all existing documents, and no one would admit they'd ever known her. It would be as if she'd never existed.

I turned away and walked down the block to my car.

***

A pale light was leaking out the window of my office when I reached the front door. I turned my key in a lock that was nearly frozen. When I stepped inside, Cindy Shipper was sitting on the floor leaning over the damaged painting and studying it with downcast eyes. Her body glowed faintly with a yellow-tinged light, and her scarlet dress stood out starkly against skin that was white as ivory. Her hair, strawberry blond in my memory, but orange and yellow on this specter, hung down her shoulders and flickered like cold flames.

Cindy turned to look at me, and it was the face I remembered, though drawn and unsmiling. Her red eyes were wet with tears, and black makeup ran down her cheeks. She spoke to me in a voice that quavered, but it was Cindy's voice. "What happened to my painting?"

"I'm sorry," I replied, lowering myself next to her. "It was damaged in a fight."

Cindy's features hardened. "Why didn't you look for me? I sent you my painting so that you would come looking for me."

"Then you should have included a note. How was I supposed to know that's why you sent it? It didn't even have a return address." My breath turned to mist as it left my mouth.

Cindy's head shook. "You should have looked for me."

"I barely knew you," I pointed out. "I had my own life to live."

A faint smile appeared on her lips, and it sent a shiver down the back of my neck. "We had something. You cared for me."

I shrugged away the shiver. "Maybe I did. I didn't forget you."

The smile disappeared. "You should have looked for me. You should have protected me."

"From who? Yourself? You weren't a dame who needed protecting. Not you. Others needed to be protected from you."

She shook her head again, and moisture filled her eyes. When she spoke, her words were almost inaudible. "They killed me."

"Who killed you?" When she didn't answer, I asked again. "Who killed you, Cindy? The Hatfields? Your husband?"

Cindy's eyes closed, and when she opened them again, they were dry. "Alu."

"Alu? Your husband? Did he kill you?" The cold in the room was oppressive, and I pulled my coat closed against it.

She smiled a smile that reached her eyes, the kind of smile men want to see when a beautiful woman looks at them. "Alu is sweet."

"But did he kill you?"

"Puppy," she said.

I wasn't sure what to make of that. "What? Puppy? Are you saying that Alu is a puppy?"

The dreamy smile didn't leave her lips. "Puppy," she repeated, turning her eyes away from me.

Where was this coming from? "Cindy. Look at me. What are you trying to tell me?"

Although I could still see her clearly, she seemed to be somewhere else, as if she occupied two places at the same time. "My puppy came for me," she said, but I couldn't be sure she was still talking to me. "My cute little puppy."

Leiti La'aka had warned me that *qaitus* were largely composed of jumbled memories, and that memories weren't always reliable. 'Puppy' might have been Cindy's pet name for her husband, or she might have been remembering a dog she once owned. Or maybe her attention had been focused on a dog at the time she died. I had no way of knowing, so I tried to regain control of the conversation. "How did you die, Cindy? Do you remember?"

Cindy's eyes hardened, but she didn't say anything at first. She blinked and stared at me, as if she were seeing me for the first time. "Alex? Did you know about the elves?"

That caught me up short. "Elves? What do you mean? Did you see an elf?"

Her eyes lost their focus again, and she gazed off over my shoulder. "Elves and elves," she muttered. "Elves, and elves, and elves." I wondered what she was seeing but resisted the urge to turn and look.

This was getting me nowhere. It was as if Cindy's *qaitu* had come loose from its anchor. I reached down and put my hand on the painting. "Cindy. I need you to tell me what happened to you. Can you do that?"

Cindy blinked again, and her eyes narrowed into a frown. "The crates are gone. They took the crates away."

"Crates? What crates?" A mist was settling over the room.

"The crates. Crates and crates. All gone. Elves and elves. My pretty puppy..." Her voice was losing its strength, and I could clearly see through her translucent body to the wall behind her. But just when it seemed she would fade away altogether, her eyes suddenly bore into mine. "Go see Claudius. He'll know."

"Claudius?" The name didn't ring a bell. "Who's that?"

Cindy's face slackened, and whatever focus she'd managed to find began to fade along with her shimmering form. "Claudius.... Find Claudius."

"Cindy, I—wait!" I remembered then. "You mean Claudius Silverblade? The lawyer?"

She refocused with an act of will, and her body regained its solidity. "Claudius. Claudius will know."

Silverblade had been head of legal services for Emerald Bay Mortgage, Donald Shipper's company. He'd also run an escort service on the side, and some of his featured attractions had been as young as thirteen. My lip curled into a snarl at the memory.

Cindy's flickering hair looked too much like flames, like her head was on fire. I tore my gaze from her hair and concentrated on her soft brown eyes. "Claudius Silverblade? Does he know who killed you?"

"Claudius knows everything." Her smile faded. She'd stopped drifting and was entirely present now. "Alex. You should have looked for me. You should have protected me."

I started to answer, but my lips had turned to unfeeling blocks of ice, and my tongue was swollen in my mouth. I reached up to touch my face, and my cheeks were numb, too.

A dense mist filled the room. Cindy reached out and put a solid hand on my shoulder, and the burning cold from her touch scorched my skin. "Come with me, Alex. You didn't come for me then. We should have been together. Come with me now."

I shook off her hand and tried to stand, but my legs groaned at the effort and collapsed. Cindy reached for me again and caught my elbow in her hand. I tried to pull away, but she slid her hand up my arm to the back of my neck. I froze from head to toe, the cold penetrating my bones, as Cindy pressed against me, and I felt the full weight of her body on mine. I gasped and the air froze in my lungs. Cindy cupped the back of my head in the palm of her hand. Her head lowered, her lips parting, and her eyes soft, until her face was inches from my own. I tried to resist, but her lips, colder than ice, brushed against mine. My heart froze, and my heartbeat slowed. A shroud of darkness descended through the mist....

A noise, like the ripping of a thick carpet, sounded from nearby, and a vibration shook the base of my skull. The sound grew louder, and I recognized it as the growling of an animal coming from within my own head. A feline scent tickled my nostrils.

"Cougar?" I breathed. Or maybe I just thought it to myself.

About a year earlier, more or less against my will, I'd undergone a mystical experience and been adopted by a spirit animal called Cougar. The spirit occasionally offered me advice, often too cryptic to be helpful, allowed me to detect the presence of magic, and sometimes lent me strength when I needed it. He didn't always come to me when I called on him, but now and then he showed up at opportune times. Like this one.

Cougar growled again, louder and longer than before, and my eyes snapped open. I pulled back from Cindy and felt skin peel off my lips. I forced myself away from her with lifeless arms that no longer seemed my own, letting my instincts, or perhaps the will of Cougar, rule my senses.

Cindy rose until she was standing over me, cold flames rising from her head. She reached out to me. "Come with me, Alex. Take my hand and we'll be together."

Cougar's growl sounded again. Warmth flowed into my arms, and I found the strength to push myself across the floor until my back bumped against the door. The flames on Cindy's head grew and spread over her face. She reached toward me again, and her voice emerged from the flames, pleading: "Come with me, Alex. Come with me."

If I'd been holding a gun, I would have plugged her. "No." The word came out in a hoarse whisper through my frostbitten throat. "No. I can't follow you where you're going."

The fire spread to Cindy's shoulders, and her dress erupted in flames, flames that did nothing to drive the freeze from the room. She raised both arms into the air and screamed, a blood-curdling wail, as fire rose from her fingertips.

"Cindy!" I cried. And she was gone, leaving nothing behind except the cold, cold mist.

***

I don't know how long I sat against the door, huddled inside my coat and trying to catch my breath. A long time, maybe. I called for Cougar, but my spirit animal had disappeared without a word. I thanked him anyway, assuming he'd get the message. Finally, I stood, rolled up the painting, and carried it out to the alley, where I stuffed it into a garbage can. After staring at it for a few moments, I went back inside and returned with a book of matches and a can of lighter fluid.

I stood by the flames and warmed myself in the clear night, stars shining down on me like curious eyes in the darkness.

Chapter Ten

I woke after sunrise tangled in sweat-soaked sheets with the remnants of half-remembered nightmares drowning in my subconscious. With a groan, I forced myself to my feet and into the shower. I stood under the hot water until it turned cold, and then for another two minutes after that, trying to drown a hangover caused by too much whiskey and the nearness of death. After toweling off, I brushed my teeth, but after running a hand over the stubble on my chin I decided shaving wasn't a priority that morning. Coffee was, however. I stumbled into the kitchen, plugged in the coffeepot, and filled the biggest mug I could find with reheated sludge left over from the previous day.

Still in my robe, I carried my coffee downstairs to my office and sipped it slowly, savoring the aroma and letting the strong, bitter elixir burn the pains and memories of ghosts from my brain. When the mug was empty, I refilled it halfway with fresh brew from my office coffeemaker and placed a call to the main office of Greater Olmec International, a prominent holding company that owned Emerald Bay Mortgage and a number of other financial institutions in the Realm of Tolanica and elsewhere. After the death of Donald Shipper, Claudius Silverblade had been promoted into the parent office. He had an office in GOI's corporate headquarters in Yerba City's financial district. By all rights, Silverblade should have been doing time for trafficking underage girls and boys, but the charges that had been brought against him a couple of years earlier had been dropped because of "lack of evidence," which was a chickenshit way of saying that the city's lawmakers wanted no part of crossing Silverblade's employer: Madame Citlali Cuapa, the CEO of Greater Olmec and the most powerful witch in western Tolanica. I'd met Silverblade when I was helping Madame Cuapa find out who had compelled her to cast a spectacularly fatal spell on Cindy Shipper's late husband, Donald. Silverblade was a sharp-minded troll with no morals, and I'd hoped I would never have to run into him again.

After navigating GOI's phone tree and sitting on hold for five minutes, I reached a human being, a young-sounding woman, who put me on hold for another five minutes while I was transferred to another human being, a more mature-sounding woman, who politely informed me that Mr. Silverblade was in a conference and would call me back at his earliest opportunity. Since I was the one who'd alerted the Yerba City Police Department two years earlier that he'd been operating an illicit child-sex racket, I assumed that Silverblade would never find an opportunity to call me.

Cindy's *qaitu* had told me that Silverblade was the man to see for answers regarding her death, so I was going to have to find a way to make him talk with me. Knowing what I was going to have to do, I took a half-empty pint bottle of rye from my desk drawer and poured a shot into my coffee. After a few sips, I steadied my breathing and placed another call.

The phone was answered after eight rings by a strong male voice. "Madame Cuapa's residence."

"Cody, it's Southerland."

"Mr. Southerland! How nice to hear from you, sir. To what do I owe this pleasure?"

I hesitated. "You didn't know I'd be calling?"

"Indeed, I did *not*, sir. Should I have known?"

"Whenever I've called before, she anticipated it. I don't think I've ever surprised her before."

"You surprised *me*, sir. The Madame may have known we'd be hearing from you and neglected to tell me about it. She's been wrapped up in something of a secretive nature for the past several days. Lots of mysterious phone calls and lots of communication through other less mundane channels."

"And she hasn't been keeping you in the loop?"

"No, sir."

I knew Cody was not only Madame Cuapa's personal assistant and protégé, but that the Madame had sponsored Cody's upbringing and kept close contact with him as he was growing up. The relationship between the two was akin to that of a grandmother and her favorite grandson. "Isn't that unusual for her?" I asked.

"Yes, sir. It is. Just between you and me, I'm concerned."

"And you have no idea what it's all about?"

"Well... as you know, sir, the Madame has an aversion to the telephone. I answer all phone calls that come into the house. Without mentioning names, I can tell you that she has not only been in contact with many of her peers around the world, but with a number of notable politicians, including representatives of several of the Dragon Lords. Whatever it is, it's big. Although the news media hasn't mentioned it, I can't help but believe that something of tremendous import has occurred recently."

"But she hasn't mentioned anything to you?"

"Not as of yet. I'm sure she'll inform me when she feels it's appropriate." He sounded disappointed.

"Cheer up, Cody. It's probably something so catastrophic that it threatens the lives of everyone on the planet, and she doesn't want you to worry."

"That's what I'm afraid of, sir. Your attempt to cheer me is having quite the opposite effect."

"I don't suppose the Madame is available to speak with me?"

"I'm afraid not, sir. The world-shaking catastrophe with which she is consumed occupies a great deal of her time. She's quite frazzled. She'd neglect to eat and drink if I didn't nag her. But I will let her know you desire to contact her. Perhaps she would welcome a respite from her current dilemma. Can I tell her what it is you wish to speak with her about?"

"It's Silverblade. I need to see him, and I don't think he'll talk to me without some motivation. I was hoping the Madame would intervene on my behalf."

"I see. Perhaps I can be of some help. What do you need from Mr. Silverblade?"

"It's regarding Cindy Shipper. I've... uh... well, I've been visited by her ghost."

"Her ghost?"

"Ghost, apparition, specter, spirit, *qaitu*... whatever you want to call it. I think she wants me to investigate the cause of her death."

"Intriguing! And how does Silverblade fit in?" I couldn't help but notice Cody's professional assistant persona had slipped a bit, and a new note of childlike enthusiasm had entered the young man's voice.

"Cindy's ghost told me that Silverblade knows all about it."

"Ah! And you want to interrogate him."

"That's right. Preferably, in person."

"Hmmm.... Let me see what I can do. I assume you want to brace the goon as soon as possible?"

Brace the goon? Cody was going all private gumshoe on me. I decided to lean into it. "Sure, pal. That would be copacetic. And sooner would be better than later, if you get my drift."

"Then leave it to me, boss. I'll be persuasive."

"That's swell. Maybe you can bring Mr. Whiskers as an ace in the hole. Never hurts to have an enforcer along when you wanna put the muscle on a troll."

"Please, sir. I'm sure it won't come to that. And, anyway, Mr. Whiskers has a gentle soul."

"Oh, he's a real pussycat. For a manticore."

"He wouldn't hurt a rabbit, unless I wanted him to. And then he would rip it apart and eat it. Silverblade knows that."

"Wouldn't hurt to remind him of that," I offered. "Maybe give him a little demonstration."

"Good point. I might just do dat liddle t'ing."

I chuckled and abandoned the tough guy banter. "Well, I'll be grateful for whatever you can do to help. I'll at least owe you a beer."

"A beer? I'm thinking more like a night on the town. I know just the place, too, and I've got a new outfit I've been *dying* to show off. With that get-up and a rugged he-man like you on my arm…. I can assure you that we'll turn every head in the room."

"Yeah, um, you know that's not the kind of attention I'm looking for."

"Don't knock it if you haven't tried it. Anyway, the drinks are fabulous, the company is outrageous, and some of those crazy mugs have very agreeable sisters, if that's what you're going to insist on."

I groaned. "Get me in contact with Silverblade, and we'll negotiate something suitable for both of us."

"You're on, sir. And you can count on me."

***

That afternoon, I got a call from a jane with a sultry-sounding voice who told me that a car would be arriving for me within the next half hour to take me to see her boss. She wouldn't reveal the name of her boss over the phone. Silverblade? Probably, although I couldn't think of a good reason why the sultry dame wouldn't just say so, and she was not one of the women I'd spoken to when I'd called Silverblade's office earlier.

I gulped the last dregs of the cup of coffee I'd used to wash down the chicken and rice I'd thawed and microwaved for lunch and grabbed my coat and hat. A brisk wind had swept away the morning fog, but the chill that had settled over the city during the night refused to yield to the sun beaming down from partly cloudy skies. I considered packing some heat but dismissed the idea. Some bigwig was sending a car for me, and the chances I'd be able to get close to "the boss" without getting frisked and disarmed were slim. If I got into trouble, I'd have to rely on my razor-sharp wit to get out of it. It could work. There's a first time for anything, right?

A luxury sedan almost as large as the beastmobile was double-parked and blocking traffic in front of my office, and a troll wearing a black suit and tie with a leather driver's cap was standing stiff and tall outside the back door.

"You're Mr. Alexander Southerland?" he asked when I reached the vehicle.

When I said that I was, he pulled the door open and waited for me to enter.

I slid over the rich leather back seat and noted the double-paned glass partition separating me from the front seat. It appeared to be soundproof. Probably bulletproof, too. After the troll took his place behind the wheel and started the engine, the bluesy sounds of a trumpet-fronted band emerged from unseen speakers. The tunes were probably meant to discourage me from trying to start a conversation with the driver through the soundproofed glass. I didn't recognize the band, but the music appealed to me. I found a control on the armrest and turned the volume up a notch.

The sedan wound its way through the downtown area before stopping at the front entrance of the Capricorn Hotel, a luxury joint near the north waterfront. My driver hopped out of the car, handed the keys to a valet, and held my door open as I climbed out.

After he'd closed the car door behind me, the troll looked down at me from a foot over my head and said, "If you don't mind?" I extended my arms out from my sides while he patted me down. It was a professional job, and I knew I wouldn't have been able to sneak a pocketknife past him.

"This way, sir," he said, and I followed him into the lobby of a hotel that would have cost me a month's pay to stay in for a single night. Two months' pay if I ordered room service and snagged a drink or two from the liquor cabinet. The troll guided me past the main elevators to a special one at the end of the hall. When we were inside, he pressed the single button, and we rose twenty-five floors non-stop to the penthouse at a speed that made me wonder if we'd been launched into near orbit.

The elevator door opened into a suite large enough to stage a tennis match in front of a small audience, although the carpet was thick enough to eat tennis balls for lunch. The troll showed me to a brown leather chair that might have been delivered new for the occasion.

"Mr. Hatfield will be with you in a moment," the troll informed me.

"Mr. Hatfield?"

"Mr. Ferrell Hatfield." The troll took up a position to one side of the elevator door.

"Not Claudius Silverblade?"

"Mr. Ferrell Hatfield," the troll repeated.

Well, isn't this cozy, I thought to myself. I'd been expecting to see Silverblade, but instead I'd been summoned by Fats Ferrell, oldest living son of Old Man Bowman Hatfield and the de facto leader of the most powerful criminal syndicate in the city. And I managed to allow myself to be led without a struggle or a gun into the penthouse suite of a luxury hotel that might as well have been a fortress. I needed an exit strategy, and fast. I did a quick scan of the suite, using all my enhanced senses, and found three ways out of the room. The first was past a quarter ton of troll down a private elevator. The second was a set of stairs next to the elevator, just to the other side of the troll. The third was out the window, twenty-five stories above the city streets.

Letting out a quiet sigh, I sat in the chair and waited for Fats. At least the chair was comfortable.

I didn't have to wait long. I'd been settled in the chair for less than a minute when Fats Ferrell, all two hundred eighty pounds of him, sauntered into the suite from a side door with a dark look on his bearlike mug. I made to rise, but Fats waved me back down.

"Don't get up," he told me in a voice that was used to being obeyed. "This isn't going to be that kind of meeting."

Fats fell into a nearby chair large and padded enough to hold his weight without groaning. He leaned forward and pointed a finger at my chest as if it were a loaded gun. "I assume you know who I am, but, in the interests of clarity, which is what this meeting is all about, I'm Ferrell 'Fats' Hatfield." He paused for a moment to let that sink in before lowering his finger and continuing. "Mr. Southerland, you've been poking your nose into the death of my brother's late wife, Cindy. You will stop, immediately. Her death is a private family affair, and it's none of your concern. Cindy's death was a tragic accident. Everyone in the family is still mourning her loss, and you'll only make things worse for us all by stirring things up. Am I making myself clear?"

I leaned back in my chair. "I'm a little confused, Mr. Hatfield. I was under the impression that I was being taken to see Claudius Silverblade. Did he contact you after I called his office?"

Fats frowned. "Silverblade? I'm not sure I know that name." He stopped frowning and pointed his finger at me again. "You haven't answered my question."

"I've been told several times now that Mrs. Hatfield's death was a tragic accident. No one has offered me any details. Can you tell me how she died?"

Fats glared back at me through narrowed eyes, no doubt wishing he was holding a gun instead of pointing a finger. "How do you like that? I asked you if I was making myself clear, and I can see that I've failed to do so. Let me try again. Mr. Southerland, I didn't bring you here to answer your questions or to satisfy your morbid curiosity. Neither I nor anyone else in my family owes you an explanation. I brought you here as a courtesy to let you know in person that your interference in our family matters is not welcome, nor will it be tolerated. You will desist immediately. That's a given, Mr. Southerland. You will cease to investigate poor Cindy's death. Let me be *crystal* clear. You have no say in the matter. I am asking you to cease willingly. That's the way I'd prefer it. But make no mistake. If you decide to oppose me in this matter, I can assure you that you will cease unwillingly." He held my eyes for a bit to make sure he had my attention. He thrust his pointed finger in my direction. "Does that clarify matters, Mr. Southerland? Or would you like details on how I will put a stop to you if you refuse my request?"

I waited a beat, then nodded. "I understand perfectly, Mr. Hatfield."

A thin smile found its way onto Fats's fat face, and he lowered his finger. "Good. Before you leave, Mr. Southerland, I have one question for you, and I'd appreciate an honest answer. I know that you're a private detective. I want to know who hired you to investigate Cindy's death. Who was it, Mr. Southerland?"

"I'm sure you'll understand that a person in my profession wouldn't stay in the business long if he made a habit of giving up his clients' names, Mr. Hatfield."

Fats stared at me for a couple of tense seconds before slowly nodding. "Okay, you've got your professional ethics. I can appreciate that. I'll find out soon enough, and that's a fact. Tell that to your client next time you see him. Or her," he added, as if it were an afterthought.

Fats looked me up and down as if he were seeing me for the first time. His tight smile relaxed. "I'm glad we've come to this understanding, Mr. Southerland. I guess you're losing a paycheck by dropping this matter, so let me make it up to you. Give Dreadshadow," he indicated the troll by the elevator, "a figure representing your loss in this case and he'll see that you are fairly compensated. And now...." Fats planted the palms of his hands on the arms of the chair. "If you'll excuse me," he said, preparing to lift himself out of his cushioned seat.

I stayed in my seat. "If I may, Mr. Hatfield...." Fats glared at me from beneath a hooded brow, and I endured it for a beat before holding up a hand. "Don't worry, this has nothing to do with Mrs. Hatfield."

Fats eased himself back into his chair, and I continued. "There's a man who works for your family. Not high up in your family, just a fella in one of your labs. You might not even know him. His name is Tom Kintay. He's got himself in a jam, and a couple of contract guys are targeting him. Now, I don't know what it's all about, but Tom's not a bad joe, and it seems to me that maybe this could all be sorted out to everyone's satisfaction without anyone suffering anything too permanent, if you know what I mean."

Fats lifted an eyebrow. "Tom Kintay, you say? Can't say I've heard the name before. He mean something to you?"

I kept my expression neutral. "Not that much. Maybe I'm just sentimental. I ran into him when I was an MP back in the Borderland. I ran into him again yesterday, and he's a mess. He asked for my help, but I'm a little over my head when it comes to contract killers. Sitting here just now, it occurred to me that hitmen might be more in your area of expertise. I gather they're from out of town, and I thought maybe they might be infringing on your territory. Let me know if I'm out of line, but if there was something you could do about the situation, well, I guess that would put me in your debt."

The hint of a smile appeared on Fats's face. "Hitmen, you say? I wouldn't know anything about that sort of thing. But if I get the chance, I'll put out some feelers and see if anyone I know might have heard something." He held up a finger. "No promises. I've got a lot on my mind today. But you say this Kintay fellow works for the family? Well, we wouldn't want anything to happen to one of our own, right? That would be bad for business."

He stood and scowled down at me. "Now hit the bricks, peeper. And stay off my radar. If I hear you been asking more questions about Cindy, things won't go well for you." He turned and disappeared through the door he'd come in from.

Dreadshadow followed me into the elevator and hit the down button. As we were plummeting to the earth, the troll asked me how much I needed to compensate me for the loss of my case. "Give me a fair figure," he said. "Mr. Hatfield is a reasonable man. He doesn't want you to feel like you've been cheated."

I waited until the elevator finished its descent before answering, mainly because I didn't trust myself to speak with my stomach in my throat. When we were safely on the ground, I looked up at the troll. "Tell Mr. Hatfield to forget about it. I don't need his money."

I started to step out the door, but Dreadshadow stopped me in my tracks with a heavy hand on my shoulder. "Mr. Hatfield won't like that. He'll take it to mean that you don't intend to honor your part of the bargain."

I stared at the troll's hand. "What Mr. Hatfield likes or doesn't like is none of my concern."

Dreadshadow kept his grip on my shoulder. "I can assure you that it most definitely is."

I looked up at the troll. "Don't bother getting the car. I'll call a cab." I continued staring into his face until he released me.

"I'm looking forward to seeing you again," Dreadshadow said. I turned and walked into the hallway, feeling the blood pulse through the bruises forming on my shoulder.

Chapter Eleven

My front door was unlocked when I got back to my office, and Tom Kintay, covered in fresh tinfoil, was sitting behind my desk holding a pistol in one hand and a coffee mug in the other. As I stepped inside, he swung the pistol in my direction. "Are you alone?"

I shut the door behind me. "You didn't happen to see a goat-headed monster when you came in, did you? Glowing red eyes that mess up your stomach and make you want to puke?"

Kintay tilted his head. "Uh-uh. Why? Is he supposed to be your watchdog?"

"Not a very effective one. I see you found the coffee."

Kintay pointed with his cup. "Nice coffeemaker. It looks like the ones we used to see in the mess halls back in the service."

"I got it at the Army-Navy Surplus."

"That's awesome. Go ahead and grab yourself a cup."

"Of my own coffee? Gee, thanks, Dad. You mind getting out of my chair?"

Kintay took a brief sip from his cup. "I'd rather sit here. I've got a good view of the door." He rested his gun hand on the desktop, but kept the barrel pointed in my direction.

My coffeemaker sat on a small table on one side of the room next to a watercooler, and I kept several water glasses, cups, and mugs of various sizes on hand for my own convenience, and for the convenience of any guests or potential clients who might walk into my office. I poured myself some coffee into the biggest, heaviest mug on the table and brought it over to the desk. When I was close enough, I slammed the mug down hard on Kintay's wrist. Kintay's gat slipped from his hand to the desk, and I scooped it out of a puddle of spilled coffee.

"Son of a *bitch*!" Kintay wrapped his hand around his wrist. "I think you broke it!"

"I doubt it, but it would serve you right. Next time you point a gun at me, I'll make you eat it. Now get out of my chair."

"Right, right, right," Kintay whined. "You don't have to get sore."

I slid a guest chair to the side of my desk. "You'll still have a good view of the front door from here."

I tossed Kintay's piece, a twenty-two semi-automatic, into a desk drawer and took my accustomed seat, while Kintay, holding his wrist, plopped sullenly into the guest chair. I slid his coffee cup to the corner of the desk next to him and gave him the once over, noting the dark bags under his bloodshot eyes. "You look terrible," I told him.

His shoulders slumped. "I've had a rough few days."

"You're still here, so I'm assuming those gunmen never caught up to you."

He sighed. "No, not yet. But I don't know how much more of this I can take. I keep hearing their footsteps right behind me."

I was pleased to see that not all of the coffee had splashed from my mug when I'd used it to disarm Kintay, and I took a sip of what remained. "What are you doing here, corporal? Have you talked to Lubank? I thought you were going to work something out with him."

Kintay let out a breath. "I called him this morning. He said he spotted one of the gunmen—the dwarf—casing his office from the street. He's been there all day."

"Makes sense," I said. "They must have figured you would either come to him, and the dwarf could nab you there, or Lubank would go to you, and the dwarf would follow him. The troll must be looking at some other likely places you could be. Good thing he didn't follow you here."

Kintay gulped some coffee and grimaced. "I was careful. It's not the first time I've been on the run." He looked across the desk at me, a small grin on his face. "You remember, right? We had some fun back in the day."

I snorted. "I remember. I also remember you weren't that hard to catch."

Kintay chuckled. "I was young and stupid back then. And it still took you a couple of days to bring me in."

"Right. And what are you now? Old and stupid?"

"Hey, I'm not old."

"Uh-huh." I gave him a sidelong glance and slurped more coffee.

"Anyway, Mr. Lubank told me to lay low and he'd get back to me, but I never heard from him. I've been trying to get hold of some guys I know, but the word's out that I'm hot, and no one wants anything to do with me. Fuckin' rats. So I came here, because I know you don't scare off so easy." He glanced at the clock on my desk. "I got here a couple of hours ago. Did you know you're out of butter?"

"Come again?"

He pointed up in the general direction of my kitchen. "I found some frozen waffles, but you don't have no butter. I had to toast them up and eat them with nothing but syrup. They're better with butter, you know."

"I eat them with peanut butter."

"Peanut butter?" Kintay considered this for a moment, then nodded. "Yeah, I can see that. But with syrup, right?"

"Of course. Or honey. Sometimes I add banana slices or a scoop of ice cream, but I'm all out."

"Hunh. Too bad. That sounds pretty good. Your cupboard's kind of bare, sport. Either you eat out a lot, or the private eye biz must not be all that lucrative."

"It has its ups and downs. I'm in one of those downs at the moment."

Kintay flashed a smile. "Well, you're in luck, pal. Because I'm flush! Don't ask me how I got it. Never mind, I'll tell you." He cupped his hand against the side of his mouth, like he was giving away a secret. "I mixed up a bag of primo capsules for Fats Hatfield. A *big* bag. And he gave me a serious chunk of change for it. But don't tell anyone! Fats has a side hustle going that none of the others know about. Not even the Old Man."

"Fats is running an independent operation?"

"And cutting the other family members out of the profits. Fats has always been greedy. He wants to run the whole syndicate, but his father won't die, and he's getting impatient."

"That's interesting," I said. I'd always thought about the Hatfield Syndicate as one unified family. But that's the problem with families: internal dissension is inevitable, especially when the kids start thinking they've grown up. I remembered the knock-down drag-out arguments I'd had with my own parents. Throw an almost unlimited amount of money into the picture, and it made sense that even little fractures in the family structure would shake things up in a hurry.

Kintay waved his hands as he spoke, causing the tinfoil to come loose and hang from his arms. "The Old Man likes to operate at a high level, to control politicians and judges, that kind of thing. He's also hands-on when it comes to the gambling rackets and the sex trade. But for Fats, it's always been about the drugs, and he's been running that part of the business for years. That's who I used to do most of my work for. But the Old Man took me out of designing drugs and put me on this other project, the secret one. You know, for the space alien. Fats didn't like that, but there was nothing he could do about it. I've been doing a bang-up job on the secret project, but it's fuckin' snoozeville. I take care of my piece of the fabric without knowing what the final product is going to be. Where's the fun in that? It feels like I'm on an assembly line. They keep track of my time! If I wanted to punch a clock, I'd get a job in a fuckin' factory! Working with those mutated stem cells is the only thing that makes the job worthwhile. That shit is dynamite! I played around with it a little and came up with a way to use it to mix up a batch of happy-happy on the side. I mean, it's what I do, right?"

I stared at him. "You used the stem cells to make recreational drugs?"

"Not just stem cells—fuckin' mutated *alien* stem cells! I cloned off a few and used them as the base in my mix." A maniacal smile lit up his face. "That shit is crazy, man! I could do a *lot* with it if they'd let me."

"And you sold the drugs to Fats?"

"Sure! We sampled some caps and he positively flipped! I'm telling you, that shit makes you feel like you can do fuckin' *anything*, like you're a god or something. It destroys inhibitions. I mean, you take one of these and you just don't care. Fats paid me for everything I'd made and started up his own operation. It's fuckin' clever, too! He made a deal with a couple of street speakers who are all bent out of shape about the war in the Borderland. He arranges for them to hold impromptu rallies on the streets and provides them with security from the cops. And then his dealers circulate through the crowd and give away samples of the stem-cell mix. You better believe that after a taste of the euphoria those caps give them, they come back with their wallets open, begging the dealers to take their dough. Fats is making a fuckin' fortune, and he's cut me in on it."

I'd run into one of those activists a few weeks earlier and seen Fats's operation at work. It had all seemed overly elaborate to me, and the cops weren't all that keen on it. But the woman I'd seen taken away by the LIA the day before didn't look as if she'd had much protection. Had she been operating on her own? I wondered if Fats's staged rallies had sparked a larger and more genuine movement, rather than one that operated as a front for Fats's narcotics racket. Maybe the elf knew. Maybe he hoped these rallies would catch on and help undermine the general public's faith in the integrity of Lord Ketz.

I thought about the conversation I'd just had with Fats. When I'd asked him about Tom Kintay, he'd played it coy, giving no indication that he knew him. And now Kintay was telling me that the two of them were business partners. Was that information I could use to my advantage? I'd have to think about it when I had more time.

The last rays of the day's sun were streaming through the blinds of my front window and casting shadows that crisscrossed my office floor. I caught Kintay's red-streaked eyes with my own and held them. "Anyone die after taking those drugs?"

The smile disappeared from his face. "How would I know? Look, sergeant. Users are gonna use. I just give them something worth using."

I shook my head. "No wonder you're on the run."

Kintay took a sip of coffee and rewrapped the tinfoil around his arms. He let out a sigh. "Lord's balls. Life was good when the family just had me producing party candy for them. That was a fun gig. Where did it all go wrong? Remember that old lab the Hatfields set me up in? It was fuckin' sweet. They'd supply me with anything I asked for, and I could spend all day just messing around with hallucinogens and pharmaceuticals, experimenting and refining.... I had a big-screen TV and a satellite hookup.... Man, it was crazy! I could watch anything I wanted. The porn they got coming out of Huaxia? You wouldn't believe it, man. Lord's flaming pecker—those guys over there are fuckin' demented!"

I rolled my eyes. "Yeah, sounds like the good life all right. You think that's why those hitmen are after you? Maybe the Old Man found out what you were doing with Fats."

Kintay shook his head so vigorously the tinfoil hood slid over his face. "No, man," he said, rearranging the foil. "It's this thing with Papadopouli and the proof about what this project is really all about. Hey, are you sure those goons didn't follow you here? No?" He let out a breath. "You got a nice little setup here. Or you would if you had some decent food." His face brightened. "We should make a grocery run."

"Look, corporal." I found a dry spot on my desktop and set the mug down on it. "Tonight's Thursday, and that's my poker night. I'd invite you to stay here, but I was serious earlier about that goat-headed monster. I call him Chivo. He stays in my laundry room and minds his own business, but he takes a dim view of intruders. The last joker who broke into my office got his throat torn out. You're lucky Chivo was out when you broke in. What'd'you do, pick my lock?"

Kintay grinned. "Wasn't hard. Piece of advice, sergeant: if you don't want uninvited guests, don't make it so easy for them to get in. Anyway, I wasn't planning on staying the night." He reached into his pocket and held up a thumb drive. "I just wanted to give you this. It's

Papadopouli's data files. I'm not going to try to sneak it past that gunman, but I figured you could get it to Mr. Lubank somehow. And maybe if I don't have it on me anymore, those goons will forget about me."

"It's not the gunmen you need to worry about. It's whoever hired them. Maybe the Old Man. Or maybe Fats. You know when I mentioned you to him, he denied knowing you. I'm wondering if you did something to piss him off."

Kintay's hands flew into the air as he launched into a manic speech, the words tumbling past his lips at breakneck speed. "But that's where Mr. Lubank comes in. That's why I called him in the first place. If he can return the data to the Hatfields and let them know I was never able to read the files, he can convince them to leave me alone. I don't know why I didn't give it to them in the first place. I don't know why I ran. I panicked! But no harm, no foul, right? I don't know what's in the files, and I don't want to know. Even if it's secret plans for an alien invasion. I mean, what do I care? Hell, I'll even go back to work for them if they want me to. I'm good at what I do, and they know it. The project is pretty far along, and if they have to replace me now it would really fuck things up. He can tell them I've learned my lesson, and that I won't fuck with them again. And if they don't want me to work for them no more, well that's okay, too. Lord's balls, I'll leave town if that's what they want. They'll never hear from me again. I'll—"

"Slow down," I said, cutting him off. "You're foaming at the mouth. You didn't take any of those caps of yours today, did you?"

"No, no—of course not!" Kintay lowered his eyes. "But I might have popped a couple of them the day I decided to run. It seemed like such a great idea at the time. In retrospect, that might have been the drugs talking. It's possible that they made me a little bit paranoid. That might be a side effect." He looked up. "I told you that shit was dynamite."

The sun had finished setting, leaving the two of us sitting in darkness. Gio's poker game would be starting soon, and I didn't want to miss it. I closed my eyes and sighed. "Look, corporal. It's getting late. I'll put the drive in my safe for the night and take it to Lubank in the morning."

His eyes widened until the bloodshot whites completely circled his pale blue irises. "But what about the goons?"

"Leave them to me," I assured him. "You got a place you can go? I've got somewhere I want to be, and while you might be a pain in the ass, that doesn't mean I want to leave you alone with a flesh-eating monster."

He sighed. "Maybe I'll just hit the highway. I'll give Mr. Lubank a call tomorrow from the road."

I took the drive from him. "That might be best."

I'd just opened my safe when I sensed a pair of approaching footsteps. I tossed the drive into the safe and slammed the door shut. My own gun was upstairs. I hurried to my desk and pulled Kintay's gat from the drawer.

"Okay," I said, gripping the twenty-two. "Let me do the talking."

Kintay stared at the gat in my hand, his upper lip twitching. "Shit, sergeant. I emptied that gun when those goons caught up to me the other day. I never got the chance to reload it."

"Shit."

One thing I'd learned through the years was that pointing an unloaded gun at two professional hitmen was a good way to eat a lead sandwich, so I tossed the useless piece to my desktop. A moment later, Breakspear and Tavish stepped through the door, hard looks on their faces and dark gray semi-automatic pistols in their hands.

I assumed *their* guns were loaded.

Breakspear looked my way and grimaced. "Evening, Southerland. I was hoping it wouldn't come to this."

I grimaced back at him. "You and me both. Let me ask you this. Are you after the data that Kintay stole?"

Kintay jerked his head toward me. "I didn't steal it! I just—"

"Shut up, corporal," I said, keeping my eyes on Breakspear. "I told you to let me do the talking."

Breakspear nodded. "Yeah, we need the data."

"If you kill either of us, you'll never get it."

Breakspear pointed at Kintay with his gun barrel. "I can make him tell me where it is."

"Don't bother," I said, indicating the safe with a nod. "It's in my safe, and I'm the only one who knows the passcode. Kintay doesn't know it, so you can't get it from him. And if you hurt him—if you so much as muss his hair—you'll never get it from me."

Breakspear glared at me with burning eyes. "I'll get it from you."

I shook my head. "Trust me, you won't. Not by force, and not by drugs. The cops have tried. The LIA has tried. They couldn't force information out of me, and neither can you."

Breakspear's eyes narrowed. "We'll knock you off and carry the safe out of here. Tavish here has cracked tougher safes than this one."

Tavish rapped on my safe with his knuckles. "This one wouldn't take me long."

"Go ahead. Try." I leaned against my desk, obscuring his view of its contents and using my senses to find what I was looking for.

The dwarf took a step toward the safe and stopped. "Wait. Did you rig something up? Is it boobytrapped?"

I kept my face blank and said nothing.

Tavish glared at me. "Let me guess. If you don't open it with the passcode, a bomb goes off. Or gas? Is that it?"

I let a smile settle on my face. "Only one way to find out."

Tavish continued to glare. "You're bluffing."

"Maybe."

Tavish took another step toward the safe, looked at it, and frowned.

Breakspear threw up his hands in disgust. "We're wasting time. Let's put these two mutts down, take the safe, and have it checked for traps."

I sighed and stood away from my desk. "Ah, I'm just puttin' one over on you. There aren't any traps. I wouldn't want to risk making a mistake on the passcode some night after I'd had a few too many and blowing myself up."

Tavish took another step toward the safe and ran his fingers through his beard.

I waved him on. "Go ahead. It's all right."

The dwarf waved me over to the safe with his gun. "You open it."

"Me? Nah. I don't think so."

He raised the gun. "Get over here and open it, or I'll fuckin' blow your head off."

I stared him down. "You sure that's the way you want to play it?"

"You've got to the count of three to get over here and open this safe. One..."

I sent out a mental command. Siphon who'd been drifting, still as an invisible pocket of air, in a corner of the ceiling, whooshed into the mug I'd used on Kintay's wrist and sent it shooting at the dwarf. It smacked the side of Tavish's skull with enough force to send him tumbling to the floor. His gun fell out of his hand and slid to the center of the room. I shoved Kintay into the filing cabinets on the far side of the room as my coffeemaker hurtled itself through the air toward Breakspear and crashed square into his shin. The troll roared and dropped to one knee.

I made a dash for Tavish's gun. It was a spur-of-the-moment, desperate plan that could have worked if luck had been on my side. But luck is a fickle spirit. The dwarf's gun had slid too close to Breakspear, and the troll backhanded me across the side of the head before I could reach it. I saw stars and fell against the wall in a heap. Siphon hurled every cup I owned at Breakspear, and they shattered against the troll without causing him any significant damage. The air spirit was giving everything it had, but the coffeemaker was the heaviest load it could manage.

Breakspear aimed his gun at the center of my chest. "Call it off, Southerland. Do it now or your heart will be pumping lead."

It was over, and I knew it. With no options left, I sent Siphon back to the laundry room. I dragged myself to a sitting position and wiped blood off the side of my mouth. Across the room, Tavish groaned, climbed to his feet, and sent a glare in my direction. Kintay cowered in the corner, adjusting tinfoil as if it could ward off whatever was coming next.

Breakspear glared at me, his glowing red eyes burning cold. "Got any more cute tricks?"

I rubbed at my jaw. "I've got a bloodsucking creature living in my laundry room, but I guess he's out for the day. Other than that, nah. It looks like I'm out of aces."

The troll pressed his lips together. "Hmm. All right, here's what's gonna happen. You're gonna open that safe. If you don't, I'll drop you and carry the safe out of here. Eventually we'll get inside, so you might as well make it easy. Either way, we're gonna have to take you both out. Nothing personal, but you know the drill. Cooperate, and we'll make it quick. Give us trouble, and it won't be so quick." He pointed toward Kintay with his chin. "We'll make you watch while we take your crazy friend apart piece by piece. You might be a tough nut, but he don't seem that tough to me, and I'm betting he'll make a lot of noise. You might not like that so much. You getting this?"

"I get it. You've got a job to do, and you don't want to get rough if you don't have to. Under the circumstances..." I nodded meaningfully at the fragments of glass and ceramic clay on the floor, "...that's decent of you. Before we get there, can I ask you a question? I don't have the right to, and there's nothing I can do with your answer, but I'm a curious guy, all the way to the end."

The troll narrowed his eyes. "What do you want to know?"

"Who hired you? I know it's against your professional ethics to tell me, but it looks like I'll be taking the information to the grave."

Breakspear stared at me, his face unreadable.

"Was it Bowman Hatfield—the Old Man?" I asked. "Was it Fats? Someone else?"

"Don't tell him," Tavish interjected. "There's no point. Besides, this place might be wired. He might be recording us."

I turned toward the dwarf. "You know, that's not a bad idea. I wish I had thought of it. But it's not anything I'd ever thought I'd need."

Breakspear took a step in my direction. "Enough. Are you going to open that safe?"

I shook my head. "No. You're going to have to work for it. But why don't you go easy on Kintay. He was never able to open the files he copied. They're passcode protected, and he doesn't have the code. He doesn't know what he copied."

Breakspear let out a breath. "I was bluffing when I said I would torture the little rat. We'll do it right. One bullet to the back of the head. Any last requests? Anything you want us to do for you when it's over? Got any friends you want notified, or any papers you want mailed?"

I rose to my feet. "Nah, I'm good. But none of this back of the head stuff for me. I always told myself that when my time came, I'd want to look into the eyes of whoever did it to me."

Breakspear nodded. "If that's the way you want it. You're a good man, Southerland. You went down fighting. I want you to know that I'm not going to enjoy this, but it's gotta be done."

Tavish carried Kintay from the back corner of the office and set him on the floor next to me with his back to the killers. "Is this it, sergeant?" he asked, his voice surprisingly calm. "I never thought I'd live to a ripe old age, but, damn, I never thought I'd go out with a clear head. I sure wish I'd've brought along a couple of those caps."

"All right," Breakspear announced. "Party's over."

A feline scent filled my head. Breakspear had said that I'd gone down fighting, but to my way of thinking, as long as you're still standing, you're not done. With the spirit of Cougar guiding me and giving me strength, I aimed a quick kick at Tavish's gun hand and struck metal with the heel of my shoe, spoiling his aim. In the next instant, I plunged the brass letter opener I'd scooped off my desk and slipped up my sleeve into Breakspear's wrist, ducking away from the blast as he reflexively pulled the trigger of his gun. Kintay did his part, too, whirling on Tavish and wrapping his arms around the dwarf's broad chest in a bearhug, pinning his arms to his side.

We never had a chance. Tavish lifted Kintay into the air and flipped him over his head, sending him crashing to the floor amidst the shards of shattered coffee cups. Breakspear wrapped his undamaged paw around my neck and lifted me off the floor. He growled and tossed me on top of Kintay just as he was struggling to his feet. Kintay collapsed under my weight, and my head slammed into the floor. Darkness flooded in.

I didn't quite lose consciousness. I was aware that I was lying at an awkward angle atop the limp form of Kintay. My animal spirit was with me, but distant, breathing life into my lungs and helping my heart to beat, but unable to do much else. I tried to move, but my limbs were numb, and they weren't responding to my mental commands. My first thought was that I was paralyzed. My second thought was that, at this point, it didn't matter. I'd made my last play, and it had come up bust. For what it was worth, I could truly say that I'd fought to the bitter end.

Breakspear pulled the letter opener from his wrist and tossed it to the floor. He slowly turned his head to regard me with all the passion of a bug collector sizing up a specimen in a kill jar. I took a deep breath, long and slow, drawing it out and wondering if it was true that your life passed before your eyes when you finally bought it. I wondered what mine would look like. Would there be some kind of grand revelation, some great moral lesson? Nah. What would the reel of my life show but endless hours of drinking alone punctuated by bouts of snooping into other people's affairs. When I was gone, I'd be forgotten in short order, and the world would continue to spin. A smile came to my lips at the thought. I was a mug. Just another mug. I waited for the blast that would put out my lights for keeps.

The temperature in the room plummeted.

Chapter Twelve

Darkness filled the room as the specter of Cindy Shipper appeared out of nowhere to stand between me and the two gunmen. Tavish backed against the wall, his eyes wide and his mouth open, a black hole behind his bushy beard. Breakspear tilted his head at the apparition, a frown over his glowing eyes. Blood from his wrist dripped over the gun he still held in his hand. He lifted the gun toward Cindy's ghost, hesitating to fire, maybe because he knew it would be fruitless or perhaps because he hadn't been paid to kill it. Without a word, the specter thrust its hand deep into the troll's chest.

Breakspear's bellows were muffled by the darkness and sounded as if they were coming from somewhere far away. His eyes flickered and turned into shining black marbles that reflected the unearthly glow from the shimmering specter. He twitched as if he were being electrocuted, and a shot from his gat punched a hole in my filing cabinet. An instant later, the pistol fell from his hand to land with a thump on the floor. A dark stain spread across the front of his pants at the crotch and down one leg.

The specter pulled its hand from Breakspear's chest and turned to face Tavish, who stood pressed against the wall. If he could have clawed his way through it, he would have. Breakspear remained standing, wobbling on rubbery legs and muttering to himself through chattering teeth.

Beneath me, Kintay stirred. The numbness had left my limbs, and, after some careful flexing, I untangled myself from him and rose unsteadily to my feet.

"Cindy?" My voice seemed muffled in the frigid air.

The specter turned its head, and I was overcome by a wave of terror as I stared into a parody of Cindy Shipper's face. Black oily slime oozed from jagged cracks lining her cheeks. A long, forked tongue slid between pointed fangs the color of iron and slipped back into her mouth. Two wells of blackness filled the space that had once been a pair of lively brown eyes. The blackness grew as I gazed into those wells, and I felt it pulling at me, inviting me to climb into its depths.

Behind me, Kintay was rising to his feet. A lingering sheet of foil slid from his shoulder and drifted toward the floor, losing speed as it fell.

Halfway down, it ground to a stop in midair. The air around me ceased moving. Time itself stopped.

Something flickered deep inside the blackness in Cindy's eyes, a tiny, but bright flame of yellow and red. I wanted to investigate that flame, to see it up close. I felt the silent rushing of wind, and the flame grew as I drew nearer. Or maybe the flame was drawing nearer to me. I couldn't tell, and it didn't matter. The flame spoke to me without words, promising answers to questions I didn't know how to ask, but answers I needed to know. The flame grew ever larger and ever brighter.

A voice came to me in the freezing wind. "You're not ready, Alex."

I pushed the voice away.

The voice persisted. "You're not ready. That flame means your death, which will come all too soon. But not yet."

My nose twitched. "Cougar? Is that you? Where are you?"

My spirit animal growled. "Come back, Alex. It is not your time."

The flame shrank, or maybe it receded in the distance.

"Wait!" I shouted. "The flame. I need to know."

Cougar's voice was firm. "There is nothing to know. The promises offered by the flame are lies. They are the promises of death, and the answers offered by death are no more meaningful than the answers provided by life. Life's only answer is to live. That's the true meaning of life. All other meaning is nothing but self-justified motivation to continue existing before the inevitable arrival of death, which comes eventually to all. It is up to the living to find their own reasons for continuing to live, their own meaning for life. Life is temporary, but death is forever. Why do you rush toward it? It will come to you soon enough. You should not be in a hurry to abandon life while you yet have a choice."

I opened my mouth to speak, but I had no words.

Cougar supplied them. "You have much to do."

"I have nothing to do," I replied.

"You must live."

"I'm tired."

"You don't have time to be tired."

The flame in Cindy's eyes tempted me with answers more fulfilling than the empty existential nihilism offered by my spirit animal. "There's something in the darkness I need to know. The flame can show it to me."

"The flame is a lie. The darkness is only darkness, and it will be there on that hour when you depart the world of the living. For now, you live, and you must investigate the murder of Cindy Shipper."

Cindy. She'd come to me. She was counting on me to release her from whatever was holding her to this world. I hesitated, and the world came back to me. "So it's true?" I asked. "She was murdered?"

"It is for you to find out. If you do not, no one else will. Her death will remain unresolved. No one will be held accountable. Justice will not be served."

I took a last, long look at the flame and turned away from it. As reasons for living went, solving the riddle of Cindy's death was as good as any. A cloud lifted from my mind, and I felt like I was waking from a dream. "You're right. I need to find out how she died. I need to know if she was murdered. That's the answer I need now. The rest of them can wait."

"Then extricate yourself from this situation and start investigating."

"Great. Got any ideas?" I waited. "Cougar?"

The sheet of foil falling from Kintay's shoulder reached the floor. Cougar was no longer with me. Apparently, he'd provided all the help he was going to give me in my present situation. Spirit guides. Just when you think you can depend on them....

The flame in the specter's eyes gave a last flicker and disappeared altogether. The all-consuming blackness shrank in on itself until it was once again contained in the eye sockets of Cindy's ghost. Or maybe I'd been thrust from the emptiness of that well. I took a step back and bumped up against the edge of my desk. It was solid enough.

Breakspear stood behind Cindy, muttering and seemingly unaware of where he was or what was happening around him. Braced against the wall, Tavish tensed and prepared to make a run for the door, but he froze in his tracks as a blood-curdling shriek emerged from the specter's throat. The shriek sent a shiver up my spine, and I felt my knees buckle. I braced myself against my desk, my mind racing.

The specter shrieked again, and I pressed my hands against my ears. Another shriek echoed through the room and didn't stop. Its volume rose and fell like an unearthly siren. I thought my mind would break under the weight of that scream. I pushed against it and struggled to concentrate through the sound.

Something.

My thoughts brushed against something, but it slipped away. I tried to run it down. If only the scream would stop long enough for me to think. Something I'd heard recently.... Something I should know.... Something about ghosts, or... or...

Qaitus! I recalled Leiti La'aka telling me about *qaitus*, how Cindy's *qaitu* was as much my memory of her as her own memory of herself, and how I could mold the *qaitu* to some degree through our interaction. I kept my hands on my ears and closed my eyes, screened out the shrieking and the pressing darkness, and remembered Cindy as I'd known her. I remembered her strawberry blond hair, the mischievous light in her eyes, the spray of freckles across her nose, her softly smiling lips.

I opened my eyes. "Cindy?" I ignored her scream and kept my voice steady. "Cindy? Do you hear me? It's Alex. You remember me, don't you?" I was dimly aware of Tavish rolled into a fetal position on the floor, not daring to breathe as he held his ears and tried to bury his face into his arms.

The shrieking eased, faded, and stopped. The specter's snakelike tongue darted in my direction, tasting the air between us. I focused on the specter's mouth, remembering Cindy's smile.

"Cindy," I said, forcing myself to smile. "You know who I am. You came to me when you needed my help. Now I need *your* help. Will you help me, Cindy? Will you do that?"

The specter tilted its head. Her head. *Cindy's* head, I told myself.

"Cindy, it's Alex. I need you to help me help you. I need you to be the Cindy I remember. I need you to be the Cindy who came to me for help."

The specter heard me. The darkness faded from its eyes, its tongue retreated into its mouth, and it... no, not it—*she*—smiled. I enlarged my focus to take in the specter's face, and it was Cindy Shipper's face with her familiar smile, sweet and a bit sad.

Cindy's lips parted. "Alex? What... where am I?" Her eyes fell on Breakspear, and her lips curled in a scowl. She disappeared in a brief flash of light and reappeared an instant later with her hand stretched over her head and gripping the troll's throat. She spoke, and her voice seemed to emerge from a great depth. "This man tried to hurt you." She turned to me, her face distorted and harsh.

Frozen mist swirled slowly through the room. I gazed at Cindy's face, the face I'd carried with me in my memories of our brief encounters, until her expression softened. "It's okay, Cindy," I assured her.

"Everything is okay now." I extended my hand, reaching for her. "You did good, Cindy, and I'm grateful to you, but I can take it from here." I took a step in her direction.

After a moment of hesitation, Cindy released Breakspear's throat and reached for me from across the room. In the next instant, she was beside me taking my hand gently in hers. Her skin was cold, so cold that it burned, but I held on. "I'm going to find out how you died, Cindy. I promise. I'm going to find who was responsible and make them pay."

Cindy lifted her head and gazed at me with hopeful eyes. "Claudius," she said. "Talk to Claudius."

"I will. I promise." Cindy's ice-cold hand softened in mine.

"Claudius will know what to do." I strained to keep my vision on Cindy, but the specter was fading rapidly. Her voice came to me from a distance. "Find Claudius. Tell him I want him to tell you everything. Everything...."

Her voice faded, and I was no longer holding Cindy's hand. The unnatural darkness in the room dissipated, and the temperature began to rise. I blinked, and when my eyes opened I found myself looking at Breakspear, who had stopped muttering and was squeezing the bridge of his nose. Cindy was gone.

I picked Breakspear's gun off the floor and pointed it at Tavish, still lying curled against the wall. "Give it," I said.

With a sigh, Tavish picked his pistol off the floor where it had fallen and handed it up to me.

I took a step back from Tavish. "Stand up."

Tavish braced himself against the wall and tried to rise, but his leg gave way, and he plopped down on his backside. He tried again, and this time he made it to his feet.

Behind me, Kintay was checking himself for injuries. Most of the foil was now on the floor. He stared at it for a moment and kicked it aside. He came up next to me and put a hand on my shoulder. "Lord's flaming pecker, sergeant. You never told me you were a damned necromancer."

"I'm not," I said, keeping my eyes on Tavish and Breakspear. "I'm just haunted."

With a gat in each hand, I directed Breakspear and Tavish to the two guest chairs. They sat without objecting, shoulders slumped and eyes directed at the floor. Kintay stood behind my desk leaning against the wall near the door to the back hallway, arms folded across his chest. I tucked the gats into my pockets and stood in front of the gunmen, saying nothing until first Tavish, then Breakspear looked up to meet my eyes.

Breakspear was the first to speak. "Lord's balls, I pissed my pants."

I suppressed a smile. "You're lucky you're still with us."

The troll shuddered. "I almost wasn't." His voice was hollow. "It was so cold... so cold I thought my bones would crack. And it was pitch black. Voices were muttering in my ears, millions of them. I was being dragged somewhere... I think it was Hell." He glanced at his partner. "I know our ancestors came from there, but if that was Hell, I never want to go back. There's nothing there, man. Just... emptiness."

Tavish stroked his beard. "That doesn't make any sense."

The troll wrapped his arms around his chest and shook. "I don't know, man. I don't know."

Tavish turned back to me. "What *was* that thing?"

"I'm not entirely sure," I admitted. "A ghost, I suppose."

The dwarf's eyes widened. "It sounded like you know her. You called her Cindy."

"It's complicated," I said.

Breakspear's jaw hardened. "You sent it away. If you hadn't...."

"You'd be dead. Both of you. And suffering in ways I can't imagine."

The two gunmen looked at each other. Breakspear turned back to me and said, "I guess that means we owe you."

"Both of us," Tavish agreed.

I looked into their faces, one at a time, and was satisfied with what I saw. "Your contract on Kintay is null and void."

Tavish gave Breakspear a quick glance. "We figured that."

Tired of standing, and no longer needing to look down on them, I moved to the other side of the desk and sat down in my office chair. The two gunmen turned their chairs around to face me across the desk.

"Tell me what you were hired to do. Kill Kintay and bring back the thumb drive?"

Breakspear reached up with a hand and pulled at his jaw, stretching his face. He let out a breath. "That was pretty much it, yeah. We were also supposed to question Kintay and find out if he had made any copies, or if he had told anyone what was on it."

"I never got past the passcode." Kintay said. "I wasn't lying about that. I still don't know what's in those fuckin' files. And I never made any copies, either."

Tavish glared at him. "Someone still wants you dead."

"Who?" I asked.

The two gunmen shifted in their chairs, looking uncomfortable. Breakspear glanced across the desk at me. "Debt or no debt, we can't give up our client. You know that."

Kintay dropped his arms to his sides. "Alkwat's balls," he hissed.

"It's got to be one of the Hatfields," I said, studying the faces of the gunmen. "Fats or the Old Man."

Neither of the gunmen gave anything away, and that reminded me of something. I groaned. "Son of a motherfucking bitch. I'm gonna miss my poker night!"

Tavish snorted. "Well, don't let us keep you."

A sharp chuckle burst from Breakspear's chest.

I looked from one to the other. "How soon can the two of you be on your way out of town?"

"Fu-u-ck," Tavish drawled. "I guess that depends on the traffic. You know any shortcuts?"

I smiled. "I'll draw you a map."

Kintay pushed himself from the wall. "Hey! Are you kidding me? You're going to let them go?"

I turned to him. "Why not? Their business here is done. I've got no reason to detain them any longer."

Kintay's pale face reddened. "What about the fact that they were going to kill us?"

"Water under the bridge." I turned to the gunmen. "Right, boys?"

Tavish grimaced. "Unfortunately. We were only paid half up front, but I guess we'll have to take a loss on this one."

Breakspear grunted. "You win some, you lose some."

I stood, and the gunmen followed suit. "All right, boys. Maybe I'll see you around. But you don't come after Kintay or me again, you follow?"

The gunmen glanced at each other. "We follow," Tavish confirmed. "You see us again, hopefully it will be over drinks. Breakspear will buy."

I walked them to the door and held it open. "I'd sure like to find out who hired you," I said as they stepped through.

Breakspear turned as he was leaving. "You think we can get our guns back? We feel kind of naked without them."

I gave the troll a long look, then gave the dwarf another one. "Sure," I said, taking the gats from my pockets. "I don't have any use for them."

Breakspear took the guns from me and handed one to his partner. He turned to leave, then stopped. "By the way," he said, looking back over his shoulder. "You dropped a couple of names, Fats and Old Man Hatfield? We know them by reputation, be we've never met either of them."

I stared after him. "That so?"

"Never talked to them, either. See ya around, Southerland."

The odd pair of gunmen walked off into the night.

Chapter Thirteen

Kintay wasn't happy, even when I reminded him that he no longer had a pair of professional hitmen on his tail.

"For now," he whined. "But whoever hired them still wants me dead. And they want that data. I'm still fucked."

"I'll get the thumb drive to Lubank in the morning," I assured him, "and he'll take it from there. You should be okay."

"Maybe. But I still need to disappear."

"Heading out of town might be a good idea," I suggested.

Kintay threw me a sidelong glance and looked away quickly, giving me the feeling that whatever he said next would be a lie. "You're right," he said, confirming my suspicion. "The Hatfields will expect me to run south to Angel City, or east to New Helvetia. Somewhere with a lot of people to get lost in. I'll go north, instead. I've always wanted to check out the redwoods."

I wished him good luck and told him to call Lubank from the road in the late morning. "Be sure to use a burner," I added.

Kintay smiled. "That's all I've got anymore. Good luck with your poker game!"

I checked the time once Kintay was gone and calculated that if I hustled, I'd only be an hour late for the game. That would be okay. I'd probably miss out on the cheese sandwiches, but there'd still be plenty of beer, especially if I stopped off at a convenience store on the way and picked up a six-pack. I'd make sure I won enough to pay for it, but not so much that anyone would fuss about me showing up late and taking their money. I ran a wet comb through my hair, changed into a clean shirt and pants, and stepped carefully through the mess in my office. I'd clean it up in the morning. Or maybe the next day. It wasn't as if I was expecting company.

I hurried up the block to pick up the beastmobile from Gio's, but when I reached the entrance to the lot, a black town car drove up on the sidewalk to cut me off. The back door opened, and a booming baritone voice cut through the night. "Get in, Southerland."

I stared through the doorway and saw a massive figure—a troll in an expensive pin-stripe suit—sitting in the shadows. After a second, I realized I recognized him. I groaned inwardly. With only a moment's hesitation, and just a bit of trepidation, I bid goodbye to poker night and slid through the door into the back seat.

Claudius Silverblade straightened the knot on his tie. "Good evening, Mr. Southerland. I hear you wish to speak with me."

I pulled the car door shut behind me, aware that I was now trapped in close quarters with a troll who had good reasons for hating me. But he was someone I wanted to talk to, and I was willing to take some risks in order to make it happen.

I'd learned over the years that when dealing with a troll, the best approach was to be direct and upfront and to show no weakness. Easier said than done when confronted by a quarter-ton gorilla whose ancestors had been bred in Hell to be killers. Over the centuries since the Great Rebellion, trolls had adjusted to life in a civilized world about as well as humans had, which maybe isn't saying much, but at least they had overcome their natural instinct to kill first and to hell with the questions. Most of them, anyway. I had no doubt that Silverblade was a tough number, but he was also a corporate lawyer, which meant he probably would derive more pleasure from ruining my life than ending it.

I jumped right into the matter at hand. "Thanks for seeing me, Mr. Silverblade. I've been visited by the ghost of Cindy Shipper, that is, Cindy Hatfield. I believe that she wants me to investigate the circumstances of her death. She explicitly told me to contact you. She said you could tell me what I want to know."

Silverblade's eyes pierced the shadows, lighting his hairless face in scarlet. He stared at me with those burning troll eyes for what seemed like an eternity before speaking. "That's quite a story, Mr. Southerland, and I can't imagine why you would tell me such a tale unless it were true."

I waited for him to go on, but he turned to his driver, a human, instead. "Lionel, please get us off the sidewalk and back on the road."

The driver—Lionel—glanced back over his shoulder. "Sure thing, Mr. Silverblade." I did a double take at the snake tattoo circling his neck above his collar, but quickly turned my attention back to Silverblade.

After Lionel had pulled the town car into traffic, Silverblade shifted in his seat and regarded me from what seemed a great height. If trolls had eyebrows, his would have been arched. "I have no reason to love you, Mr. Southerland," he said, his baritone voice clipped, "but neither do I hold any grudges against you. You inconvenienced me a bit, but the fact is I'm more highly positioned within the structure of Greater Olmec now than before you alerted the police to my other activities. In any case, Madame Cuapa wishes me to cooperate with you, and she is not someone I desire to offend. Out of respect for the late Mrs. Hatfield, whom I counted as a good friend, I will answer your questions as best I can." He folded his hands in his lap. "What is it you wish to know?"

I studied his face, looking for a hint of deception. He seemed sincere enough, so I answered. "I first saw a vision of Cindy last April. It must have been soon after she died. Her ghost, if that's what it was, caught fire in front of my eyes. Earlier this week, Cindy's ghost visited me again. Again, it went up in flames. She's visited me a couple of times since. What can you tell me about Mrs. Hatfield's death?"

"Nothing."

"Nothing?" It was my turn to arch my brow. "Cindy says otherwise."

"Truly? What did she tell you?"

"A number of things, but none of it was clear. She mentioned crates and a puppy. She also said something about elves. She told me that you knew everything, and she told me to tell you that you should tell it all to me."

Deep creases formed between Silverblade's eyes as he stared down at me. "Elves?"

"Elves, and elves, and elves, she said. And crates, and crates, and crates. Which were all gone, according to her. The crates I mean. I don't know about the elves."

Silverblade raised his hands from his lap, forming a triangle in front of his massive chest with his long, thick fingers. "Elves are extinct."

I grunted. "That's what I've heard. You still hear about sightings, though."

"Hmmm.... And crates, you say?"

"That's what she said. And a puppy. A cute little puppy, who came for her. It was all a bit jumbled, but the one thing she was clear about was that you know everything. She seems to have had a high regard for you, but then she used to work for you, right?"

The troll's face lost all expression. "That is not exactly correct, at least not in the way you are thinking."

"No? Care to elaborate?"

"No, Mr. Southerland, I do not."

"Fine. Then tell me what you know about elves and crates. And about the puppy."

Silverblade let his hands fall back to his lap. The sounds of traffic were barely audible through the luxury sedan's thick shaded windows. Silverblade let out a breath, and he spoke with a voice that was much more relaxed than it had been up until then. "Let's start from the beginning, Mr. Southerland. Cindy kept in contact with me after her husband, Donald Shipper, died and her stepdaughter inherited the house. As I said, we were friends. I helped her find a little place in the city, and, later, I introduced her to Fats Hatfield, who introduced her to his brother, Alu. A marriage was arranged."

"Arranged?"

Silverblade sighed. "As you may remember, Cindy was always attracted to two things: wealth and power. She knew that Alu, the son of Bowman Hatfield, the head of the wealthiest and most powerful extralegal syndicate in the city, was unmarried. She found out everything she could about him and enlisted my aid in gaining the proper introductions. She knew that I had business connections with the Hatfield family."

I raised an eyebrow at that. "Really? Fats told me he didn't recognize your name when I mentioned it to him."

Silverblade snorted. "Fats Hatfield is a lying sack of shit, something that I remind him of to his face frequently. It seems I will have to do it again."

"Did you tell him that I was investigating Cindy's death?"

"I most certainly did not. Why would I?"

"I don't know. I had a theory that you didn't want to talk to me, and that you arranged for me to be picked up by Fats and warned away from looking into what happened to Cindy."

"You were mistaken."

"It was just a theory. I guess it was all wet."

A low rumble emerged from deep within Silverblade's chest. "As I was saying," he continued, "I helped arrange Cindy's introduction to Alu. The Hatfields were happy about it, but, more importantly, Cindy was happy."

I considered what he was telling me. "I get why Cindy wanted to marry into the Hatfield family. Wealth and power, like you said. But what was in it for the Hatfields? I mean, sure, Cindy was a beautiful woman. But she was, what, maybe thirty? Not too old to have children, but from what I remember she'd never wanted any, and her relationship with Donald Shipper's children was hardly inspiring. She had some money, but not enough to interest the Hatfields. Her social contacts were limited...." The corner of my mouth curled into a skeptical smirk. "Say, you're not gonna tell me that Alu fell in love with her, are you?"

"He did, actually, in his own way. And I think Cindy was pleased with him, as well. But it was a marriage of convenience all around. I'm not ashamed to say that I was well paid by the Hatfields for the part I played in helping bring it about. You asked what the Hatfields gained from the marriage? That's both simple and complex."

"Give me the simple."

Silverblade opened his hands, palms up. "They gained a wife for Alu."

I grunted. "Better give me the complex."

Silverblade refolded his hands. "Alu is... unusual. He's reclusive, and for good reason. He is not an attractive man, and he's quite sensitive about it. He appears in public rarely, and he wears a facemask when he does. He was resigned to living his life without a marriage partner, but his father and brother considered that to be a bad look for the family. An attractive wife for him, on the other hand, one with the social graces Alu lacks, would be more in keeping with the image the family wishes to project. Finding one, however, was a problem."

"Why? I've run into loads of dames who were willing to marry unattractive men for their dough." A half grin appeared on my face. "Someday I might make enough money to interest a few of them."

Silverblade, apparently immune to my charm, ignored my attempt at disarming self-deprecation. "There were other complications. First, Alu is a rare creature: a fire elementalist."

I perked up. "No shit? I didn't know we had any in this city. Hmm. Al the Torch. I guess that explains the nickname—and the looks. I've only met two fire elementalists, both of them when I was stationed in the Borderland. The army used them for special operations—you can probably guess how. Both of them looked like they had set fire to their own bodies. Their faces were... well, you get the picture."

Silverblade grunted. "That's why Alu wears a mask. I've never seen him without one."

I shook my head. "And Cindy married him?"

"She was quite pleased with him. But, as I said, it was only a convenience."

"What do you mean?"

"Well, that brings us to another complication. Alu is impotent. I think he was quite taken with Cindy, but they could not be intimate. Not in the usual sense, anyway. And yet, I had the strong impression that, in his own way, he loved Cindy. And I think Cindy was happy enough with him."

"Even though they couldn't..., I mean, the Cindy I remember—"

Silverblade cut me off. "They had an arrangement."

"What kind of arrangement?"

"Cindy was allowed to be with other men. But only professional men. Professionals I supplied."

I shook my head. "Once a pimp.... I thought you were a highly paid muckety-muck at Olmec."

Silverblade's thick lips spread into a sly smile. "Old habits die hard. Besides, one can't have enough money." His smile faded. "But it didn't work out."

I met the troll's shining eyes. "What happened?"

Silverblade sighed. "That's where 'Puppy' comes into the picture. Cindy was having an affair. A real one, not a dalliance with one of my professionals. And Alu wasn't happy about it."

"Wait. Puppy is a person? Another man? You're telling me Cindy's dead because she had a jealous husband?"

Silverblade shook his head. "I am telling you nothing of the kind. Regardless of what Alu might have felt about Cindy's affair, I find it hard to believe that he would kill her, or that he would have her killed. He cared for her."

"A lot of men say they cared for the women they killed. The police and the newspapers refer to those murders as crimes of passion. Kind of gives passion a bad name, in my view, but there you are."

"Alu wouldn't have done it," Silverblade insisted.

"Al the Torch?"

Silverblade sighed. "You'd have to meet the man to understand."

"Sounds like a good idea. I'll go call on him."

The rumble emerged from the troll's chest again, sounding like the growl of a tiger in the distance. "That would be a very bad idea."

"Why?"

"Fats Bowman would take a very dim view of it. He's extremely protective of his brother."

I took a quick look out the front window to see where we were going. Apparently, Lionel had simply been circling the block.

"Alu was adopted, wasn't he?"

Silverblade scratched his jaw. "I wouldn't read anything into that. Alu is a Hatfield through and through."

"If you're trying to convince me that Alu didn't murder his wife, you're doing a bad job of it. Lord's balls, she marries a fire elementalist from a criminal family, and she dies in a fire. Are you telling me that's a coincidence?"

"I'm telling you Alu wouldn't have done it. Couldn't have done it. Alu isn't like that. He and Cindy may not have had a conventional relationship, but it was a relationship that made them both happy."

"Wait a minute. Didn't you say that Alu wasn't happy about her stepping out on him?"

Silverblade sighed. "He wasn't angry enough to kill her."

"But he might have told Fats about it. Or the old man."

Silverblade scoffed. "You've really got it in for the Hatfields, don't you. It clouds your judgment. The Hatfields might be guilty of a lot of things, but they don't do honor killings. You've been watching too many movies. If Alu had told his father or brother about Cindy, they might have brought her in for a chat to remind her how dependent she was on the Hatfield family for her good wine, her expensive shoes and jewelry, and her new social standing. They might have threatened to kick her back down to the minors if she didn't play ball according to the rules of the game. And maybe they might have leaned on the man she was seeing. Scared him a little and paid him off. Maybe even convinced the 'Puppy' that Yerba City might not be the right town for him to be chasing bitches. But they wouldn't have knocked off Alu's wife. She was family. You think Fats's wife never cheated on him with the pool boy? She's still around, and still cheating, too. But don't tell Fats I mentioned that. No, Mr. Southerland, you're barking up the wrong tree."

"It's not a tree I can ignore. You say Alu couldn't have killed his wife, but how can you be sure? Men—even stable men with good reputations—will get awfully unpredictable when they find out their wife is doing the dirty with another man. Alu is from a criminal family. His reputation? He's Al the Torch, and it isn't hard to imagine how he got that name. He's impotent: he can't satisfy his wife. In the circles he runs in, that already makes him the butt of jokes. So he tries to control the situation by giving his trophy wife a safe, quiet outlet for her sexual desires—not something a lot of men would do. He's generously sacrificing his own dignity for her. She should be grateful. But what does she do? She stuffs his generous sacrifice up his ass. She has a tawdry affair with someone she refers to as a puppy dog. It's humiliating. He can't stand to look at her anymore. And what if certain people find out about it? What if it leaks to the media? What will people say about him? This son of a Hatfield who can't get it up and can't control his wife. It's too much. Al the Torch loses his mind, lures Cindy into a warehouse, and uses a fire elemental to burn the place to the ground while she's trapped inside."

"That's how you see it?"

I shrugged. "It makes sense to me."

Silverblade shook his head. "That's because you don't know Alu. You've never met him, never talked to him. What you describe might be plausible with the riffraff *you* spend your time with, and it might fit the image you've built in your head about the Hatfield family, but it's unimaginable when it comes to Alu. You talked to Cindy, or her ghost, at least. What did she say about Alu?"

"Huh? I don't remember. Not much. At the time, I thought she was calling Alu her puppy, but you're telling me that 'Puppy' was the guy she was having an affair with." I tried to recall exactly what Cindy had told me about her husband. "Uhhh... I think she might have referred to Alu as 'sweet.' Yeah, I remember now. I asked her if Alu had killed her, and she said, 'Alu is sweet,' or something like that."

Silverblade raised his palms in a shrug. "There you are. Apparently, Cindy died believing that her husband hadn't been responsible for her death. If she didn't think so, why should we?"

I leaned back in my seat. Maybe Silverblade was right. I had to admit that he had a good argument. I also had to admit that I was biased against the Hatfields, who had tried to have me killed on more than one occasion. I let out a slow, resigned breath. "All right," I said, not defeated, but willing to at least explore other possibilities. "If Alu didn't kill Cindy in a fit of passion, and Fats and Bowman didn't do it to defend his honor, then who did?"

"You're asking the wrong question, Mr. Southerland. Cindy's death was an accident. She wandered into the wrong place at the wrong time. Simple as that." Silverblade turned to his driver. "Lionel, let's take Mr. Southerland to his home."

I held up a hand. "Wait. Cindy said you know everything. She said... she said you would know what to do."

The troll looked away. "I don't know what to make of that."

"Give me one more turn around the block," I said.

Silverblade stared back at me, considering the matter. "All right," he conceded at last. "But just one more time around. I don't have all night."

My mind raced. "All right, for the moment let's forget about *how* she died. Tell me about *where* she died."

"It was one of the Hatfield's warehouses. Down at Grayshore Point. Just a storage and transfer facility, as far as I know."

I frowned. "What would Cindy have been doing there?"

Silverblade was silent for several moments. "Last time I talked to her, Cindy seemed... not disturbed, but... curious about some special operation the Hatfields were involved with. They were developing something, she said. Something secret. I told her that she shouldn't be surprised that the syndicate was manufacturing exotic recreational drugs. That's a big part of what they do. But she insisted that it wasn't drugs. It was something weird, she said. Something different from their usual rackets. Different kinds of people were working on it. Not the usual crowd, but people who had been brought in and kept apart from the rest of the workers. She wanted to find out what was going on. I advised her to leave it alone. I told her there were some things she was better off not knowing about." The troll scratched the back of his ear. "A week later, a warehouse owned by the Hatfields went up in flames, and Cindy's body was discovered in the ruins. The warehouse was practically empty. Anything that had been stored there had already been shipped."

"Are they sure it was Cindy?"

"It must have been. You've seen her ghost."

Four times now, in fact. I sighed. "Good point."

"Are you ready to go home now, Mr. Southerland?"

"Yeah, I guess so. Say, you wouldn't happen to know the address of that warehouse, would you?"

"Not offhand. Like I said, it's in Grayshore Point. It shouldn't be hard to find." He stared at me. "Are you really going to investigate the place?"

"Sure, why not?"

"Fats won't like it."

"Fats can go fuck himself."

That got a chuckle from Silverblade. "When were you planning on going?"

"Soon. The sooner the better."

Silverblade turned his gaze to a distant point over my shoulder. He rubbed his chin a couple of times and turned back to me. "Fine. I'll call you in the morning around seven with an address, and I'll meet you there at nine."

I stared at him. "You want to go with me? Why?"

Silverblade's lips spread into a tight smile. "Two reasons. First, Cindy was, as I said, a friend. A good friend. I believe her death was an accident, but, if it wasn't, I want to know about it. Cindy reached out to you from the dead and told you to come to me. I don't know why she would do that, but what if I know more than I think I do? A visit to the site of her death might jog loose a bit of knowledge I'm not aware I hold."

"And your second reason?"

The troll's smile broadened. "Fats Bowman wants to keep Cindy's death out of the public eye. He won't be pleased when he discovers that you are investigating the remains of the warehouse where it happened. I don't like Fats. He's an odious little toad of a man, a man with no class. It would please me to see him displeased. He can indeed, as you so eloquently put it, go fuck himself."

By the time Silverblade dropped me off, I decided it was too late to crash the poker game, and, besides, I was no longer in the mood for cards. Instead, I took an hour to clean up my office and shuffled off to bed. It had been a long day, and I had another long day ahead of me. I had a date with a troll to investigate the scene of Cindy Shipper's death: the scene of an ugly crime, if, in fact, she'd been murdered.

Chapter Fourteen

I delivered Kintay's thumb drive to Lubank without incident, and the surly gnome assured me he'd take care of everything.

"Tell your pal to call me as soon as possible. And tell him if anyone bothers him, he needs to keep his trap shut and refer them to me."

"You can tell him yourself. He's going to call you this morning." I indicated the drive. "What are you going to do with that?"

"All you need to know is that it'll be a hell of a lot safer with me than it was with your pal. Or with you."

I left it at that. I had business that morning at a possible crime scene.

The warehouse where Cindy met her death had been located just off the bay on the southeast side of the peninsula in a heavily industrialized section of Grayshore Point. It had been a one-story building, just wide enough for two loading docks and a walk-in entrance to the office area, and maybe half again as deep. It was tucked into an industrial park with various other shops flanking it on either side. The warehouse itself was a burned-out ruin. The metal walls were blackened and warped, and parts of the roof had caved in. The building appeared to be beyond repair and would likely have to be razed to the ground. Damage extended beyond the warehouse, too: flames had left scorch marks on the wall of the furniture factory to the left of the warehouse, and the roof of the automotive body shop on the office side of the building was new.

Silverblade was standing outside his town car talking in low tones with his driver, Lionel, when I turned into the parking area. I hadn't paid much attention to the driver the night before, but I gave him a quick once over as I drew near. He was fair-skinned, thirtyish with an athletic build, but what stood out to me, even more than the dark green and scarlet tattoo of the snake winding around his neck, were his eyes, which were an unnaturally bright shade of gold. As I pulled up alongside the two men, Lionel tossed his half-smoked cigarette to the asphalt and crushed it underfoot. His odd eyes softened, and his lips parted as he gazed at the beastmobile. The expression of wistful longing on his mug gave me the distinct impression that he would sell his own mother for a peek under the hood. Silverblade said something to him, and, with obvious reluctance, the driver tore his gaze from my car and slid in behind the wheel of his own.

Silverblade greeted me with a broad smile. "I think Lionel would like me to buy your vehicle. Would you consider an offer?"

"Not a chance."

"He'll be disappointed. It won't be the first time, however. Lionel used to be one of my escorts, and he enjoyed the work. But I had to end his career when he turned twenty-nine. He was too old, I'm afraid. A shame. I spent a lot of money on spells and potions to get that eye color. It was a good investment, though. He was a particular favorite among very wealthy and powerful older men. Women, too, while he was still young." He sighed. "Oh well. Fortunately, it turns out he's a fine driver and mechanic, as well. He's got an instinct for automobiles. I wouldn't think a man in your line of work would be able to afford such a vehicle. There must be a story behind it, hmm?"

I nodded toward the beastmobile. "This old thing? I picked it up at a flea market. It had a few dings in it. I polished it up a little to make it presentable."

The troll shot me a sly grin. "Sure you did." He turned toward the burned-out warehouse. "Shall we go in and take a look around the place? I'm anxious to see how a genuine private eye goes about his business. Do you use any special equipment? A magnifying glass, perhaps?"

"Nah. Just a magic wand and a forty-four. But I left them at home. I'll have to get by on my powers of observation and my keen wit."

"Ah, the tools that almost sent me up the river. Almost." He raised his hand to indicate the office entrance, its door hanging open. "Shall we?"

I followed Silverblade into the blackened metal shell of the building, the enormous troll's last words echoing in my head.

We entered a dark office, and Silverblade switched on a high-powered flashlight. I scanned the area with my own magical senses, which showed me more than any flashlight beam would be able to.

"Careful," Silverblade cautioned as he stepped through the wreckage. "It doesn't look like anyone has cleaned this place up since the fire." He glanced over at me. "Where shall we start?"

"Everyone keeps telling me that the fire was an accident. An electrical short or something." I pointed down the wall to the right of the entryway. "That looks like the electrical panel over there, or what's left of it. Let's take a look."

Silverblade followed me to the panel, casting the powerful beam of his flashlight over broken and charred desks, chairs, and hollowed-out filing cabinets. The ash-covered electrical panel, a gutted slag of melted plastic, tangled wires, and scorched metal bolted into the carbonized wood like something that had been tortured to death, feebly reflected the intense light of Silverblade's flash. "What a mess," said the troll. "I'm no expert, but my guess is this is where the fire started."

"Uh-huh. Maybe. Or maybe this area burned along with the rest of the building." I leaned in to get a closer look at the cables that had burned away from the box. "I'm no expert, either," I said, running my fingers over the brittle plastic insulation wrapped around the wires. "Let me check something out."

I grabbed one of the circuit-breaker casings and attempted to rip it free from the panel, but it had melted into the metal frame and was stuck fast. After giving it my best shot, I turned to Silverblade. "Can you get that out of there?"

The troll reached in and yanked the casing free with ease. I had to give him credit for keeping his expression neutral as he handed me the unit.

"Thanks," I said, turning the casing over. "Look at this. The wiring is still attached. The plastic insulation on the wires outside the panel are blackened, but all the plastic wire covers on the inside still have their original color." Silverblade shined his light on the yellow and red wires to confirm that they were undamaged. "And see here? The copper wire inside the insulation is still intact."

Silverblade looked down at me. "What are you suggesting?"

"This plastic insulation hasn't burned away like you'd expect it would if it had overheated or shorted. It doesn't take a lot to melt plastic, and I know that copper wire burns at a lower temperature than a lot of other metals. If this had been the ignition point of the fire, it seems to me we'd be looking at some severe damage. I don't think the internal wiring leading into the circuit breakers caused the fire. I think that whatever burned this panel came from outside the surface." I looked up at the troll. "But I could be wrong. Like I say, I'm no expert."

Silverblade gave his head a little sideways tilt. "Sounds like you know more than I do. Have any of your investigations involved arson?"

"A few. Mostly during my time with the Military Police, and I was just looking over the shoulders of the specialists. But when I was thirteen, me and a few of my buddies decided we were going to set fire to this guy's car. We thought it would explode, like the cars do in movies, but it just burned. You can imagine how disappointed we were. I remember how the engine looked afterwards. The insulation on the battery cables had all melted away, and a lot of the wiring had burned, too." I pointed to the wires leading away from the panel into the wall. "That car looked a lot worse than this."

Silverblade smirked. "Sounds like you ran around with a swell bunch of friends."

"They were okay. A few of us managed not to die young."

"Still in touch with any of them?"

"No."

"Probably just as well." The troll cast his light beam over the floor directly in front of the electrical panel. "What about these burn patterns? Can you make anything out of them?"

I studied the blackened cement floor for a few moments. "An actual fire investigator might be able to see something here, but it's outside my realm of expertise. I see lots of scorching, but I can't tell if it's leading toward or away from the electrical panel. It looks pretty intense, though. The floor is blacker here than it is further in, so I guess the fire *could* have started here. I'm assuming Cindy's body was found nearby?"

Silverblade raised his eyes from the floor. "I have no idea. Let's look around and see if we can find anything."

I glanced around the burned-out office. "Right. Unless she scratched a note on the floor while she was dying—'My husband did this'—I'm not even sure what to look for. But, that's why we're here, so let's give it a go."

We spent the next fifteen minutes walking slowly through the office area of the warehouse, sticking close together. It's not that I needed the light from Silverblade's flash, but I didn't trust the troll. If he came across a scrap of evidence, would he be more interested in sharing it with me or keeping me from seeing it? I didn't know for sure. As it was, neither of us found anything remotely helpful except for scattered footprints clearly visible in the ash and soot on the blackened cement.

I pointed to a cluster of overlapping prints. "These were left after the fire."

Silverblade sucked at his lower lip through his teeth. "I see them. By whoever took the body away?"

"And by the police. They investigated the scene until the Hatfields told them it was none of their business and sent them packing."

I cast my gaze around the room. "The fire happened, what, about four months ago? It doesn't look like the Hatfields have been using this place lately, and I don't think they've bothered to guard it. But some of these prints look fresher than others. Looters, maybe?"

Silverblade wiped dust off his suit. "Maybe so. Whoever it was sure wasn't interested in doing any cleaning. I wonder why no one has cleared the wreckage. The neighbors must be thrilled."

As I scanned the office area, my eyes were drawn to a set of scorched, but intact file cabinets, the drawers open and empty. The insides of the drawers were lined with soot. "It looks like the Hatfields cleared out their records before the fire, which makes me think they were the ones who set it. It would be interesting to know what was going on in this place before it burned down." I crossed the room to the cabinets and gave them the once over, but whatever files had been stored in the drawers were gone without a trace. I was about to walk away, when I stopped.

"Hey, Muscles," I said, waving the troll over. "Help me pull these cabinets away from the wall."

"You thinking something might have fallen behind them?"

I grabbed one of the cabinets. "Or under them. It's been known to happen. And anything behind these cabinets could have survived the fire." I pulled the top of a cabinet away from the wall. "See there? The wall behind these cabinets looks unharmed."

There were five cabinets in all, and I managed to slide one out by the time Silverblade had carried the others, two at a time, well away from the wall. I found what I was hoping for under the last pair: two sheets of paper, untouched by the fire, stapled together. I studied them, hoping for some useful information.

Silverblade glanced over my shoulder. "What is it? A shipping report?"

"Looks like it."

"Anything interesting?"

"Not really. All the items are what you would expect to see. Office supplies, computer parts, restaurant and bar supplies.... Nothing unusual." I turned the page over and scanned the items listed there. The second sheet also had items listed on both sides, and none of them raised any red flags. I went back to the first page and studied it.

"You find something?" Silverblade asked.

"I'm not sure. Like I said, nothing surprising about the items being shipped. It's just that there's a lot of them. And they all went out over a two-week period in April of this year, from April eleventh to April twenty-sixth, with an especially heavy load going out on the twenty-sixth." I took another look at the second sheet.

Silverblade raised his eyes. "So what? It just sounds like an active warehouse."

"Look at this." I pointed to a blank column. "It doesn't look like anything came in during those two weeks. Everything listed here moved out. And the twenty-sixth? The heaviest day? That was the day of the fire."

Silverblade took a quick look at each sheet. "It looks like they spent those two weeks clearing out the warehouse."

"Hmm. And they worked hard to finish up by that last day. It's almost like someone knew on the eleventh that the place was going to burn down on the twenty-sixth, and they wanted to clear everything out before it happened. They worked extra hard on the twenty-sixth to make sure the warehouse would be empty."

I turned to look at Silverblade, who said, "Huh. You might be right. Could just be a coincidence, though. Coincidences happen."

"True. It's not conclusive, but as of now my working theory is that the fire was planned."

Silverblade looked up from the report. "What do you want to do now? Should we look through the rest of the warehouse?"

I sighed. "I guess we'd better. There's no reason to assume Cindy was in the office when the place went up." I pointed to the area behind where the office had been. "Let's check back there. A lot of these prints lead that way. Maybe that's where the body was found."

I led Silverblade out of the remains of the office to the warehouse floor, where enough light poured through the gaping holes in the ceiling to allow us to see most of the interior unaided. He pointed to the far side of the building. "Let's have a look at the loading dock. Cindy's ghost said something about crates, right? Maybe she was snooping around over there when she got caught in the fire."

As we crossed the floor, I stopped. A faint, but intense high-pitched whine, like the sound of a miniature drill, had settled into the base of my ear canal and was causing my back teeth to tingle.

Silverblade noticed I wasn't moving. "What is it?"

"Do you hear anything?" I asked.

The troll slowly turned his head, as if his large, pointed ears were scanning for radio signals. "No…. No, just the creaking of the building and the traffic outside. Why?"

I shook my head. "It's nothing. I thought I heard something, but it's gone now. Let's go."

In fact, I was still picking up the faint whine, which grew stronger as we moved toward the storage area. Something in the building was giving off enough magical energy for me to detect, and the vibrations grew stronger as I moved closer to the back of the building. I veered off in that direction. Nothing in the ruins seemed out of the ordinary: just a lot of broken and charred wood. I moved carefully past the remains of a stretch of collapsed ceiling and a forklift, glancing up to make sure I was in no danger from falling objects. Things appeared to be stable enough, but I was wishing I had brought along a hard hat, just in case. Something seemed a bit off to me, but I couldn't quite pin it down, and, in any case, my focus was on finding the source of the magical energy.

The energy was strongest in a portion of the back wall about halfway across the width of the building. After pacing back and forth and ducking up and down, I concluded that a square-foot section of the wall had been enchanted in some way. Some sort of magical surveillance? I couldn't tell. A security ward of some kind? I drew in a deep breath, held it, and pressed the palm of my hand against the enchanted area. The ceiling didn't fall on my head, nor was I transported through the wall. I let my breath out in a slow stream.

With a shrug, I turned away from the wall to find Silverblade staring at me with his beacon-like eyes. "Find something?" he asked.

"Nah. Nothing here. How about you?"

The troll pointed toward the section of collapsed ceiling I'd walked past. "This is odd."

"What do you mean?"

"The roof caved in here, right?"

"That's what it looks like." I jerked my head toward the forklift and then to the ceiling. "Wait a second...."

Silverblade nodded. "This pile of rubble isn't lined up with the opening up there. Somebody moved it after it fell." He indicated the forklift. "Maybe with that."

I walked toward the charred debris. "Check out those scrape marks. That's where that section of ceiling fell, but the wreckage was cleared and moved aside. There's a lot of footprints here." I studied the prints. "A lot of people were moving around here after the fire." I pointed at a size twenty-eight print. "At least one of them was a troll."

Silverblade studied the marks. "Are you thinking what I'm thinking?"

"I'm thinking this is where they found Cindy's body." I whistled softly. "I sure hope she was already dead when the roof caved in on her."

Silverblade lifted his eyes to meet mine. "Alkwat's balls! What the fuck was Cindy doing here, anyway?"

I pushed my hat back on my head and wiped sweat off my hair. "I wish I knew. She talked to you. She told me you know everything. Think, Silverblade. Did she tell you anything at all that might hint at why she would have been in an empty warehouse at night?"

Silverblade scratched behind his ear. "I don't remember anything useful or specific. She said the Hatfields were 'developing something.' Those were her words. I assumed she'd found a shipment of drugs, but she insisted that wasn't it." He glanced in my direction. "Cindy would have recognized drugs. That was something she knew a thing or two about from earlier in her life. Before she married Shipper."

"When she was working for you?"

"Like I told you before, she didn't work for me. We were friends."

I snorted. "Yeah, I'll bet." I turned away from the troll and moved toward the remains of the ceiling to see if I could find any evidence that it had been lifted from a dead body.

Silverblade stepped in front of me. He was surprisingly quick and quiet for all his bulk. "Do you know anything about Cindy's childhood, Mr. Southerland? She had it rough. She was fourteen and on her own when she came to me out of the blue one day. She'd heard about my escort business, and she wanted in. I talked her out of it."

I looked up at the troll, somewhat dismayed by how much taller he seemed when he was crowding me. "Why? Don't try to tell me she was too young for your operation. I know better."

"Someone who spent his younger years trying to make other people's cars explode is in no position to judge what I do, or, rather, used to do." He held up a hand to cut off my response and took a step away from me, giving me room. "Leave it, Mr. Southerland. I don't need to justify myself to you, and that's not why either of us is here. I talked Cindy out of entering my business because I could see she had a brighter future than that. I put her in a rehab center and paid for her care. I put her in school and paid for that, too. After she graduated, she did office work for me. Not in my escort business, but in my law firm. I recommended her to other lawyers, and she did legal work for them, too." He paused for a moment before continuing. "She had relationships with a couple of those lawyers, but that was her doing, not mine. To put it bluntly, she wanted a rich husband, and she wasn't above using her pretty face and body, as well as her immense charm, to find one. I introduced her to Donald Shipper, who was coming off a divorce. He was respectable, single, and he wasn't a lawyer." The corner of his mouth curled into a half smile. "The two of them found what they needed in each other."

"And later," I added, "you introduced her to Fats Hatfield."

"Yes. As I explained to you before, it's what she wanted." He stared at me for another moment. "Anything else you'd like to ask me?"

I met his eyes, but, eventually, I allowed myself to relax. "Let's finish checking this place out. We're probably wasting our time, but you said you wanted to watch an investigator in action. Well, this is what we do. I hope you've been entertained."

Silverblade chuckled. "Scintillating. I wouldn't have missed this for the world."

"Mr. Silverblade?" We both turned at the sound of Lionel's voice. He was standing in the entrance to the office area with a rough-looking bruiser on either side of him pointing flashlight beams into the shadows in our direction.

"Is he here?" Silverblade called back. I cast a sidelong glance at the troll.

"Yes, sir."

Silverblade shot me a brief smile before turning back to Lionel. "Then show him in."

I turned toward Silverblade and raised an eyebrow. He gave me a half-smile in return and jerked his chin toward the doorway. "I thought it would be a good idea for you to meet somebody. I wasn't positive he would come."

Chapter Fifteen

    I turned back to see a short, slight figure step into the warehouse, the two bruisers towering over him and lighting his way with their flashlights. Lionel let the door close behind him and remained by himself just inside the entrance. The figure walking our way was covered head to toe in black, with black boots, black gloves, and a black hood. He wore a pull-down black mask over his face with openings for his eyes and nose, and, oddly, his red and scarred throat. I knew instantly who he was and sent out calls for every air elemental in the vicinity.

    Silverblade clapped a hand on my shoulder. "Relax, Mr. Southerland. I told you he didn't kill Cindy. You need to talk to him and find out for yourself."

    I fixed him with a glare. "You planned this."

    Silverblade didn't bother to deny it.

    I turned to watch Al the Torch approach with his henchmen.

    Silverblade stepped forward until he was between me and Al the Torch. "Thanks for coming, Alu." He indicated me with a raised arm. "This is Alexander Southerland, the P.I. I told you about. We've been going over the warehouse looking for anything that might shed light on your late wife's death, but so far we haven't found much. We think we found where her body was recovered."

    Alu locked eyes with me but didn't offer to shake my hand. He reached up and pressed one end of a black tube against his exposed neck. When he spoke, his voice was synthetic and monotone, and I realized he was using an electronic larynx device to produce the words he shaped with his throat and mouth. "Mr. Southerland. Claudius tells me you think I was responsible for the death of my wife. He also told me that you have met Cindy's ghost. Is this true?"

    I tried to peer beneath his mask with my enhanced awareness. "It is."

    "And why would she have come to you, rather than me?"

    "I met her while I was investigating the death of her former husband, Donald Shipper."

    "So I've been given to understand. May I ask you a question, and please forgive me for being blunt, but I would appreciate an honest answer." He paused for a moment to catch his breath before asking, "Did you sleep with her?"

I held his eyes for a moment before answering. "We both passed out in my bed one night after drinking too much. This was long before she met you. I don't remember what happened after that, but we woke up fully clothed, and she told me I never touched her. I believe her."

Alu lowered the electrolarynx and held my eyes for a long moment before letting out a ragged breath. He nodded and raised the electrolarynx to his scarred throat. "Good. It shouldn't make a difference to me, but it does." He turned to one of the bruisers. "Give me your flashlight and wait for me by the entrance. I wish to speak with these gentlemen alone."

The bruiser gave Alu an "Are you sure?" look, but Alu pointed toward the entryway with his chin, and, after handing his flash to his boss, the bruiser and his fellow goon obediently walked off in that direction.

Alu shined his light on the nearby forklift, scorched and badly damaged by the fire. "Would you two gentlemen mind if I sat? I have respiratory problems, and I tire easily."

Silverblade stepped aside to give him room. "Sure, no problem." We walked to the forklift, and the troll helped Alu up the step to the seat where he sat sidesaddle dangling both legs out the side of the lift.

After taking a moment to catch his breath, Alu turned his light on me and pressed the electrolarynx to his throat. "Did you find out who killed Donald Shipper?"

"I did."

"Hmm. Maybe that explains why she came to you," he muttered. In a louder voice, he asked, "Did she ask you to find out who killed her?"

"Not directly. But I got the feeling that's what she wanted."

Alu peered at me through the eye openings in his mask. "Mr. Southerland, do you believe I killed my wife?"

"It makes sense, doesn't it? Your wife died in a fire, and you're a fire elementalist."

Alu took a slow and cautious deep breath through his nose, afraid to draw in too much air too quickly. "Yes, I can see why you suspect me. It's logical up to a point. But your theory fails to account for a few facts. First, I loved my wife." A wry smile formed behind his tight-fitting mask. "I suppose you've heard that from murderers before, and I know that women are often killed by men who professed great love for them." He took another slow and careful breath. "But Cindy was the only good thing that ever happened to me. I miss her every day. Mr. Southerland, you have to believe me when I say that I was too devoted to her to ever want to lose her."

I held his eyes. "I understand you had cause to be angry with her."

Alu dropped his eyes. "It's true that she was having a... a ...." He lowered his device, took a breath, and raised it again. "That she was fucking a man against my wishes. I don't know who he was, only that he worked for the family. An engineer or a technician of some sort. We talked about it. We even fought about it, but I never asked her to tell me who he was." He looked back up at me. "You probably think I'm a coward, Mr. Southerland, and maybe I am. I don't like confrontations. And I'm not a killer."

I met his liquid brown eyes. "You come from a family of killers."

Alu nodded. "It's true, and I don't deny it. But I'm not like the others."

I scoffed. "Sure you aren't. They call you 'The Torch' because you light their cigarettes for them."

That forced a series of short wheezes from Alu, and it took me a few moments to realize he was laughing. The wheezing was followed by a short fit of coughing. He turned his head to one side, pulled the mask off his mouth, and spat a glob of goo into the ashes on the floor. When Alu had regained control of his breathing, he pointed his flashlight beam at his feet. "Al the Torch." He shook his head. "Mr. Southerland, I'm told we share something in common. I hear you're an elementalist. I'm an elementalist, too. I hear your talent is with spirits of the air. I command and control fire elementals. Do you know what it's like to command fire? Do you think it makes me strong? It doesn't. Look at me, Mr. Southerland. I've burned every part of my body, both inside and out. Because of my talent, I have survived these burns, but they've transformed me into a freak. My family is ashamed of me. But we Hatfields have an image to protect. I'm 'Al the fucking Torch' because it sounds tough and strong. It's all for show. That's all." He took another slow breath. "Fact is, I would be a weak man even if I were physically normal. I wasn't born a Hatfield. I was adopted. I didn't get the tough and strong genes. Just a fucking talent with fire."

"Some people would say that talent makes you dangerous."

A single sharp wheeze came through the mask. "I'm dangerous enough, I suppose, and not just to myself. But I have no inclination for causing harm, much to the consternation of my father and brother. And I never had a desire to cause harm to my wife no matter who she might have slept with." His eyes shut behind the mask. "Cindy was a high-spirited woman with needs. And Lord knows, she couldn't get what she needed from me."

I leaned against the forklift to take some weight off my tired feet. "You set some fires for your family, though, didn't you."

Alu's eyes opened, and I continued. "You burned down Medusa's Tavern, the hangout for the Northsiders. And when the gang moved their operation to The Dripping Bucket in the adaro settlement, you burned that down, too."

Alu stared at me from behind his mask. "Yes, I did those jobs for the family. My participation in the family business is limited. I'm not privy to much of their operations. I'm not stupid. I'm aware of the kinds of things they're involved with, but I'm not a part of it. Not unless they need something burned down. Like the headquarters for an uncooperative street gang. But no one was hurt in those fires. I've never started a fire that hurt anyone. I've never hurt anyone badly. I've never killed anyone." He indicated the front of the warehouse with an outstretched arm. "And I didn't set this fire. I know that doesn't fit your version of what happened to Cindy, but it's true."

I sighed. "Yes, I know."

Both Alu and Silverblade jerked their heads to stare at me.

"I've seen your handiwork, Alu. The fires at the Medusa and The Dripping Bucket were controlled. In both cases, the inside of the building was devastated, but nothing outside the buildings suffered any damage at all. Dry weeds outside the Medusa showed no signs of charring. The asphalt outside the walls of The Dripping Bucket showed no scorching. Those buildings imploded, and one hundred percent of the damage occurred within the walls. I'm no expert, but that must have taken some doing. I don't know that anyone but someone with tight control over fire elementals could have pulled it off."

I pointed at the charred warehouse floor. "This fire was a sloppy mess. It burned out of control. The buildings on both sides of this one were damaged. And the fire left enough of Cindy's body intact that it could be identified, even after the roof fell in on her." I looked at Alu. "If you had been angry enough to murder your wife, would you have left enough of her behind to indicate she'd been here on the night of her death?"

Alu made a choking sound and looked away, lowering his electrolarynx. Silverblade jerked his head toward me. "Mr. Southerland, please. You're talking about his wife!"

"I'm sorry, Alu," I persisted, "but I need you to answer my question. Are you capable of obliterating a person so completely in a fire that you'd leave no evidence of that person behind?"

Silverblade glared at me. "Mr. Southerland! Show some decency."

Alu straightened and raised the electrolarynx to his neck. "It's all right, Claudius. I know he's trying to help." He forced himself to look at me. "Of course I could do that, Mr. Southerland. Give me enough time, and I could set off a firestorm that would melt this whole city to slag."

I hesitated, staring at the little man in black. "You could do that?"

"Easily. I'm very good at what I do, Mr. Southerland. But only a monster would even contemplate such a thing. And, despite my appearance, I'm not a monster." Silverblade reached up and put a comforting hand on Alu's shoulder.

I let out a breath. "That's... good to know."

Alu looked up at Silverblade and patted his hand.

Turning back to me, Alu asked, "Are you saying you no longer believe I killed my wife? Because the fire was too chaotic?"

"After what I saw at the Medusa and The Dripping Bucket, the aftermath of this fire must be offensive to your sense of aesthetics."

Alu smiled beneath his mask. "It is indeed, Mr. Southerland. Lord's balls, look at it. It's an embarrassment. It would grieve me to no end to know that some people might believe I was responsible for such a grotesque display of unprofessionalism. When it comes to fire, I'm an artist. This isn't art—it's incompetence. It's pure amateur hour."

I glanced at Silverblade, who shrugged. I turned back to Alu. "I assume you've already had a look at this place?"

Alu's eyes dropped. "Actually, Mr. Southerland, this is the first time I've ever been inside this building."

I stared at him in disbelief. He met my eyes briefly before resuming his examination of the tops of his shoes. "When I heard that Cindy's body had been found in the remains of a burned building, I couldn't bring myself to come here. My father had me brought to his house to break the news to me, and I've been there ever since. I couldn't even go back to the house I shared with Cindy." He turned toward Silverblade. "Claudius came to my father's house to speak with me last night. He told me that I'd been hiding long enough, and that I needed to come out and see where my wife had been found. He said it would be a good idea to talk to you."

When Silverblade had told me I needed to see Alu in order to understand why he couldn't have killed his wife, I hadn't known what he meant. I was beginning to figure it out now.

After steadying his breath, Alu, with an assist from Silverblade, slid out of the forklift to the floor. "Please show me where Cindy's body was recovered. I'm ready now."

Silverblade put a hand across Alu's back to steady him. "We're not a hundred-percent positive, but we think it was right here." He turned the beam of his flashlight on the site we'd identified earlier.

"Let me take a look," Alu said. He stashed his electrolarynx into his pocket and crouched to examine the marks on the floor. Silverblade and I stood to one side to give him room, only guessing at what was going through his mind as he studied the spot where his wife's body had been recovered. Alu remained motionless for what seemed like a long time.

After a few minutes, Alu twisted and turned the beam of his flashlight on the floor behind him, slowly tracing a path toward the back wall with the light. He stood and paced one deliberate step at a time toward the wall—toward the source of the magical energy I'd spotted earlier. He crouched again to examine the floor in front of the wall, and then the wall itself. He stood and waved us over to him as he retrieved his electrolarynx.

Shining his flashlight at a particularly dark area of the floor near the back of the forklift, Alu said, "The fire started there. There was an explosion. Someone ignited several gallons of grease on that spot, and it was blown out into the room." He swept his light across an area extending from the front wall to the middle of the warehouse floor, and, once he'd pointed it out, I could see that the cement floor was burned marginally blacker in the area he'd indicated. The back of the forklift was also badly scorched, as if it had been in the line of fire. Alu continued his analysis. "The burning grease ignited the wooden structures in this area, which spread the fire." He turned his flashlight on the area we'd examined before, the area where Cindy's body had been discovered beneath the fallen ceiling. "You can see how the grease scorched the floor in that direction. See how the color and texture are different?"

I squinted. The area he'd pointed out didn't look that different to me, but I took his word for it.

He hesitated, scanning the room before resuming. "As fires go, this one wasn't that big a deal. The overall damage wasn't actually very extensive. It looks worse than it really was."

I glanced at Silverblade before turning back to Alu. "I don't know. It looks like a total loss to me."

Alu made a wheezing sound that might have been intended to indicate scorn. "This building could be cleaned up and rebuilt, I think. Most of the support pillars are still standing, and the wall isn't all that badly damaged." He looked up. "The roof would have to be replaced, of course, but the structure of the building is intact." He cast his gaze about the room, breathing slowly. "I could have brought this whole place down in about five minutes and left nothing standing."

Alu walked back to the site of Cindy's death and stood with his head bowed. After half a minute, he looked up. "I've seen enough," he declared, and set off toward the entrance.

I didn't move. "Wait."

Alu didn't stop.

"Wait a minute, Alu," I said, calling after the retreating figure. "I need to get a picture of what happened here."

Silverblade snorted. "It's obvious, isn't it? Someone set off a bomb, and Cindy was in range of the blast."

I started to reply, but after a glance at Alu I decided my thoughts were best kept to myself. I nodded, instead. "Okay, thanks for your help. You were right, talking to him made a difference. I'm going to stay here for a bit. I still want to take a look at the rest of this place."

Silverblade hesitated for a moment before turning to follow Alu. "All right. Uhh.... Do you need a light?" He held out his flash.

"I'm okay," I assured him.

"Whatever you say. I'll call you later." He turned and hurried to catch up to Alu.

Alone in the warehouse, I crouched in the darkness to examine the spot on the floor where Alu said a 'grease bomb' had exploded. I didn't know a lot about bombs, but I'd seen some creative IEDs—improvised explosive devices—in the Borderland. Or the remains of them, anyway. Someone must have rigged up a device, probably something simple, like a small plastic container filled with gunpowder, nitroglycerine, hydrogen peroxide, or even fertilizer, and attached it to the side of a water tank filled with grease. Once detonated, the material would have ignited the grease, causing it to explode away from the wall and burn everything—and anyone—it touched. I suppressed a shiver as I thought about Cindy's body engulfed by an explosive wave of molten grease. She would have died where she had fallen. Instantly, I hoped, although the memory of flames consuming her specter's face suggested otherwise. Once the fire spread, the ceiling must have fallen in and covered her body, but she would have been dead before that happened. The rubble had just made her body harder to find and remove.

I saw no obvious remains of an IED, which meant that Silverblade had been wrong: someone *had* done some cleaning up after the explosion and fire. Not much, just enough to remove anything that would have pointed to a bomb as the source of the blaze. The cleaning hadn't been thorough, however. I got to my knees to conduct a careful search of the area and found a few traces of melted plastic burned into the floor. It appeared that Alu had been correct in his assessment, not that I'd doubted him. The fire had indeed been started by a bomb. But had Cindy been the target? Was this murder, or a tragic accident? Had Cindy simply been in the wrong place at the wrong time?

The bomb had almost certainly been detonated remotely. Homemade IEDs didn't require a lot of technical expertise or sophisticated equipment. An ordinary cell phone makes a great remote detonator. Strap it with a small bag of gunpowder to the bottle of grease, call the number, and an electrical current running through the phone sets off a small charge, which ignites the gunpowder. Then—*BOOM!* Blazing grease blasted all over the place. But cell phones, like almost all detonators, leave traces, and I hadn't found any. Of course, a fire elemental could detonate a tank of grease without leaving any trace at all, but now that I'd met Alu I was convinced he hadn't started this fire. Maybe he'd taken me in. I'm not easily fooled, at least not by men, but it happens. I shook my head. Most likely, whoever had set off the explosion had come back and removed any obvious remains of the detonator along with all but a few traces of plastic. Maybe when they'd removed Cindy's body? That would imply that a Hatfield had done it.

I stood up and used a handkerchief to wipe grease from my hands. I sighed when I saw my pants. They were a lost cause. Lord's balls—I'd only had them for, what, five years? Six at the most. I sighed again. If I didn't get a paying client soon, I wasn't going to be able to leave the house.

I walked to the pile of ceiling rubble and sorted through the pieces someone had pulled off Cindy's corpse. After moving and picking through some of the wreckage, I found some broken pieces of melted plastic. One of the pieces looked like it might have come from the neck of a large plastic bottle, a big one, maybe five gallons, like the one on the watercooler in my office. I stood and scanned the floor, taking another look at the extent of the damage. It was easy to believe that five gallons of burning grease could have done it.

I was about to walk away when I spotted something that seemed out of place: a strip of white plastic about five or six inches long and three or four inches wide. I bent down to examine it. In the heat of the fire, the plastic had partially fused itself to a fallen overhead beam, but it didn't look as if it had been part of the ceiling or rooftop. I ripped it carefully from the wood, trying to preserve as much of it intact as possible. Torn and melted, its original shape was hard to discern, though it appeared to have been a pouch of some sort. After studying it for a few seconds, I stuffed the pouch into my pocket.

I wanted to take another look at the wall where I'd detected the magical energy, but the sound of sharp voices from outside the building caused me to freeze in my tracks. One of the voices clearly belonged to Silverblade: there was no mistaking that booming baritone. I jogged toward the entrance and paused at the partly open door, listening and reaching out with my awareness.

Silverblade, Lionel, Alu, and Alu's two bruisers were in a group just past the door. A half dozen other men were approaching the entrance. "Come on out of there, Southerland," a familiar voice shouted, "or we'll come in blasting."

I let out a slow breath, counted to three, and stepped through the doorway. Six pieces of iron swung around to point themselves at my chest. I stopped and lifted my empty hands away from my sides. "Something I can help you with, Fats?" I asked.

Chapter Sixteen

Silverblade stepped between me and the men with the guns. "This isn't necessary, Fats."

Fats kept his eyes on me. "I told the snoop to leave Cindy's death alone. It's none of his business. But he wouldn't listen."

Alu walked over to join Silverblade. "Put the guns down, Fats. You're overreacting."

Fats jerked his head toward his brother. "Go back to Pop's house, Alu. I'll take care of this."

Alu took a step toward Fats, putting himself squarely in the line of fire. "Fuck off, Fats. Cindy was my wife. This is my concern. Not yours."

Fats's eyes narrowed. "Get out of my way, Alu!"

Alu and Fats glared at each other, neither moving for a handful of moments. Then Alu reached up, pushed his hood back from his head, and tore off his mask. Standing behind him and a little to the side, I saw a mass of black and red welts and scars with patches of matted gray hair scattered about the surface of an otherwise hairless skull. His ear was nothing but a stub of burned tissue. More scarring covered the side of Alu's charred face. Alu walked toward Fats until his brother's gun barrel was poking into his midsection. Staring straight into Fats's eyes, he raised the electrolarynx to his throat. "Are you going to shoot me, brother? Do it. You'll be doing me a favor."

Fats lowered his gun and took a step back. His eyes moistened, and a tear rolled down the side of his face. "Alu. What are you doing here?"

"I came to see where Cindy died. She was killed, Fats. And it wasn't an accident. It was a bomb, and she got caught in the blast. She was murdered."

Fats glanced past his brother to Silverblade and me. "Is that what they told you?"

If Alu could have raised his voice, he would have. "They didn't tell me. I told them!" The veins in the side of his neck bulged. "You think I can't walk into a room and tell you how it burned?"

Fats put his gun away and reached for his brother's elbow, "Let's go home and talk about it. Let's go see the Old Man."

Alu shook off his brother's hand. "Someone killed Cindy, Fats. Was it you?"

Fats's eyes widened. "Me! How can you say that, Alu? How can you accuse me of such a thing? You know it wasn't me. Cindy was family!"

"I want to know who did it. I want to know who killed my wife. Do you know who it was?"

"It was an acci—"

"Don't tell me it was a fucking accident." Alu gasped once and began coughing uncontrollably.

Fats reached out to his brother again, and this time Alu fell into his arms. The two continued to embrace until Alu ceased coughing.

"Let's go see the Old Man, Alu. If Cindy's death wasn't an accident, then he'll need to know. We'll find out who did this thing, and we'll have vengeance."

Alu pushed himself out of his brother's embrace. "I don't trust Pop. And I don't trust you. And I don't want vengeance. I just want to know what happened." Alu turned toward me, and I got a good gander at a marred and pockmarked face that looked like the surface of an angry planet. "Mr. Southerland," Alu said, extending his hand in my direction. "I want to hire you to find out who murdered Cindy."

Fats spoke before I could. "Alu, I don't think—"

Alu whirled on him. "I don't give a rat's ass what you think, brother. I'm hiring Mr. Southerland to find Cindy's killer. And if it turns out to be someone in the family, then I'll take care of the vengeance."

He raised his hand, and the air above his head shimmered. The shimmering glowed, first yellow, and then orange, before deepening into a bright red whirling inferno, a twenty-foot-tall whirlwind of flame and heat that threatened to melt the skin off my face from twenty yards away.

Fats and his henchmen backed away from Alu and tried to shield themselves against the heat. Hell, so did everyone else except me, but only because I had nowhere to go but inside the warehouse, and I didn't want to do that. Instead, I called on the air elementals I'd summoned earlier and put on standby. At my command, three dozen whirling funnels of air, none of them larger than a loaf of bread, but collectively as strong as a storm-force gale, lifted Alu's fire elemental into the air and redirected the heat of its flame harmlessly away from us.

"Alu!" I shouted. "We get the point."

When Alu turned to me, I added. "And I'll take the case. But only if you disperse your elemental. I think we'd all appreciate it." I looked directly at Fats, catching his eyes. "Isn't that right, Fats?"

Fats hesitated for a moment before nodding. "Yeah, sure. I think we can all come to a suitable arrangement."

***

An hour later, I found myself in the den of a twelve-bedroom, three-story house in the Galindo District, face-to-face with the last man I'd ever hoped to meet in person: "Old Man" Bowman Hatfield, Yerba City's most notorious criminal mastermind, the architect of the mighty Hatfield Syndicate, and the undisputed kingpin of the city's underworld.

I couldn't have been more disappointed in the man sitting in his underwear in the patched, overstuffed rocking chair across the room from me if I'd hit on a twelve and drawn the king of diamonds.

"Old Man" Hatfield was, indeed, old: about eighty, I guessed, though he looked twenty years older. The thin strands of white hair combed over his scalp failed to hide much of it, and the hair hanging limply from his head to his shoulders wasn't much thicker. The thickest patches of hair on his head sprouted from the insides and tops of his ears. The skin beneath his rheumy eyes sagged like melted candle wax, dragging the corners of his mouth down with it. The shoulders under the straps of his undershirt slouched as he bent his narrow chest over a gut the size of a beach ball, and the legs emerging from the bottom of his loose-fitting briefs were thinner than my upper arms. As Old Man Bowman regarded me, he reached with bony fingers for a porcelain cup and loudly slurped lukewarm coffee.

The old bastard hadn't even offered me a drink.

Fats leaned toward the family patriarch from an easy chair. "Pops, if Mr. Southerland can find out who killed Cindy, then I think his fee is money well spent."

Bowman kept his watery eyes on me. "That's assuming Cindy was murdered," he said in a rasping voice that spoke of decades of cigarettes and whiskey.

"You heard what Alu told you," Fats said. "That fire was started by a fuckin' bomb."

Bowman rested his coffee cup on his bare thigh and looked up at the old troll standing at his side. "It's fuckin' hot in here, Slaywood. Go turn up the ceiling fan." Bowman turned back to Fats. "And how do we know the bomb was intended for Cindy? How did the bomber know she would be there? Lord's balls, maybe she just happened to be in the way when it went off."

Fats sighed. "That's what Southerland is going to find out for us."

Bowman coughed once, covering it with the back of his hand, and set his coffee cup down carefully on a side table. "What does it matter? The girl is dead." He flicked the hand that had been covering his mouth in my direction. "What's this asshole going to do, bring her back?"

Alu, sitting next to Fats in a chair that matched his brother's, raised his electrolarynx. "Cindy was my wife! I have a right to know whether or not she was murdered." The effort to get the words out sent him into a fit of coughing.

Bowman stretched his arm over his head and snapped his fingers. His aide, Slaywood, removed a pack of cigarettes from his pocket and handed one to the old man. After Bowman slipped the cigarette into his lips, the troll lit it with a silver lighter.

Bowman blew a cloud of smoke into the air in front of his face. "Alu, Alu, Alu," he said, once his son had regained his breath. "Why do you want to put yourself through this? You miss Cindy. We *all* miss Cindy. She was a lovely girl. A little fast for you, but, eh...." He lifted his shoulders and one arm in an exaggerated shrug. "She made you happy for a few months. But she's gone. And, I'm going to be honest with you now, she was cheap. She was a fuckin' opportunist, which I told you right from the start, but when do you ever listen to your Pops, eh?"

"You're talking about my wife."

"Not anymore she's not!" Bowman shouted. He inhaled sharply on his cigarette and immediately blew the smoke out the side of his mouth away from Alu. "For two months she was your wife. Two fuckin' months. You want a pretty dame to look at? I'm tellin' ya, there are plenty more where she came from." He gestured with his cigarette toward Silverblade, sitting on a sofa on the other side of the room. "He's got a whole fuckin' catalog of 'em he can show you."

Alu leaped to his feet. "You're so full of shit. I can't talk to you." He stomped past me toward the door.

"You can't speak to me that way, boy," Bowman shouted after him.

Alu turned. "No? What are you going to do, Old Man—ground me? Send me to my room without supper?"

"Your room? You don't have a fuckin' room. You don't live here, remember? I've allowed you to stay here while you were grieving for that golddigger, but it's been long enough. Two months you were married to that piece of eye candy, and you've been moping about it for twice that long!" Bowman waved Alu away with his cigarette. "Go back to your house! Go home! Forget all this bullshit about hiring a fuckin' snoop. Especially this pain in the ass. He should'a been fuckin' dead a long time ago."

I leaned back in my chair. "I'm sitting right here, you know."

Bowman glared at me, but before he could say anything, Silverblade cut him off. "If I may, Mr. Hatfield." When Bowman turned his way, Silverblade continued. "Your attempt to keep young Mrs. Hatfield's death from becoming a media spectacle has met with only limited success. It's too good a story to keep under wraps. The death of the beautiful wife of the most mysterious member of the infamous Hatfield family.... A gossip-hungry public feasts on stories like that, and every ratings-hungry newshound and would-be investigative journalist in the city is champing at the bit for a chance to serve it up to them. You've managed to clamp a lid on it for four months, but that's only made it more appealing. Certain news sources are starting to show an interest." He raised an arm toward Alu. "A couple of them have contacted your son."

Bowman turned to Alu. "Is this true?"

"Yes, Pops. I've received some calls. And I'm ready to talk to them."

Bowman threw his cigarette to the floor. "You can't do that! Why do you always have to be such a fuckin' diva?"

"I'm not a diva."

"You're a fuckin' diva. You always have been, ever since we brought you into this family. What have we ever done to earn your disrespect? They were going to throw you into a volcano on that shithole island you were born in. We rescued you, gave you food and shelter and a good life in the world's greatest city. We kept the government from taking you and exploiting you for your talents. You didn't want to be a part of the family business, and I said, 'Fine.' You weren't cut out for it anyway, and that's jake with me. I had Terrell, and I had Ferrell. I let you do what you wanted. I spoiled you. And what did it get me? Now you want to betray me. This is how you repay your family for all the kindness we've given you."

Alu raised his tubular device slowly and theatrically to his neck. "Nice performance, Pops. I'm touched." He glared through the eyeholes in his mask. "And you call me a diva. Yeah, I know all about how you 'rescued' me from those savage islanders. How could I forget when you remind me every day? You think I'm disrespecting you? When did you ever show me any fuckin' respect?"

Bowman slammed his fist on the side table hard enough to send his coffee cup falling to the floor, where it shattered and spilled coffee in all directions. "We showed you all the respect you needed by making you a part of our family. By making you my son! By not forcing you to be like Terrell and Ferrell. By letting you find your own path, whatever that might turn out to be. And by loving you as much as I love them, regardless of what kind of man you turned out to be. What more could you possibly want from me?"

Fats chimed in. "Pops is right, Alu. You're my brother. But I can't let you bring scandal down on the family."

Alu choked out a wheezing laugh. "You think so? Watch me."

Bowman glared at him. "I forbid it!"

Alu stepped toward his father. "Why? What are you afraid of? Are you afraid they'll find out you had Cindy killed? Is that it?"

Fats stood. "Don't be fuckin' ridiculous, Alu. No one in this family wanted Cindy dead."

"No?" Alu turned toward me. "Then let Mr. Southerland find out the truth."

Bowman sputtered, but no words from him were immediately forthcoming.

Fats turned to his father. "Pops, please. Alu is right, and so is Silverblade. None of us had anything to do with Cindy's death, but you know what the fuckin' media is gonna do with this. I told you before that no one was going to buy the idea that Cindy's death was an accident, even if it was. Which is what I thought when it happened. But Alu found evidence of a bomb, and that changes everything. If anyone else, like the cops, finds out about a bomb, then this whole thing is gonna blow up in our faces."

Bowman jerked his head toward Fats. "Is that you're idea of a fuckin' joke?"

"Huh?"

Bowman shook his head and sighed. Looking up at his aide, he said, "Give me a fuckin' cigarette."

The rest of us were silent as Bowman filled the room with smoke. Finally, the old man looked around at the rest of us. "Where's Anton? Why isn't he here?"

Fats sighed. "I told you, Pops. He's in a meeting with the mayor. He'll call you when he's out."

Bowman pulled the cigarette from his lips and scowled. "Fuckin' Anton. He told me he had this all taken care of. He told me not to worry about Cindy's death coming back to bite us in the ass." He pushed the cigarette stub between his lips, and the tip lit up like a troll's eye. "All right," he said, nearly obscuring his face with a cloud of smoke. "Here's how it's gonna be." He turned to Alu. "You're gonna keep your fuckin' mouth shut with the media. And I want the names of anyone who contacts you."

Alu started to object, but his father threw up a hand to cut him off. "And you," Bowman's eyes met mine. "You're going to find out how Cindy died, and why. If someone killed her, you're gonna tell me who." He pointed at me with a bony finger. "And you're only gonna tell me. Personally. Not the cops. I find out you told the cops, you're a dead man. Not the fuckin' media, either. You ain't sellin' this story to nobody. I find out you tried to sell this story, you're dead. You aren't gonna tell Silverblade. You're not gonna tell Fats. You're not gonna tell Alu. You're not gonna tell Anton, even if he asks you to, which he probably will once he finds out we're fuckin' hiring an outsider to find out what happened to Cindy. You aren't gonna tell anyone unless they happen to be with me when you tell the *only* person you're gonna fuckin' tell, and that's *me*! You understand, you piece of shit?"

"Sure," I said. "I've got it."

Silverblade cleared his throat. "Just one thing, if I may, Mr. Hatfield."

Bowman turned to glare at him, his eyes clear and his sagging face suddenly hard as granite, and in that moment I could see the Bowman Hatfield that had built an empire.

Silverblade was unperturbed. "I'm going to assist Mr. Southerland with his inquiries. I have a personal investment in this matter, and I have a feeling he's going to need some help."

I shook my head. "That's not necessary, Silverblade. I work alone."

The troll fixed his glowing eyes on me. "Not this time. I've been in communication with Madame Cuapa. She... had a feeling about the outcome of this meeting, and she's instructed me to lend a hand."

Everyone stared at Silverblade, jaws dropped and mouths hanging open. Bowman spoke first. "Madame Cuapa? Well, fuck me. Fuck me sideways. What's her stake in this?"

Silverblade shrugged. "Beats me. But she's interested."

Bowman flung his cigarette to the floor, almost hitting the first one. "Who says she gets to be interested!"

A slight smile appeared on Silverblade's face. "You want to go tell her she shouldn't be?"

The Old Man's eyes widened briefly, and he cleared his throat. "Nah," he muttered. "Fuck her."

Silverblade's smile widened a bit, but he held his tongue.

Bowman turned his attention to me. "Email me a fuckin' contract and I'll sign it. Your standard rates. Don't even think about trying to gouge me because I'm rich. And don't try to pad a phony expense report, either. Anton Benning will go over everything with a fine-toothed comb, and if he finds any discrepancies...."

"I'm a dead man?"

Bowman smiled. "You catch on quick, smart guy." He jerked a thumb at Silverblade. "If you want this son of a bitch to help you out, fine, but his cut comes out of your end. If Cindy was murdered, you find out who the scumbag was that did it. And no fuckin' around. I want answers, and I want them fast. Any questions?"

"No, it's all very clear, Mr. Hatfield. I'll get right to work on it."

"Good." His head swiveled from one side to the other. "Alkwat's balls! Slaywood! Where's my fuckin' cigarette! What the fuck happened to my cigarette!"

Chapter Seventeen

After we left the Hatfields, I walked Silverblade to his car and tried to talk him into letting me conduct my investigation without his help, by which I meant without his interference. He wasn't buying it.

"Madame Cuapa insists I tag along and extend whatever resources I can to your aid. I promise I won't get in your way. You're in charge, and I'll lend a hand in any way I can. Lionel will take us wherever you think we need to go."

"I don't need your driver, and I don't need your car. I've got a car of my own, and I'm perfectly capable of driving it myself."

Silverblade was persistent. "Don't be petulant, Mr. Southerland. You're involved with the Hatfields now. Take it from someone who has dealt with them firsthand. They're a shifty bunch. Old Man Bowman has given you his blessing, but he's capable of turning on you at a moment's notice if he doesn't think he's getting a proper return on his investment. He'll have people checking your every move and making a nuisance of themselves. You may need someone like me to keep them off your back."

I had to admit that he had a point, but I wasn't going to give in that easy. "Don't you have a job of your own?"

"Yes, I do. And I have a few things to take care of this afternoon. But Madame Cuapa wants me to help you, and she's the one who signs my paycheck."

"Speaking of money...," I began, but Silverblade cut me off.

"Don't worry about it. I will aid you without compensation, and Lionel comes with the deal. He's a very capable young man, beyond his services as a driver."

I remembered then that the gas gauge in the beastmobile was reading less than a quarter tank, that I was out of cash, that my rent was coming due in a few days, and that my credit card had gone out with the rest of the Golden Gate Hotel's garbage two nights before. I should have demanded a retainer on the spot from Old Man Hatfield.

I let out a breath. "Any idea why Madame Cuapa is insisting on sending you to me?"

Silverblade shook his head. "I don't have the foggiest. But, as you know, the Madame sees things the rest of us don't. My guess? It has something to do with your supernatural visitations. That would be squarely in her realm. But it's not in mine, so...." He pressed his lips and raised his hands in a "who knows" gesture. "When she spoke to me this morning, she seemed very anxious that Cindy be sent along her way without unnecessary delay."

"You talked to her this morning?"

"She rousted me out of bed with a phone call."

"Wait—she called you? On the telephone?"

"She placed the call herself. A couple of hours before sunrise."

That brought me up short. "She hates using the phone."

Silverblade grimaced. "Don't I know it. Her instructions to me usually come through Cody or one of her staffers."

I whistled under my breath. "She must be serious."

"Indeed." Silverblade kept his eyes on me, waiting.

I made a decision. "All right. Call me tonight and we'll discuss strategy. You'll follow my lead, and you won't do anything to tie my hands. Lionel, too. That work for you?"

Silverblade made a crisp military salute. "Yessir!"

"And one other thing," I said, rubbing sweat off the back of my neck. "Loan me a double sawbuck and don't ask me any questions." I figured that would get me enough gas to see me through the weekend.

***

I was most of the way through my second peanut butter and banana sandwich when Kintay buzzed me on the phone.

"What's up, corporal?" I asked.

"I'm being followed." Kintay was breathless.

I pulled the phone away from my ear and groaned. "You're not being followed. Those two gunmen hit the bricks last night. They're probably halfway to Azteca by now."

"Well if it's not them, it's someone else," Kintay insisted. "A blue minivan has been on my ass for the last ten minutes."

"Have you been taking those caps?"

"No man—I swear! Well... maybe one or two, but that's all!"

I took a deep breath and kept my voice calm. "Where are you, corporal? I thought you were leaving town?"

"I was going to," Kintay whined. "I had to pick some stuff up. You know, in case I needed to earn some cash."

"I thought you were flush?"

"I was, but I can't get to it right now. It's a long story. I need to meet you somewhere."

"Wait a minute." Peanut butter from the last bite of my sandwich was sticking in my throat, and I washed it down with a swallow of coffee. "Did you call Lubank this morning?"

"Ummm...."

"Kintay!"

"Just meet with me somewhere, sergeant, and I'll tell you what's going on."

I sighed. "Where do you want to meet?"

"I don't know yet. I'll call you back when I lose this tail."

The call disconnected.

Fifteen minutes later, Kintay called again. "I'm at a place called The Lion's Lair. Do you know where that is?"

"Yeah, it's a gin mill near downtown. I can be there in twenty minutes."

"Ten would be better."

"I'll bet it would. But it's gonna be twenty, and that's if the traffic is light, which it never is on a Friday afternoon."

"Whatever. Just hurry."

It wound up taking me a full half hour: fifteen minutes to get within a block of The Lion's Lair, another ten to find a parking space, and another five to walk out of the bright sunshine into the shadowy dive. I spotted Kintay with his back to the wall in a dark corner booth, slouched so low that he was almost under the table. He straightened when he saw me and motioned me to join him with a frantic wave of his hand. At least he'd ditched the tinfoil.

I used some of Silverblade's dough to get a bottle of beer from the bar before joining Kintay. He didn't look like he'd slept in a while. "Why are you still in town?" I asked him.

He sighed. "I was going to leave, but I wanted to stop by my place first to pick up my money and some other things. But a couple of goons were sitting in a car parked up the block from my house. Trolls, I think. I didn't get a good look. They were in a blue minivan that I'd never seen before. I went around the block so I could sneak in through my back door. But when I got inside, I heard someone trying to jimmy the lock on the front door, so I ran back out again."

"Uh-huh. Are you sure you heard someone picking your lock? You sure that wasn't the drugs?"

"No, man. I hadn't taken any yet."

I frowned. "You told me you'd taken a couple."

"I didn't have any on me then. I took a couple later on."

I frowned some more. "Where'd you get them?"

"From my house. I grabbed them before I ran out."

I sipped a swallow of beer without tasting it. "Let me get this straight. You went back to your house to get money, and you left with nothing but drugs?"

Kintay's eyes dropped. "I grabbed the caps first. I was going to get the money when I heard them messing with the door."

"So, the drugs were your first priority?"

Kintay raised his eyes. "My stash was handy!"

I shook my head. I was drinking a lousy beer I couldn't afford, so I had no room to be judgmental. "All right. Where did you go when you left the house?"

Kintay lowered his eyes again. "I don't know. I drove around. I tried to hook up with some people I knew, but no one's talking to me." He squeezed the bridge of his nose. "I tried to get some sleep over at Bunker Park, but it got a little noisy when an antiwar demonstration broke out. The cops busted it up, and the whole thing turned into a riot. I hotfooted it out of there and walked around the Humback for a while. Finally I decided I would go back home and see if they were still watching my house. The blue minivan was still there, and they must have seen me. That's when I called you. But I lost them, so I don't think we have to worry about them for now."

"You were in the middle of an antiwar rally?"

Kintay looked up. "Huh? Oh, that. I don't know. I wouldn't call it a rally. More like a spontaneous uprising."

"Did you see anyone strange there?"

Kintay snorted. "They were *all* strange. It was Bunker Park at midnight."

I stared at him for a few moments before shrugging. "So, what do you want from me?"

Kintay sat up. "I need you to go to my house and get my money. It's zipped up inside my mattress."

I guzzled half my beer and let out a quiet belch. "I don't think so," I told him.

Kintay reached across the table and grabbed my coat by the collar. "Come on, man—I'll owe you!"

I pulled his hand away. "I don't want you to owe me. I want you to call Lubank and do what he tells you."

Kintay slouched in his seat, sulking. "Lubank is going to want money!"

"Sell your stash."

"I've only got a few, and I need those. I've got more in my desk at the project, but I'll never be able to get in there."

"Why not? Isn't the place empty?"

Kintay glared at me. "Are you kidding? They've got security guards there round the clock. Lord's balls, that place is laced up tighter than a fuckin' girdle. Especially since the fire."

I blinked. "Fire? What fire?"

Kintay wiped his nose with his sleeve. "The one that burned down the warehouse a few months ago. We had just finished moving into the new lab, and they got real uptight about security in the new place."

"Wait. Your lab was at the warehouse at Grayshore Point?"

"Sure." Kintay scratched his chin. "Until the fire. It shook everybody up pretty bad when they found out Al the Torch's wife got caught in it." He gave me a sidelong glance. "I'd tell you where the new lab is, but they'd kill me for sure."

"Cindy Ship... Cindy Hatfield was killed at your lab?"

Kintay sat up straight. "Not *in* the lab. The lab was under the warehouse. Mrs. Hatfield was found in the warehouse outside the entrance."

"Was the entrance magically protected?"

"Sure. You had to get your face scanned in order to get in. You couldn't even *see* the door without passing the scan."

I put my elbows on the table. "But you'd already moved out of that lab before the night of the fire?"

Kintay's eyes lit up. "We had just finished the move the day before, and you'll never convince me that was a coincidence. The way I figure it, someone must have set that fire on purpose. Probably to cover something up. Maybe the old lab was supposed to burn, too, but something went wrong. Maybe Mrs. Hatfield had something to do with that. Maybe her being there messed things up. Maybe she got in the way of something. I never talked to her, but I saw her once when we were all invited out to a shindig at Fats Hatfield's place. She was a real doll."

I sat back, thinking. When I'd thought long enough, I asked, "When did Papadopouli go missing?"

Kintay chewed on his lower lip. "About two weeks before the fire. Give or take a couple of days."

"How soon after that were you told to start packing up for a move?"

"The next day. Coleridge called a meeting and told us that we had two weeks to move. Again, no way was that a coincidence."

"Could Papadopouli have set the fire? Was he capable?"

"Oh, I'm sure he's capable. They say it was an electrical malfunction, but that's probably hooey. Even if it isn't, Papadopouli is certainly capable of making an electrical system overload. But no one saw hide nor hair of him after he was called into Coleridge's office that day. We all figured he was gone for good."

"Maybe...." A few pieces had come together, but too many of them were floating just beyond my grasp. "Tell me more about Papadopouli," I said.

"Not much to tell. Hey, are you going to finish that beer?"

I passed him the bottle. It was almost empty, and, anyway, it tasted like it had come from the bottom of a bucket of pesticide.

Kintay finished it and wiped his mouth. "Like I said, not much to tell. Your typical nerd. A good gee, I guess, but serious about his work. I mean, he'd really get wrapped up in it. We worked ten-hour shifts and half a day on Saturdays, and sometimes he'd be so into it that he wouldn't say a single word all day. I can't imagine he had much of a social life." Kintay chuckled. "Although.... A few weeks before he disappeared, he claimed that he'd found himself a dame."

"A girl?"

"Yeah. Crazy, right? One night, here comes this baby-faced geek, all dreamy-eyed, you know, and he says he's got himself a girl. A real dream, he says. I'm like, bullshit you do, but he just smiles, and, I swear to you, sergeant—he giggles! Like a fuckin' schoolboy!" Kintay slapped the tabletop and shook his head in disbelief.

"Okay," I prompted. "Then what happened."

"Right, right, right. So there he is, all goofy and drifting off into lala-land for the next few days, and then, one day, he comes to me all agitated. He makes sure no one else is around to hear him, and he says to me, 'My girl'—he never would tell me her name, but, anyway, he says, 'My girl wants to know what we're doing here.' And I say, '*We* don't even know what we're doing here,' and he says, 'She wants to see.' And I'm like, 'She wants to see what—our work?' And he's like, "Yeah, she wants to see our work. She says what we're doing could be a massive breach of realm security. She told me it might be treason! And she might be right, so I'm going to bring her here and show it to her. Because if what we're doing is treason, then I want out.'"

Kintay's pale skin had turned nearly purple as he tried to tell his story without breathing, and he paused to suck in some air.

"Slow down," I said.

Kintay went on, slowing his pace by only a degree. "So I tell him there's no fuckin' way she can get into the lab because even then our security was tight, but he says he's going to get her in when no one's around and show her what it is that we're working with. And I go, 'Hey, is she a fuckin' cop or something?' Because I figure if the Hatfields are in it with a space alien then everything we're doing is more illegal than fuckin' murder probably, you know what I mean? And he goes, 'No, she ain't no cop.' But then he stops and says, 'I don't *think* she's a cop. Unless she's something big, like the Lord's Investigation Agency.' But then he goes, 'Nah, no way. She couldn't be Leea. No way.' And I go, 'Well, you better find out for sure before you try to let an LIA agent in here.' And he says he will, but there's no fuckin' way it could be true."

The bartender came by to see if we wanted any more drinks, and scowled at me when I waved him away. "Did you ever find out who this dame was?" I asked Kintay.

"Nah, but he never got her inside the lab, I can tell you that."

"Did he ever try to sneak anything out?"

Kintay thought about that for a few beats, then shook his head. "Man, I don't know how he could have. The magical protections in that place would have sounded an alert if he'd've tried. But, I wonder.... It wasn't too long after that when he comes to me with that thumb drive and tells me he has proof about what the project was doing. What its final goals were." He looked over at me. "Do you think the twist was involved?"

I considered the idea. "She could have been. She made him suspicious about your project, and she might have put him up to trying to find out more about its purpose. She might have even helped him find this proof he put on that drive."

Kintay's lips spread into a wry smile. "A wonk like Papadopouli.... He'd have done anything a good-looking dame told him to do. And, let's face it, she was probably a cop, or LIA. Ten will get you twenty we were under investigation. She probably got whatever information she wanted from him and then turned him over to her superiors. You know what they say about fuckin' Leea: they can make you disappear so completely that your mother will forget she ever gave birth to you. I'll tell you one thing, no one at the project ever even mentioned his fuckin' name after he went missing."

Kintay snapped his fingers. "Hey! If the twist was Leea, and she got Papadopouli nabbed, and he talked, and if Coleridge or the alien found out about it.... Then maybe that's why they moved the lab and burned down the warehouse: to keep the LIA from shutting it all down! Whaddaya think?"

I didn't think much of Kintay's theory, and I told him so. "I don't think you would have had a chance to move your lab before Leea raided the place and took all of you into custody. Your bosses gave you two weeks to move, right?"

"Right! But we really had to scramble. Moving an operation like that ain't easy. It's hard to imagine we could have been out of there and installed somewhere else any faster. We were lucky to finish when we did. First, the warehouse catches fire the very next day, and then we get that killer rainstorm just a couple of days later. Remember that? When the whole city flooded? Wow—that was crazy!"

I grimaced at the memory but didn't want Kintay to get sidetracked. "So you think your bosses were in a rush to get you to a new place as soon as feasible."

Kintay's eyes widened. "That's right! That means they were on the run, right?"

I shook my head. "I don't think so, at least not from the LIA. Two weeks would've been plenty of time for Leea to make a move on you. And if your bosses were really on the run from the LIA, they would have moved your operations somewhere far away from here. Maybe even into one of the other realms. But you're still here talking to me, so your new place can't be too far away. And I'm not buying your idea that your pal's dame was LIA. I don't think she was a local cop, either. I think she was just a gal who preferred her men to have brains rather than brawn."

"Do dames like that exist?"

I chuckled. "That's what I've heard. But it helps if you have dough." I sniffed the air between us and grimaced. "You might also want to pay some attention to your personal hygiene."

Kintay snorted. "Will they settle for one of the two?"

I picked up the empty beer bottle that the bartender hadn't bothered clearing from our table, confirmed that it was truly empty, and set it back down again. "You don't know anything else about this woman? Think!"

Kintay lifted his hands to his sides. "All I know is that he was nuts about her. And he claimed she was crazy about him, too. Who knows, maybe she was. Stranger things have happened."

"But he never mentioned her name?"

"Never. It's like her name was some kind of big secret. Sometimes he called her Ginger, but that was just his private pet name for her. And he says she called him Puppy."

More pieces fell into place. Kintay saw something in my face and sat up straight. "What? What is it?"

"Let's go," I said, pulling out my phone as I slid out of the booth.

Kintay followed me out of the Lion's Lair and into the sunshine. "Where are we going?" he asked.

"Grayshore Point," I said, walking fast and trusting Kintay to keep up.

Chapter Eighteen

On the way to my car, I called Silverblade's office and told his secretary to have her boss call me back as soon as he was available. Next, I put in a call to Lubank's office.

"Sorry, honey." Gracie coughed and took a puff from her cigarette to soothe her throat. "Robbie's in a meeting, and from the sounds of all the shouting coming out of his office, it sounds like it's going to last all afternoon."

"That's all right, beautiful. Tell your old man that Tom Kintay is with me, and that the two of us need to see him *today*, without fail. Oh, and tell him to keep that thumb drive safe until we can all get together."

"Will do, honey."

"Oh, and Gracie. That thumb drive is hot, and some bad guys may have a notion that Rob's got it."

"Don't worry about a thing, sweetie. Robbie's already taken precautions. Two slabs of dreamy beefcake are sitting in my waiting room entertaining me with their rapid-fire repertoire. To be honest, I don't think either of them has much going on upstairs, but, honey, we're talking about some gorgeous staircases. I hope I'm not making you jealous, baby."

"I'm crushed. I thought I was the only one for you."

"Oh, you are, sweetheart, you are! Well, you and Robbie, of course. But that don't mean a girl's gotta sit around with her eyes shut when a couple of living statues come around and start flexing their pecs in front of her."

I left Gracie to her voyeuristic pleasures and hoped the muscle she was gazing at would be sufficient to stop any determined intruders.

Kintay was incredulous when I told him that his pal's "Ginger" was none other than the wife of Al the Torch Hatfield.

"You can't be serious! Lord's flaming pecker." He smiled and shook his head. "That crazy bastard. I guess I underestimated him. But who'd'a thought a dreamy looker like Mrs. Hatfield would ever see anything in a geek like Papadopouli."

"She might have been using him," I pointed out.

Kintay nodded slowly. "I can see that. If she was curious about what we were doing, she might have pegged him as her way in. Hey! Do you suppose that's why he went missing? If the Torch got wind that he was seeing his wife...." He jerked his head toward me. "The fire! The Torch trapped his wife in that warehouse and burned it down!"

I shook my head. "A week ago I might have agreed with you, but I don't think so now. I've already done some investigating into Mrs. Hatfield's death, and the evidence leads away from Alu."

Kintay smiled. "Alu? You're on a first-name basis with him?"

"He wants me to find out how his wife died."

That got a long stare from Kintay, who finally shook his head. "Wow. You're working for the Hatfields?"

I didn't say anything.

Kintay turned his eyes to the road ahead. "Huh."

I broke a lingering silence. "You're on the right track, though. If Alu or one of the other Hatfields found out that Papadopouli was Mrs. Hatfield's 'Puppy,' that might explain why he disappeared."

Kintay turned to me, eyes wide and his lip twitching. "Lord's balls!" His eyes fell. "Poor sap. Of all the dames to fall for. I sure hope she was worth it." He looked up again. "Wait. Could the fire have been meant for him?"

"You think they set a fire just to get rid of some computer tech who was keeping time with the wrong woman? Not likely. I'm thinking more along the lines of a bullet in the brain and a six-foot hole somewhere. Or, if they were really upset, they wrap him in chains and toss him into the Nihhonese."

"But you think Papadopouli is dead?"

I shot him a quick glance. "I wouldn't bet against it."

Kintay spotted no fewer than three "suspicious" blue minivans on the way to Grayshore Point. One of them was closer to green than blue, but I indulged him by taking the time to lose all three of them in traffic. As a result, it took us more than an hour to reach the warehouse. On the plus side, I was reasonably certain that no one had followed us there.

Neither of us had brought a flashlight, but summer days are long in Yerba City, and enough sunlight peeked in through the openings in the ceiling to dimly illuminate the interior. Kintay took me straight to the back wall and stopped where I'd detected the magical ward. "This is the entrance."

"Did you need to flash an identification badge or anything?"

"Nah. I'd walk up to the wall and stare into it, like this, and then the door would open for me." He frowned. "It's not opening now, though. They must have deactivated the scanner."

I could still feel the magical vibrations emanating from the wall. "Or at least the part of it that unlocked the door. Is there any other way in?" I asked.

"Sure." Kintay pointed down the wall toward the far side of the warehouse. "The lab stretches out that way. A tunnel leads out the back of the lab just past Coleridge's office. It was only supposed to be used in the case of an emergency, but I used to duck back there to... well, let's just say to take care of personal needs."

"You mean to get loaded?"

Kintay grinned. "To stimulate my creativity. Genius doesn't just need an open mind. Sometimes it needs the mind to be expanded."

"Uh-huh." I led him to the pile of debris near the hidden entrance. "Mrs. Hatfield's body was recovered near here. Take a look around and let me know if you see anything that sticks out."

"That's your department, isn't it?"

"I never saw the inside of this place before the fire. You saw it every day. Just take a look around and tell me if you notice anything odd."

Kintay raised his eyebrows. "Anything odd? Sure. It's all burned down. That's freakin' odd. Anyway, I never spent much time in here. I just passed through on my way to the door."

"Just take a look."

Kintay took in the ruined interior with a broad sweep. He pointed toward the front of the building. "No trucks. There was always a couple of trucks parked there, waiting for a load. But they wouldn't still be here now, so I guess that's no big deal."

"You must have produced a lot of product."

Kintay shook his head. "The trucks weren't for us. They used this warehouse for a lot of different things. Mostly for short-term storage. The only time we ever used the trucks was during those two weeks when we were moving our stuff out to the new location."

"What did they store here?"

"I don't know. Odds and ends. I never really noticed." He scratched his jaw. "Office supplies, I guess. Computers. I think I saw kitchen appliances one time. Refrigerators and stoves and shit. I didn't pay much attention to any of it, to be honest. What we were doing down below had nothing to do with what was going on up here."

That matched what I'd seen on the shipping report I'd found. "You didn't receive your supplies or ship anything out in crates?"

Kintay stared at me. "Crates? Nah. The stuff we worked with, you know, the mutated alien stem cells? It always arrived by courier in refrigerated containers. Boxes, you know, like the one you brought me that time. Only without the trick locks and the booby traps." He grinned at the memory.

"And the warehouse?"

Kintay made a scoffing sound. "That was a totally different operation from the lab. None of the workers up here knew what we were doing down there. I mean, they must have known something was going on, but curiosity wasn't encouraged. The warehouse operated from eight to five. Us techies came in at seven in the morning and we left at six in the evening. We hardly ever crossed paths with the warehouse workers, and we were under orders not to fraternize with them, not even during our lunch hours." He shrugged. "I don't know what I can tell you about what they did on this level."

He swept his eyes around the warehouse. He pointed to the loading bay. "Like I said, the trucks came in from there." He turned and nodded toward the back of the building. "The stuff they brought in was stored over there. This area we're in now was usually clear. They had some tables and benches here. I think it was their break area." He turned in a circle… and paused, a frown on his face.

"What is it?" I asked.

He pointed. "This forklift. I mean, maybe it's nothing, but I've never seen it here before. It was always in the storage area. They left it in the same spot every night. Why would it be in this part of the building? No need for a forklift in the break room. As far as I know, nothing was ever stored here."

I indicated the pile of scorched timber and roofing material a few yards from the forklift. "They most likely used the lift to move that debris." I pointed toward a section of floor lit by the sun shining through the opening in the ceiling. "It appears that Mrs. Hatfield was over there when she died, and her body was buried when the ceiling collapsed."

Kintay's face screwed into a knot. "The roof fell in on her?"

"Not until after she burned to death, I think. Hard to say, but I'd lay odds she was already dead when that section of ceiling fell and buried her underneath."

"Ugh. I don't want to think about it." Kintay wrapped his arms around his chest and shivered.

"Someone uncovered her body from the rubble. They probably used the forklift to lift the heavier debris off of her." I took a good look at the forklift. "Interesting," I said, walking toward the back of the lift.

Kintay followed me. "What do you see?"

"Hmm? Nothing, nothing.... It's just that...." I stood next to the mechanized lift and looked backwards and forward. "Hunh."

Kintay moved next to me. "What? I don't see anything."

"This fire wasn't caused by an electrical malfunction," I told him. "It was caused by a grease bomb."

Kintay stared at me. "A grease bomb! Are you sure?"

"I have that from an expert. The grease bomb went off in this area. Now, if the bomb had been set up right here behind this forklift, then it would have been out of the view of anyone walking toward that hidden entrance from the building's main entrance." I turned to Kintay. "Were the doors to the loading dock ever open at night?"

"I don't think so. They were always closed when I got off work."

"Did anyone working in the lab have a key to the loading bay doors?"

"Not that I know of. I never did. We didn't even have keys to the front entrance. Coleridge and her security goons always got here before the rest of us and opened them."

I took several steps toward the office area and did an about-face. "So you all entered through the office, then walked this way toward the entrance to the lab."

"That's right."

I followed the path I'd described and stopped at the forklift.

"And if a container of grease was left here, behind this forklift, you wouldn't be able to see it until you were practically on top of it, because the forklift would have been standing in the way. You can see how the back end of the lift is badly scorched." I ran my finger over the machine and held it up. Blackened grease covered my fingertip.

Kintay turned to me and met my eyes. "Which means anyone coming this way would have been walking into an ambush."

"That's what it looks like. Someone set a trap and waited for Mrs. Hatfield to walk into it."

Kintay studied the forklift and the floor leading away from it. He scratched the back of his head. "I don't know, sergeant. I agree that it looks like an IED went off here, and the blast mark extends that way across the floor." He pointed away from the forklift to the center of the warehouse. "But it doesn't make any fuckin' sense."

"What do you mean?"

"Think about it. If you wanted to kill someone—a woman, let's say—on a dark lonely night in a warehouse, how would you do it? I mean, would you blast her to smithereens with an IED?" He pointed at the floor. "I mean, look at the marks. That blast was a motherfucker. You set up an IED like that to take out an armored personnel carrier. Whoever set off this blast was expecting a fuckin' invasion, not a single individual."

I ran my eyes over the floor. "The Hatfields aren't exactly known for their subtlety."

Kintay's lips stretched into a tight smile. "The Hatfields might plant a bomb in a car, but they're not going to burn down an entire warehouse to kill one woman. We aren't talking about subtlety here. We're talking about necessity. And the use of resources. Why ambush her with a grease bomb? If you wanted her dead, wouldn't you just, I don't know, shoot her? Or hit her over the head with a hammer? Or strangle her? Doesn't a bomb seem just a little fucking excessive?"

I didn't want to give up. "What if they wanted to make a point?"

Kintay shook his head. "What point do they make by blasting Mrs. Hatfield with a firebomb that destroys their own warehouse, and then insisting that the fire was caused by an electrical malfunction, and that Mrs. Hatfield's death was an accident? It's too complicated. Lord's balls, sergeant! That's the kind of scheme I see in comic books, not real life."

He was right, and I knew it. I threw up my arms in surrender. "All right, corporal, I see your point. But who set up this IED? And why?"

Kintay raised his hands, palms up. "I don't know. It's crazy."

I stood in thought for a few moments while Kintay wandered idly about the warehouse. After a minute, he wandered back to where I was standing.

"You know," he said. "This place looks really different when it's empty. I mean, it's weird. This place is a mess, but I would have expected a bigger mess, you know what I mean? What happened to all the stuff they were storing here? Did someone clear it out after the fire? Did it get looted?"

"There wasn't anything here," I said.

Kintay turned to me. "There was *always* stuff here. I mean, I didn't know what any of it was, but this place was always busy."

I indicated the far side of the warehouse. "You said that trucks were usually parked in the loading dock. Mrs. Hatfield's ghost talked about crates, and how they were all gone. You said your bosses had you scrambling to move your lab. I found evidence that the stuff they kept stored in here was being moved out in a hurry before the day of the fire. The Hatfield's knew something was going to happen that night, like maybe a bomb was going to go off, and they cleared everything out before it could be damaged or destroyed."

Kintay considered it. "I guess that makes sense. But it doesn't tell us much."

We walked through the storage area and found nothing but the charred remains of shelving and partitions, strengthening my theory that everything of value had been shipped out before the fire.

"The crates are gone," Cindy had told me. *"They took the crates away."*

I turned to Kintay. "Cindy—Mrs. Hatfield—saw them move everything out of here the night of the fire. She must have been watching."

"Okayyy...." Kintay was skeptical. "But what was she doing here in the first place?"

"That's a good question," I said, moving toward the main entrance. "Maybe the answer is on that drive you got from Puppy."

***

After we left the ruined warehouse, Kintay accompanied me while I talked to a few of the employees of the establishments on either side. No one in the furniture factory would give us the time of day, except the owner. "The Hatfields owned that warehouse," he said as he hustled us off the premises. "Whatever they did or didn't do is their business, not mine."

We had better luck at the body shop, where a mechanic confirmed that a crew had emptied the warehouse the day of the fire. "Trucks were in and out of there all day," he told me. "And they were in a hurry to clean the place out. I could see them loading them up every time they came in. They worked late, too. They usually knocked off at five, but on that night they were still at it at six or six-thirty, at least."

The last thing we did before leaving Grayshore Point was find the end of the emergency tunnel leading out of the lab. After driving past a wholesale plumbing parts distributor, a lumberyard, and a hat making factory to a point about a quarter mile behind the Hatfield's warehouse, we reached a small wooden shed wedged between a leatherworks shop and the studios of KYRB, a thousand-watt AM radio station that blasted feel-good government-sanctioned news, traffic, and weather reports to a citywide audience of bored married couples and elderly shut-ins.

"That's it there," Kintay told me, pointing at the shed.

We parked the beastmobile in front of the radio station and walked to the shed, which was unmarked and unadorned apart from several years' worth of faded graffiti. I extended my awareness, trying to pick up signs of enchantment, but detected nothing unusual. Predictably, the door was locked, and Kintay didn't have a key. We each reached into our pockets and pulled out a set of lock picks.

Kintay lips stretched into a wide smile. "Lord's balls, sergeant. I'm surprised at you. Don't you know that breaking and entering is against the law?"

"Only if you get caught."

Kintay looked at my set of picks with a grin. "What fuckin' toy store did you get those from? You couldn't break into a piggy bank with those pieces of shit."

"I do okay." I started toward the door.

Kintay reached out a hand to stop me. "Uh-uh, sergeant. Better leave this to someone who knows what they're doing."

I stepped aside. "Be my guest."

After examining the doorframe with care ("Checking for tripwires," he muttered), Kintay selected a pick from a varied and elaborate set he pulled from inside his coat. "This'll do it," he said, inserting the pick into the lock. He had the door open in under ten seconds.

He stood and gestured for me to enter. "Age before beauty."

I shook my head and stepped through the door into an unlit corridor.

"Uhhh...." Kintay hesitated at the entrance. "You wouldn't happen to have a flashlight, would you?"

"No, but I don't need one. You can wait outside if you want to."

"All right. I'll hold the door and make sure no one's watching us. But hurry, would you? If I see that blue minivan again, I'll give you a holler."

Thanks to the elf's augmentation of my senses, making my way through the dark corridor was as easy as walking down a city sidewalk in broad daylight. Since receiving the elf's gift, I'd learned to stop trying to strain my eyes to see in the dark and trust entirely to what my brain told me was there. At least, that's the way I described the process of navigating my way through pitch-black darkness to myself. I had no idea how it all actually worked. In any case, there wasn't much to see. After a climb down a short flight of stairs, the corridor extended straight as a ruler in front of me, with nothing on either side but walls, and nothing above but a ceiling.

My plan was to follow the corridor all the way back to the abandoned lab and take a look around, but after about fifty steps, I was distracted by a faint tingle in the back of my jaws just below my ears. I slowed and traced the source of the vibration to a section of unmarked wall to my right. I pushed against the wall, but it didn't budge. *Another enchanted door*, I thought to myself, and let out a sigh. I was going to pass by, but the vibration in my jaw shifted slightly, stopping me in my tracks. I pressed my palms against the wall. As I moved my hands, the vibration changed, growing stronger or weaker depending on where I placed them. Seeking the strongest vibrations, I slid my palms across the wall until the vibrations were at the peak of their intensity. I pushed, and a section of the wall swung open on soundless hinges. I held my breath and stepped through.

I looked up into a star-filled sky. To my left, a new moon shone over a distant range of snowcapped mountains. A single tree, maybe thirty feet tall with a multitude of branches and dark green leaves, stood directly in front of me, growing from a grassy mound. The dirt floor beneath my feet was packed, smooth, and bare. A gentle breeze filled my nostrils with the scent of something earthy, yet sweet. Green fields and forests stretched away from me on all sides to distant hills and mountains. I turned to look back the way I came, and, apart from the open doorway leading back to the corridor, I saw fields stretching away in that direction, as well. I breathed the air and was struck by an overwhelming sensation of wandering through a long-past age before the advent of cities, industry—before the emergence of human life itself.

My awareness told me it was all an illusion, that I was standing in an empty room about the size of my own office, bounded by walls of metal. Air entered the room through a ventilation grate above the door. When I concentrated, I discovered an adjoining room to my left, one filled with modern kitchen appliances, but no food or any indication that the kitchen had been used recently. No water came from the faucet, and the oven didn't activate when I turned it on. I turned my attention to the back of the main room and discovered another door, an ordinary wooden one with an ordinary doorknob. It opened easily enough, and I couldn't keep the grin off my face when I spotted a very ordinary looking toilet, along with a sink and a bathtub. No towels or toilet paper, though, and the bathtub was bone dry. I turned the handle on the faucet over the sink, but no water emerged.

Leaving the bathroom, I walked back to the tree. To my surprise, the bark was as soft and smooth as leather. I sat on the grassy mound, and it was as if I had descended into a form-fitting chair. When I wished to lean back and lift my feet, the tree's surface accommodated me. I closed my eyes, relaxed, and let the tension drain from my muscles and bones. I could have slept there for the rest of my life.

I opened my eyes, sat up, and sniffed the air, recognizing something familiar in it. I smiled to myself. I knew who'd been living in this strange, beautiful place, and regardless of what Kintay might want to believe, he wasn't a space alien.

Chapter Nineteen

I wanted to continue down the corridor to the lab, but it felt good to relax against the tree, or whatever it really was, and I found myself in no hurry to get up. The gently moving air washed over me, cool and refreshing, and I gazed with half-closed eyes at the grate above the door. Something brushed against my awareness. Frowning, I put some sigils together in my mind, and the world of winds came into clear focus. Directly in front of the grate, unmoving, was an air elemental the size of a drop of water. It could have been any of the millions of tiny spirits that drifted through the air, but the sight of this one caused my pulse to pound and something cold to form in my gut. I sat up straight and stared at the elemental.

Several months earlier, I'd seen an elemental just like this one inside Walks in Cloud's shop. It had fled when it knew I'd become aware of it: odd behavior for an elemental. When I'd spotted the air elemental in her office, my first assumption was that it had been planted there in an attempt to discover the whereabouts of the RAA formula, or perhaps something else equally sensitive. But Walks had suggested that the object of the elemental's surveillance had been me, rather than her, and I had reason to believe that she'd been right.

Could this be the same elemental? Something in the back of my brain told me it was. I still didn't understand the full capabilities of the enhanced awareness the elf had given me, but I'd learned to give credence to certain insights and intuitions I couldn't explain, or even articulate. I sent out a wordless call to the elemental, seeking a connection and trying not to scare it off.

My call, gentle as it was, rolled off the tiny spirit as if it were surrounded by a steel shell casing. Before I could try again, the elemental zipped through the grate and disappeared.

I got to my feet and stepped through the door into the corridor. I'd wanted to follow the corridor to the lab, but I hurried back to the entrance instead.

Kintay was crouching next to the half-open doorway when I emerged from the corridor. "We need to leave," I said when I saw him. "Someone's been watching us."

Kintay's eyes widened. "How?"

"An air elemental. It took off after I spotted it." I shut the door, and the two of us headed for the car.

"You're sure about this?" Kintay asked.

"Not entirely," I admitted. "But it's a strong possibility. And I don't know how long it's been watching."

Kintay stopped in his tracks. "Long enough," he said.

I followed his gaze and spotted a blue minivan speeding around the corner and hurtling down the street in our direction. I didn't know who was in the minivan, but I didn't want to find out while unarmed and in the open. Kintay ran in the direction of the radio station, and, with no better ideas, I hurried after him.

The ground in front of us erupted as the sound of automatic rifle fire filled the air. Warning shots, I realized, given that the two of us were still breathing. For now, at least. I grabbed Kintay by the shoulder and pulled him to a stop. "It's no good," I told him, and he lowered his head. With our escape route cut off, we turned and lifted our hands in surrender.

The van stopped in front of us, and we weren't gunned down where we stood. I took that as an encouraging sign. The passenger door opened, and the troll who emerged aimed the barrel of a combat-issue assault rifle at our feet. He nodded toward the van. "Get in," he commanded. "The boss wants to talk to you."

Kintay gaped at the troll. "Quarrelmace?"

The troll's head was shaped like a six-sided die, and the large pointed ears that framed his face looked like wings. His square face broke into a smile that exposed the tips of a mouthful of long, pointed yellow teeth. He was perhaps the ugliest troll I'd ever seen. "Hello, Kintay," he growled in a voice that sounded like gravel in a garbage disposal. "Long time no see."

I turned to Kintay. "Friend of yours?"

"He works security at the lab. That mug behind the wheel is Blazearrow. He's the head of security."

Quarrelmace lifted the rifle barrel until it was pointed in the direction of Kintay's chest. "Let's go," he said. "Both of you."

Kintay shot me a glance. "Guess we'd better go."

"Guess so," I agreed.

Quarrelmace opened the door to the rear seat of the van and waved us in with the point of his rifle. Once we were settled, the trolls drove us south down the peninsula.

"Where we going?" Kintay asked.

Blazearrow answered in a voice that, in contrast to his partner's, sounded like velvet. "Coleridge wants to see you."

Kintay pointed at me with his chin. "Him, too?"

"My instructions were to bring you both."

"To the lab?"

Neither troll responded.

We drove out of the city to Milltown, an industrial town about ten miles down the eastern coast of the peninsula. Blazearrow pulled the minivan into a parking complex adjoining a twelve-story office building. The trolls ushered us out of the van toward an elevator, Blazearrow in the lead, and Quarrelmace following us with his assault rifle at the ready. On the way, we passed by several men and women in business attire. None of them gave us a second look, although two men and a woman standing at the elevator when we arrived elected to wait for the next one rather than join us. Blazearrow stared into a panel in the wall, and the elevator shot upwards.

I glanced at Kintay. "Your last place was more secret than this one."

Kintay grinned. "Hiding in plain sight seems to work just as well. Besides, no one can get to the top floor without passing the facial scan."

Quarrelmace smiled at Kintay, displaying his demonic fangs. "Can't get down from there without a scan, either. And your access has been deactivated."

Kintay gave me a sidelong look.

When we reached the twelfth floor, the elevator door opened into a carpeted reception area. Blazearrow indicated a row of chairs. "Wait here," he told us. We sat, and Quarrelmace remained standing near the elevator door while Blazearrow stepped past the unoccupied reception desk and disappeared through a doorway. No more than a minute passed before he stepped back through and held the door open. "This way," he said.

We walked through a laboratory and down a hall past a row of offices that looked like any offices in any office building in the world: desks, computers, telephones, copy machines, filing cabinets, clipboards, folders, stacks of paper in in-boxes and out-boxes, stick-on notes, waste baskets filled with wadded sheets of paper.... No people, though, which wasn't surprising since it was after seven. Blazearrow led us to an open door at the end of the hall, where he stepped aside and waved us through.

The woman sitting at her desk on an elevated chair had a face that was neither attractive nor unattractive, framed by unremarkable hair cut into a forgettable style tucked behind her large, rounded ears. She might have stood three feet tall in two-inch heels. She was staring at a computer screen.

"Sit down," she said without looking up.

Kintay and I sat and watched the gnome key data into her computer for a solid five minutes. Finally, without ceasing her work or looking away from her screen, she spoke in a placid, uninterested voice, utterly devoid of emotion. "Did you get past the passcode?"

"No, ma'am," Kintay replied. "I have no idea what that drive contains."

Coleridge continued her typing. "And you?"

I assumed she meant me. "Nope. I never had the chance to try."

After another minute of typing, Coleridge spoke in the same disinterested voice. "Blazearrow, please open the window."

"Yes, ma'am." The troll did as he was told, pushing the window open and exposing the office to the breeze blowing in from the bay.

Coleridge kept her eyes on her screen, checking over whatever she was entering into the computer. Raising her voice only enough to be heard over a passing plane and the distant sounds of traffic, she said, "Blazearrow, please take Kintay to the window, and hold him over the ledge. Quarrelmace, if Mr. Southerland attempts to interfere, please shoot him in the head."

Before either of us could react, Blazearrow yanked Kintay out of his seat by his wrists and dangled him out the window. Kintay's screams rang out into the late afternoon, nothing but gravity between him and the sidewalk, twelve stories below. I tensed, but Quarrelmace had me squarely in his rifle sights from across the room. He showed me his teeth, letting me know how much he would enjoy putting me down. I breathed away my tension and settled back into my chair.

For the first time since we'd entered her office, Coleridge looked up from her computer screen. "Mr. Southerland, was Mr. Kintay telling the truth when he said he had no knowledge of what is on the thumb drive he stole from our lab?"

"That's what he told me," I said, folding my hands in my lap. "And I believe him. He told me the drive was passcode protected, and that he didn't know the code."

Coleridge held my eyes for a few heartbeats and nodded once. "Where is the drive now, Mr. Southerland."

When I didn't answer right away, Kintay screamed, "His lawyer, Robinson Lubank! He gave the drive to Lubank!"

Coleridge continued to hold my eyes. "Is this true Mr. Southerland?"

I let out a breath. "It's true. Lubank knows nothing about the drive. I told him to hold it for me in a safe place until I came back for it."

"He's not attempting to break into the files?"

"No, ma'am. I expressly told him not to."

Coleridge released me from her gaze and sat back in her chair, thinking. "Blazearrow," she said at last, "please bring Kintay back inside."

The troll did as he was told and helped Kintay back to his chair, where he slumped, red-faced and open-mouthed, his chest wheezing as he forced deep gulps of air through a throat as tight as a drinking straw.

"Are you okay?" I asked him.

His lips spread into a broad grin. "That was *crazy*! I'm lucky I didn't shit myself."

I stared at him for a long moment, shook my head, and turned back to Coleridge. "Ma'am, I'll be happy to get the thumb drive back from Lubank and bring it to you. I honestly don't care what's on it. In return, I'd like for you to lay off Kintay. He made a mistake, but there's no harm done. He doesn't know what's on the drive, and he doesn't want to know." I turned to Kintay. "Isn't that right, Kintay?"

Kintay's eyes were wide, like a child's. "Absolutely, ma'am. I'm sorry I ran off with it. The whole experience has been a nightmare for me. An absolute nightmare."

If I hadn't known him better, I would have believed him. I wondered how well Coleridge knew him.

The stone-faced administrator considered the matter for another few moments before nodding. "Hmm. You may or may not regret taking the drive rather than turning it over to me, as you ought to have done, but I'm certain you were sorry you were caught. I trust you will be less impetuous should a similar occasion arise."

Kintay swallowed. "Yes, ma'am."

Coleridge held his eyes for another beat before turning to me. "Mr. Southerland, please call Mr. Lubank and let him know you are on your way to retrieve the drive. Blazearrow and Quarrelmace will take you there, pick up the drive, and take you back to your car. They will return with Mr. Kintay, and the two of us will discuss his future with the project."

"That sounds fine to me, ma'am. Just one thing. I would like your assurance that Kintay will come to no harm. I know he can be erratic, but he means well, and he's good at what he does. I'm sure Fats Hatfield will vouch for him if you ask him. I know that Fats respects his work, and I don't think he'd be happy if he heard that his best candymaker slipped and fell out a window."

A small smile appeared on Coleridge's face and disappeared just as quickly. "We've missed Mr. Kintay. It is my firm hope that he return to the project. We are in a delicate stage, and we have use for his skills. But much will depend on whether we receive the thumb drive from your attorney, and whether the information on that drive is still secure. It's true, as you say, that Mr. Kintay is highly regarded within the syndicate, but the members of the Hatfield family place a premium on reliability, loyalty, and respect. Those who forget this lose their value to the family. Do I make myself clear?"

"You do, ma'am. Crystal clear. And Kintay understands, too. Don't you, Kintay."

"I do," Kintay assured me, his face glowing with the most innocent look he could muster. "I absolutely do."

"Hmm," Coleridge muttered, turning back to her computer. "We'll see."

***

After calling Lubank and making sure he still had the thumb drive, I told him I'd be bringing people to his office to pick it up. He said he would have it waiting for us, but Gracie was going to be disappointed when he sent her two bodyguards home.

"I'm gonna be good and glad to get those two lugnuts out of my reception room," he told me. "Gracie hasn't done a lick of work since I brought them here."

"Keep them handy until we're done," I told him. "Just to be on the safe side."

We arrived at the attorney's office without incident, and Blazearrow took the thumb drive from Lubank.

"I'm glad to get rid of this thing," Lubank told the troll. "I don't need the headache."

Blazearrow's eyes narrowed as he looked down at the attorney from more than twice the gnome's height. "You didn't make any copies, did you?"

Lubank glared back up at the troll, his fists on his hips. "Th'fuck would I do that for?"

Blazearrow's upper lip curled into a sneer. "Let's hope not. My employer would be most unhappy if she found out otherwise."

"Your employer can kiss my ass. You've got what you wanted, now get the fuck outta here before I charge you for a consultation."

The trolls dropped me off at the beastmobile in the KYRB parking lot, and I told Kintay to call me as soon as he could. He gave me a smile and a thumb's up as the trolls were driving him away. I hoped this wouldn't be the last I'd ever see of him.

As soon as the minivan disappeared, I called Lubank. "Did you make a copy of the thumb drive?" I asked him.

"Of course I did. I gave the drive to Walks in Cloud, and she cracked the passcode in about two minutes. Lord's flaming pecker, Southerland.... You ain't gonna believe what's on it. Get over to Walks's office pronto. I'll meet you there."

Chapter Twenty

The sun had set by the time I left Grayshore Point, and traffic became increasingly thick as I drove north. It was stop-and-go, and soon I could see why. Up ahead, a traffic cop was waving drivers off the main road to an alternate route. Farther up the road, police were herding a few dozen scowling high school kids and young adults into prisoner transports, clubbing anyone who resisted across their backs, hips, and knees with nightsticks. A couple of the cops were lugging away homemade signs with messages like, "WAR NO MORE!" and "LET LORD KETZ FIGHT HIS OWN FUCKING BATTLES." I thought the first one was kind of catchy, but the second one was too wordy.

As I reached the traffic cop, he put out a hand to stop me. He turned and waved through a familiar looking vehicle: the unmarked black prisoner transport I'd seen hauling away the speaker at the antiwar rally two nights earlier. As the wagon wound its way past me, I looked past the driver at a thin face whose bushy eyebrows and hawklike nose formed a distinctive profile. It was the wraithlike man I'd seen from a distance outside the Golden Gate Hotel. As soon as I laid eyes on the figure, he sat up with a start and turned to face me. A wave of what could only be described as dread descended over my thoughts like a veil. Our eyes met and locked for a long moment before the wagon passed me by and headed down the main road in the direction from which I'd come. The veil of dread lifted as the wagon moved away from me. I shivered, feeling as if I'd been pulled from the brink of a sudden and certain death.

I peered back over my shoulder at the departing vehicle, wondering if it held another rabblerousing antiwar activist in the back, but the piercing sound of the traffic cop's whistle brought me back 'round again. The cop's stern eyes held vague warnings of dire retribution for my inattentiveness as he motioned me toward the alternate route.

Silverblade called while I was detouring around the rally. I gave him directions to Walks in Cloud's place in Nihhonese Heights and told him I'd meet him there as soon as I could. By the time I arrived at the shop, passing the LIA surveillance van parked a half-block up the street, Lubank and Silverblade were already inside drinking coffee.

Walks in Cloud looked up from her computer screen when I walked through the door. "What kept you?" she asked, removing a cigarette from her lips. Her voice contained a distinct note of excitement that was uncharacteristic of the world-weary computer wizard. "Never mind, Jack. Come around here." She indicated a folding chair on her side of the worktable. Lubank was already propped up on a padded seat on the other side of Walks's wheelchair, and Silverblade was crouched on one knee behind her. A smile was on the computer wizard's broad face, deepening the dimples in her cheeks, and she stroked the long braid hanging over her shoulder to her lap. "You aren't gonna believe this."

Lubank pointed at the blurred photo filling Walks's computer screen. "Turns out the only file on the thumb drive was a video. It looks like it comes from a hidden surveillance camera, and there's no audio. The quality ain't great, but take a look." He nodded at Walks. "Go ahead and fire it up."

Walks started the video and the motion caused the image to sharpen. At first, all I saw was the back of someone wearing a hooded white robe standing directly in front of the camera and blocking the view. After a moment, the figure moved forward toward what was now revealed to be someone lying on a hospital bed, head turned away from the camera. Tubes pumped fluid into the patient's wrist, and cables led away from the patient to monitors on the far side of the bed. Another robed and hooded figure stood at the foot of the bed, facing the patient. This figure turned, revealing the face of a middle-aged woman with a pair of large oval eyes over a mask that covered the lower part of her face. The first figure placed a hand over the patient's forehead, and the patient's head turned toward the camera. For the first time, I saw that the patient was a woman with large, pointed ears and pale skin.

My heart nearly exploded out of my chest. There could be no mistaking it. I was looking at an elf, only the second elf I'd ever seen, and the first female. For a moment, the camera caught the elf's green eyes, and I could see that she was in pain. Her face suddenly tightened into a grimace, and the muscles in her neck bulged as if she were lifting something heavy. The woman at the foot of the bed crouched and reached toward the elf's lower body. She stayed in that position for what seemed like an eternity. The elf's mouth opened, and I knew she was screaming. The figure standing at the side of the bed dabbed at the elf's forehead with a cloth.

The patient let out another scream and slumped into her pillow. The woman at the foot of the bed stood suddenly and held up a wriggling baby boy with slick, red-brown skin, a wrinkled face, and pointed ears, an umbilical cord dangling from his midsection. I closed my mouth, suddenly aware that it had been hanging open for some length of time. The woman walked around the far side of the bed, and, as she leaned to place the baby in his mother's arms, her hood parted, and I caught a clear glimpse of pointed ears. The first hooded figure turned to say something to the other two, and I got a good look into the depths of her hood. She, too, was an elf, and, judging by the deep lines extending from and surrounding her dark green eyes, either an especially ancient one, or one who had seen hard times. Probably both, I thought.

I fell back into my chair. "Lord's balls," I muttered. "Is this authentic?"

Walks nodded. "I've been over the data with the Cloud Spirit. This video hasn't been tampered with in any way. No electronic special effects at all, and the Cloud Spirit has detected no magical energy." She turned to the screen. "They could all be wearing make-up or prosthetics, but the Cloud Spirit has enhanced the video in ways that only she can do, and neither of us can detect anything that suggests a hoax. That's as close to a guarantee as you're going to get."

"Can you tell when it was filmed?"

"Yes. April sixth of this year. The birth occurred at precisely one-seventeen in the afternoon. The Cloud Spirit has confirmed the time."

Just a few days before Papadopouli gave the thumb drive to Kintay and disappeared. "Any idea where this happened?" I asked.

Walks shrugged. "Somewhere in our time zone, but I can't pin it down any closer than that. Could be a hospital, but I don't think so. Someone's home, maybe?"

"Or a private lab," I said, studying the screen. "Wow. If it gets out that elves have not only survived over the centuries, but that an elf baby has been born...."

Walks grabbed my arm with stubby fingers. "Hang on, Jack. We're just getting started."

Curious, I leaned forward once more.

Walks fast-forwarded the video a bit, and when she reset it to normal playing speed, I watched as the elf gave birth to a second baby boy.

"Twins," I said, astounded.

Lubank let out a chuckle. "Keep watching."

I shot him a glance. "There's more?" He indicated the screen with a nod.

Again, Walks nudged the video forward, and I watched a third elf, a little girl this time, make her way into the world.

Walks smiled at me. "Triplets. Three baby elves."

My eyes were still on the screen. The elf mother now had three tiny offspring nestled into her arms. The two figures who had helped deliver the triplets stood over the mother, observing.

Silverblade's voice came from behind Walks, "Show him the rest."

Walks again moved the video forward and stopped it. "The video was edited, but I was able to determine that what you are about to see occurred less than two hours after the births." She re-started the video.

The triplets, each now in tiny cloth diapers, were moving about on the floor, crawling quite vigorously on their hands and knees. I pointed at the screen. "I don't know much about newborn babies, and even less about baby elves, but that's not possible, is it?"

Walks gave me a sidelong glance, a wary look on her face. "Wait for it."

As I watched, first one of the babies, then the other two, stood upright and took their first faltering steps on two feet. Within minutes, all three were running around the room, mouths open and eyes bright. If the film had come with audio, I guessed I would be hearing squeals of excitement and joy.

I shook my head. "Well, I'll be damned."

Lubank chuckled. "The little fuckers sure grow up fast, don't they?"

Silverblade laughed. "Raising them must be a nightmare."

I glanced at Walks and was surprised at the intensity in her eyes as she watched the screen, frowning.

As we were watching the triplets exercise their newfound ability to dash about the room, a new figure stepped into the range of the camera, either from an unseen part of the room or from outside it. My heart skipped a beat when I saw him. He wore a mask and a robe, but his hood was down, and I stared into the familiar face of the one elf I'd met in the flesh, the one who had pushed a crystal into my forehead and magically enhanced my awareness. I'd given him the vials of mysterious stem cells and the formula for Reifying Agent Alpha, and he'd contracted with the Hatfields to set up hidden labs and provide security for a discreet personal project. Having seen the video of an elf giving birth to three tiny babies, and after watching these newborn rascals scampering about the hospital room within two hours of leaving the womb, I thought I finally had an inkling of what the elf had been cooking up in those labs.

"Elves, and elves, and elves...," I muttered under my breath.

Walks turned to me with a questioning expression.

"Cindy Shipper's ghost has visited me a few more times."

Walks gaped at me. "Lord's balls, Alex."

I gave Walks a brief rundown on Cindy's visitations, updating Lubank and Silverblade, as well. "Elves, and elves, and elves," I repeated when I was finished filling them in. "According to Kintay, Papadopouli was in a relationship with Cindy, and he told her about the project. She wanted to know more. Papadopouli copied this video to a thumb drive. He probably planted the surveillance camera himself and then showed the video to Cindy. And now Cindy is dead, and Papadopouli is missing. He's probably dead, too." I pointed to the screen. "Because of this video. Someone is willing to kill in order to keep this from getting out."

"The LIA?" Lubank suggested. "The Dragon Lords want everyone to think elves are extinct."

Silverblade, still crouched behind Walks, spoke up. "Was that an LIA surveillance team I spotted on my way in?"

Walks twisted her head to speak to the troll over her shoulder. "Don't worry about them. They've had me under observation for months. I have pizza delivered to them sometimes. But the Cloud Spirit watches over this place. Between her and my own security measures, they can't pick up anything from inside this shop. Mostly they just want to know who comes in asking for my services." She turned to address the rest of us. "Which means they know you're all here tonight, and that might make them curious. You all might expect a visit in the near future."

Silverblade rose from his crouch. "That won't be a problem," he said, reaching for his coffee cup. "If anyone is questioned, here's how it will go. Madame Cuapa hired Lubank to look into a personal and confidential legal matter. Lubank hired Southerland to do some investigating related to the matter." He sipped from his cup before continuing. "Southerland recovered some relevant computer files and turned them over to Lubank, who brought them to Walks in Cloud for analysis. Walks in Cloud prepared a report for Lubank and Southerland, and I'm here as Madame Cuapa's representative. If the LIA wants to know the nature of the legal matter, or anything about the computer files Southerland found, they should contact Madame Cuapa."

Lubank chuckled. "That'll work. Not even the LIA will fuck with the Barbary Coast Bruja. As soon as they hear she's involved, they'll send us on our way with an apology for the inconvenience."

The edges of Walks in Cloud's lips turned downward. "That takes care of the surveillance team, but it doesn't mean the LIA wasn't involved in Mrs. Hatfield's death."

I considered the possibility for a moment before shaking my head. "The LIA might have taken out Papadopouli, but not Cindy. Cindy got in the way of a homemade grease bomb. That doesn't sound like an LIA op to me."

Lubank grunted. "Unless they got an amateur to do their dirty work for them."

I was skeptical, but I gave Lubank a tentative nod. "Maybe."

Walks stroked the braid hanging over her shoulder. "A grease bomb sounds more like a mob hit."

"The Hatfields?" I scratched the stubble on my jaw. "I'd like it to be the Hatfields, but I don't know. Bowman Hatfield—with his two sons encouraging him—hired me to find out how Cindy died. I think that rules them out."

"You don't think they hired you to throw you off their scent?" Walks persisted.

"Not a chance," I said. "That only happens in cheesy novels and bad TV shows."

Lubank climbed down from his chair to pace. "The question we have to ask is who wants to keep this video secret. If not the LIA, then who?"

I pointed at the computer screen. "What we just watched is the result of a secret project that Papadopouli and Kintay were a part of. A woman named Coleridge runs the project. She's a gnome, by the way."

Lubank chuckled. "Then you know she's a smart cookie. Devious, too."

"We know for a fact that she wants that video suppressed. She sent her two security goons to your office to retrieve the thumb drive. She knew you had it because she had one of the goons hang Kintay out a twelfth-floor window until he told her. She probably sent those two hitmen after him, too. Last thing they told me was that the Hatfields hadn't hired them."

Lubank held his arms out in a shrug. "There you go, then. This Coleridge dame sent her security goons out after Mrs. Hatfield. They were a little heavy-handed about it, but they got the job done."

"I don't see it, Lubank. Coleridge had Kintay and me in her office with two trolls and no way out. Once she had your name, she could have let her goon drop Kintay to the sidewalk and then had me tossed out after him. She could have stormed your office with her entire security team. She didn't do any of that. In fact, after you gave up the thumb drive, her goons drove me safely back to my car, and I think she's giving Kintay his old job back."

"But she doesn't think any of us saw the video," Lubank pointed out. "Unlike Mrs. Hatfield and that other guy."

"Why take the chance? She could have eliminated all of us, just to be sure."

Walks, who had been listening intently, turned to me. "Maybe she didn't want to draw any more attention to herself, or to the project."

"You're all forgetting something."

We all turned to look at Silverblade, still crouching behind Walks.

The troll made sure he had our attention before proceeding. "Who does Coleridge work for?"

I sighed. "The Hatfields."

Silverblade shook his head. "Who initiated this secret project in the first place? Who hired the Hatfields to set up these labs and provide security for the project?" The troll's eyes glowed like burning charcoals as he stared down at me. "Do you really think Madame Cuapa wouldn't be aware of a conspiracy launched by surviving elves to take this world back from the Dragon Lords?"

I returned the troll's stare. "Are you trying to say that the elf killed Cindy to keep his project secret?"

"Makes sense to me," Walks said.

I turned to her. "You think so?"

"Why wouldn't he?" Silverblade interjected. "And now that we've seen this video, the four of us could be next on his list."

Chapter Twenty-One

"Wait a minute," Lubank said, and pointed a finger at me. "Is this the elf you say messed with your awareness and gave you magical healing powers? Are you saying he hired the Hatfields to help him with a secret project to kill off the Dragon Lords? And that these babies we just saw are part of that? And now he's going to kill us all in order to keep his secret?"

I pushed my hat back on my head and wiped sweat off my forehead with the palm of my hand. "I can't talk about it," I said.

"I can," Silverblade said, nodding in my direction. "This elf of his, along with others of his kind, are plotting against the Dragon Lords. He's made a deal with the Hatfields, and they're in on it. Southerland here is involved, but only in a small way. Madame Cuapa doesn't think he knows much. Is that right, Southerland? Have you been in the dark about what this elf has been doing?"

"I can't talk about it," I repeated. I pointed at the computer screen, frozen on the last image we'd seen. "But that's him. That's the elf I've been dealing with."

Walks turned her chair to face me directly. "If Silverblade is right, this elf is going to give us trouble."

"I need to talk to him. But I don't think so. This elf is more powerful than you can believe. If he wanted to keep Mrs. Hatfield quiet, the last thing he would do is take her out with something as crude as a grease bomb, and then burn down a warehouse to try to cover it up." I shook my head. "That bomb was overkill. It was sloppy. It wasn't the work of a professional, and it sure wasn't the work of an ancient creature capable of crawling into your head and talking to you during your dreams."

Walks blinked. "The elf does that?"

"It's a wonder I ever get any sleep."

A sly smile spread across Walks's face. "I don't know. The Cloud Spirit visits me in my dreams all the time. I enjoy her company."

I narrowed my eyes at that but decided to leave it for later.

"Look," I said, turning to the others. "I don't know what this elf is up to, although after watching this video I have my suspicions. But it's clear that his secrets are starting to get out. I'll talk to him. I don't believe any of us are in any danger from him, but I'll find out what he has to say about it and let you know. Fair enough?"

Walks nodded. Lubank grunted. Silverblade kept his face blank.

"In the meantime," I continued, "we need to keep this video under wraps. Walks?"

"Not a problem. The Cloud Spirit will put it somewhere where no one can get to it." She'd no sooner finished speaking when the video disappeared from her computer screen.

I blinked at the blank screen. "Uhh.... I'm assuming you can bring that back if you need to, right?"

Walks smiled. "Of course."

***

I wanted to speak with the elf right away, but I knew that wasn't how it worked. I had no way of directly contacting the elf, who usually found some way of finding me when he wanted to talk. I thought about calling Ralph, the elf's embedded agent in the LIA, but that could be a time-consuming process, and I was in a hurry. Besides, I had another idea.

After a brief stop at my house for a couple of toasted waffles with peanut butter and bananas, I made my way to Grayshore Point. Parking my car in the KYRB parking lot, I entered the tunnel to the abandoned lab and found the door to what I was convinced had been the elf's living space when the lab had been operational. I placed the palms of my hands on the spaces marked by magical energy and pushed.

The door opened, and I paused at the entrance, looking in. The place looked the same as it had earlier in the day, and I concluded that no one had come by since my brief visit. If the elf had indeed been staying there, it appeared that he'd left it behind when the lab was moved after the warehouse fire.

And yet, I wondered. I entered the room, pulling the door shut behind me, and, as I'd done earlier, I sat against the tree and studied the ventilation grate over the entrance. As before, air entered through the vent and circulated throughout the room. But if the elf no longer used this place, why bother pumping in air?

I put sigils together in my mind and searched the air currents for the teardrop-sized elemental. I had a theory regarding that little spirit. Someone was using it to keep tabs on me, but who? The Hatfields? I'd asked Anton Benning a few months back if he had been using an elemental to tail me, and he'd denied it. The oily fixer could have been lying, of course, but his surprise at the question had struck me as genuine. He denied it again when I talked to him on the phone earlier that week, and I was leaning toward believing him. I couldn't be sure, though, and I hoped I wasn't being duped. Benning was a hard man to read.

The cops? They had no reason to, and tracking by elemental was neither their style nor in their budget. The LIA? Again, unlikely. When I'd first discovered the elemental, I'd asked Ralph to find out if I was the target of Leea surveillance, and the agent had been unable to uncover any such operation.

Who did that leave? As I was pondering the question, I felt a familiar feathery brush at my consciousness. I scanned the waves of air, unmoving, using only my awareness. Focusing on a current drifting to my left, I spotted a tiny air spirit buried inside it, a droplet of still air invisible to anyone without the talent and the magical skill to "see" it.

Without moving, I sent out a gentle nudge, nothing more than a wordless acknowledgment of the spirit's presence. I knew it was skittish, and I didn't want to spook it again. The elemental began whirling, but it continued to drift with the current. I watched it move languidly around the room as the air slowly circulated. After a minute, I sent out a query: "Do you have a name?"

An almost inaudible hiss filled my head. "This one is called Tracker One Four Epsilon Six Three."

Eh? "Do you mind repeating that, slowly?"

It took me a couple of tries before I could fix it in my memory.

"Greetings Tracker One Four Epsilon Six Three," I said, finally. "That's quite a mouthful for a little guy. May I call you Tracker?"

"No."

Fine. "Do you know who I am, Tracker One Four Epsilon Six Three?" I asked.

"You are Target Zeta Three Phi Nine Nine Seven."

Seriously? "If you wish," I suggested, "you may call me Alex."

After a few beats, the hiss returned. "That is permitted, Alex."

"How long have you been tracking me, Tracker One Four Epsilon Six Three?"

I didn't expect the elemental to answer, so I wasn't surprised when it didn't. Elementals typically have little concept of the passage of time. After waiting half a minute, I tried a different question. "Who commands you, Tracker One Four Epsilon Six Three?"

This time the answer was immediate. "This one is not permitted to say."

Well, it'd been worth a shot. I decided to try another approach. "Is the one who commands you an elf?"

I'd been told that all elves had the natural ability to command air, water, and earth elementals: all types of elementals except fire. As far as I knew, only the Dragon Lords could command all four types of elementals, and most human elementalists, like me, could command only one type. I was fairly convinced that the elf had been using this particular undersized elemental from time-to-time to keep tabs on me. Benning had sent his people to pick me up on a couple of occasions when I was out of my office, and, although he'd denied using an elemental to track me, the fixer revealed each time that an unnamed source had provided him with information regarding my whereabouts. Since the elf had contracted with the Hatfields for his secret project, I had to wonder whether it was the elf who had been Benning's mysterious source on those occasions. I just didn't know why.

The elemental, however, was not inclined to be helpful. "This one is not permitted to answer that question," it said.

Getting information out of an elemental was always a tricky business, and this one wasn't as loquacious as, let's say, Smokey. I tried another question. "Did you track me to this place?"

"No."

No? "Were you here when I arrived?"

"Yes."

"Were you waiting for me?"

"No."

"Who were you waiting for?"

"This one is waiting for Target Alpha One Beta Three."

Needless to say, that name didn't ring any bells. "What species is Target Alpha One Beta Three?" I asked, not expecting an answer.

I didn't get one. But if the elemental hadn't been waiting for me, then it could only have been waiting for the elf. And if the elf had been designated as a target, then I'd been wrong in thinking that the elf must have been the one commanding it. If not the elf, then who? I was more confused than ever.

I tried several times to formulate a question that might enable the elemental to tell me how long it had been since Target Alpha One Beta Three had last been in this room, but the little spirit simply had no concept of time beyond 'now,' and 'not now.' When I asked Tracker One

Four Epsilon Six Three where its target was now, it, of course, could not answer.

Still, if the tracking elemental was waiting to pick up the elf at his old digs, maybe that meant it had reason to believe he might be on his way there.

"Are you expecting Target Alpha One Beta Three to arrive here soon?" I asked, but 'soon' was an unknowable concept for the little fellow. So, I tried a different question: "Have you been commanded to wait here for Target Alpha One Beta Three?"

"Yes," came the answer in my mind.

Well, I thought, if the elemental could wait, so could I. I leaned back into the "tree," kicked up my legs, and closed my eyes.

In the best-case scenario, the elf would contact me in my sleep, and, for once, luck was with me. In my dream, we stood together on the end of the familiar old Placid Point Pier under a sky full of stars shining down on a calm sea.

The elf turned, and I felt a pair of emerald eyes, bright as the stars, gazing at me from deep within the weather-beaten hood that covered his head. "Matters have reached a point where we need to speak," he said, his voice filling my head. "You have discovered one of my homes and are present there now."

Speaking to the elf was always difficult because my own voice grated at my ears like the sound of fingernails scraping across metal after listening to the elf's commanding, yet somehow soothing tones. "I need to know once and for all: do you track me with an air elemental?"

A frown darkened the elf's eyes. "I do not, nor have I ever used a spirit of any kind to determine your location. I don't need to, as you well know."

I turned to face him. "What are you talking about?"

"I speak, of course, of the...." He hesitated, frowning once more. "Ahhh... you have no word for it. We call it an *edthrrildohn*, a word perhaps best rendered in your language as 'heritage stone.' I refer to the crystal I gave you when first we met."

"The one that enhanced my awareness," I noted.

"Indeed, it has that effect in a human. It gives you selected physical abilities that are similar to those of an elf. It affects you in other ways, as well. It is through the heritage stone that I am able to communicate with you in your dreaming mind."

"Wait," I said. "You wouldn't be able to do this if you hadn't pushed that crystal into my forehead?"

"That is correct. Although human thoughts and emotions are more open to the perceptions of elves than to most of their fellow humans, it is the heritage stone that allows me to focus our communication with each other in a much more precise manner. It allows us to speak to each other with the clarity we are currently experiencing. But I thought you knew that."

"First I've heard of it."

The elf shook his head. "The fault is mine. I spent too many centuries dismissing, and later resenting humans for their role in The Great Betrayal, when humans abandoned the elves and threw their support to the Dragon Lords, helping them to wrest dominion over the peoples of the earth from the elves. Only recently have I made an effort to understand humanity, but the more I think I know about humans, the more I discover how little I've learned. Talking with one of you can be a most curious and frustrating experience."

I stared at him for several moments before asking, "You can use the crystal—the 'heritage stone'—to climb into my head?"

A smile crept into the elf's lips. "If by 'climb into your head' you mean 'enhance our mutual communication,' then, yes, of course."

"Can I use it to climb into yours?"

The elf shook his head. "Of course not. The human mind would be overwhelmed by the workings of the mind of an elf. Allow me to use a crude analogy. A portion of the electrical energy from a lightning bolt, properly contained, could provide enough power to cause a light bulb to glow. But if that light bulb were exposed to the full force of the lightning bolt, the bulb would be rendered forever inoperable."

"You're saying I'm a light bulb, and you're a lightning bolt?"

"It is, as I said, a crude analogy. Hmm.... And I now sense a somewhat inflammatory one. You are angered by it."

I consciously tamped down on my growing ire and frustration. "I never asked you to shove an enchanted crystal in my head," I noted. "You did that against my will."

"That is not quite correct. You were unaware of what I was doing until the deed was done. Therefore, you were not in a state of opposition to my action."

I waited until I'd relaxed my jaws and unclenched my teeth before speaking, and I kept my voice even. "If you had understood humans, or, more specifically, this particular human, you would have known before you acted that your action would be against my will."

"You are, perhaps, correct. I've already admitted that my understanding of the human mind is, let us say, a work in progress. Still, giving you the heritage stone was for our mutual benefit—yours as well as mine—and for the greater good. And you have not regretted receiving the stone. It has preserved your life on numerous occasions. Indeed, it will allow you an extended lifespan and an effective barrier against pathogens and other threats to your health. And all with no ill effects. Additionally, the heritage stone has also allowed us to communicate when a physical meeting would have been inconvenient."

"Nonetheless," I insisted, "it was invasive. You could have asked first."

The elf nodded. "I concede your point. I, however, do not regret acting as I did. I sensed you would have refused the stone had I asked permission, and I needed you to take it. My plans took precedence over your personal concerns."

I glared into the elf's green eyes. "You say you can read my emotions. What am I feeling now?"

"You are angry and growing increasingly so."

"Give the elf a cigar. Did you ever consider that I might not want you tracking my every move or poking around in my head at your leisure?"

The elf's eyes narrowed. "If you didn't want me to know your whereabouts or contact you, then why have you left the gateway function of the heritage stone open?"

I blinked, and it's possible that my jaw might have dropped. "Are you telling me that I have the power to shut you out of my head?"

"Of course. We elves have a great respect for privacy. More than you humans, I find."

I closed my eyes and reined in my raging thoughts. When I was under control, I opened my eyes and asked in the most measured tones I could manage, "When you forced that elf rock into my head—"

"Heritage stone."

My eyes slammed shut again of their own accord. "When you crammed that fucking piece of crystalized lightning shit into my head—*why didn't you provide me with a fucking instruction manual?*"

The elf's expression remained bland. "When you were given arms and legs, did you require a manual to determine how to use them?"

We stood facing each other for what seemed like a hellish eternity, me glaring into his maddeningly composed features. Finally, I drew in a deep, slow breath, waited for ten heartbeats, and let it out. "I have some questions," I said, once my pulse rate had slowed a notch or two, "and, under the circumstances, I feel you owe it to me to answer them."

The elf nodded. "That is acceptable to a point. I will provide you with answers to questions I feel are appropriate, as you say, under the circumstances."

Chapter Twenty-Two

"First question," I said, holding the elf's eyes. "What is the purpose of the project you've been conducting in the labs the Hatfields have provided for you?"

The elf's gaze didn't waver. "I will answer this question, but the answer is complex, and I can safely maintain this connection for only a limited time. I could answer more efficiently if you told me what you already know or suspect."

"Fair enough," I said. "I've seen a video recording of an elf giving birth to three little elves, who were up on their feet and running around the room within two hours of their birth."

The elf's eyes widened and his lips parted as he drew in a quick gasp. "Ah...." His head tilted slightly to one side. "Ah, yes. I see. Yes, indeed. You have, somehow, seen the initial encouraging results of my work. A recorded video, you say. Before we proceed further, may I ask how you came by this video? The fact that you have viewed this event on a surveillance device is most disturbing, and your answer to my question could be quite important."

I found myself oddly reluctant to tell the elf more than I needed to. This was his time to answer *my* questions, not the other way around, and the awe I'd always felt in the presence of this ancient figure of legend had diminished, burned away by suspicions and my smoldering anger. But I thought his question to be a fair one, and I resolved to give him a bare-bones account of how I'd found myself watching a remarkable clandestine birth.

"One of the workers on your secret project came to suspect that his contribution might not be beneficial to the Realm of Tolanica. I believe he did some digging and discovered your covert hospital room. I'm guessing he got curious and planted a hidden camera, which captured the birth. It also captured your presence at the birth, or at least soon afterward. You may have been there all along, but out of the camera's view."

The elf sighed. "I was there. I had never seen a birth of one of our kind, and I was curious, though not curious enough to stand so close as to be in the way of the delivery." He smiled at the memory. "It was... breathtaking." His smile disappeared as quickly as it had arrived. "But also distracting. That's the only excuse I have for being unaware that the event was being recorded."

I continued. "One of your lab workers acquired a copy of the video. He concluded that possessing the copy put his life at risk."

The elf frowned. "What drove him to that conclusion?"

"The worker who made the video disappeared shortly afterward. He had been having a secret affair with a woman, someone not directly associated with your project. I believe that she knew about the video. She may have even been the one to plant the camera. Regardless of her role in all of this, she was killed just outside your lab soon after the other mug disappeared. I can't help but think the mug is also dead, but I have no evidence of it."

"You're talking about Cindy Hatfield, the wife of Alu Hatfield."

"I am. And now I have another question. An important one, and I want you to answer honestly with no attempts at deception or deflection. Were you involved in the death of Mrs. Hatfield and the man who exposed her to your project?"

The elf held my eyes long enough for me to study his expressionless face. "I was not, at least not in any way that I am aware of. I was told that the death of Mrs. Hatfield was an accident, that she was caught in the fire that burned down the warehouse after we moved our work to another location."

"Milltown."

The pupils in the elf's eyes widened almost imperceptibly. "Indeed."

"Are you telling me you are unaware that the warehouse fire was caused by an improvised bomb, and that Mrs. Hatfield died in the explosion?"

The elf broke eye contact and peered out over the water. He placed both hands on the remains of the wooden fence that had once surrounded the pier. "I am ashamed to admit that I witnessed the fire once it was underway, albeit from a safe distance. It was only later that I found out Mrs. Hatfield had been trapped inside. I was not, until this moment, aware of an explosive device, though I knew the story I'd been told was incomplete. I also know that you are telling me the truth."

"And what about Papadopouli?"

The elf turned to me. "He's the one who recorded the birth and subsequently vanished? I knew him to be a data processing engineer on the project, and that he had been provided by the Hatfield Syndicate. I was unaware he had disappeared."

"How could that be?" I asked. "How were you so 'unaware' of so many of the odd occurrences associated with your operation? Are you in charge of this project or not?"

The elf stroked his chin. "I am. It is my 'operation,' as you put it. But I have delegated the actual management of the project to others."

"The Hatfields."

"That is correct. Other than inspecting the new location to ensure it was properly established, I have spent little time there until recently. I had my own belongings to relocate, and it has taken time to settle." He turned to me with a wry smile and a gleam in his eye. "Time in *your* sense of its passage. For me and my kind, it seems I have moved at a most rapid pace. I am, however, only now beginning to resume a closer oversight of my project." His smile faded. "But I can see that you humans have been rather busy in the interim. Such impetuous, childlike creatures. I stepped away from the project for a mere one-third of a revolution around the sun and came back to find many unacceptable developments. Do you humans never take the time to think things through before you act upon your impulses?"

Knowing the elf was almost supernaturally persuasive, I considered his words carefully before responding. "You're telling me you had nothing to do with the death of Mrs. Hatfield or the disappearance of Mr. Papadopouli?"

The elf shook his head. "As I said, not in any way in which I am aware. You have my assurance of that. I would be most displeased—most displeased, indeed—if others undertook these actions as a result of anything I may have said or done."

"Perhaps by telling the Hatfields to keep your operation secret at all costs?"

The elf paused a beat before answering. "It has become apparent—glaringly so, I can see—that I will need to take some time to recall the content of some of my conversations with my associates."

"Bowman Hatfield?"

"Yes, along with his son, Ferrell, their lawyer, Anton Benning, and their project manager, Clarissa Coleridge."

"Next question," I said, cutting into his thoughts. "Did the results of your project enable that elf mother to give birth to three unusually powerful offspring?"

The elf's face twisted into a puzzled expression. "What do you mean?"

"Those babies went from birth to crawling to running about like a bunch of six-month old kittens in a matter of minutes! They'll be jumping out of airplanes without parachutes in another week."

The elf chuckled, a musical sound. "Dear fellow, I most sincerely hope not. You, of course, have no knowledge related to the development of infant elves. An elf in the womb has a twelve-month gestation period. During the final month, the mother forms a mental bond with the fetus, which accelerates its development. When the baby is born, the newborn begins to walk within hours. The infant elf assumes other activities, such as hunting, within a few days. A week at the most. No, my dear fellow, what you saw was unusual only in that the mother gave birth to more than one infant—three of them, in fact. Oh, they may have been a bit more robust than is typical, but only just. But, Mr. Southerland, my dear fellow.... You have seen something truly remarkable, and yet you have entirely missed its significance."

I frowned. "What do you mean?"

"The question you should be asking is how an elf was able to give birth in the first place. To my knowledge, and I believe most firmly that I am correct in saying this, prior to the birth you witnessed on that video recording, no elf child has been born into this world for more than five thousand years!"

"You're kidding!" I exclaimed, startled.

"I can assure you that I am not. What's more, twins are a rarity among elves, and triplets are unheard of." The elf stared out over the water. "The birth recorded on that video represents a major development in a plan I helped initiate more than four hundred years ago."

When the elf didn't elaborate, I prompted him. "And the stem cells I found had something to do with this plan?"

The elf continued to gaze at the calm sea. "It had a great deal to do with it. But the reifying formula you handed over to me turned out to be the breakthrough we needed." He shook his head. "To think that a formula developed by a human for the purpose of enabling a Dragon Lord to produce an offspring would turn out to be the key development in a scheme to drive the Dragon Lords from this world.... My boy, life is filled with glorious irony."

"Right," I said. "It seems I've been helpful. So, maybe you can tell me a little more about this plan of yours."

Reflected starlight made the elf's eyes gleam. "You have indeed been most helpful. As for the plan...." He took a few moments to gather his thoughts before continuing. "As I said, it's complex, and I have little time remaining for our visit. But I owe you at least a brief explanation." He gazed back out over the sea, as if his memories lay beyond the horizon. "After our defeat at the hands of the combined might of the Dragon Lords and the multitude of human armies that had left the care of the elves and aligned themselves with the opposition, the elves were nearly exterminated, and the survivors were scattered to the ends of the earth. But, eventually, some of us found each other again and resolved to reverse our fortunes. Having been overwhelmed by numbers, and with our own numbers severely reduced after our defeat, we realized we would have to take radical steps to repopulate if we were to have any hope of overcoming the Dragon Lords."

I shrugged. "Makes sense. But you say that no elf had been born in five thousand years. What happened?"

The elf's eyes fell. "Dragon magic. As elves were hunted down and destroyed, our deaths fueled a powerful enchantment, a spell that resulted in a decline in the fertility of elven women. The more elves that died, the harder it became for our women to conceive. Finally, after about a thousand years, not only had elves grown few in number, but the surviving women stopped conceiving altogether."

Inwardly, I shuddered at the power and sheer malevolence of such a spell, and at what the spell said about the genocidal creatures who had been ruling the Earth for time out of mind.

The elf continued. "Elf biology works against us, too. Though our natural lifespans are long, unlike shorter-lived humans we've never been a numerous people. Neither deaths nor births among elves are commonplace. An elven woman might live for tens of thousands of years, yet give birth only once every century. Indeed, it was long before we realized that an enchantment was preventing new births, as conception among elves is a rare occurrence even in the best of times." He looked at me. "So you can see why this birth you have witnessed is such a monumental event. And there have been others. Twins and triplets born secretly to elven women in Huaxia, Sindhu, Nyungara, and Ghana, all within the past few months. All as a result of the serum we developed in our lab here in Yerba City."

I thought about Kintay. I wondered how much he knew about the substance he'd been working with, a substance he'd seen primarily as a foundation for a new recreational drug.

"My connection to you fades, and little time remains," the elf said, a sudden urgency in his voice, "and I fear I may have already strained those limits to some degree. Nevertheless, I must ask a question of you. You asked earlier about whether I'd been tracking you with an air elemental. Why? Speak quickly."

The beginnings of a dull pain were forming in my temples. "An air elemental, a small one, about the size of a drop of water, has been tracking me. I saw it earlier in your abandoned home and again when I came back. It may still be here. It has been given the name Tracker One Four Epsilon Six Three. I thought at first that you had been using it to keep tabs on me, but it says that's not the case. I think that both of us have been designated as its targets. It calls me Target... something or another. I can't remember. And I strongly suspect that you are Target Alpha something. I think. It won't tell me who is commanding it."

My headache had grown while I was speaking, and I was having trouble focusing on the elf. "Any ideas?" I asked.

"Yes." The elf's voice sounded distant and was fading fast. "It means my project has been compromised, and it means I must disappear for a time. I must say goodbye for now, Alexander Southerland. I will return when I am able."

My eyes popped open, and I immediately slammed them shut again as searing hot pain sliced its way through my brain. My head throbbed, my heart pounded, and I wondered who had shoved a red-hot poker up my ass all the way to the back of my skull. I buried my knees into my chest, hating everyone and everything in the universe, along with the universe itself. I lay curled in the fetal position for what seemed like a million years until the pain subsided.

Carefully and with great reluctance, I opened my eyes and scanned my surroundings. I was inside the elf's former home, alone. My stomach was churning, and I needed coffee the way a gun needs lead. I dragged myself to my feet and collapsed back into the tree, or whatever the fuck it was, stubbornly refusing to feel grateful that it had cushioned my fall. I was drained and exhausted, but instead of taking the time to recover, I scrambled to my feet and glared at the tree stretching its way over my head into the illusion of a sky. The starry sky reminded me of my conversation with the elf. He'd told me that he could only safely hold his connection to my mind for a limited time, and I cursed him for miscalculating those limits. Then I cursed myself for asking so many questions and cursed him again for his long-winded responses. I wondered about the elemental but lacked the concentration to bring the airways into view. Cursing Tracker One Two Fuck You for refusing to be visible, I staggered out of the elf's deserted lair.

The rising sun was low in the sky when I emerged from the tunnel, meaning I'd spent the night inside. Just one night, I hoped. I had no way of knowing for sure. Wait, I did have a way. I found my phone in my pocket and was inexplicably relieved to find that it had only been a night. Any longer without coffee and I might have killed the first person I saw for breathing.

As it was, the first person I came across was a casually dressed chubby gent standing in the doorway of the radio station, blinking at the sun and smoking a joint the size of a small cigar. He looked over when he saw me. "That your car?"

"Yep."

"It's a beast."

"It's got plenty of legroom."

The gent sucked on the blunt and held the smoke in his lungs. "You could hold a party in there," he said, squeezing a minimal amount of air through his pinched throat. After another beat, he released the smoke from his lungs and offered up the joint. "Want some?"

"No thanks. But, if you've got some coffee available...."

"Sure, man. Come on in."

I followed the gent through the door into a small reception area. A computer and a landline telephone sat on a desk on one side of the room, and a large, double-paned window revealing an on-air studio dominated the wall on the far side. On the other side of the window, a skinny mug wearing headphones sat in darkness and read from a lamp-lit sheet of paper into a microphone. A speaker next to the soundproofed window fed the broadcast into the reception area at a nearly inaudible volume.

The chubby gent lifted his arms to indicate the entirety of the premises. "Welcome to KYRB, 'All the News You're Allowed to Hear.'"

"That's your slogan?"

"Not officially. I'm Chet Sugarman. I run the place." He took another hit on the blunt.

"Alexander Southerland." I didn't offer a hand.

"Grab a seat, Southerland, and I'll get you some coffee. Cream? Sugar?"

"Black is fine," I said, easing myself into a cushioned chair along the wall opposite the desk.

After Sugarman disappeared through a door leading to the business end of the station, I focused my attention on the news broadcast coming through the speaker. The announcer was deep into a story on the antiwar demonstrations breaking out in the city:

"When asked whether he was alarmed at the increase in the number of public protests in recent weeks, the mayor denied that the demonstrations were a concern."

On cue, a recording of Mayor Harvey sounded through the speaker: "A few agitators from outside the city have been doing their best to stir up trouble, but, apart from causing a few minor disruptions in the smooth flow of vehicular traffic, they've had a negligible impact on the lives of the citizens of our fair city. Police response has been rapid and thorough, and I'd like to commend the YCPD on the tremendous job they've been doing to keep our streets safe."

The radio announcer's voice jumped in: "When asked if the demonstrations were the result of an organized plan, Mayor Harvey responded by saying...."

The recording of Mayor Harvey's voice came up again: "I have good reason to believe that these outside agitators have been bussed into several major Tolanican cities by the Quscan government in an attempt to undermine faith in the rule of Lord Ketz-Alkwat, and I'm happy to hear that the loyal citizens of Yerba City have turned a deaf ear to the rants of these foreign agents."

The announcer again went live: "Mayor Harvey concluded his remarks and left the press conference without taking further questions. In other news...."

I thought about the "outside agitator" I'd met a few months earlier. Far from being a Quscan agent, he'd been a discharged soldier in the Tolanican army who'd lost an arm in the Borderland. Or, at least, that's what he'd claimed, and I had little reason to doubt him. His opposition to the long-running border war between Tolanica and Qusco had been genuine enough, even if Fats Hatfield had financed his activities as a front for selling Kintay's exotic drugs. It occurred to me then that not only Fats, but Anton Benning had been a part of that scheme. At least that's who Stormclaw, the troll acting as the agitator's bodyguard and driver, had taken me to see after I'd inadvertently wandered into the middle of one of those demonstrations. I wondered if Kintay knew about Benning's involvement.

Sugarman interrupted my musings when he re-entered the room bearing coffee and a plate of doughnuts.

"These are a couple of days old," he said, indicating the doughnuts, "but I think they're still good."

I thanked him and tested the coffee with my lips to make sure it wasn't going to scald the roof of my mouth before taking a healthy sip of the brew. It was scorched and bitter enough to make my jaws pucker, but it was coffee, and it was as strong as a stockbroker's love for money. I put half the cup away before selecting a half-stale chocolate frosted doughnut from the plate.

Sugarman pulled on the remains of his blunt and smiled dreamily. "Can I ask what brings you out this way, Southerland? Your car's been parked here all night. Our receptionist says she heard gunshots out here yesterday afternoon."

Instead of answering, I took a bite of the doughnut and let the dried chocolate frosting melt on my tongue. The coffee was already working its magic on my headache, though my stomach was queasier than ever.

Sugarman sighed. "I don't mean to be nosey, but I *am* a newsman, which means I've got a heightened sense of curiosity."

I gave him a sidelong glance as I sipped my coffee. "You ever get a *real* news story, or just the pablum they give you to comfort this city's loyal citizens?"

A smile split the newsman's face. "A nugget or two of actual news sometimes slips through. You run into any of these antiwar protests?"

I kept my face neutral. "A couple of times. I had to take a detour around one last night."

He gave me a conspiratorial look. "There's more to them than meets the eye. I'm just sayin'."

I looked back at him over the top of my coffee cup. "You better be careful who you tell that to. I could be a cop."

He laughed and took another toke. "You're no copper. You came out of the tunnel. I figure you must work for the Hatfields. Anyway, you look like you do."

My eyebrows lifted. "I do?"

Sugarman gestured toward me with the last of his blunt. "Sure you do. I've seen a few of you mugs coming out of there at night. Trolls mostly. A gnome chick. I saw Fats Hatfield come out of there one time. And Anton Benning, the mayor's fixer. You got the same look about you."

"Same look as Benning?"

That elicited another laugh from the newsman, followed by a fit of coughing. "Nah, not Benning. He's a smooth fucker. More like Fats. Tough, you know. You aren't a torpedo, are you?" He held up his hands.

"Don't answer that. Sometimes I get a little *too* curious, if you know what I mean."

A thought struck me, and I asked, "Did you see anyone come out of the tunnel the night that warehouse caught fire?"

Sugarman took a paper clip from the desk and attached it to the stub of his joint, which burned away to almost nothing under the force of his last, long drag. Tossing the blackened nub, clip and all, into a wastebasket, he turned to me. "Does that tunnel lead to the warehouse? I always thought it did, but I've never been able to see where it comes out on the other end."

I held his eyes until he asked, "You aren't actually a cop, are you?"

"I'm a private detective," I admitted.

"No shit? Huh! I didn't think those guys existed except in movies."

"I get that a lot."

His eyes narrowed. "So, I was wrong? You don't work for the Hatfields?"

"I'm not with the syndicate, no. And I'm interested in what you might have seen on the night of that fire."

Sugarman nodded slowly. "I was working that night. I did the afternoon drive shift and hung around afterward for a while, shooting the shit with Mick Stone." He pointed toward the window looking in on the studio. "That's the joker on the air right now. Anyway, a little before seven I start to get hungry, so I go off to get some dinner. There's a nice little diner about a mile from here that serves a mean octopus salad."

I let out a breath. "I'm sure."

Sugarman chuckled. "You probably want me to get to the point, don't you. People tell me I talk too much. But I'm a reporter, so talking is what I do. Anyway, I'm coming out of the station, and that's when I see him. That spooky lug in the hood. He came out of the tunnel and headed off that way."

"And this was around seven?"

"Somewhere between six-thirty and seven. Just before the fire started. I watched him until he got to the corner, and he turned toward the warehouse. I thought it was odd. If he wanted to go to the warehouse, why didn't he go through the tunnel and get in that way? But I've seen him come out and head in that direction before. Like I say, I'm a curious kind of guy. I think maybe he's either going somewhere other than the warehouse, or the tunnel doesn't actually lead to the warehouse after all."

"You ever try to follow him?"

Sugarman smiled, and his red-rimmed eyes gleamed. "Once. A joker like that, with that big fuckin' hood... I'm guessing he doesn't want anyone to know who he is. But I lost him. It's kind of weird when you think about it. He was there one second, and then he wasn't. I think there might have been some magic at work." The newsman leaned toward me like he was going to tell me a secret. "I've got a theory about him. You know Al "the Torch" Hatfield? The younger brother? He hardly ever appears in public, but whenever he does, he's always covered up. Head covered, face covered.... That got me to thinking. And then, after the fire, I become even more convinced. If I was a betting man, and I just might be, I'd put a couple of c-notes on it. I think that hooded lug is Al the Torch. Thought so the first time I saw him, and now I'm more convinced than ever."

"What makes you so sure?"

"Well..." he began, leaning even closer to me, "like I said, I spotted him coming out of that tunnel before the fire started that night and walk around the corner in the direction of the warehouse. Remember, now, I already thought he might be Al the Torch. Well, a few minutes later, I see the flames shooting up on the other side of the block. Naturally, I ran over there to see what was going on, and I see the warehouse all lit up. Flames everywhere. I don't see the hooded man anywhere, but he was headed in that direction just before the place went up." He leaned against the side of the desk. "I mean, it's not conclusive, but when you put two and two together...." He shrugged. "Where there's a Torch, there's fire, right?"

Chapter Twenty-Three

The first thing I did when I got home was open a bottle of beer and email a contract to Bowman Hatfield. I insisted on a retainer. It was Saturday, my credit card was shredded, and my calculations told me I'd be out of beer by Monday. Tuesday, if I was careful, but I wasn't planning on being careful.

It had been a rough night, and I napped all morning. Or at least I tried to. A few minutes before noon, I was awakened by someone banging on my front door. When it didn't stop, I rolled out of bed, threw on some clothes, and dragged myself down the stairs to my office. I refrained from grabbing my gun to shoot whoever was threatening to beat my front door in.

Opening the door stopped the pounding, but my mood didn't improve when I saw who was standing in the doorway.

"What do you want, Bronzetooth?"

The troll in the custom-made pinstriped suit glared down his nose at me. "How come you don't answer your phone, peeper?"

"I turned it off. I was sleeping."

"Yeah? Well, wake up, Buttercup. Benning wants to see you."

"Why doesn't he come here?"

Bronzetooth peered over my shoulder into my office and sniffed. "Maybe he doesn't like the smell. You coming without a struggle, peeper? Or do I have to knock you out and carry you like a sack of garbage?"

I remained standing in the doorway. "What's your hurry? I haven't had my morning coffee. Come in and I'll put on a pot. I think I can even dig up a bowl of yonak for you. Bloody and spicy. Room temperature, too, just the way you trolls like it."

Bronzetooth tried to bore a hole into my forehead with his laser-red eyes. He knew that I knew that he disdained traditional troll food, like yonak.

I let out a sigh. "No? All right, I'll get my hat."

After cleaning up a bit and packing away a peanut butter and banana sandwich in near record time, I allowed Bronzetooth—Anton Benning's bodyguard, personal assistant, and chief enforcer—to drive me to his boss's midtown home. I slurped coffee from a thermos, and he remained silent during the entire trip. Once there, the troll searched me for weapons I wasn't carrying, confiscated my cell phone, and demanded that I leave my shoes by the door before leading me down the carpeted hallway to Benning's office.

The fixer was sitting at his desk when Bronzetooth announced me, and he wordlessly waved me to a chair. He didn't look happy to see me. He didn't stand to offer me a limp handshake, and he didn't offer me a drink. Too bad. I'd been dreaming about the shawnee whiskey he kept stocked in his office bar all the way to his house.

When I was seated, Benning adjusted the carnation in his lapel, making sure it was in the optimum position, and fixed me with a firm stare. My nose twitched at the honeysuckle scent of his cologne. His lips, almost hidden beneath his bushy salt-and-pepper mustache, were stretched taut, and his clenched jaw caused the skin over his cheeks to stretch until his cheekbones were as sharp as a pair of knives. He wasn't sweating, though, not even in his three-piece cashmere suit. Men like Benning don't sweat. They make other men sweat.

Benning got right down to business. "I have received a copy of your contract from Bowman Hatfield. He wishes you to investigate the circumstances surrounding Cindy Hatfield's death." He paused to let that information sink in. "This past Tuesday, I informed you that Mrs. Hatfield's death was the result of an unfortunate accident."

"And 'tragic'," I said, leaning back in the chair and adjusting my tie. "You called it a 'tragic' and 'unfortunate' accident."

Benning raised one eyebrow, and Bronzetooth, standing near his boss's shoulder, fixed me with a glare.

"Why don't you leave him alone with me for a few minutes, Mr. Benning," said the troll. "Let me teach this rodent a little respect."

Benning gave the troll a tight smile. "That won't be necessary, Bronzetooth." He turned back to me. "You recall our conversation?"

"Yes," I continued, "I remember. But things are different now. The Old Man's boys—both of them—want me to find out how and why Mrs. Hatfield died, and their father hired me to do it. He's a hard man to say no to."

Benning kept his firm stare on me for several heartbeats until he'd confirmed I wasn't going to wilt under its severity. Without a word, he picked up a pen and scratched something out on a piece of paper. He ripped it out of a notebook and pushed it across his desk in my direction. "That's a check, Mr. Southerland. I believe you'll find that it will cover your costs and any likely expenses you would incur over a two-day period. I've also included a bonus for bringing your investigation to a rapid and satisfactory conclusion. A substantial bonus."

I leaned over to examine the check. With the bonus, I wouldn't have to worry about food, gas, or rent for the next three months.

I sat back into my chair. "All I need is a retainer, Mr. Benning. I haven't concluded my investigation yet."

Benning folded his hands atop his desk. "Ah, but you have, Mr. Southerland. Your investigation has proved beyond doubt that Mrs. Hatfield died in a fire caused by an electrical malfunction in a warehouse that, to the embarrassment of our family, should have been shut down for repairs years ago. It is shameful that we kept the building in operation for as long as we did without a thorough inspection resulting in needed upgrades to the building's infrastructure. Mrs. Hatfield's death was entirely the fault of our negligence. Bowman Hatfield won't like hearing this, but, fortunately, you won't have to be the one to tell him the bad news. I will take care of that myself."

"I see. There's just one thing, Mr. Benning. What was Cindy doing in that warehouse that night? That was rather a strange place for her to be, don't you think?"

Benning nodded, his expression still tight. "Yes, it was. It seems that Alu's wife had been conducting a clandestine affair with one of our engineers. The two of them had planned to meet that evening at the warehouse."

I let out a chuckle. "A sophisticated woman like Mrs. Hatfield? You'd think she'd conduct such business in a hotel room. A nice one, like the Huntinghouse. But a warehouse? I'm having a hard time buying that one, and I don't think Old Man Hatfield will buy it, either."

Benning's smile broadened a bit. "Ah, but, what you don't know is that the Hatfield family maintained a facility beneath the warehouse, its entrances hidden by enchanted security equipment. The facility was used for a project of a sensitive nature, one that we don't want exposed to the public. The offices there were rather nicely apportioned, and the engineer in question had brought Mrs. Hatfield into the facility a few times to see some of his work. Doubtless for other reasons, as well." Benning shook his head. "Unfortunately, the young engineer had grown increasingly unreliable. I believe that he had become addicted to narcotics. Mrs. Hatfield was, dare I say, an adventurous woman, and she herself may have introduced her lover to some rather exotic recreational substances. We had to let the engineer go. Soon afterwards, we were forced to move our operations to a more suitable location. The old building had become a problem. It was falling apart. The greatest concern was the electrical wiring, which had been allowed to decay over the years and had begun to malfunction."

Benning paused long enough to make sure I was keeping up. After a few moments, he continued with his story. "I'm not sure what happened between the two lovers. I only got his side of the story. He was quite smitten with her and overly romantic. She, I suspect, regarded him as little more than a plaything. Their relationship cooled once he was no longer working on the project. Mrs. Hatfield undoubtedly lost interest in the young man once he was no longer associated with something that interested her. At any rate, he decided to return to the lab to beg for his job back, not knowing that the operation had relocated. Mrs. Hatfield must have learned of his intentions and gone to the warehouse herself to intercept him. She arrived early, however, well before Papadopouli. While she waited for her lover, the fire unexpectedly broke out." Benning shook his head, a sad look in his eyes. "Ironically, she may have caused the fire herself in an attempt to turn on the lights in the front office of the warehouse. It was a dark, dreary place, and a vulnerable woman like Mrs. Hatfield would not have been comfortable waiting alone in the dark. It's possible that she hit a wrong switch at the wrong time, upsetting the faulty wiring in that place."

I nodded along with the story, keeping my face blank. "I see. And how do you know all this?"

"The morning after the fire, the engineer in question came directly to me, right here in my home, and confessed the details of his affair and his plans for that evening. He was upset and contrite, and he begged me to keep what he'd told me from the Hatfield family. He greatly feared what their reaction would be to his story, and rightly so. I sympathized and agreed to help him. His indiscretions could not be overlooked, of course. It wasn't just that he was involved with Alu's wife, but he had revealed the presence of the underground facilities to her. Under the circumstances, I felt that his best recourse was to make himself scarce. I made that clear to him. I informed him that he would have to leave the city, the farther away the better. I procured for him transportation to a location I will not disclose. Needless to say, I made it clear that he was never to return to Yerba City, nor to make contact of any kind with any of his former colleagues. He agreed to these terms in return for his continued wellbeing, and he fully understands the consequences that would result for violating his side of the bargain."

I looked at the check. "And that's what I'm supposed to tell Old Man Bowman?"

The fixer's smile failed to soften the intensity in his eyes. "It is indeed. And I assure you, he will accept your story, as will his sons. Write your findings up in a report and send it to me. I will deliver it personally to the Old Man."

I turned in my chair. "Hey, Bronzetooth. Why don't you fix me up with a glass of your boss's shawnee."

The troll fixed me with his deadliest gaze, his eyes glowing like the burning tips of lit cigars. "Why don't you come over here and kiss my ass, you fucking piece of shit!"

I turned back to Benning. "He gets less friendly every time I see him. I've never been able to figure out why he doesn't like me."

The fixer lifted an eyebrow. "Have you not considered that he might be having a bad day? You know nothing about Bronzetooth. Do you know that he's married and, like most troll fathers, hoping for an offspring? Trolls are not prolific creatures, and most parents are disappointed when they realize they are destined to be childless. You really should strive to be more empathetic." He waved a hand in dismissal. "But enough of that. Are you having a problem with the details of your upcoming report?"

"Alu found evidence that the fire was started by a grease bomb."

Benning chuckled softly. "Oh, dear—Alu found grease in a warehouse?" He rolled his eyes and waved the idea away with a dismissive gesture. "Yes, I've heard Alu's theory. He is, however, mistaken. Alu is a recluse, given to many elaborate fantasies. A 'grease bomb' indeed. Grease, as I'm sure you know, is hardly uncommon in a storage facility, and any heavy accumulation of grease he or you found in the ruins of that warehouse was doubtless left behind when heavy equipment was moved from the facility that morning."

Benning stood. "And I believe that concludes not only your investigation, but our business. Bowman has a great many things on his mind at the moment, and he will be relieved that you were able to wrap up this little matter so quickly. I congratulate you on a job well done, and I look forward to receiving your report by the beginning of the day on Monday. An attachment to an email will be satisfactory. Bronzetooth will provide you with my address." Without turning, he lifted a hand and snapped his fingers. "Bronzetooth, please return Mr. Southerland to his home."

Bronzetooth flinched ever so slightly, but quickly composed himself. "Yessir, Mr. Benning."

I gave Benning a long look, stood, and picked up the check.

"Oh, one last thing, Mr. Southerland. That matter of the surveillance video we discussed before. I'll personally drop it in the mail to you once I have your report. I give you my word that there are no copies. Consider it an additional bonus for your excellent work." He held out a hand, and after giving his extended fingers a quick shake, I preceded Bronzetooth out the door, keenly aware of the troll's red glare burrowing into the back of my head.

***

Benning's alternative version of Cindy's death was hooey. I knew it was hooey, and Benning knew that I knew it was hooey. It made me wonder why the oily fixer was so anxious to sweep the whole thing under the rug. Was it simply a matter of trying to insulate the Old Man from a worry he didn't need, or was it something darker? Had Benning been involved in Cindy's death? Had he killed her, or, more realistically, had her killed? And, if so, why? Did it have something to do with the elf's project and the video of the newborn triplets?

Sitting at my desk early that evening studying Benning's check, I felt as if I were circling in on something, but I couldn't quite make the moving parts stand still. If Benning had been responsible for Cindy's death, I could understand why he'd want to keep it from the Hatfields, especially Al the Torch. But why would Benning want Cindy dead? He wouldn't have liked that she'd discovered the purpose of the elf's project, but would he have been sore enough about it to have her killed? Cindy's death was clumsy, a clusterfuck. Sure, Benning was a smarmy, patronizing son of a bitch with the morals of a viper, but he was too sharp an operator to eliminate a loose end by setting off a grease bomb and burning down a warehouse. That had been a hack job. Benning was a surgeon.

He was also keen enough to write me a check I wouldn't be able to cash until the banks opened on Monday. Sure, I could deposit the check electronically with my phone, but it wouldn't be credited to my account until after the weekend. An instant payday joint down the block would cash it for twenty percent of the check's value, but I wasn't desperate enough for a sucker play like that. I flicked the check with a finger and shoved it into my desk drawer.

Benning wanted my bullshit report by the beginning of the new work week. If I didn't send it to him, I could not only expect him to cancel his check, but to gift the police with a security camera feed featuring Alexander Southerland, P.I., breaking into the Peninsula Property Management Company under the light of a nearly full moon. Since the company was owned by the Hatfield Syndicate, it was a sure bet that I'd do time for it. Not even Lubank would be able to get me off. But that threat would vanish if I gave Benning what he wanted.

I wrote the report exactly as Benning had dictated it to me. It's not that I didn't have a choice, it was just that the other choices—prison or taking it on the lam—didn't appeal to me. Alu would be disappointed in my findings, but fuck him. I didn't owe him anything. Besides, he wouldn't be half as disappointed in me as I would be in myself. I read and re-read the report before attaching it to an email addressed to Benning. I moved the cursor to the send button and stared at it, my finger resting on my mouse's clicker.

I didn't click on send. I didn't delete the report, either. Instead, I saved the email as a draft, grabbed my coat and hat, and stepped outside in time to watch the last gleam of the setting sun as it disappeared over the horizon. A cold wind was sweeping in from the west across the peninsula, and I pushed my lid all the way down to my ears to keep it from flying off my head as I made my way up the block. I didn't have a destination in mind; I just needed to feel the chill of the night air on my face and hear the symphony of the city playing out in the noise of the traffic on a Saturday night.

I knew that my life would change the moment I sent my report to Benning, and not because I'd be in the clear for the break-in. It's possible that Benning had lied when he told me he hadn't made copies of the security video—he'd lie to his mother, his wife, and his youngest child if it meant more money and power for Anton—but I knew that in this particular case he'd told me the truth. He didn't need those copies. By sending him a falsified account of Cindy's death to give to Old Man Bowman, the smooth-talking fixer would have me by the shorthairs. If I crossed him in the future, Benning would see to it that the Old Man and his sons knew I'd lied to them and taken their money. The Old Man would consider it a grave insult, and he'd make sure the entire city found out what it meant to try to play the head of the Hatfield family for a sap. I'd be lucky to come out of it with a quick, clean death.

If I didn't send the report, I'd most likely end up in stir, my career finished. If I sent it, I'd be deep in the pockets of the Hatfield Syndicate, with Benning's honeysuckle-scented fingers around my throat. It wouldn't be all that bad to begin with. I'd have plenty of work—Benning would see to that. "Looking for a case? The Hatfields have got something for you. Just a little something to show my gratitude for helping me out with that Cindy Hatfield matter." Next, it would be: "Working on something, Southerland? Drop it. The Hatfields need you to do a thing for them. A little shady, but nothing that'll get you into trouble with the law. The family would be grateful." Gradually, the cases would drag me across lines I didn't want to cross. "Yes, I know it's not the kind of thing you would normally consider, but just this one time, Southerland—the Hatfields would greatly appreciate it." It would get worse: "Squeeze this palooka, Southerland. It's okay, he's a bad gee, and what he's got would not only hurt the family, but a lot of innocent people, besides." And: "Rough this mug up, Southerland. Turn his face into something his mother wouldn't recognize. Don't worry about it, he deserves it. He's as dirty as they come." And finally one day it would be: "Punch this scumbag's ticket, Southerland. He's got it coming. Believe me, no one's gonna miss him when he's gone." I thought about Breakspear and Tavish, two stand-up pros who had crossed the line and found out there was no coming back. I'd have plenty of dough, enough to frequent Yerba City's better clubs and drink myself to a stupor whenever I wanted to, which would be often, until I drank myself to death.

    I was in over my head, and I couldn't see an acceptable way out. I needed a different perspective on my situation. I needed a different kind of brain, one more devious than my own. Fortunately, I knew who to call.

    I punched in Lubank's number and outlined my dilemma in detail as I made my way around the block. Lubank listened patiently, asking questions only when he needed me to clarify a point or provide some further context. He made sympathetic noises in all the right places and encouraged me to elaborate in detail. I made it all the way around the block and was halfway through my second circuit when I'd explained my situation as thoroughly as I possibly could. "And that's it," I finished, my voice raw from the cold. "I've got to admit that I'm stumped. What do you think?"

    "What do I think?" Lubank responded. "What do I *think*? Lord's flaming pecker, Southerland—I think you're fucked! It's been a fun ride, son, but it's time to hop off the grill—you're cooked! Good luck, peeper. See you in the funny papers."

    He disconnected the call.

Chapter Twenty-Four

I wasn't worried about Lubank. I knew he'd handle the legal side of things for me. He wouldn't be able to resist the challenge, nor would he pass up the opportunity to push me farther into his debt. In the meantime, Benning wanted my report first thing Monday morning, which meant I had less than thirty-six hours to find out how Cindy Hatfield had died, and why.

Silverblade was leaning against my office door when I got back to my place, and he greeted me as I approached. "Good evening, Mr. Southerland. Ready to return to the scene of the crime?"

I pushed my hat up on my forehead to get a good look at the troll. "First of all, we're not positive that a crime has been committed. Second, what makes you think I'm going anywhere tonight?"

"Madame Cuapa told me you were returning to the warehouse tonight." He held out a plastic bag. "She said you'd be hungry, so she made you a chicken sandwich and a thermos of hot tea for the trip."

I stared at the bag without taking it. Accepting food or drink from the Madame had not always worked out well for me in the past.

A wide smile split Silverblade's clay-like face. "Take it. The Madame said to assure you it was harmless."

I took the bag from Silverblade's hand and carefully removed a sandwich wrapped in clear plastic cling wrap.

"It won't bite you," Silverblade told me, the smile still on his face.

"All right," I said, removing the wrap. "But I'm not drinking the tea until you've had a taste of it."

The troll's lips parted, exposing pointed teeth. "Ha! That's jake with me. I've got my own thermos in the car, but I'll be more than happy to take some of yours, too. I can't get enough of the Madame's tea."

"How did she know I'd be hungry?" I asked.

Silverblade looked down at me. "You know she trafficks with enormously powerful spirits, don't you? She's reaching a state where I think she's more spirit herself than human."

I shuddered despite myself. "Yet she still takes the time to make sandwiches?"

Silverblade's lips twisted into a half smile. "Well, I suspect she had Cody make the sandwich. But I'm sure she brewed the tea herself."

He turned toward his car, which was parked a few yards up the block. "Ready to go? Lionel's drinking some of the Madame's tea right now. You can wait to see whether he's turned into a toad before you try any."

Lionel drove us to Grayshore Point, and I'd finished the hot tea before we reached the ruined warehouse. It was delicious, and I was genuinely relieved when the brew neither plagued me with hallucinations nor sent me packing to Mictlan, the Aztlan land of the dead. *Not this time*, I thought to myself.

On the way, Silverblade asked me what I planned to do once we got to the warehouse. "You think you missed something when we were there before?"

"We won't be going into the warehouse," I said. "We'll be going under it."

Silverblade gave me a questioning look, and I continued. "The elf's operation was run out of a facility under the warehouse. They moved the operation just before the fire, and as far as I know it's been deserted ever since. There's probably nothing there, but I want to take a look."

When we reached the warehouse, I had Lionel drive us around the block to the entrance to the tunnel. The door to the shed was still unlocked, a good sign that no one had been there since I'd walked out of the tunnel the day before. Silverblade and Lionel, each holding a flashlight, followed me inside. We walked past the hidden entrance to the elf's abandoned home, and I gave no sign that I knew about it. Putting together sigils in my mind, I shifted my vision to the realm of winds, but saw no sign of the tracker elemental. The tunnel continued straight as a rod down an almost imperceptible slope for a little more than a hundred yards until it stopped at a concrete wall. The three of us stood and stared at it.

"Looks like a dead end," Lionel said, shining his light at the wall.

"Maybe," I agreed. But I was feeling the telltale vibrations of magical energy in my upper jaws just below my ears. I pressed the palms of my hands against the wall, looking for the source.

Silverblade was eyeing me curiously. "What are you doing?"

"I'm detecting residual magic. The door that opens from the lab into the warehouse was enchanted. It was invisible, and anyone entering had to pass an identification check by a magical scanner. I think the door on this end was equipped with a scanner, too, but it's not operational." I slid my hands carefully across the surface. "I think the scanner was located right… about… here." I tapped on the wall's surface. "That means the door should be here, too."

Lionel gawked through the dim light. "I don't see anything."

I knocked on the wall. "It's here. This part is wall...." A dull thud sounded as I knocked. "And this is the door." My knocking produced a different sound, louder and with more echo. "That's definitely metal."

"Okay," Lionel said, frowning. "But how do we open it?"

I looked up at Silverblade. "You want to do the honors?"

The troll shot me a glance and moved closer to the seemingly blank wall, rapping his knuckles on various parts of it. "That's metal, all right. Thick, too." Stepping back, he turned to me. "I sure hope this door isn't rigged to explode. Or worse."

I reached up and rubbed my chin. "I'm only picking up traces of energy, probably left over from when the scanner was operating. I think they shut it all down when they left. The door's still invisible, but that's passive magic. I'm not detecting anything active."

Silverblade hesitated. "I was unaware you could detect magical energy."

I allowed myself a brief grin. "I'm full of surprises."

The troll rubbed his hands together. "All right, here goes. You two might want to step back a little."

Lionel and I followed Silverblade's advice and gave him plenty of room. Silverblade took three troll-sized steps back and crouched. Lionel leaned against the wall of the tunnel and wrapped his arms around his head. I stood well behind Silverblade in the center of the tunnel. After taking a deep breath and holding it for a second, Silverblade let out a fierce roar and launched himself at the door, striking it with his shoulder. With a deafening screech, the door burst inward, and Silverblade fell into the room.

I braced myself for some kind of magical attack that, thankfully, never came. I hadn't expected one, but you never knew. After a few moments, Lionel lowered his arms and gaped at the hole in the metal wall. "Lord's balls," he muttered.

I walked through the door and found Silverblade sprawled on the floor.

"Fu-u-uck," the troll drawled. "That hurt."

"You okay?" I asked.

"Fuck if I know." He sat up and tested his shoulder. "Bruised, not broken," he proclaimed. "Just don't expect me to do that again for a week or two. I'm not as young as I used to be."

I took a long look at the doorway. The doorknob latch had pushed its way clean through the door jamb under the impact of Silverblade's charge, and the door's frame was bent and twisted. The mounting plate for the deadbolt was lying in pieces on the floor. The door itself was hanging crooked, its upper hinge torn and loose. It appeared that the doorway had been blown open by a cannonball. The monitor screen on the wall next to the door was blank.

I looked down at Silverblade. "Right. Let's have a look around."

Silverblade rose to his feet. "What are we looking for?"

"Anything that doesn't look right."

"That's awfully vague."

I glanced around the room we'd forced our way into and saw nothing to indicate what it might have been used for. A number of brown stains on the carpet suggested spilled coffee. An employees' lounge, perhaps? I turned to Silverblade and Lionel. "Start by looking for anything that was left behind after the move."

We searched the facility from back to front. Stairs in the front of the underground lab led up to a door, and the floor and walls on the landing at the top of the stairs showed fire damage. A large viewing screen on the wall was blank, but I assumed it would reveal the warehouse above the lab outside the door when it was operating. I climbed the stairs to the door and felt the vibrations of magic that kept the door hidden from the outside. In the course of our search, we found a surprising number of odds and ends lying about the various offices and lab space, confirming that the move had been hurried and ill-planned. None of the objects, however, proved to be of much interest: paperclips, a few pens, some empty soda bottles and candy wrappers, a wrinkled blue tie, an empty wastepaper basket…. I told the others to place anything they found in the basket, and we'd soon filled it.

After a half hour of searching, I turned the wastepaper basket over and spilled the objects to the floor. As I was sorting through it, something caught my attention. Looking up at the others, I asked, "Who found this?"

"The old pocket protector?" Lionel asked. "I did. It was in one of the offices."

"Show me." Silverblade and I followed Lionel to an abandoned office near the front of the facility.

Lionel stepped to a small closet and opened the door. "It was on the floor next to the tie I found."

I gave the room a good going over, stopping at a wall outlet. "This must have been Papadopouli's office. He was in charge of data processing, and I've seen fancy outlets like these in Walks in Cloud's shop. Did you find anything else in here, Lionel?"

"Just the tie and that thing."

I studied the pocket protector. The initials 'PP' were embossed in small print on the front of the protector. The inside of the plastic pouch was covered with ink stains of various colors. The bottom of the pouch had torn in one spot, and it appeared that blue ink had spilled through the hole. Papadopouli, or whoever had used the protector, had most likely bought a new one to replace it.

I reached into my coat pocket and pulled out a melted strip of white plastic. Setting the strip next to the pocket protector, I turned to the others.

"What do you think?" I asked.

Silverblade bent to study the two objects. He pointed at the melted strip. "Those marks are stretched, but it could be a double-P monogram. It looks like a match for the letters on this pocket protector. Where did you find that?"

"In the debris that had been moved off Cindy's body."

Lionel looked up from the plastic strip. "Did the chick wear one of those?"

"No. But her boyfriend, Petros Papadopouli did." I remembered Kintay telling me how the computer nerd always carried a dozen or so pens with him in a monogrammed pocket protector.

Silverblade stared down at me. "You think Papadopouli was there the night of the fire?"

"I do. I think he died in it, same as Cindy."

Silverblade considered it. "If that's true, then whoever cleared away Cindy's body must have cleared the other one away, too."

"Uh-huh," I agreed. "Which means someone knows that Papadopouli is dead."

Silverblade scratched the bottom of his pointed ear. "You think Papadopouli could have been the target? He probably filmed that birth. Maybe someone wanted to make sure he didn't tell anybody about it."

"He told Cindy," I said. "I'm sure of it. Elves, and elves, and elves."

"And now they're both dead," Silverblade said. "And they both died in the same place."

I nodded. "Looks that way. Unless...." I toyed with a thought. "Unless it was only Papadopouli who died in the fire."

"Huh?" Silverblade gave me a hard look. "What are you saying?"

"We're assuming that Cindy died in that fire, and that someone cleared the rubble off her body and took it away. But what if it didn't happen that way? Maybe it was just Papadopouli who died that night?"

Silverblade didn't buy it. "You saw Cindy's ghost. You said she was burning."

"She could have burned to death somewhere else."

"She was alive the morning of that warehouse fire. I talked to her on the phone. The idea that she burned to death somewhere else on the same day that warehouse caught fire…. It's quite a leap."

I had to agree. "Right. Just a thought."

"Someone took them both out at the same time."

I scratched the stubble on my jaw. "With a bomb?"

Silverblade shrugged. "Someone wanted to make sure. And they wanted to burn the place down to cover up the evidence."

"Hmm. Maybe."

"You don't sound convinced."

"I keep trying to put the pieces together, but I can't quite make them fit." I looked up at the troll. "Is that how you would do it?"

Silverblade chuckled. "I wouldn't know. I've never had to kill anybody before."

I thought about that. "Maybe whoever built that bomb had never killed anyone, either."

Lionel, who had been standing near the door, jerked his head in our direction. "Someone's coming," he stage-whispered.

"Shh!" I hissed. I extended my awareness, listening with more than my ears and feeling the changes in the wind currents. After a few moments, I smiled and stepped to the door. "Chet Sugarman? Is that you? Come on back, it's all right."

I turned to the gaping Lionel and the frowning Silverblade. "Either of you ever been on the evening news?"

***

"Hi, Southerland. Who are your friends?"

Silverblade looked from the newsman to me and raised one arm in a half-shrug.

"What are you doing here, Sugarman?" I asked.

"Just curious." He held up a paper bag. "Anyone want doughnuts?"

I started to say something, but Lionel was quicker to the punch. "You got chocolate?" he asked.

Sugarman opened the bag. "I got a couple of chocolate frosted. Will that do?"

Lionel held out a hand. "Perfect!"

What the hell. "Yeah, okay, I'll take a chocolate frosted if you've got another one in there."

"I've got one more. I've also got maple and vanilla coconut."

The glow in Silverblade's eyes intensified. "Vanilla coconut?"

The newsman looked up at the troll. "I've got two. You can have them both."

I frowned. "No coffee?"

Sugarman pointed back over his shoulder. "Got some back at the station."

I glanced around the room. "Fine. I guess we're done here anyway."

On the way back through the tunnel, Sugarman turned to me. "What's the story here?"

"No story. The three of us were just poking around."

"They your associates?"

I glanced at Silverblade. "Let's just say yes."

"Uh-huh." Sugarman gave the wastepaper basket I was lugging a meaningful glance. "Looks like you found something."

"Just some trash," I said, swallowing the last of my doughnut.

"Anything interesting?"

"No."

Sugarman chuckled. "Sure. You're an investigator picking up trash, and none of it is interesting."

"Not interesting enough for a news story."

When we emerged from the tunnel into a cloud-covered night, I handed the wastepaper basket to Lionel. "Put this in the car," I told him. "And make sure it's locked."

Inside the radio station, Sugarman asked, "What was that place?"

I set my coffee cup down on the desktop. "The Hatfields were running some kind of operation down there. Don't know what, but it's connected to an investigation I'm conducting. I was hoping to find something there. It was a longshot, but I'm paid to be thorough."

Sugarman peered at me over his coffee. "You don't know what they were doing in there? Hmm. I might be able to help you out there."

Silverblade and I glanced at each other. I turned back to Sugarman. "You know something?"

Sugarman smiled. "I know they're manufacturing drugs down there. Something special."

"That right?"

"Yep. A guy who worked there gave me a few samples. It was dynamite stuff, let me tell you!"

I groaned inwardly, but kept my face expressionless. "This guy. He got a name?"

Sugarman chuckled. "I'm sure he does, but he never shared it with me."

"Skinny blond joker? Pale skin, like he's never seen the sun? Light blue eyes?"

"Those eyes were more red than blue whenever I saw him, but, yeah, that's the guy all right."

I picked up my coffee cup. "He ever tell you about his work?"

Sugarman shook his head. "Not much. We smoked a little weed together from time to time, and one day he comes by with these white capsules. He says it was something he was developing and that it would make me feel like I've got laser vision, super strength, and knowledge about the secrets of the universe. He wasn't wrong!" He laughed. "We tripped on the stuff a few times, and each time it was better than the last. I never seemed to remember anything about those secrets once I came down, though. If I ever pop one of those caps again, I'll be sure to set my phone to record."

Lionel had been watching the studio announcer behind the window drone on about something inconsequential. He turned to Sugarman. "You wouldn't happen to have any more of that shit, would you?"

Silverman glared at his wheelman, who shrugged.

Sugarman chuckled. "No, man. Sorry. That crazy jasper hasn't been around since the fire. I miss him, and not just because he always had something for me. He used to talk about the Hatfields, especially Fats. I guess the two of them were tight. That's the way he made it sound, at least, but maybe he was bragging. You know, trying to make himself sound cool by association with a bigtime mobster. He used to talk about Benning, too. You know, the fixer? I guess he didn't like him much. He liked Fats better." Sugarman snapped his fingers. "I just remembered something he said about Benning. He said it was too bad that he was working for Benning now instead of Fats. He said Benning didn't appreciate his talents the way Fats did, but Fats didn't have much to do with whatever was going on in his current operation. Benning oversaw all that. Well, Benning and the space alien."

I perked up at that. "The what?"

Sugarman laughed. "The two of us were a little high, and he started going on about aliens from outer space. I'd seen the mug in the hood. This was before I started thinking he was Al the Torch. Anyway, I mentioned him, and he said the mug was an alien from outer space. I didn't take him seriously, but he went on about it for a long time. He said this alien had the power to cloud minds." He laughed again. "I told him his mind was clouded enough from all the weed we'd been smoking, but he was convinced this other guy was not from this earth."

I was thinking I needed to have another talk with Kintay. "Did this guy ever mention a man named Papadopouli?"

Sugarman shook his head. "Nah. He was pretty cagey when it came to names, except for Fats and Benning. And Cold Fish. That's what he called the gnome woman who managed the project. He said that this Cold Fish and Benning were pretty tight, and that while she might be the on-site manager, he said it was Benning who called the shots. But it was all done for the space alien, he said, although what space aliens want with primo hallucinogens is anybody's guess. Maybe they eat them for breakfast." He pulled a hand-rolled joint from his pocket. "Anyone want to get wasted?"

"Thanks, but I'll pass," I said.

"I'll pass, too," Silverblade said. Pointing at Lionel, he added, "And so will he."

Chapter Twenty-Five

Cindy was waiting for me when I got back to my office, and she wasn't the only one. Chivo was with her, and Siphon hovered nearby, drifting lazily between the floor and the ceiling like a half-deflated helium balloon. The air in the room was frosty.

"Baaaalek," Chivo bleated, catching me with eyes that glowed red, like a troll's. I readied myself for a bout of nausea but experienced only a light wave. Chivo blinked and looked away before it could get worse. He turned toward Siphon, and, after a few moments, the elemental began translating Chivo's thoughts: "I am learning to control the effects of my eyes on other living things. Soon, others will be able to look upon me face to face and suffer no ill effects. That is if I desire it to be so. I am also learning to intensify those effects. One day, I may be able to drain the life from another through their eyes by concentrating my gaze upon them. The process will be painless and humane."

"That's considerate of you," I said, trying and failing to suppress a shudder. Mist flowed from my mouth as I spoke. "Where have you been?"

I waited for Siphon to receive and translate Chivo's response. "I have been places where few can go. I returned and found this one mired in this place, stuck on her journey to Xibalba." Chivo indicated Cindy's transparent form as Siphon spoke. She looked more ghostly than ever, floating a foot above the floor in an upright position, but with her eyes shut, her face blank, and her arms hanging loosely at her sides, as if she were sleeping. After a few more moments, Siphon continued: "She told me you were holding her here while you sought to discover the cause of her death."

"That's not true," I said, my eyes on Cindy's spectral form. "She came to me. She wants me to find out how she died and who was responsible."

Siphon spoke Chivo's thoughts: "I see. She asked this of you?"

I hesitated. "Not in so many words. She speaks as if she's dreaming. But I believe that's what she wants. She even told me to speak to a mutual acquaintance who she thought would be able to shed some light on it."

"Aaaave yoouu?" Chivo bleated.

"I've met with him. So far, he hasn't been as much help as I hoped he'd be, although he seems to be trying." I indicated the floating specter. "Cindy said he knew everything, but I think she's mistaken. Either that, or he's not aware of what he knows."

I looked at Cindy. Chivo saw me studying her and turned to Siphon, who spoke: "If you are not holding her here, then I believe it is her desire to know why she died that ties her to this place. She is counting on you to untie this knot so that she may be released to continue her journey. Would you like me to awaken her so you can question her further?"

I shuddered and stuffed my hands in my coat pockets to warm them. "I don't know. Our conversations tend to end with her trying to drag me to the land of the dead."

Chivo's snout twisted as he let out hissing bleats of laughter. "Aaaiii... caaaan... preeevennnt... daaaat."

I allowed myself a tight smile. "All right. Wake her up."

Chivo turned his gaze on Cindy. After a few seconds, her eyes popped open and darted this way and that before settling on me. "Alex," she breathed, her voice sounding far away.

"Hello, Cindy," I began. "I've been investigating your death."

The specter's eyes widened. "Claudius...."

"Yes, I've spoken with him. He doesn't know how you died."

Cindy's form grew less transparent. "Puppy. Ask Claudius."

"Puppy? That's Papadopouli, right?"

A smile lit up Cindy's dead face. "Puppy. He came for me." Cindy seemed more present and more coherent than she had during her other manifestations, and I figured that must be Chivo's doing.

"Cindy? Did... Puppy... die in the same fire that took your life?"

Cindy's face hardened, and the already frigid room grew colder. "Puppy... burning.... He came for me."

"In the warehouse?" I asked.

A faraway look came into Cindy's eyes. "Crates and crates. They moved the crates."

"When, Cindy? When did they move the crates."

"Crates and crates. They moved them all."

"Was this the day of the fire?"

Cindy met my eyes. "They took me away."

"Who did? Cindy, who took you away?"

"Trolls. They took me through the wall. Then Puppy came. He came for me." Her eyes widened. "Puppy? What are you doing? I'm in here! What are you doing? Come and get me!"

"Where are you, Cindy? What is Puppy doing?"

Cindy gazed over my head in silence, watching something only she could see. Suddenly, she raised her hands to her face and let out a screech that curdled my blood.

"What is it, Cindy? What happened?"

"Fire!" She screamed. "Puppy! Look out! Fire! No, no, no, no, no! Don't burn! I'm coming, Puppy! Stay away from me! I'm coming! I'm coming!"

The temperature plummeted. Sleet formed in the air and fell to the floor.

"Cindy!" I shouted, but it was no use. Cindy screeched, and I had to clap my hands over my ears. Siphon shot across the room and darted from wall to wall like a trapped bird. The spikes on Chivo's back shot upright and stood rigid down his spine. His skinless, rat-like tail curled around his back legs. The screams went on and on, and I fought the temptation to run from the room. When I didn't think I could stand it any longer, Cindy's screams faded into the distance. She grew more and more transparent until she faded from view.

Tiny balls of ice covered the floor, but the room began to warm as soon as the specter disappeared. When the echoes of the specter's screams faded from my head, I turned to Chivo. The spikes along his spine relaxed and lay down on his back. He turned to Siphon, who had settled near his shoulder, and, after another moment or two, Siphon's voice sounded: "I apologize. The specter's agitation grew too strong, and she escaped my influence. I was forced to banish her. I can call her back if you wish to try again."

I studied the melting sleet on my floor. "Maybe another time."

Chivo turned to me. "Guuuuuud."

I crossed the room and sat behind my desk. Siphon's voice reached me as I searched through a drawer for a bottle of whiskey that wasn't there: "Did you learn anything?"

I shut the drawer and let out a slow breath. "I think so."

Chivo's lips twisted as he tried to speak. "Yuuu... aaaave sawwwved..."

I looked across my desk at him. "I've solved the case? Not entirely. I think I know how she died, but I don't know who set off that bomb. Coleridge? Maybe. But why? To kill Papadopouli?" I shook my head. "I don't see it. Using a bomb to kill one poor lovesick dope makes no sense. Not when you've got two trolls at hand who could snap his neck with a backhand slap. No, I'm missing something."

I leaned back and stared into the ceiling.

"Yohhh naaak."

A smile broke out on my face, and I sat up in my chair. "You hungry, Chivo? You need some yonak?"

Chivo lowered himself to all fours. "Huhhhn... greee."

"I've got some in the fridge. I've been saving it for you. Hope you don't mind it cold. I had it out, but the smell was getting to me." I got out of my chair and walked upstairs.

∗∗∗

I stood at the end of the pier and watched the turbulent sea send waves rolling through the pilings to crash against the shore. When I heard his voice, I didn't have to turn to know who was standing behind me.

"You have not closed the heritage stone's gateway to me. I conclude that you welcome my visit."

"I still don't know how to shut you out. As it happens, I wanted to speak with you again anyway, so it's copacetic."

"You are still investigating the circumstances surrounding the death of Mrs. Cindy Hatfield?"

"I am. I received another visit from her, and I think I'm closer to finding out how she died. And why."

"I have come to ask you to cease your investigation."

The waves continued to roll beneath the pier, and I could feel them shaking the pilings. It all seemed real as can be, yet I knew I was sleeping in my bed, and that all this—the waves, the pier, my conversation with the elf—was taking place somewhere inside my head, and that the elf was providing the virtual reality show.

I turned to regard the elf. "Why do you want me to stop investigating Cindy's death?"

"I have met with Bowman, Ferrell, and Anton. It was a productive meeting, one in which I learned a great many things. My project is proceeding at a most satisfactory pace, and I am quite pleased with its progress. But it is a delicate operation that depends greatly on timing and secrecy. The Dragon Lord knows that a conspiracy has been launched against him. He knows that a major part of it is centered in

Yerba City, and he has sent his agents here to discover more about it. It is my judgment that your investigation into matters so close to the project could be disruptive to the timing of my operation. Therefore, I am asking you to cease your activities for the time being. It is for the greater good."

My heart was racing, and I focused on keeping my breathing steady until it slowed. I met the elf's eyes and held them for a few moments before speaking. "What about Cindy? Don't you think she deserves a little justice?"

The elf lowered his eyes and sighed. "We all deserve justice. The reality is that sometimes justice must be delayed, or forgotten, in order to serve the greater good."

I snorted. "I hope you aren't trying to tell me that the needs of the many take precedence over the needs of the few, or of one person. Don't you think that's a little trite?"

The elf tapped his chin with an index finger. "Putting the desires of one before the wellbeing of the community at large strikes me as a rather selfish attitude."

"Isn't that what you're doing? Putting your own desires ahead of the needs of others?"

"Not at all, my dear fellow. I would love nothing more than to find a quiet place in this world to pursue leisure activities. I once took a great deal of pleasure in tending a garden and studying the green things that grow from this earth. I have elected to sacrifice these desires in order to pursue a larger matter: wresting control of this world from the dragon usurpers and handing it back to the elves. It is for the benefit of all of the creatures native to the earth that I do so."

"Is that right? Well, tell it to Cindy's trapped spirit. She can't finish her journey unless someone tells her why she had to die. And if I don't do it, who will?"

The elf let out a breath. "I am not unsympathetic. It is my wish that everyone could live and die in peace and happiness. But such dreams are out of keeping with the universe we live in. All I can tell you is that justice can take time, more time in many cases than you short-lived humans consider appropriate. And sometimes justice comes not at all. That is the way of things. It is my nature to view such matters on a larger scale than you perhaps do."

"And it's my nature to help people who ask me for it if I'm able, and if I feel like they deserve it."

The elf arched an eyebrow. "And you feel Mrs. Hatfield deserves it?"

"Why ask me? What do I know? I'm just a working-class private snoop, and it's not up to me to make those kinds of calls. But stop calling her Mrs. Hatfield. Someone who knows told me that these things we call ghosts consist largely of our memory of the living person. Well, I never met Mrs. Hatfield, but I knew a Mrs. Cindy Shipper. I didn't know her well, or for long, but that doesn't matter. It was Cindy Shipper who came to me looking for help, or maybe just some kind of combination of her distorted memories of me and mine of hers. You might say it's not Cindy Shipper at all, but just a phantom image of who she was. A specter. But whatever she might be now, a part of her is the Cindy Shipper I remember. She came to me, and I'm going to help her. Maybe in the end we *all* get the justice that's coming to us no matter what we do. But you're asking me if I think Cindy Shipper deserves justice, and I say she does. Don't ask me to explain it to you any further. I say she deserves justice, and that's the end of it."

The elf's lips curled into a tight smile. "I see. Or, rather, I see that you are determined to follow that path. Very well. But I will not aid you. Nor will Cougar, your spirit guide. Itzamna has spoken to him and forbidden it. The spirits native to this region of the earth are in alignment with my goals. They all wish to see the Dragon Lords driven from this world. Pursue your investigation if you must, but know that the justice you seek may not be forthcoming."

I turned back to look at the waves. "If I can see Cindy off on the rest of her journey, I'll be satisfied with that."

The elf's voice came from behind me. "Anton Benning has given you an account of Cindy's death that, while not accurate, will move my project along in a timely manner. It would behoove—not just you—but the collective community you are a part of to accept it as truth."

"And will it help Cindy?" I asked. "The way I see it, this 'greatest good for the greatest number' crap is all fine and dandy until it affects someone you care about. Maybe I'm not seeing the bigger picture, and maybe I don't want to. Maybe I'm just a big dope, and the universe is playing me for a sucker. All I know is that Cindy needs me, and I wouldn't be able to look at myself in the mirror if I turned my back on her. Can you understand that?"

But the elf was gone, and the sea was already vanishing from my sight. Darkness descended over me.

***

A voice reached me in the darkness. "Sleep easy, my son. When you need me, I will be with you." For the briefest of moments, the scent of wild cat filled the air before it faded into the night.

Chapter Twenty-Six

It wasn't that I wanted to stand in the way of the elf's plans to rid the world of the Dragon Lords. Their treatment of the adaros and their interminable war in the Borderland were two good reasons to want them gone. But I wasn't going to stop trying to help Cindy simply because the elf had made a deal with the Hatfields. While it was true that I owed a debt to the elf, I didn't work for him, and I didn't need his permission to do my job as I saw fit. Bowman Hatfield had hired me to uncover the truth about Cindy's death, and I was going to complete that task whether he, his sons, or his associates—the elf included—liked the results or not. If anyone had asked me, I would have said it was the professional thing to do. But I wasn't kidding myself. This case was personal, and it became more personal every time someone told me to back off.

I knew who I needed to talk to next, but I didn't know how I was going to make it happen, especially without the cooperation of the Hatfields. Cindy had said that she'd been grabbed from the warehouse by trolls and taken "through the wall." My best guess was that Coleridge had been in the recently abandoned lab, probably making sure nobody had left anything important behind. She'd spotted Cindy on the viewing screen next to the door to the inside of the warehouse and sent her two security trolls to bring her into the lab. I wanted a conversation with Coleridge. Or, if not with her, then with Quarrelmace or Blazearrow. Those three knew what had happened to Cindy. Maybe they'd made it happen.

The trick was getting any of them to talk to me. Actually, the first trick would be to find them. I didn't know where any of them lived, and an internet search came up empty. I thought about enlisting help from Detective Kalama, but it was Sunday morning, and in twenty-four hours Benning was going to have me arrested for breaking and entering the offices of the Hatfield-owned Peninsula Property Management Company. I didn't have the time or, as far as Kalama would be concerned, sufficient reasons to ask the police to do my investigative work for me. Besides, I couldn't be sure that Coleridge, Quarrelmace, or Blazearrow would be home. They all struck me as workaholics.

I didn't know where they lived, but I knew where they worked. Even if they had Sunday off, I figured they'd respond to a security breach at their office. A break-in, for example. Why not? I was already on the hook for one. Might as well go for broke.

As plans went, well, it wasn't so much a plan as an induced clusterfuck. That was jake with me. Like I'd told Lubank, plans are for suckers.

I grabbed my hat and debated whether to bring my gun. Concluding that I wasn't likely to come out ahead in a shootout with Quarrelmace and Blazearrow, I decided to leave it behind. I put on my hat and headed for the door.

Silverblade's car was parked outside my office, and the back passenger door opened as soon as I stepped outside. With a muttered, "Lord's balls," I walked to the car and climbed in.

I looked up at Silverblade. "Been waiting long?"

The troll smiled. "Just got here. I didn't figure you'd be taking the day off. So, where are we off to?"

We? Well, why not. I settled back into the seat. "I need to talk to Coleridge or one of her security goons. I thought I'd go to their office and see if they were in."

Silverblade stared at me. "You're just going to knock on their door?"

I grinned at him. "Sure. And if that doesn't work, I'll kick the door in and wait for them to show up."

Lionel turned his head to stare at me, too. I was drawing quite a crowd.

Silverblade snorted. "You were going to take them on by yourself?"

"I was until *you* showed up. Now I guess we'll go see them together. But I wasn't going to 'take them on.' I just want to talk to them."

"Without an appointment?"

"I didn't have time to make one."

A smile snuck its way onto the troll's face. "You heard the man, Lionel. Let's get going."

I told Lionel how to get to the Milltown office and filled Silverblade in on my visit with Cindy's ghost. "You think Coleridge and her security team saw what happened to Cindy?" Silverblade asked when I was done.

"I'm sure of it. What I don't know is how directly involved they were."

"You think Coleridge was responsible for the bomb?"

"I don't know," I admitted. "It's possible, but my gut says no. Of course, my gut's been wrong before. It doesn't make sense, though. Who was her target? Papadopouli?" I shook my head. "I don't buy it."

Silverblade frowned. "Something's been bothering me. They closed that lab site down before the fire. Why? Maybe the whole purpose of the bomb was to burn down the warehouse. And maybe that's why Coleridge was there, to set the bomb off. Maybe Cindy—and Papadopouli, too—were simply in the wrong place at the wrong time."

I thought about that. "Maybe. But it still doesn't add up. There are simpler ways of burning down an old warehouse than setting off an IED. And why burn down the building in the first place?"

"An insurance scam? Sounds like something the Hatfields would do."

I shook my head. "According to the police, the Hatfields never even put in a claim. No one did."

Silverblade let out a breath. "We're definitely missing something."

I stared at Silverblade. "Cindy's ghost insists that you know something. Last night she asked me to ask you about Puppy—Papadopouli. What do you know about him?"

The troll leaned back in thought. "He's an engineer, a computer tech. Not Cindy's usual type. She's always been attracted to power and money. Execs, bankers. Mobsters. Techies? That's not Cindy's style."

"Maybe he had something else going for him. I've heard he was a genius. Maybe she thought he had potential. Maybe she thought she could guide him."

Silverblade snorted. "Now *that* sounds like her. She had a lot of power over men. I found that very useful when she was...." He turned to me as if he'd forgotten I was in the car with him.

"When you were pimping her out to rich bastards?" I offered.

"When we were more closely acquainted."

I shot him a sidelong glance. "Sure."

Silverblade continued as if I hadn't interrupted his train of thought. "I think she was using her 'Puppy' to get inside the lab, to find out what the project was really all about."

"Why?"

The troll pulled at the lobe of his pointed ear. "She was bored? She was curious? She'd married into the most powerful crime family in the city, and she wanted to know more about their inner workings. Alu wasn't a big part of the syndicate. Fats hardly ever talked to her. Bowman treated her like an ornament for Alu. All he was concerned about was whether she was making his son happy. I think he wanted her to cure Alu's impotence. To make a man out of him."

Something tugged at me. "The elf's project. It's all about fertility." I looked across the car at Silverblade. "You say Alu didn't play a big role in the Hatfield operations. Did he know anything at all about this secret project?"

Silverblade shrugged. "I couldn't say. But he was around people who did."

"The elf told me that before the birth we saw on that video it had been five thousand years since an elf had been born into this world. What if Alu was familiar enough with the project to know it had something to do with restoring fertility? Maybe he said something to Cindy, something that got her thinking. It's possible she got the impression that the Hatfields were working on something that might cure Alu's impotence."

Silverblade's upper lip curled, as if he were smelling something a bit off. "I don't know. Sounds like you're reaching."

"Think about it," I insisted. "Her father-in-law is hoping she'll have an impact on his son's inability to 'be a man.' He says something garbled about a project that might cure infertility... she puts two and two together... and gets five because she wants it to be more than it is. She's bored. That fits her. Her new family is involved with something big, but she's excluded. She wouldn't like that. She's curious about this project she's heard a bit about from her husband and maybe her father-in-law, and she wants to explore a possibility that will make her more important to the family's inner circle." I locked eyes with Silverblade. "This is a woman who almost certainly arranged to have her former husband and her stepson murdered. She's not the kind of woman who sits around and waits for things to happen."

Silverblade, who had been slouching, sat up so suddenly that he bumped his head against the roof of the car. "Cindy told me once that this new man in her life might help her gain status with the Old Man. I had no idea what she meant by that at the time." He took off his hat and rubbed the top of his head.

I looked up at him. "Did she say anything else about it?"

Silverblade's eyes narrowed as he tried to dredge up the memory. "She'd been talking to me, and she probably thought I was paying more attention than I was. It was like that with her sometimes. She'd chat, and I'd have my mind on other things. I confess that I liked the sound of her voice, but I didn't always listen to what she was saying."

"When was it? What were the circumstances? Was she on the phone? Was she with you in person? Where was it?"

The troll waved me off with a scowl. "Shut up and let me think."

I waited. After a few seconds, his eyes widened. "We were having lunch at the Huntinghouse." He gave me a sidelong glance. "My old stomping grounds, as you recall. She was excited. She'd mentioned Alu's inability to satisfy her sexually, and the license he gave her to... well... to pursue other avenues. She laughed at the idea that Bowman thought she could cure her husband of his 'affliction.' That's the word Bowman used. She said this new man—an engineer working on a special project—could.... Let me think.... That he might hold the key to 'making her husband whole.' But she would have to use him... somehow. She was going to take advantage of him, she said. I don't think she really cared for him much. I got the feeling she was willing to endure being with him in order to help her husband."

I waited some more. Finally, Silverblade turned to me. "He was going to be her ticket to get inside the lab. This was a while back, and I don't remember exactly what she said, but it was something to that effect. Maybe he'd shown her the video? She might have said something about that, but I don't remember. But.... But I think she said that he was going to show her something else. A surprise. But not anything to do with helping her husband. Something more... what was it... more 'sinister'! Yes, that's the word she used. He was going to show her something sinister about what the Hatfields were doing. Something at the lab?" He thought for a second, trying to remember. "Hmm. Yes, Papadopouli was going to take her into the secret lab when no one was around to show her something. But I don't remember her mentioning anything specific." He gave his head a quick shake. "She certainly never said anything about elves, I can tell you that. I assumed it had something to do with drugs, or marketing drugs. I'd heard that Fats and Benning were giving away some new designer drug at those antiwar protests. That's why I shrugged off what Cindy had been trying to tell me. I figured she was close to finding out something I already knew and didn't care much about."

I stared at the troll. "And you're just now remembering all this?"

His lips flattened. "Like I said, it was a while back, and I had other things on my mind at the time. I was involved in a complicated legal matter involving financial manipulation at Greater Olmec. A lot of money was changing hands, and not all of it was strictly on the up and up. It was my job to make sure we wouldn't get our fingers singed. Cindy was quite exuberant that day, and she no doubt told me a lot more than

I remember. You're lucky I can recall as much as I do. I'm not sure how accurately I remember any of it. But that's the gist."

I sat back and watched the traffic through the front window. "All right, that's helpful. It explains why Cindy wanted me to talk to you. Let me know if anything else comes to you."

Silverblade pulled at his ear again. It was an annoying habit. "I wish I knew more. I don't see how this helps us explain why Cindy died, though."

"Coleridge and her goons should be able to tell us. All we have to do is make them talk."

A wry smile crossed Silverblade's lips. "What are you going to do—beat it out of them?"

I shot him a quick glance and a wry smile of my own. "Nah. I thought I would try asking them nicely."

"After you kick down their door?"

"I'll leave that part to you."

***

"We've got a problem," I said, indicating the panel on the elevator wall. "We can't get up to the twelfth floor without passing a facial scan."

Silverblade smiled. "You forget. I've worked security in buildings like this. Lionel?"

Lionel opened the briefcase he was carrying and handed Silverblade a troll-sized electronic tablet with a stylus.

Silverblade turned to me. "Do you have any pictures or video of anyone who works at this lab?"

I shook my head. "No. But you could probably find a photo of Fats Hatfield online. He never met a camera he didn't love."

It didn't take long for Silverblade to pull up a close-up shot of a smiling Fats shaking hands with Mayor Harvey. He held up his tablet screen for me to see. "This will work. Give me a second to make some magic."

The 'magic' Silverblade made wasn't supernatural, but it was impressive. He used editing software to isolate and zoom in on Fats's fat mug, brighten his eyes, darken his eyebrows and lips, and sharpen his jaws and cheekbones. The whole process took less than a minute. When the photo was altered to his satisfaction, Silverblade held his tablet screen a few inches away from the scanner and moved it back slowly until the scanner beeped. The elevator shot upwards.

The troll snorted. "Lord's balls. I hate to think how much this piece of shit system cost the Hatfields. They didn't even spring for magical protections against basic hacking."

We exited the elevator into the reception lounge. Silverblade noted the unoccupied desk on the far side of the room. "No one working on Sunday," he noted.

I extended my chin toward the door past the desk. "There's at least one person on the other side of that door. According to Kintay, they've got security guards here around the clock."

Silverblade glared down at me. "You couldn't have mentioned this earlier?"

"It just now occurred to me."

Silverblade glared at me for another moment. Finally, he sighed and nodded at Lionel, who moved to the door. After trying the handle, he looked back over his shoulder at us. "It's locked."

Silverblade looked at me with an eager gleam in his troll eyes, but I held up a hand. "Let me try knocking."

I wasn't surprised when my knock was answered, nor by the man who opened the door.

"Sergeant?" Kintay's eyes shot from me to Silverblade and Lionel before jerking back to gaze at me. His pupils were tiny dots in the middle of his pale blue irises. "What are you doing here?"

"I wanted to make sure no one had tossed you through a window." I sniffed the air. "Working overtime?"

Kintay raised a hand and wiped beads of sweat off his neck. "Right, right, right. You know me. I can't sit still." He studied the moisture on his fingertips and giggled.

"I *do* know you, corporal. Let me guess. You're baking up some of your special capsules. And sampling a few for yourself."

A smile practically ripped Kintay's face in two. "I might have sampled a couple earlier this morning. Crazy, right? Fats needs more freebies for the antiwar crowds, and follow-up paying orders are coming through like you wouldn't believe. That shit is hot, and demand is increasing. My little capsules are going to fuckin' kick this city in the ass!"

I eased my way past Kintay, and he stepped aside, but not without a show of protest. "Hey, man," he said, waving his arms frantically in my face. "You can't come in here. Hey! Who are these mugs? Lord's balls, sergeant—you're going to get me in big trouble here!" He stopped suddenly, the grin returning to his face. "Oh, what the fuck. Come on in, man. Caps for everyone! Let's get this party started!"

I looked around the lab to confirm that no one else was there. "Anyone working in the back?" I asked.

Kintay shook his head. "No, man. It's just me." Sweat dripped from his forehead into his eyes, and he wiped it away with the back of his hand.

I fixed him with my sternest stare. "Where are the security guards?"

Kintay reached up and scratched the side of his face. "Fats doesn't like a lot of prying eyes in the office when I'm doing my special work for him. He doesn't trust the security team. They all report to Coleridge."

"He pulled them?"

"They probably aren't far. Maybe down a floor or two. But they aren't up here."

With a glance at Silverblade, I jerked my chin toward the hallway leading out of the lab, and he and Lionel stepped off to see if Kintay was telling the truth.

"I need to talk to Coleridge," I told Kintay when we were alone. "Any chance you can call her?"

Kintay's eyes widened. "I don't want her to see what I'm doing here, sergeant. I mean, she knows she can't stop Fats from using me to do a little side work for him, but she doesn't like it much. She's real fussy about what goes on in her lab. And I'm just, you know, kind of stuck in the middle of those two, you know what I mean? I mean, you're kinda putting me in a bit of a jam here."

I shrugged. "That's the problem with too many chains of authority, right?"

Kintay giggled. "Reminds me of the army. Captain Cold Fish and Colonel Fats, both with their own plans for us grunts."

"Sure does, corporal. But I still need to see Coleridge."

Silverblade returned with Lionel in tow. The troll shook his head. "Nobody home."

"They'll be here soon enough." I looked at Kintay. "How long does it take Coleridge and her goons to get here if they're in a hurry?"

Kintay's shoulder jerked. "How would I know? It's not like Cold Fish has ever had me over for fuckin' dinner." He frowned and rubbed sweat from his forehead. "Shit. The cap's wearing off. I'm starting to get a little worried about all this. I should have taken a bigger dose. What time is it? I need to make a note." He looked up at me, his eyes suddenly tired. "Fuck, sergeant—why did you say you were here again? And where's my fuckin' notebook! I've gotta figure out a way to make this latest batch of caps less crashy. Gotta add some time-released mellow."

"You don't know where she lives?" I asked.

"Who, Cold Fish?" Kintay grimaced. "No clue. Hey, man. Do me a solid, okay? I don't want her to see me... you know...." He flailed his arms about searching for the right word.

"Hyped to the gills?" I suggested.

Kintay pointed at my chest. "Exactly!" His face contorted into a pained expression. "Well, half to the gills, now. I could sure use a beer."

I waved him away. "Go ahead. Scram. I don't need you here."

"Let me clean up a little first. I don't want to leave my shit laying around. Coleridge will have a hissy fit."

Lionel, who was standing by the door to the reception lounge, shouted back over his shoulder at us. "Too late. Elevator's on its way up."

Kintay's eyes looked as if they would pop out of his head. "Oh, shit!" He dashed toward his workstation, which was littered with a jumbled array of powders, liquids, implements, and containers.

Silverblade turned toward the door. "It might not be coming all the way up.

"Gotta assume it is," I said. "She probably knew something was amiss the minute you hacked the scanner. Could be security guards. Or maybe Coleridge herself. I wouldn't be surprised if she lived somewhere in the building."

Silverblade's face hardened. "All right. Follow my lead. Kintay, find a janitor's closet or something to get good and lost in. And keep quiet. Southerland, follow us, but stand back and give me and Lionel room to move." He pulled a gat the size of a cannon from somewhere inside his coat.

The three of us moved into the reception lounge, where Silverblade and Lionel, who had left the briefcase in the lab, took up positions on either side of the elevator.

I frowned at Lionel. "You don't have a gun?"

He smiled back at me. "Don't need one."

I glanced at Silverblade, who shrugged.

The elevator continued to rise, and I took up a position where I'd be easily seen when the door opened. I took a deep breath and let it out slowly. "Remember," I told my two fellow combatants, "I just want to talk with her."

Silverblade trained his heater on the elevator door. "Let's hope she gives you the chance."

Chapter Twenty-Seven

Coleridge, emptyhanded, stood in the middle of the elevator. Towering over the gnome on either side stood Quarrelmace and Blazearrow, each pointing the business end of a semi-automatic rifle at my chest. I stood in the center of the reception lounge, my hands raised at the sides of my head.

Coleridge turned to Silverblade as she stepped into the room a few paces ahead of the two security goons. "Are you intending to use that weapon, sir?"

Silverblade kept his heater trained on the gnome. "Not unless I have to."

"I wouldn't advise it. We appear to have you outgunned."

Silverblade pointed at me with a quick movement of his chin. "The boss says he wants to talk."

The faintest of grins pushed the edges of Coleridge's lips. "There's only one boss here, and it's not him."

I decided it was a good time to try to diffuse the situation. "I'm sorry for the intrusion, ma'am. No disrespect intended. I had a couple of questions for you, and I was in a hurry. I had no way to contact you, and I figured coming here might attract your attention."

Coleridge faced me for the first time, all traces of a smile gone. "You have broken into a secure facility. Tell me why I shouldn't let my men shoot you."

"Then you'd never find out why I wanted to talk to you."

"I'm not a curious person by nature, Mr. Southerland."

"I don't think the elf would take it well if you had me shot."

The gnome's eyes flickered, but her expression did not otherwise change. "I don't care what the elf thinks."

"Don't you? Maybe not. But I wonder what he'll think about *you* when Papadopouli's video hits every news outlet on the internet."

Coleridge kept her eyes locked on mine for a couple of beats before responding. "You're full of surprises, Mr. Southerland, but you're bluffing. I've looked into you, and I've concluded that, although you may lack formal education outside of your military training, you are a reasonably intelligent man. You're smart enough to realize that the Dragon Lords control all of the major sources of news on the internet, and that they would never allow that video to appear on any of them. While some fringe elements might display it for its shock value, in short order the video will easily be demonstrated to be a hoax, and, after some initial minor disruption, the whole matter will be dismissed and forgotten. You got anything else?"

My nose began to itch, and I lowered a hand—slowly—to scratch it. "Just one more. If I don't leave this place alive, I've arranged for the cops to discover that the drugs the Hatfields have been distributing at the antiwar rallies are being manufactured from this lab by a fellow named Tom Kintay. A police raid on this place would most certainly be against your interests."

Coleridge smiled. "Oh, Mr. Southerland. Do you really believe the police don't already know? I may have to reevaluate my opinion about your intelligence."

I let out a breath. "In that case, I suppose you should let your goons shoot me. That is, unless you have any reasons of your own for keeping me alive."

That caused a frown to appear on her face. "Such as?"

"I don't know. Maybe you abhor violence? Especially when it's unnecessary? Or when you're likely to be caught in the crossfire?"

Coleridge's features softened to some degree. "I don't encourage unnecessary violence, but 'abhor'? No, that's too strong a word. And violence may be advisable in this case. As for getting caught in the crossfire, Blazearrow has never failed to protect me in similar circumstances in the past, and I don't think he'll fail me now."

Something in her words, or her tone, must have been a signal, because she clearly expected to hear the sound of a rifle blast eliminating Silverblade as a threat. What she heard instead was the sound of Blazearrow's rifle clattering to the floor. She turned and her eyes widened in shock at what she saw.

While I'd been negotiating for my life with Coleridge, I'd become aware of an intense magical energy emanating from Lionel, who was standing unarmed and barely noticed to the side of the elevator opposite Silverblade. Out of the corner of my eye, I'd detected movement around his neck as two green and scarlet tattooed snakes slithered soundlessly over his collar and down the length of the sleeves of his jacket. When they reached the ends of his outstretched arms, they reared up, heads swaying gently in unison from side to side, and stared intently with eyes as black as death at the two security goons. As I kept Coleridge distracted, her protectors were staring back at the snakes with empty eyes and all expression drained from their faces.

Coleridge watched in confusion as Silverblade picked Blazearrow's weapon off the floor and plucked the other rifle from the hands of an unresisting Quarrelmace. The lab manager's cool demeanor crumbled at the sight of the snakes, and her face was white with fear when she turned to stare at me.

"Why don't we all sit down," I suggested, indicating the chairs in the lounge. "It looks like you won't be having me shot after all."

Coleridge decided that would be a good idea, and she shuffled wordlessly to the nearest chair. Lionel indicated a couch with a movement of his eyes, and Quarrelmace and Blazearrow shambled across the room as if under a spell, which I suppose they were. Soon, all of us were seated, except Silverblade, who leaned against a wall with a rifle in each hand, barrels pointed at the floor. The snakes had wound their way back up the inside of Lionel's jacket, and their heads poked up from his collar, staring into the eyes of the security trolls and tasting the air with their slender darting tongues. I moved my chair so that I was sitting a couple of feet opposite Coleridge, who glared at me with cold eyes.

I met her glare and absorbed it. "You were in the old lab when the grease bomb went off and burned down the warehouse," I began. "Cindy Hatfield was in the warehouse as the last of the crates were hauled away. You saw her on the viewing screen next to the hidden door. You sent your two security goons into the warehouse to grab Mrs. Hatfield and bring her into the lab. How am I doing so far?"

Coleridge didn't answer, so I continued. "Papadopouli showed up. I'm less clear about what happened next. An IED went off and caught Papadopouli in the blast. Mrs. Hatfield somehow slipped past you and ran into the blaze to help Papadopouli. She died in the fire." I paused for a few beats, studying the lab manager. "I'd appreciate it if you could help me out by filling in some details."

Coleridge's eyes never left mine as she slowly lifted a hand to her face, extended her index finger, and pushed it into her nostril. After digging around a bit, she pulled her finger out of her nose and stared at the crud on her fingertip before wiping it off on the side of the chair.

I had the feeling Coleridge wasn't going to be cooperative.

I stood and turned to Silverblade. "Watch her for a while, would you?" I walked past the reception desk and through the door into the lab.

Kintay was nowhere to be seen. I quieted the thoughts in my mind, searched for sounds, and sniffed the air. Turns out the hyped-up lab rat had taken Silverblade literally and hidden himself in a janitor's closet behind a stack of toilet paper.

"You might as well come out of there," I told him. "But keep your voice down. That new drug of yours... you said it removes inhibitions, right? And when you let us in, you didn't seem to care much that we were breaking into a secure area. Am I right in assuming that the drug would encourage someone to talk to me, even if she doesn't want to at the moment?"

Kintay's eyes widened. "Are you talking about Coleridge?" he hissed in a strained stage whisper. "Lord's balls—you want to get her cranked?" He giggled. "I'd pay good money to see that!"

"I just want to know if it will work."

Kintay thought about it. "She'll get real cocky," he said, then giggled. "That won't be much of a stretch, because she already thinks her shit don't stink. But she's extremely cagey and guarded. Hides behind a wall as thick as dragonhide. But once she's under the influence of my wonder drug.... Yeah, I think she'll let her guard down because she won't care what you know. She'll talk because she'll think she can get away with it. That's what that shit does to you—makes you think you're fuckin' untouchable!" A wide grin dimpled his cheeks. "It's an amazing feeling."

I thought about that. "The trick is going to be getting her to take it, and I'm going to need it to work fast. I don't want to have to force-feed it to her."

Kintay made a scoffing sound. "Have you considered a suppository?"

I scowled. "Not this time."

"Right, right, right. Although that might be fun! No? All right, no problem, sergeant. As it happens, I've been working on turning the stuff into poppers. You know, inhalants. In fact, I've got an experimental batch in a nasal spray bottle in my desk. I mixed it up a few days ago, and I was going to test it on myse—... umm... on a willing subject as soon as I got the chance. But it's ready and waiting. One big squirt up the nostril, and she should be singing and dancing in no time."

That's great, I thought to myself. *She's already cleared a passage.*

When I returned to the room, Silverblade came to meet me. "We've got a problem," he said, keeping his voice low. "Lionel is channeling a spirit called Ometeotl to keep those trolls in line."

I glanced at Lionel, whose eyes were narrowed in concentration as he muttered something under his breath. I'd seen those snakes tattooed on Madame Cuapa, and I knew Ometeotl, a dual representation of the male and female principle, was an extremely powerful, if volatile spirit.

Silverblade went on. "The problem is that Ometeotl is a spirit of *this* world, and their influence is strongest over the peoples of this earthly realm. But trolls are native to Hell, an *un*earthly realm. Lionel can only maintain his control over them for a limited time, and I'm afraid that time is running out fast.

"Then we'd better hurry. Let's go."

We crossed the room to Coleridge, who watched me with the hint of a smile. I glanced at Silverblade. "Keep her still."

The troll moved more quickly than anyone had a right to expect from a creature standing in excess of seven feet tall and carrying more than five hundred pounds on his hulking frame. In an instant he was crouched behind Coleridge, one beefy arm wrapped around her upper body.

"Hold her head," I said. I shoved the nozzle of the spray bottle into the nostril she had picked clean, and emptied the contents with two forceful squeezes.

Coleridge tried to stand, but the gnome was no match for Silverblade's grip.

She fixed me with a glare that would have wilted flowers and set them ablaze, but when she spoke, her voice was measured and deadly in its calm. "You'll pay for this. The Hatfields will have you skinned alive."

"I don't doubt it," I said, taking the chair opposite her. "But this was all so unnecessary. All I want is clarification as to what happened to Mrs. Hatfield the night of the fire. The Old Man himself is paying me to find out."

Coleridge's lips spread into a smile that threatened to crack a face that was not used to expressing joy. "Old Man Hatfield already has his story. Mrs. Hatfield's death was an accident caused by faulty wiring in that old warehouse. She was in the wrong place at the wrong time. As for Papadopouli, he's missing. You have no evidence that he was killed in the fire, or that he was even in the warehouse that night. No one has seen him for months. He no doubt moved out of the city after he was fired from the project. Anton—Mr. Benning, that is—decided to move the operation to a more secure location after that, just to make sure that the little shit engineer didn't do something to compromise us."

"Benning decided to move the project?"

"That's right. Anton is a smart man. Always thinking. And he's already assured Bowman that your report will confirm this story. His sons are also satisfied."

"Oh? And when did you last speak to *Anton*?" I made sure she knew that I'd caught her calling Benning by his first name.

Her smile disappeared as quickly as it had arrived, and it appeared that she was going to clam up. A short laugh escaped through her lips before she could stop it, and a confused frown wrinkled the bridge of her nose.

I wondered about the amount of drug I'd squeezed up Coleridge's nose. I'd all but emptied the bottle. Maybe I should have asked Kintay for more detailed instructions concerning dosage. Too late now, though. "What were you doing in the warehouse that night, ma'am? Giving it one last once-over after the move?"

She didn't answer at first, but her eyes widened suddenly, and her lips twitched into something resembling a grin. "Sure. One last look around to make sure those idiot lab drones hadn't left anything important behind." She snorted. "Like drugs. The lab tech Fats Hatfield stuck me with is more interested in manufacturing his pleasure pills than doing the work we hired him to do. And that fat fuck Fats encourages him." She smiled up at me, a harsh thing, and her pupils compressed into pinpoints. "He's a complete degenerate, you know. Fats, I mean. We're doing important work here, and none of the Hatfields seem to care. Except An—Mr. Benning. He's the only one amongst them with an ounce of intelligence. Or good sense."

"Was he with you that night?"

"Mr. Benning? What would he be doing there? Of course not. I went there on my own accord."

"With your security team."

"Hmm? Oh, you mean those two? Yes, they were with me, being useless, as usual."

"You sent them out to get Mrs. Hatfield off the floor."

Coleridge, still restrained by Silverblade, lifted an eyebrow, and I could hear her heart pumping. "Well, what if I did?" She gave the trolls a sidelong glance. "That's what they're there for. To fetch and carry. Sure, I sent them out to scoop Alu Hatfield's trophy wife off the warehouse floor before she fell down and bruised her pretty face. She had no business being there in the first place." Coleridge shot another glance at the trolls and scowled. "They had one job. Keep that dizzy dame out of my hair. And they botched it. Like I said: useless. All muscles and no brains."

I leaned toward her to regain her attention. "What do you mean? What happened with Mrs. Hatfield?"

Coleridge narrowed her eyes at me and shook her head. "That's none of your beeswax. I'm getting tired of your stupid questions. I've got nothing to say to you. What do you think you were doing, breaking into this place.... You've got no right to be here. You and your knuckleheaded ape are holding me against my will. That's kidnapping. When Anton finds out about this, he'll have your asses in a sling."

"My associate will release you if you agree to answer a few simple questions."

She made a halfhearted attempt to pull herself out of Silverblade's grip. "You've got no right to hold me," she shouted. "I'm not saying another word." She tried to spit in my face, but her mouth had gone dry.

Behind me, one of the trolls squirmed in his seat, and I heard a hiss come from one of the snakes wrapped around Lionel's arm. Turning my attention back to Coleridge, I asked, "What's the harm in filling me in on what happened to Mrs. Hatfield? Like you said before, no one's going to let the truth become public knowledge anyway. Why don't you let me in on what you know?"

Coleridge let out a loud mocking laugh. "Why should I? Who do you think you are? You're nobody. You and your brutish friends. You don't deserve to know the truth."

"We're the brutes? All I wanted was a polite conversation. It was your security goons who burst into the room with combat-issue weapons."

Coleridge cast a disdainful glare at the two trolls on the couch. "Some security officers they are—look at them! A couple of drooling idiots. Good for nothing except strongarm work. 'Goons' indeed! But they're *my* goons." She called out to Quarrelmace and Blazearrow, both now visibly struggling to emerge from the control of Ometeotl's hypnotic influence. "Aren't you, boys? You're *all* mine, aren't you. Fuckin' trolls. You'd still be living in caves and eating grubs if we gnomes hadn't taught you to use what little sense you've got. Not good for anything that doesn't involve muscles. And you couldn't keep one little human frail from rushing out to her death! Fucking useless, those two," she finished, grumbling through her last words.

"Boss?" Lionel's shout caused Silverblade to look past me at his assistant. I turned to see Quarrelmace struggling to his feet.

"Take it easy now," Silverblade advised, raising one of the rifles for emphasis. "Let's not make this ugly."

"Oh, do sit down, you big oaf," Coleridge said, a scowl in her voice. "We wouldn't be in this mess if you hadn't screwed up."

Quarrelmace straightened to his full height, his head nearly grazing the ceiling. "I shhcreweddup?" His words were slurred. "If you'd'a led Blazenme teg care uvvat keyboard joggey liigwe wanded'a—"

"Shut up! Not another word!" Coleridge's face had turned red as a ripe tomato, and her heart was racing like a jackhammer. "You don't speak unless I tell you to. Don't forget who you work for, you buffoon!"

A growl rose from deep within Quarrelmace's chest, and he took a step toward Coleridge.

Silverblade pointed the barrel of his rifle at the other troll's chest. "That's far enough."

Quarrelmace halted, but the arm Silverblade was using to restrain Coleridge slipped up to her neck. She tucked her chin and lowered her mouth to the troll's massive upper arm. Silverblade let out a yelp as Coleridge's teeth clamped onto his bicep. Before I could react, the gnome was out of the chair and running for the elevator.

Lionel started after her, but I stopped him. "Let her go," I said. "We don't need her."

Silverblade stared at me, a quizzical look on his face, as Coleridge disappeared into the elevator. We heard it descend immediately after the door slid shut.

Silverblade shrugged a question, and I nodded at Quarrelmace. "We don't need her, because we've got him."

Quarrelmace looked from me to Silverblade and back again but didn't otherwise move.

"You godd me, too."

We all turned toward the new voice.

Blazearrow lifted his eyes to me, a hard look on his face. He spoke slowly, trying to focus on his words. "I never liiged dad heardless coleblooded bidjj. Idwas Benning's idea to pud-der in charge of the lab, but she never tolddim we were there the night Mizzuz Haddfield died. Fats was the one who assigned us to prode... to protect Coleridge...." He shook his head and grit his teeth for a moment before resuming. When he did, his voice was clear. "And she convinced us not to say anything about that night to Fats or anyone else. She thought she'd be able to ride it through.

But it's all going to come out now, and they aren't going to like what they hear. Not Benning, and not Fats. Coleridge is cooked, and that most likely means that we are, too. The way I see it, Quarrel and I have two choices. We can go to Fats with our hats in our hands and hope for the best. Or we can take it on the lam." The glow in his burning eyes deepened as they met mine. "Well, I'm not one for begging. If you keep those snakes out of our heads and promise not to stop us from leaving, we'll tell you what you want to know. Right Quarrel?"

Chapter Twenty-Eight

"Blaze and me hustled the broad out of the warehouse and into the lab," Quarrelmace explained. "Like Coleridge wanted. But the broad isn't having it. She's yelling her fool head off about 'Don't you know who I am?' and 'Alu is going to burn the hide off your bones'.... Shit like that. So Coleridge tells us to lock her into the bathroom until we're done. But there ain't no locks on the bathroom door, so I push her in and hold the door closed. I gotta stand there while she pounds on the fuckin' door and tries to pull it open. And all the time she's screaming like crazy. It's a fuckin' nightmare."

Blazearrow picked up the story. "So we're cleaning up, and Coleridge sees that computer guy, Papadopouli, on the wall monitor. I come in from the back, and there he is, getting into a forklift. I'm thinking he's going to try to break his way in with it, but he parks it a little ways away from the door. Then he goes off and comes back with something. I can't see what it is at first, but he sets it down next to the forklift, and I can see that it's one of those coolers, you know, like on a water dispenser. I ask the boss lady if she wants me to go get him, but she says to wait and see what he's up to. Seems like a bad idea to me, but she's the boss, so I sit tight."

"And Coleridge is just watching all this?" I asked.

"Right. Me and her, just watching."

"And the Hatfield broad is throwing a fit in the bathroom," Quarrelmace said. "A regular ing-bing. Especially once she hears that 'her puppy' is outside. Lord's balls! I gotta tell ya: anyone ever calls me a puppy, I'll have to wring their neck!"

I'd pulled my chair opposite the couch to question the two trolls. Silverblade stood listening while Lionel sat at the receptionist desk tapping away at his cell phone. Kintay was back at his workstation. Fats had given him a quota, he'd explained, and he intended to fulfill it.

I nodded at Blazearrow. "All right. Then what?"

The security officer squeezed the bridge of his nose, still trying to shake off the effects of Ometeotl's spell. After a moment, he raised his eyes and continued. "Then I see him strapping a cell phone to the side of the water tank, and that's when I know he's putting a detonator on a bomb. I seen enough of that kind of shit in the hills outside Tenochtitlan when I was hunting down rebels during my mandatory. So I tell Coleridge that the computer tech is gonna set off a bomb, and I start up the stairs to stop him. I get about halfway, and I see the bomb go off in the monitor. The little fucker couldn't have been more than ten feet away when a watercooler full of blazing grease took him down. Poor sap never had a chance."

Something about Blazearrow's story nagged at me. "Papadopouli used his own cell phone as the detonator?"

"We figure he had a burner," Blazearrow said. "We found the remains of another phone on him later when we were cleaning up. That must have been his regular phone."

Blazearrow glanced at Quarrelmace, who dropped his eyes before answering me. "I heard Blaze yell 'bomb.' Then I hear the blast through the ceiling. I wanted to see what was going on, you know, to make sure Blaze and Coleridge are all right. The broad took advantage of the fact that I wasn't holding the door closed anymore and ran in past me." He looked up.

Blazearrow picked up the story. "When the bomb went off, it lit up the monitor by the door. Coleridge must have jumped back from it, because I heard her cursing a blue streak, which was unusual. Normally, she's cold as ice and almost never raises her voice. I turned and saw her laid out on the floor, so I guess she must have tripped. Anyway, I ran over to help her, and that's when the broad—Mrs. Hatfield—came running into the room screaming 'Puppy! Puppy!' She was up the stairs and out the door before I could catch her. And then, when the door opened, flames poured through the doorway, and I had to let her go." He shook his head. "There wasn't nothing I could do but slam the door shut before the flames burned down the lab along with the warehouse."

I remembered the fire damage I'd seen on the landing. "The door protected the lab from fire?"

"Sure," Blazearrow said. "As long as it was closed. It had enough enchantment stored in it to hold back anything short of dragonfire."

Silverblade glanced my way. "Then it was Papadopouli who set up the bomb. But it went off before he could get clear of it. Why? Who set it off? Not Papadopouli himself, unless he did it accidentally."

My teeth clenched. "Whoever set it off, Papadopouli was setting a trap with that bomb. Why? And who was his target?"

"Coleridge thinks he was after us," Blazearrow said. "Her and Quarrel and me. He probably didn't know that we had moved the operation, but he must have known somehow that we were going to be there that night. But we got there earlier than he expected, and we came in through the back way."

"Through the tunnel?"

"You know about that? Yeah, we came in through the tunnel. We spotted Mrs. Hatfield about twenty minutes after we got there, and Papadopouli showed up about fifteen minutes after that. So, maybe, what, six thirty-five? Six forty? Something like that. We think he planned to hide out somewhere in the warehouse, probably in the office, and then call the burner phone once we were in range. The blast would have taken all three of us out, easy. Coleridge thinks he had it in for us because we got him fired." A chuckle forced its way through his lips. "Who knew the little geek had it in him? Sure, he was a little high-strung, but I had him pegged as harmless. Losing his job must have really screwed with his head."

I turned to Quarrelmace. "Anything you want to add?"

The troll shook his winged block of a head. "Nah. That's about it." He grunted. "It wasn't our finest hour, I'll say that. Coleridge has been pissed at us ever since. I guess that's why she wouldn't send us after Kintay. She was afraid we would fuck it up."

I stared at him for a moment. "Why was she after Kintay?"

"She found out he had the video that the other geek made. Blaze and I figured she'd want us to go get him, but she sent those out-of-towners after him, instead."

Blazearrow held up a hand. "Coleridge didn't send them. Benning did. Coleridge told Benning that Kintay had a copy of Papadopouli's video, and he hired a couple of button men to take care of it."

"Benning hired the hitmen?" I asked. "You're sure?"

"Positive," Blazearrow said. "Coleridge mentioned it to me. She said she didn't trust Quarrel and me not to make a mess of it, so she asked Benning to handle the matter. That was fine with me. I don't have anything against Kintay. He seems like an okay gee when he's not running off and getting toasted. I'm glad I didn't have to drop him out the boss's window."

I considered the security officers' story. "What did you do while the fire was going?"

Blazearrow rubbed his eyes with the heels of both hands. "We spent the night in the lab. It wasn't comfortable, let me tell you. Coleridge bitched at us all night long. The warehouse went up quick, but we were safe underground. First thing in the morning, Quarrel and I went in and retrieved the bodies, or what was left of them."

"The fire was out?"

"Mostly. Coleridge had a couple of fire proximity suits delivered during the night, troll-sized for Quarrel and me. She stayed in the lab, of course. The warehouse ceiling had collapsed, and we had to dig the bodies out from underneath the rubble."

"Did you use the forklift?"

Blazearrow sneered. "Of course not. A forklift would have damaged the bodies. Besides, it wasn't anything Quarrel and me couldn't handle."

Some of the pieces of the puzzle were in place. It was Papadopouli who had planted the bomb, but I still didn't know who he was targeting. Not Coleridge. Despite what she wanted to believe, that story made no sense. It had more holes in it than hallstatt cheese. And I didn't know why the bomb had gone off prematurely, although it was possible that Papadopouli had simply screwed up. Cell phones make great detonators, but they can be touchy.

Quarrelmace coughed. "Are we done here? Coleridge has probably talked to Benning by now, and we need to be in some other part of the world when Fats finds out we let his brother's wife walk into a burning building."

"Almost," I said, holding up a hand. "Do you know what was on Papadopouli's video?"

The two trolls looked at each other. Blazearrow turned to me and shook his head. "No idea. We just know he saw something he wasn't supposed to see. Coleridge was pissed, but I got the feeling she was more scared than anything else. Maybe she thought she was going to be blamed for losing control of one of her employees. She's big on controlling people. Maybe you picked up on that."

I thought about that. "So, Coleridge finds out somehow that Papadopouli has made a video recording of something he's not supposed to know about. She sends one of you to bring him to her."

Blazearrow nodded. "That was me. I took him to see Coleridge. Benning was there, too."

"Benning was there?"

"Yep. With his bodyguard, Bronzetooth. Coleridge eighty-sixed me from the office, so I don't know what went on after that. But that was the last I saw of Papadopouli until he showed up with that bomb." He chuckled. "I figured Benning had put the quiet on him permanently, if you get my drift. Surprised the shit out of me when I saw him on that monitor with a damned IED."

"All right. Just one more question before you go." I looked from Blazearrow to Quarrelmace, making sure I had their full attention. "The hooded man. Neither of you has mentioned him. What can you tell me about him?"

Both trolls dropped their eyes and shifted in their seats. Quarrelmace turned away from me, shaking his head. Blazearrow looked up again, studying my face. "You wouldn't believe me if I told you," he muttered.

I smiled. "I already know he's an elf."

Blazearrow's eyes widened, and Quarrelmace jerked his blocky head around to face me in openmouthed astonishment.

"How can you know that?" Blazearrow asked.

"Well, I kind of work for him. Sort of. He's done some things for me, and I owe him." On impulse, I made a decision. "The two of you have been helpful. It's been a tough day. You're right, Blazearrow: Benning is going to be a lot more pissed off at Coleridge than she expects. She fucked up, and none of the Hatfields are going to like it. Neither is the elf once I tell him what went on here today, and he's going to want answers from the Hatfields. They're going to point the finger at Coleridge, and she's going to try to shift all the blame to the two of you. I agree: it looks like the three of you are out. But here's what I'm going to do. I'm going to put in a good word for you with the elf. Leave it to me. I'm sure that he's got use for a couple of professionals like you. I'll ask him to keep the Hatfields off your back and see to it that he takes good care of you. I think he'll go along with it. Is that jake with you?"

It was. I let Blazearrow and Quarrelmace go after that, and they agreed to call me when they found a place to lay low. They'd been remarkably cooperative, and I laid that on Coleridge. People in her position need to have more respect for the mugs who do their dirty work for them. You can buy a man's loyalty, but if you don't give him nothing more than money his loyalty will end the minute you cut off his supply of dough. The two trolls didn't owe anything to Coleridge, and soon they wouldn't owe anything to the Hatfields, either. But if everything went the way I planned, they would owe plenty to the elf, and they would owe me plenty, too.

***

That night, I wrote up a report and emailed it to Benning. I knew he wasn't going to like it, and I wasn't surprised when my phone buzzed five minutes after I hit the send key.

Benning spoke before I could say hello. "You're fired, Southerland. You're fired, and you're fucked. I hope you enjoy prison food."

He disconnected the call before I could respond. I had a feeling the check he'd given me had already been canceled. That's the problem with money. Most of it is just data in a universe made of radio waves. A push of a button is all it takes to make it vanish into the ether.

I found two nickels lying loose in my desk drawer and stacked them, one on top of the other, on my desktop. If I left them alone overnight, I thought, maybe they would mate. I went to bed hoping for triplets.

I was awakened soon after sunup by the sound of rapping. Not a light, persistent tapping on my windowpane this time, but a series of repeated heavy-knuckled thumps at my front door. I put on the first shirt and pair of pants I could find, slipped on some shoes and socks, and made my way downstairs, where I found Chivo on all fours staring at the entrance, ready to ambush any unlucky sap who came through.

"It's all right, Chivo," I said, a tight smile on my face. "It's just the police. Lubank should have me back home sometime later today, but, if not, you've got enough yonak in your room to last through the week if you don't get greedy."

Chivo looked up at me, and a low growl sounded from deep in his throat.

"You should make yourself scarce for a couple of hours in case the coppers decide to search the place. They don't have any cause to, but you never know when a couple of bulls will take advantage of a situation like this to look around for some loose change or a couple of bottles of hootch. If they see you, they'll be obliged to notify Animal Control, and then you'll be obliged to rip out their throats. I'd just as soon avoid all that, if it's all the same to you."

Chivo gave me a last look and ran a thin tongue over his snout before shuffling, reluctantly, through the rear door on his way to the back alley.

I opened the front door just as the three cops on my porch were about to break it down with a portable battering ram.

"Hello, boys. I hate to spoil your fun, but you won't be needing that bosher. Mind if I grab my hat and coat before you haul me off?"

A red-faced bull with an unfortunate mustache planted himself in my face. "Alexander Southerland? You are under arrest for breaking and entering, burglary, and the willful destruction of property." Without taking his eyes off me he signaled to one of his compadres. "Cuff him."

"You don't need to do that," I said, going out of my way to be non-threatening. "I'm not planning on giving you any trouble."

Despite my assurances, the other two cops forced my hands behind my back and slapped my wrists in irons, and they weren't gentle about it. I thought it was overkill, but I endured it. I didn't say anything when one of the cops took my cell phone from my pocket and tossed it back through my office door before pulling it shut. But when I saw the gleaming black unmarked transport van roll down the street and stop in front of my office, I pulled up short.

"What's with the wagon?" I asked the lead cop, my eyes narrowing. "Isn't that a little much for a simple B&E?"

"Shut your mouth, motherfucker!" The red-faced bull's mustache twitched as he pushed me toward the van. When I dug in my heels, the other two bulls came to his aid, and the three of them dragged me to the back of the carrier.

The door opened. When I saw who was waiting for me inside, things began to click, and I kicked myself for not seeing it coming. The three cops picked me off the ground and gave me the old heave-ho headfirst into the van. When I rolled to my side and peered up at the figure hunched over me, his hairless head scraping the ceiling, I knew, then and there, that Benning was right: I was well and truly fucked.

I groaned. "I should have asked those bulls to show me their buzzers. I didn't have them pegged as LIA."

Bronzetooth sneered down at me from what seemed like a mountaintop. "They're not LIA. They're all real city coppers with real legit badges. And they're all on Mr. Benning's pad."

I closed my eyes as more pieces floating around in my brain fell into place. I knew almost everything I needed to about Cindy Shipper's death, and much more besides. More than Bronzetooth, I realized. Much, much more than I should.

The transport was designed to carry up to ten human prisoners in a secure compartment separated from the driver by a reinforced wall and a locked door, but I found myself alone in the back with Bronzetooth. The troll slapped twice at the separating wall with the flat of his hand, and the van began to move. I rolled to my back and gazed up at the roof.

"You're taking me to see your boss? You could have just come around in your car."

Bronzetooth reached down with one hand, grabbed my restraints, and yanked me off the bed of the transport until I was dangling in the air, my arms extended behind my back, and my shoulders strained to their limits. He pulled me close to him, until our noses were inches apart. His mouth opened, and he laughed, blasting my face with his hot, wine-soaked breath.

"*I'm* your boss, you stinking rodent!" Bronzetooth's eyes burned like red-hot lava. "We're going to take a little ride, and you're not going to give me any trouble."

The troll shook me like a ragdoll, and I roared in pain as the ligaments in my shoulders stretched to their breaking point. He dropped me to the floor, only to pick me up by my aching shoulders and toss me onto the bench that lined the wall of the van. Before I could make a move, Bronzetooth attached the restraints on my wrists to a clamp embedded in the wall. As he stepped away, I unleashed a kick that connected with a solid thunk just beneath the troll's knee, and he nearly knocked me cold with a short backhand slap to the kisser that I knew would turn my jaw an interesting shade of purple. When the little birdies stopped circling my head, I lowered my chin to my collar and wiped blood off my lip.

Bronzetooth lowered himself into a seat on the bench across from me. "Mr. Benning doesn't want to see you today, Southerland." His lips stretched into a leering grin. "As a matter of fact, you reprehensible piece of filth, he doesn't ever want to see your ugly mug again."

Chapter Twenty-Nine

I leaned against the wall of the van, working my bruised jaw and wondering why I was still alive. Maybe Benning didn't want my blood on his hands, though I couldn't imagine why it would bother him much. I wouldn't be the first person he'd sent on his way to the great unknown. I figured he must want something from me, but I couldn't imagine what it would be.

Bronzetooth wasn't volunteering any explanations, but I thought it wouldn't hurt to be sociable. "How's your knee?"

Bronzetooth dismissed my question with a snort and offered nothing further.

"I take it Coleridge called your boss. What's with the two of them, anyway? I thought I picked up something from the dame. Is he banging her? She doesn't seem to be the type who would sleep with her boss, or anyone else, for that matter, but it's not always easy to tell what someone's like once they leave the office and let their hair down."

Bronzetooth sneered and shook his head a couple of times before turning away from me.

"No? Well, she speaks very well of ol' Anton. She gets a little gleam in her eye when she mentions his name. If he's not doing her, ten will get you twenty she's wishing he would."

Bronzetooth's face screwed up as if he were sucking a lemon.

I chuckled. "Yeah, I know what you mean. I don't see the appeal, either. But Anton? Who knows. Maybe his wife doesn't give him what he needs anymore. Does he have a thing for gnomes? He's so tightly wound, so dignified and proper, what with that immaculately trimmed shrub over his lip and that fresh carnation he always wears in his lapel. It wouldn't surprise me if he had a secret yearning for the exotic."

Bronzetooth's eyes glared like scarlet beacons as he locked them on mine. "Anyone ever tell you how boring you are, Southerland? Are you trying to put me to sleep with your incessant bullshit? Is that your plan?"

I shrugged, testing the strength of my restraints, and I grit my teeth as a burning flame lit up both my shoulders. As I suspected, the restraints were plenty strong enough to keep me out of trouble.

"Why am I still alive, Bronzetooth?" I asked once the pain had subsided. "Is it because you enjoy my company?"

Bronzetooth's massive chest swelled, and a single sardonic "Ha!" escaped his lips.

"How come you don't like me?" I asked. "I can tell that you don't. I could tell the first time we met. You really had it in for me. How come? I'm not a bad guy once you get to know me."

The troll crossed his arms over his chest and turned his eyes away from me.

"Did I do something to you that I don't know about? Did you hear something about me? I'll bet it's all the result of some sort of misunderstanding. Deep down underneath it all, I'm an okay gee." I tried to slide over on the bench to pull myself closer to him, but the wall clamp prevented me from moving more than a few inches.

"What is it, Bronzetooth? You don't like humans? You like to beat up on humans, don't you. I'll bet you don't have anything in particular against me after all. It's not personal between us. It's just that I'm human, and you regard us humans as small and weak, like grubs. Like worms. We cook our food and we can't drink your homebrewed troll whiskey without choking on it and burning a hole in our gut."

I shook my head. "And yet, you work for a human, and I get the impression that you're remarkably loyal to Mr. Benning. Devoted to him. I'm sure he pays you well, but it's more than that, isn't it. You admire the man. Sure, he's a low-life chiseler in a custom suit, lethal as a cobra and cunning as a cornered rat, but I'll admit he's a charmer. Smart, too. And refined, with impeccable taste. He's money, and he carries it well. Is that what makes him appealing to you? That's it, isn't it. He's as human as I am, but he's a rich human. You like it, don't you: that heady fragrance of wealth? It turns your head, makes you want to impress the man, makes you want to show him how tough you are by hurting his enemies. But only enemies who are smaller than you are. I'll bet a month's salary you'd never tangle with another full-grown troll."

Bronzetooth forced a yawn, but I could tell he was listening.

I pressed forward. "A lot of trolls would be repelled by a man like Benning. Trolls are fighters—warriors! Or at least their ancestors were. You know, I like trolls. In general, I mean. A little rough around the edges, maybe, but that's jake with me. Of course, most of the trolls I've met have been working-class mugs, like me. Cops, bruisers, security personnel. Even a few button men. But that's not you. You're more refined than most trolls, aren't you. More like Benning. More... human.

You turn up your nose at yonak, and I'll bet you don't drink trollshine, either. That's Mr. Benning's expensive wine I smell on your breath. A little early for it, if you don't mind me saying so. I've seen you drink your boss's shawnee, too. Good human whiskey. I'm guessing that's more to your liking than trollshine. Benning's probably a role model for someone like you. Trolls? Nah. They're too common for a high-living gentleman like yourself."

Bronzetooth jerked his head around to glare at me. "Lord's *balls*! If you don't shut your fuckin' yap, I'm gonna shut it for you."

I put a thoughtful expression on my mug. "Hmm, now that was interesting. 'Lord's balls?' 'Shut your fuckin' yap?' That's not the kind of talk I would have expected from an upscale chap like yourself. What would Benning say if he heard you speaking like a gutter rat? Wait a minute. Is that what you used to be? Did Benning raise you up from the gutter and introduce you to a better life? Give you nice clothes and an education? Teach you manners and how to hold in your farts in public? Is that why you fawn over him the way you do? I've got to tell you, Bronzetooth. Most trolls I know wouldn't have a lot of respect for a pompous suck-up like you. They've got too much pride in their Hellborn heritage. Too much respect for themselves. Ha! You think you've turned away from them, but they're the ones who've turned their backs on you."

Bronzetooth's face was turning red, and I knew I had struck a nerve. It was sitting there, begging me to poke at it. I dove in with both feet.

"Benning told me you and the missus were hoping for a child. A son, no doubt. Someone you can raise to be like you. Someone who will appreciate the finer things in life. I hope it happens. We've got enough belligerent trolls already. It's practically a cliché. Tough trolls. Strong trolls. Trolls who eat nails and spit fire. You know what I mean: the kind of troll your wife wishes she had married. The kind of troll who could make her blood run hot and give her a son. She'd like a son, too, wouldn't she. She'd like a son she could raise to be a real troll, instead of a lapdog who jumps to attention at the snap of his human master's fingers. The kind of troll she thought she was getting when she married you."

With a roar, Bronzetooth launched himself off the bench with a suddenness that almost surprised me, even though I'd been hoping and waiting for it. While we'd been talking, I'd been aware of the subtle presence of Cougar, my spirit guide, filling my bones, ligaments, and muscles, dulling the pain in my shoulders, and augmenting my vital functions and my strength. It wasn't enough to snap my restraints, but when the toe of my shoe snapped upwards like a bolt of lightning and smacked the soft tissue squarely in the center of the charging troll's parted thighs, it felt as if I'd punted his tackle so far up his gut that it tickled the bottom of his throat.

Even trolls have their weaknesses. The momentum of Bronzetooth's attack, combined with the Cougar-aided force of my foot in his groin, propelled the troll up and over my head. I ducked just far enough to evade the troll's noggin as it cracked against the wall with the force of a cannonball. The van swerved, and the air left my lungs as a quarter ton of troll crashed into my body and slid down to the floor. Bronzetooth groaned and rose up on his knees. I snapped my foot into the side of his head with all the strength Cougar had to give me, and the troll hit the deck like a sack of wet cement.

He lay still, but his ragged breathing let me know he was still alive, and I knew it wouldn't be long before he regained his senses. He was, after all, a troll. If I wanted to live to a ripe old age—or through the afternoon—I needed to be free of my restraints before he came to. I used my left (non-kicking) foot to slip the shoe and sock off my right foot, which was now red and throbbing. I hoped I hadn't broken anything, but I feared the worst. After slipping my bare foot into the troll's coat pocket, I used Cougar's strength and dexterity to pull a set of keys free and raise them with my toes, which were disturbingly numb. As I was lifting the keys to the bench, my foot spasmed, and the keys slipped away and fell to the floor with a clatter. As luck would have it, the van made a quick turn at that point, and the keys slid across the floor. Cursing, I extended my leg as far as I could, but the keys lay just beyond my outstretched foot. I took a deep breath and let it out slowly. I extended myself toward the keys, sliding off the edge of the bench and screaming as hot coals burned deep in my damaged shoulders. I felt something tear in both shoulders as I pushed myself another inch from the wall, and it was all I could do to stay conscious. My foot touched metal, and I managed to drag the keys back across the floor to my side of the van.

A change in Bronzetooth's breathing told me he wouldn't be out for much longer. I grasped the key ring with my toes, now red and visibly swollen, and this time I was successful in lifting the keys to the bench. After another minute of trial and error, during which time Bronzetooth rolled to his stomach and attempted to push himself up from the floor, I heard a satisfying click and removed the cuffs from the clamp.

Bronzetooth rose to one knee. My arms refused to work, and bright white lights exploded noiselessly in my head as I tried to use them to push myself off the bench. Acid rose from my stomach and burned the back of my throat. I called out to Cougar in my mind. My right foot—bare and already injured—launched itself, and I didn't know if it was Cougar or me who had willed it to do so. I yelped in pain as the side of my foot smacked into Bronzetooth's neck just below the lobe of his pointed ear. The troll fell to the floor of the van as if the marionette strings holding him upright had all been cut at once.

I fell to one knee next to the troll, clutching my swollen right foot. Kicking Bronzetooth in the groin had been like kicking concrete, but kicking him in the head had been like kicking a wrecking ball. I was certain I'd broken at least one toe, and if my ankle wasn't sprained it was at least severely bruised. I didn't think I'd be walking on that foot for a while. The troll was still alive, of course, but I hoped the second concussion he'd received would keep him quiet for a while. The problem was that my arms were still restrained behind my back. I lowered my backside to the floor, trying with only limited success to muffle a scream as I stretched my already strained shoulders and slid the restraints under my butt, legs, and the soles of my feet. I lifted my hands, restraints and all, and used the metal bracelet to scratch my nose, which had been itching like a sonuvabitch from the moment the cops slapped the cuffs on my wrists.

Satisfied for the moment, I pushed myself toward the moaning Bronzetooth. With nearly nerveless fingers, I fumbled at his coat and removed a handgun so large I doubted that I'd be able to fire it without breaking my arms. I had to draw on more of Cougar's strength to retrieve my sock and shoe and stuff my bruised and swollen bare foot into them. My fingers shut down completely when I attempted to tie the laces, so I settled for stuffing them inside the shoe to keep from tripping over them. I sat back on the bench, Bronzetooth's hand cannon in my lap, and took a moment to catch my breath.

I knew I didn't have much time before the troll woke up. I closed my eyes, called up a sigil in my mind, and sent out a call for Smokey. It took several precious minutes to establish a telepathic connection and issue a series of hurried commands.

"Do you understand what you need to do?" I asked.
"Smokey understands."
"Good. Now scoot, and don't be slow."

Bronzetooth sat up suddenly and tensed himself to spring. He froze when he found himself staring down the barrel of his own gun. I hoped he wouldn't force me to try to use it. My arms were numb from my shoulders to my fingertips, and I wasn't sure I had the strength to pull the trigger. And if I did manage to get a shot off, I knew I wouldn't be able to handle the recoil. I'd be as likely to shoot myself in the head as hit the broadside of a troll, even from five feet away.

I had enough strength to motion the gun toward the bench on the opposite side of the van, and, with a sigh, Bronzetooth took the hint. I kept the gun pointed his way.

"Where are you taking me? And don't try to tell me we're going anywhere near a cop house. We've been heading steadily southwest since your johns tossed me in this van, and we're way out of their jurisdiction."

The troll carefully lifted a hand and rubbed the spot under his ear where I'd kicked him. "A guy wants to talk to you. He's got some questions."

"What guy?"

"Friend of Mr. Benning's."

"This friend got a name?"

"Probably. Most people do."

I was getting impatient. I waved the gun a little to make sure he remembered I was holding it. "Give me a reason why I shouldn't shoot you where you're sitting."

Bronzetooth looked from the gun to my face and his lips twisted into an evil grin. "You sure you can handle that thing? You'd better be sure you don't miss." He jerked his chin toward the cab of the van. "I've got two friendlies on the other side of this wall, and two more friendlies following us in a prowl car. They're all packing iron. Are you going to shoot them all? And then what? You wouldn't last another day in this city. You'd have the whole YCPD after you, and cop killers never make it to court."

He was right about that. And even if I managed to plug Bronzetooth, those four cops would see to it that I never made it out of the van alive. I'd be just another dangerous prisoner—a murderer—gunned down while trying to escape justice.

Bronzetooth's grin was still on his face, and I returned it with one of my own. "Sounds like you've got me cornered, like a rat. You ever seen a cornered rat? They get to feeling desperate. And when they're desperate enough, they'll do anything, no matter how unreasonable it might be." I gritted my teeth and lifted the gun off my lap, aiming the barrel between the troll's eyes.

Bronzetooth's grin disappeared. "Hold on, Southerland. There's no need to get crazy. No one has threatened you. Mr. Benning just wants you to see a guy, that's all."

"A guy with questions. Right. And what happens to me when he's done asking them?"

Bronzetooth shrugged with the side of his face. "I don't know. I guess he lets you go."

My eyes narrowed. "Sure he will. That's why your bulls had to slap these bracelets on my wrists and throw me into an armored carrier. Because Benning's friend is going to let me leave when he's done with our friendly chat." I stared hard at Bronzetooth. "You must think I'm dumb as dog shit. How about it, Bronzetooth? Am I dumb enough to blow your fuckin' head off?"

Bronzetooth's eyes widened, then narrowed. He looked like he was going to force me to use his gun and find out whether I could make the shot count. He tensed, and I braced myself for a shot.

The van slowed and turned. Neither Bronzetooth nor I moved as the van coasted to a stop.

Bronzetooth relaxed, and a smile came to his lips. "If you're holding that gun when those coppers open the door, they're going to shoot you before you can turn around."

Once again, he was right. I hated that he was always right. I lowered the weapon to the floor and kicked it toward Bronzetooth with my undamaged foot. He picked it up and pocketed it just as the back door swung open.

Two coppers, including the red-faced bull with the unfortunate mustache, stepped inside to retrieve me. He pulled up short at the sight of my cuffed hands in my lap. Bronzetooth stood and promptly stumbled, bracing himself against the wall of the van to keep himself upright.

The bull jerked his head toward Bronzetooth. "You all right?"

Bronzetooth sucked in some air through his teeth. "Just a little carsick." He shot me with a glare. "The air in here is a little ripe."

The bull chuckled. An involuntary yelp escaped me when he grabbed my restraints and pulled me to my feet. Stabbing pain raced down my arms from my shoulders, and my injured foot gave under my weight, causing me to fall against the wall and slide back down to the bench. The bull shot Bronzetooth a leering grin, and I let him draw his own conclusions about what had been going on in the transport while we'd been on our way to wherever we were now.

The bull picked my hat up from the floor of the van and pushed it down on my head. "Get up. We're here."

"Where?" I asked. But the bull wouldn't answer. A haunted look came over his face, and his eyes dropped. I didn't like that look. It didn't bode well for me at all.

Pushing with my one good foot, I managed to stand, and I let the bull guide me as I limped out of the carrier. I told myself that my foot was bruised, not broken, and that my rotator cuffs were overstretched, not torn. Just because I wasn't a doctor didn't mean my diagnosis wasn't on the money. I must have done a good job convincing myself I was essentially okay, because I managed to lower myself out of the transport without help, though not without an agonizing convulsion that caused my eyes to fill with tears.

When I wiped my eyes, I was distracted from the waves of stabbing pain pulsing through my shoulders and foot by the sights and sounds that greeted me outside the transport. I was surrounded by a milky gray sky tinged with a diffused silvery glow, as if a dozen suns were striving with only minimal success to shine through heavy fog. I blinked at the sight and was nearly overwhelmed by oppressive vibrations of magical energy pounding noiselessly at me from all sides. My breathing came in ragged gasps, and the sounds of the footfalls around me were muffled by the gravity of the air, which filled my ears like water. I was standing on enchanted ground, and I concluded that we'd driven through a portal into a place that stood outside the world I knew.

The van had parked in front of a gray one-story building whose walls gleamed with a pearl-like sheen. The edges of the building blended so well with the surrounding sky that I couldn't get a fix on its size. The more I stared at it, the more the front entrance seemed to open into the strangely glowing sky itself. The pain subsided enough to convince me I was suffering from only a few minor aches and pains, and I made the short walk to the unmarked entrance with only a noticeable limp and a continual stream of grunts and groans.

The bull and Bronzetooth ushered me through the front door and down a short hallway into what could only have been an interrogation room. The bull took out a key and removed my cuffs, and Bronzetooth guided me to the only piece of furniture in the room: a steel folding chair facing a surveillance camera and a wall speaker. Once I was seated, my escorts left the room without a word. The door shut behind them with a solid click, followed by the sound of a bar sliding into place. I wouldn't be leaving this room without help. I noted the air vents at the base of the walls on either side of me. If anyone decided to pump the room full of lethal gas, I wouldn't be leaving it at all until they carted me out on a gurney.

The flow of magical energy in the room was more subtle and less oppressive than it had been outside, but it was still enough to fill the air and dull my senses. I felt as if I were sitting inside a thunderbolt that had frozen in mid-strike. Static electricity strained to be released from the pores of my skin on every part of my body.

I sat back in the chair and flexed the fingers on both hands. My upper arms still ached as if someone had jammed ice picks into my shoulders and left them there, but at least I could lift my elbows as high as my chest for a few seconds without passing out from the pain. Any higher than that was currently out of the question. I lowered my hands to my lap and stared at the camera.

"If anyone can hear me," I announced, "I could use a cup of coffee. And about a dozen aspirin."

An unrecognizable voice, distorted to sound deep and robotic—or demonic—came through the speaker. "Would you like cream or sugar with the coffee?"

"Black is fine," I replied, my voice sounding insubstantial in the stifled atmosphere of the room. "I like my coffee to taste like coffee."

Chapter Thirty

I didn't get the aspirins, but they gave me coffee. I figured it would have to do.

The demon robot voice sounded through the speaker after I'd gulped down a couple of swallows of the brew. "Tell me about the elf." I imagined a man behind the voice: thin as a wraith, bushy eyebrows, and a hawklike beak over his kisser.

I looked into the surveillance camera. "Elves are extinct."

"The elf, Mr. Southerland. The one who put the heritage stone into your forehead, which is even now allowing you to heal from the injuries you suffered on your way to this facility."

I fixed my mug with a look of innocence. "Injuries? What injuries? The ride here was quiet. Bronzetooth never laid a hand on me."

"Apart from a single slap, that's mostly true. You did more damage to him than he did to you. I'm impressed. It's not easy for a human to batter a troll into unconsciousness. In fact, I wouldn't have thought it possible. There is clearly more to you than meets the eye."

I told myself that I couldn't assume the speaker was the peculiar operator I'd seen hauling off agitators in a prison transport that looked exactly like the one that had brought me to this place, but I felt it was a good bet. In any case, the voice was right. It had been Cougar, using my leg like a club, who had rendered Bronzetooth unconscious. Unfortunately, it was my foot that was paying the price.

The voice knew a lot about what had happened inside the prisoner transport, and I suddenly realized how. "Tracker One Four Epsilon Six Three," I said, nodding. "I have to admit I never detected the elemental in the van. But I should have known it would be there. You're the one who commands it, aren't you."

"Indeed, Mr. Southerland. Or should I say Target Zeta Three Phi Nine Nine Seven."

"You must know a lot about me."

"I do. You're not it's only target, but I have observed much of your life through the tracker elemental."

"You have the advantage over me," I said, trying to shift into a comfortable position in the folding chair. "Why don't you at least tell me your name?"

"You may address me as Counselor."

"You're a lawyer, then?"

"Among other things, yes."

I guessed that was about as much as I was going to get. "Well, Counselor, that elemental was also following the elf. You must know a lot about him, too."

"Sadly, Target Alpha One Beta Three is far warier than you are and much more difficult for my elemental to track. I know the elf leads a plot to undermine the rightful and beneficent rule of Lord Ketz-Alkwat, and I know that he has recruited you to play a role in his conspiracy. I would like to know more."

I shrugged. It made my shoulders ache. "Ten will get you twenty you already know more about his schemes than I do. I've run a few errands for him, but that's about it. You say he's plotting against Lord Ketz? I don't know that for a fact. The elf doesn't trust humans much, and he hasn't exactly taken me into his confidence. He gave me that heritage stone—against my will, I might add—and I'll admit that it's been useful. I owe him for that, so I help him out when he needs me to. I've delivered some packages for him. I helped find someone for him: a ten-year-old troll with a speech problem. He didn't tell me why he needed me to do these things for him, and I didn't ask any questions. When it comes to his actual plans, I'm in the dark. You'll have to ask his other elf friends."

"You know much more than you're letting on."

I snorted. "I don't even know his name. Come to think of it, I still don't know yours, either, Counselor."

"His name is of no import, nor is mine. How many other elves have you met?"

I started to shrug but stopped at the first onset of pain. "I don't know, maybe a dozen? But I don't know their names, either."

"You're lying, Mr. Southerland. You have met no other elves."

"I haven't?"

"No."

"Huh. Say, Counselor, if you already knew I hadn't met any other elves, then why did you ask me how many I knew?"

"Perhaps I was testing your honesty."

"Oh, I see. Well, I've got to admit, I'm not an honest person. I lie all the time. I even lie to myself. In fact, I might be the least honest person I know. I'm telling you, Counselor: you can't believe a single thing I tell you. Not even that."

Silence followed, and I took advantage of it to finish my coffee. When I was done, I asked, "Hey, Counselor—you think I can get another cup? This stuff's not half bad."

That brought the voice back. "I was hoping we would have a sensible conversation, Mr. Southerland. You must appreciate the position you're in. There is no escape from this facility. Your further involvement in any conspiracy to undermine the rightful rule of your Dragon Lord has ended. You sit under the penalty of death for your crimes against the Realm of Tolanica. Yet, you are more valuable to me—and to the Realm—alive. But to live, you must aid me in stopping the elf's insane conspiracy to destabilize civilized rule and throw the world into chaos."

I leaned back in my chair. "Is that a 'no' on more coffee?"

"Don't try my patience, Mr. Southerland. As I said, you have value to me, but you are not essential."

I lowered my coffee cup to the floor. "How am I supposed to have, as you say, a sensible conversation with a disguised disembodied voice who won't even give me a name? If you were serious about talking to me, we'd be sitting in a nice restaurant enjoying baked salmon and a glass of avalonian whiskey. Or at least in a bar with a couple of beers. But this?" I lifted my hands chest high, trying not to grimace, and glanced around the empty room. "Who are you kidding?" I lowered my arms. "This isn't a conversation, it's an interrogation. Say, you didn't drug my coffee, did you, Counselor? It won't do you any good, you know. I'm resistant to most forms of drug-enhanced interrogation. Part of my training during my mandatory service to the Realm."

"No, Mr. Southerland. Your coffee has not been drugged, though I daresay we have chemically enhanced interrogation techniques here that would shatter your resistance, no matter how well you've been trained. I hope we won't have to employ them. They tend to leave the recipient in a permanent state of inactivity that makes the continuation of life impractical. I would prefer leaving you alive and functional."

"Why? Oh, I see. You want to turn me."

"That's correct, Mr. Southerland. And it would most assuredly be in your own best interest to agree to enter our service."

I scratched my jaw. "The alternative, I take it, is death?"

"Regretfully, Mr. Southerland, you are correct. It's a simple matter of justice. You have been tried and found guilty of capital crimes in the highest court of the Realm and are under a capital sentence. I have the authority to postpone that sentence indefinitely. All I need from you in return for that postponement is for you to cooperate with the body I represent for the rest of your natural life."

"The body you represent.... You mean the LIA?"

"Oh, no, Mr. Southerland. I'm not a part of the Lord's Investigation Agency."

I blinked, surprised. "You're not?"

"Certainly not." Even through the distortion and the sound-flattening magical energy permeating the room's atmosphere, I could hear the scorn in the demonic voice. "The LIA has its uses, to be sure, as do the police and other enforcement agencies. I am a part of something higher. I am a member of Lord Ketz-Alkwat's Sovereign Court."

"Sovereign Court? I've never heard of it."

"We're not widely known to the general public, Mr. Southerland. Sadly, most of the people who have encountered the Court are no longer with us. The Sovereign Court handles matters that directly threaten the security of the Dragon Lord and his ability to govern the Realm of Tolanica."

"And this is the court that has sentenced me to death?"

"Exactly, Mr. Southerland."

The pain in my shoulders flared, and I crossed my arms across my chest to ease the pressure on the ligaments. "I don't recall being present at my trial. Were you the prosecutor? The judge?"

"I was both, Mr. Southerland. And your presence was not necessary."

"Did I at least have a defense attorney?"

"A defense attorney was not necessary, either. The Court examined the evidence, and your guilt was beyond doubt. Your execution will be carried out at my discretion."

"Uh-huh. When you say 'The Court,' how many deciders of fact are we talking about? Just you?"

"That is none of your concern, and you are wasting my time. Your choice is clear. You will tell me everything you know about the elf who is conspiring against the rule of Lord Ketz-Alkwat. You will tell me everything you know about the conspiracy itself, including the names of your fellow conspirators. You will agree to aid in the capture of this elf. If you refuse to serve the government you have betrayed, your sentence of death will be carried out without delay."

I let my hands fall to my lap. "Like I said, I don't know much. I've only met the elf a couple of times. He pops in, asks me to do something, and then he disappears. I don't know anything about any conspiracy, and I don't have any names to give you. Sorry."

"You are lying, Mr. Southerland. I had hoped you would be more cooperative, if for no better reason than to preserve your life. I must admit that I do not understand you. I have spoken with many dissidents throughout the Realm. They tend by and large to be misguided fanatics. Often, they have suffered some form of misfortune and found a way to blame their troubled condition on the government, or, in some twisted way, on Lord Ketz-Alkwat himself. But I have studied your background, Mr. Southerland. I have found no strong indications of political passion or fanaticism in your personal history, nor have I found any hint of burning grievances on your part. Your two-year record of combat service in the Tolanican Army was exemplary, and you performed admirably for an additional year in the Military Police. You've earned a decent living as a private investigator and never registered any formal complaints against the Tolanican government. I happen to know that Anton Benning, Mayor Harvey's head of security, thinks very highly of you."

Really? That was news to me.

The voice continued. "Why you have chosen to aid a decrepit old monster's attempt to turn the Realm upside down is a mystery to me, Mr. Southerland. Perhaps you can enlighten me. What has our government done to hurt you?"

I shrugged involuntarily, and lances of pain pierced my shoulders. I fought to keep my breathing even. "I've got no beef with the government," I said through clenched teeth, "and I can't imagine life without the Dragon Lords." I should probably have stopped there, but I couldn't help myself. "You may have heard that I'm not crazy about Lord Ketz's policy toward the adaros, and I'll admit that it concerns me. It falls just short of genocide. Also, the war in the Borderlands has gone on for far too long. Seems to me if something was going to be accomplished by it, it would have happened by now. But only a bunch of damned fools would fight a useless battle against a Dragon Lord over such matters. Not only is it all outside the control of mugs like me, but throwing a few rocks at an immortal hundred-foot-long flying arsenal like Lord Ketz over shit like that is suicide."

"So, then. It seems you are a dissident after all."

I made a scoffing sound. "Mmph. A dissident? I've got a few gripes about how things work, that's all. Who doesn't? But I don't see how Lord Ketz or anything calling itself a Sovereign Court would be put off by a few rambling complaints by a lug like me. Maybe this government isn't as strong or secure as it pretends to be."

I sat through a long pause, so long that I thought the Counselor was finished with me. Finally, the voice spoke again. "You're right, Mr. Southerland. Lord Ketz-Alkwat has nothing to fear from the likes of you. You can be useful to your government, however."

I raised my eyebrows. "That right? What did you have in mind?"

"The elf has proved to be elusive, like a mouse in a mattress factory. We discovered where he'd been residing when he was in Yerba City, but circumstances caused him to abandon that particular lair. You know the one I mean. We believe he's still in Yerba City, but we don't know where. You, however, are in communication with him, and we believe you have the ability to entice him out of the hole he's been hiding in and out into the open."

"Circumstances?"

"I'm sorry, what?"

"You said he'd abandoned his home as a result of circumstances. Can you be more specific?"

"That's not important!" The Counselor's impatience rose above the vocal distortion. "What's important is that the elf needs to be brought to a location where he can be apprehended or eliminated."

"You want me to give you the elf."

"Precisely."

"And why would I do that?"

The Counselor was silent for a few beats, and the voice, when it resumed, was exasperated. "You are no threat to the Realm, Mr. Southerland, but I will confess that the elf is another matter. Unlike you, he poses a... let's call it a concern. You can aid us in alleviating that concern. I had hoped that a threat to your life would compel you to act on our behalf, as any sane man would. But I can see I've misjudged you, or, perhaps, misjudged your level of common sense. I have the distinct impression you would rather die than aid your government! This is beyond reason. A matter of excessive pride, perhaps? You may not be a typical dissident, Mr. Southerland, but I am rapidly coming to the conclusion that you are mentally disturbed. My most logical course of action is to have your sentence carried out immediately. But I've learned that you play poker, and I have, as you might put it, one last card to play. I must warn you, however: this will be my last effort on your behalf. If you desire to see another morning, I suggest you choose your next course of action wisely."

I turned at the sound of a sliding bolt and watched as the door was pulled open. Walks in Cloud wheeled herself into the interrogation room. Her lips stretched into a taut smile. "Hello, Jack. Quite the pickle, eh?"

I stood and whirled on the surveillance camera. "You fucking son of a bitch! Is this how you're playing it? You can't bend me to your will by threatening my life, so you're gonna threaten my friends? That's dirty! That's fuckin' dirty!"

"Relax, Alex." Walks in Cloud's voice sounded thin in the deadened air. "It's not like that."

I turned. "What are you saying, Walks?"

"I'm saying I'm here of my own free will, you big oaf. I asked the Counselor for the chance to talk to you, and he's letting me."

My fingers were digging into my thighs, and I forced myself to loosen my grip. "What do you mean? What's going on here, Walks?"

Walks sighed. "I'm with them, Jack. Your elf's project is a complete disaster, not just for us but for the entire world. He needs to be stopped. And we need you to help us stop him."

Chapter Thirty-One

I stared across the room at the friend I thought I knew. "I don't get it, Walks. Wait—they've got something on you! They're forcing you to help them, aren't they. Just like they're trying to do to me. We can get out of this, Walks."

But Walks was shaking her head. "No, Alex. I came to the Counselor of my own free will. It was the Cloud Spirit who convinced me."

"The Cloud Spirit? What does she have to do with any of this?"

"She was severely shaken by that video. After the rest of you left, she and I had a talk. Look, Alex. Try to understand. You started out helping the elf because you owe him. I get that. You were never concerned with politics. How many times have I heard you say that if you've seen one boss, you've seen them all? You never believed the elf's conspiracy would actually work, and, as far as I can tell, you still don't. You never really cared about what he was doing, what his goals were. But you owe the elf, so you're doing the little tasks he asks you to do in order to pay off your debt."

Walks wheeled herself across the room until she was within my reach. "Sit down, Alex. Things changed after the big storm last spring when you got caught up in the adaro situation. Since then, you've leaned more and more toward becoming a believer in what the elf is trying to do. But it's crazy, Alex. It's a fantasy. The Dragon Lords overwhelmed the elves six thousand years ago. By anyone's way of reckoning, that battle was over and done with a long time ago. There's no going back."

I remained standing, ignoring the ache in my foot. "You don't think the elf can succeed? Maybe not, at least not in our lifetime. But elves live for a long time—practically forever—and the groundwork he's laying today could grow into something big someday."

Walks met my eyes. "So what? Think about it, Alex. Let's say the elves somehow succeed. Let's say at some point far in the future they drive the Dragon Lords back into Hell and retake control over this world. What then? What makes you think they'd be an improvement over the Dragon Lords? Who do you think the elf is trying to help—us? Nothing he does in the next hundred years is going to have any effect on *our* lives. Our descendants?" She smiled. "And let's forget about the fact that we're both childless. I'll always be childless, but, who knows? You may produce a little P.I. someday." Her smile faded. "But let's pretend we care about the future of humanity, not to mention the descendants of trolls, dwarves, and gnomes. Does the elf? Is that what all of his schemes are about? The future of all sentient creatures? Forget about it. He's out for himself and his own people, Jack, just like everyone else. Come on, Alex. Sit down."

I lowered myself into the chair to take the weight off my bad foot, and so I wouldn't have to look down at Walks. "I'll admit I don't know a lot about elves, but I do know they were in control of this world for a long time. For a lot longer than the Dragon Lords have been around. And the elves didn't drive the adaros out of their homes. They didn't herd the adaro women into camps while trying to kill off all the adaro men. The Dragon Lords did that. The elves weren't genocidal, like the Dragon Lords are."

Walks stared back at me. "How do you know? Maybe they tried, but failed. Ever think of that?" She shook her head. "Alex, you know nothing about elves. But the Cloud Spirit does."

"How? There was no internet back then."

Walks reached over and put a hand on my knee. "The Cloud Spirit is a spirit of technology. She's been with humanity in one form or other since the first human deliberately sharpened a stone and used it to scrape antelope meat off a bone. She saw how the elves ruled the prehistoric world. The elves never had a centralized government. Before the arrival of the Dragon Lords, the elves were never united. They were tribal, and they opposed each other in violent tribal conflicts."

I blinked. "The Cloud Spirit told you this?"

"She did more than tell me. The Cloud Spirit has a long and vivid memory. She shared these memories with me in visions. She showed me what life was like for humanity under the dominion of the elves. Alex, the elves herded humans like intelligent cattle. Humans, in turn, domesticated and herded other animals for themselves and for the elves in the form of ritual sacrifices. Humans worshiped elves, as if they were gods, which, to the ancient humans, they were. And the elves cultivated human intelligence like a crop. They drew energy from humans. They used this energy to fashion spirits, which they used to further their control over humans."

I frowned. "Wait a minute. Didn't elves teach humans how to hunt and gather, and then later how to grow crops? Even the history permitted by the Dragon Lords credits elves for the survival of early humans."

Walks nodded. "Yes. And it was all for the benefit of the elves, so that they wouldn't have to do all the hard work themselves. Any benefit for humans was incidental."

I shook my head. "But that's all ancient history. What's it have to do with the world we live in today?"

Walks pulled her hand off my knee. "Don't be a jackass, Alex. The elves want to reshape the world in their own image and for their own comfort. They want a world of tribal hunter-gatherers, primitive technology, and neolithic farming villages. They want to be worshiped again by primitive herds of humans. It was the Dragon Lords who introduced civilization to the world, who taught humans how to smelt and forge metals, who supervised the construction of cities and formed centralized governments. They abolished tribalism. They encouraged ethnic mixing and unified societies."

I snorted a laugh. "Unified societies? Tell it to all the mothers whose sons and daughters died fighting the Tolanican-Quscan Wars in the Borderland."

Walks let out a breath. "Come on, Alex. It's a big lumpy world, and nothing ever goes smooth as silk. But if it weren't for the Dragon Lords, we'd all be throwing spears at buffalo and fighting wars over wells. Look at me, Alex. I'm a computer tech. Computer technology wouldn't exist if the elves were still in charge. The Cloud Spirit would be a spirit of arrowheads, wooden plows, and pottery. I wouldn't be able to exist in that world. Can you see me following herds to fresh pastures, or, at best, hoeing weeds in the furrows?"

My eyes dropped to her legs. "I thought it was the Cloud Spirit who took away your ability to walk?"

She rolled her eyes at me. "The Cloud Spirit required a commitment from me in order to become a fully attuned priestess. I was a fat, unhealthy kid. I wasn't using my legs all that much before I dedicated my life to her. It was an easy sacrifice for me to make. I'm a child of the modern world, Alex. The world created by the Dragon Lords. I couldn't exist in the world the elves would create if they succeeded in driving the Dragon Lords out of it. Maybe you could, but I'm not sure you'd like it all that much." She tossed me a world-weary smile that made her look just like the Walks I'd come to know. "You'd have to harvest your own coffee beans and distill your own hootch. Are you ready for that, Jack?"

I shook my head. "The world has changed for all of us. It's changed for the elves, too. You don't really expect elves to throw away all of our progress and go back to hunting woolly mammoths. They don't exist anymore. Things aren't the same as they used to be. The elf I know has been living in this city, and he seems to have adapted to it all right."

Walks tilted her head slightly and lifted her eyebrows. "Has he? Does he use a computer? Does he own a cell phone? Have you ever seen him driving a car?"

I thought about that. "That doesn't mean the elves are going to abolish modern technology. How would that even be possible?"

Walks sighed, and she shook her head. "Oh, Alex. You're so naïve. Do you have any idea how fast we humans would revert to earlier forms of technology if we burned books, eliminated the internet, and stopped educating our children for even ten years? Do you know how fragile the edifice of stored ideas really is? How easily it can be toppled and its contents destroyed? How quickly accumulated knowledge can be lost? How rapidly civilized humanity would revert to savagery without strong hands to guide it? With the chaos the elves plan to unleash upon the world, it could all fall apart..." She held up her hand and snapped her fingers. "Just like that."

"You seem to know a lot about their plans. Is this you talking, or the Counselor?"

"It's me, Alex. And the Cloud Spirit. And I trust her implicitly."

As Walks spoke, I heard, or thought I heard, a series of soft 'pop's from outside the room, but the sound was so muffled I couldn't tell for sure. My eyes narrowed. "Is this what you were going to tell me when we were having lunch the other day? But that was before we'd seen the video."

Walks nodded. "The Cloud Spirit has never been comfortable with the elf's conspiracy. You were told that Lord Ketz found an alternative to the RAA formula we were hiding from him. Something that would help him reproduce. That was a lie. The Cloud Spirit gave him the formula. That's what I wanted to tell you. I wish I'd had the courage to do it. The timing didn't seem right, though. But now that she's seen the video, she's more alarmed than ever. She believes with all her being that humanity is better off under the rule of the Dragon Lords than they were when they were being herded by the elves. And I'm convinced that she's right."

I heard more muffled pops and shifted in my seat until the pain in my shoulders relented. "*You* may trust the Cloud Spirit," I said, "but I have no reason to. I've never spoken to her, but I've had a lot of conversations with the elf. I never got the impression he plans to enslave the human population and take us back to the Stone Age."

"No? But he has no problems working with organized crime families, does he. You hate the Hatfields, yet you blindly follow a creature who has partnered up with them. Doesn't that at least make you uncomfortable with your choices?"

I tried to shrug and partially succeeded. "It's not always black and white, Walks. The line gets a little fuzzy sometimes. You know that. How much of your work is for the benefit of rich scumbags who shit all over the rest of humanity? But we've all got to make a living, and sometimes that means sharing a foxhole with assholes."

Walks's lips spread into a bitter smile. "Listen to you, Jack. You're judging me for standing with the Dragon Lords, and there you are sitting in a hole with the Hatfields." She reached for me with an outstretched hand. "Won't you let me pull you out while you've still got the chance?"

The door opened, and a man in a suit holding a semi-automatic took half a step into the interrogation room. I tried to spring from my chair, but my foot gave way, and I stumbled helplessly to one knee. The gunman lifted his weapon until the barrel was pointed squarely at my chest. His eyes focused and his jaw clenched. I was about to die like a wounded dog.

Before the gunman could squeeze the trigger, a tiny gray funnel of whirling wind passed in front of his face and peppered his eyes with a stinging spray of sand. A thunderous crack shattered the muffled stillness of the air, and the hot odor of phosphorus and sulfur shot up my nostrils and burned my sinuses. The round from the gat, however, went wide and plunged into the wall behind me. As the gunman reached reflexively to wipe his eyes, a series of staccato claps ripped through the hallway. The gunman's eyes widened as he crumpled to the floor.

Silverblade burst into the room, holding an automatic rifle. His eyes darted from Walks to me, and he asked, "Are you okay?"

Walks turned to me with wide eyes, and I could see that she was unhurt. I nodded at Silverblade. "We're fine, thanks to you. And to Smokey." The elemental was spinning like a miniature tornado over the fallen gunman, and it darted to hover over my shoulder at the sound of its name.

Silverblade indicated the exit with the point of his rifle. "Let's get the two of you out of here."

With Silverblade leading the way, I pushed Walks into the hallway. Lionel appeared from around a corner, his head framed by the heads of two snakes emerging from tails tattooed on his neck. Blood covered his hands and forearms, but he looked none the worse for wear.

Silverblade addressed him. "What's the situation?"

"I've got three secured in the back. I got another one, too, but he's not going to be useful."

We followed Lionel around the corner to the cops who had brought me to the facility. Three of them were seated on the floor against the wall, blank eyes staring at nothing, and zip ties around their wrists and ankles. The fourth cop, the bull with the unfortunate mustache, was also propped against the wall, but he didn't need the ties. His eyes were closed, and his round, red face was bloated almost beyond recognition. Two sets of puncture wounds on the sides of his neck had spilled a surprising amount of blood down the front of his uniform. More blood smeared the floor where he'd been dragged to the wall.

Lionel pointed at the red-faced bull. "This one fired a couple of shots at me, but Ometeotl ate the bullets."

Silverblade scowled. "That's not all he ate. Madame Cuapa wanted them alive."

Lionel shrugged. "These three are still kicking. Or they would be if they were feeling better. They'll be dazed for a bit, but the Madame should be able to get something out of them."

Silverblade grunted. "Let's hope they've got something useful to tell her."

I turned from the cops to Silverblade. "Where's Bronzetooth?"

Silverblade stared down at me, his burning eyes as intense as lasers. "Who?"

"A troll, Anton Benning's man. He's the one who brought me here."

Silverblade's face relaxed. "Oh, him." He turned to Lionel.

Lionel stared back at Silverblade with a sheepish expression. "He got away from me. Sorry, boss. The snakes couldn't hold him."

Walks pointed. "I think he went that way."

We all turned to stare down the hall to the opening where an exit door had been pulled from its hinges and was lying on the floor.

I leaned in front of Walks and mouthed the word 'Counselor' so that only she could see it. After a moment of hesitation, she used her eyes to indicate a closed door halfway up the hallway.

"Stay here," I told her.

Turning toward Silverblade and Lionel, I held a finger against my lips and gestured toward the door Walks had pointed out to me. They followed me to the door, and I extended my awareness beyond it to the room inside. The flow of magical energy fought against my enhanced senses, but I was reasonably certain the room was empty. I tested the handle, and it wasn't locked.

I opened the door to what appeared to be a security station. A bank of monitors displayed areas inside and outside the facility. One of them showed the interrogation room. A chair sat in front of a microphone. I looked for a device that might be used to transform the Counselor's voice into something demonic and robotic, but I didn't see one. I suppressed a shudder, reminding myself that I barely knew how to turn on a computer or take a photo with a cell phone. The voice-distortion mechanism was probably built into the audio system. I mean, that metallic growl couldn't have been the Counselor's real voice, could it?

Silverblade and Lionel followed me into the room, and Lionel held the door open as Walks joined us. I turned to Walks. "The Counselor.... Tall? Thin as a reed? Bushy eyebrows and a nose like a beak?"

"Yes," Walks confirmed. "And he had two attendants with him."

The room pulsed with magical energy, and I traced the flow of vibrations to the back wall. Pointing at a section of it, I turned to the others. "The Counselor—that's the guy running this circus—got out through here. I'm guessing his associates left with him. He must have opened a portal, or someone did it for him. I can sense where it was...." I pounded the wall with the flat of my hand. "But it's not open."

Silverblade turned to Lionel. "Can Ometeotl open it?" Turning back to me, the troll explained, "That's how we got here. Your elemental led us in the right direction, and Ometeotl found the entrance to this... place... and opened it. It's right outside the facility, and your elemental let us know you were inside. There was some resistance, but we took care of it."

A hissing voice sounded near my ear. "Smokey finds Alex in place beyond the winds."

I looked up at Silverblade. "I take it this place is not a part of our world?"

The troll shrugged. "Beats me. It certainly seems otherworldly, but that's the Madame's department, not mine. We just followed your elemental. That was quite an experience, by the way. It's not an ideal navigator. It couldn't figure out why we couldn't drive where the wind blows. You need to teach it the rules of the road." He turned his gaze on Walks. "I'm surprised to see you here."

I spoke before Walks could respond. "The Counselor brought her here against her will to try to get me to cooperate." I locked eyes with Walks. "He thought that by threatening my friend, I'd agree to lure the elf into an ambush." I turned back to Silverblade. "We were in the middle of negotiations when you showed up. I take it that Smokey found Madame Cuapa at home?"

"Right. The elemental delivered your message to the Madame, and she sent for me. Then she sent us to go get you. Cody, too."

My eyes widened. "Cody's here?"

The troll's face hardened. "Yep. And he's not alone."

"Wait. You don't mean…?"

A thunderous roar shattered the oppressive atmosphere. I stared at Silverblade, whose face split into a broad smile that exposed the tips of his pointed teeth. "There was about a half dozen men guarding this place, and they opened fire on us as soon as we pulled in." He shook his head. "The poor bastards never had a chance."

"Where is he?" I asked.

"Cody?" Silverblade pointed toward the front of the facility with his chin. "He's out front in Madame Cuapa's bulletproof SUV. I told him to stay inside the vehicle. I'm sure he's fine."

Another roar tore through the thick air and into the building, followed by the crack of a rifle shot. I brushed past Silverblade, Smokey riding on my shoulder, and made my way to the hall. The others followed, with Lionel pushing Walks.

Cody was sitting behind the wheel of a new model SUV with extended passenger room. I expected the vehicle to be armored, but I saw no evidence of anything that would stop flying lead, unless it was the fist-sized crystals on the front and rear bumpers pulsing with a strange bronze-colored light. When Cody saw me emerging from the entryway, he waved and pointed over my head toward the roof of the building. I turned back and saw a large lion with eagle's wings circling above the rooftop, his scorpion tail trailing behind. A shot rang out, and the manticore dove toward the roof at a speed almost too fast to follow. When he rose again, it was with a struggling troll locked in his claws. The winged monster lifted himself high into the strange silver-gray sky, where he tossed the troll over his head and pierced him with a sudden thrust of his barbed tail. The troll let out a bloodcurdling scream, and the rifle flew from his hands in a long arc before falling to the driveway a few yards from the SUV. The manticore let the troll flail for a few more agonizing seconds, the point of the flying monster's tail deep in his victim's chest. He opened his lion's maw, let out a deafening roar, and snapped his tail like a whip, sending the troll speeding away from him to the ground below. The troll hit the driveway with a thud that told me no one would be putting the pieces back together again, even if they could somehow all be scraped off the pavement.

Poor Bronzetooth, I thought to myself. He'd really had himself one hell of a day.

Chapter Thirty-Two

I climbed into the front passenger seat, and Walks, Silverblade, and Lionel squeezed into the seat behind us. We put the three cops, still dazed, but conscious, into the far back seat of the SUV with Mr. Whiskers. The manticore lay across their laps, pressing them against the back of the seat with his massive body, and licked blood off his paws.

"He took a few bullets," Cody informed us, "but he'll be fine. They just made him mad."

I stared at the blood that had soaked into the fur surrounding the manticore's mouth. "He's calmed down now, though... right?"

Cody's lips spread into a wide smile. "Of course! I think he's about ready for a nap. Aren't you, boy?"

Mr. Whiskers raised his eyes briefly, gave his mane a vigorous shake, and resumed cleaning his claws.

Cody rolled his eyes. "He'll be asleep before we're halfway home."

I took a good look at Cody and shook my head. Nearly half a foot taller than me and broader in the shoulders, Cody was wearing a fur-collared camo vest open at the chest and fastened with a single clasp just below his navel. He wore matching jodhpurs, combat boots polished to within an inch of their lives, and black elbow-length driving gloves covered with silver sequins. His long black hair was tied back with a camo-patterned cloth that appeared to have been torn from a t-shirt. He looked like a character from a burlesque show, and somehow made it look good.

Cody noticed me looking and winked. "You like the outfit? I picked it up a couple of years ago, and I've been looking for an excuse to wear it ever since."

I pointed to the bronze crystal hanging over his exposed chest on a silver chain. "That thing work?"

"Not as well as the ones on the car. Those things will turn back rockets. But this baby baffles bullets."

"Baffles?"

"It confuses them. Makes them think I'm somewhere else. The Madame insisted I wear it today. For some reason she doesn't like the idea of me getting splattered by gunfire. It was either this or body armor, and stomping around in a bulky bulletproof vest isn't my style. Not that

I needed it. Silverblade insisted I stay in the car. At least I got to share in Mr. Whisker's fun."

I knew that Cody and his improbably named companion shared a mystic link that went beyond mere telepathy. "Did you feel it when he got shot?"

Cody grimaced and rubbed his stomach. "That part wasn't as fun. I should have let him wear the crystal."

After Ometeotl led us out of the portal and onto the streets of Yerba City, I told Silverblade to thank Madame Cuapa for me. "I'm still not sure why she is so keen on having you watch my back, but I'm grateful for your help. You and Lionel, both. Not to mention Cody and his pet monster."

"Hey!" Cody interrupted. "Careful with the 'p' word around Mr. Whiskers."

I glanced over my shoulder to find the manticore staring at me with cold eyes.

"Kidding," I said. "And I thought you were going to take a nap."

Mr. Whiskers yawned, showing off an impressive set of three-inch fangs sharp enough to pierce steel, and lowered his head to his paws.

Silverblade gave the beast a quick glance before turning to me. "The Madame hasn't confided in me, but I suspect she has some kind of history with this Counselor fellow."

Cody nodded. "She does, but I don't know all of the particulars. It goes back to before I took up my position in her household. I know that he's about as close to Lord Ketz-Alkwat as you can get. If he's calling himself Counselor, I think it's because he's one of the Dragon Lord's chief advisors."

I glanced at Walks, but she didn't meet my eyes.

Cody continued. "It looks to me like a turf battle. The Madame regards Yerba City as the heart of her territory. This Counselor is definitely a witch, and maybe something more. He serves spirits that are antithetical to the spirits the Madame serves. I know she's not happy about him being here."

Silverblade turned to Walks. "Did you talk to the Counselor after he took you?"

"They put a hood over her head before they drove her out to that place," I interjected. "Right, Walks?"

Walks glanced at me before answering. "That's right. And no one said much to me. Nothing useful. I was in the room with them when they were questioning Alex. I heard him tell Alex to call him Counselor. I got a look at him when they took my hood off before pushing me in to see Alex."

Silverblade frowned down at her. "How did they treat you? Did they hurt you?"

Walks glanced up at him with a look of defiance. "They were all perfect gentlemen. They even let me use the little girl's room when we got to the facility."

Nobody asked her for details.

I had Cody drop Walks and me off at Gio's to pick up the beastmobile. Walks kept quiet during the drive, and I headed off any attempt by Silverblade to question her. I don't know what Silverblade suspected, but I noticed he was careful not to say anything about the elf or to ask about the tape we'd all viewed in Walks's shop.

After the others had driven off, Walks looked up at me from her chair. "I haven't changed my mind, Alex. I'm still opposed to your elf's plans to take the world back from the Dragon Lords and send us back to a pre-civilized life harvesting wheat and sacrificing goats to our elf gods."

I wheeled her toward the beastmobile. "I think you're assuming way too much about the elf's plans, but I'll ask him about them next time I talk to him."

After I'd helped her into the car and taken my place behind the wheel, she turned to me. "What about us, Alex? Are we still good?"

I felt something hollow in the pit of my stomach. "Sure," I said.

"Are we? Be honest with me."

"Sure," I said. "We're still good."

We spent the long twenty-five-minute drive through heavy traffic back to her place in an uncomfortable silence, nor did we speak while I wheeled her into her shop. She didn't look at me as I pulled the door shut and walked back to my car.

***

Two days later, Detectives Kalama and Blu brought me to Bowman Hatfield's Galindo Estates residence, where we were ushered into the Old Man's den by Slaywood, the old troll I'd seen lighting the patriarch's cigarettes the last time I'd been there. "Mr. Hatfield will be down shortly," the aide informed us. He indicated the portable bar that had been wheeled into the room. "Feel free to pour yourself a drink while you wait." He paused by the door to switch on the ceiling fan before stepping out of the den to tend to the Old Man.

Fats, Benning, and Alu were gathered in the office, all holding glasses of shawnee whiskey. Alu hadn't touched his, I noted. He sat in a chair in the back of the room, his head covered with a black hood and mask and gripping his glass as if he feared it would slip from his hand to the polished hardwood floor. Fats was sprawled in an easy chair, a sour look on his puss. He glanced up at me as I entered and quickly looked away, as if the sight of me hurt his eyes. He started to take a drink, scowled, and lowered his glass. It was early in the afternoon, and I had the feeling he'd all too recently been dragged out of bed after tying one on the night before. His henchman, Dreadshadow, stood at his shoulder looking as if he would rather have been almost anywhere else. I knew how he felt. Benning sat in a thickly padded chair to the right of Old Man Bowman's empty rocker, studying the liquor swirling in his glass as if he were attempting to analyze its contents. A young troll I'd never met stood by Benning, scowling at the detectives and me as only a young troll can. He was wearing a suit that looked exactly like the one I'd last seen on Bronzetooth, and he didn't bother to hide the bulge of an enormous shoulder holster under his coat.

I felt the faint buzz of magical energy in the room, but I couldn't tell where it was coming from. Probably some bauble the Old Man had picked up from somewhere. Maybe something stashed inside one of the drawers of the mahogany wardrobe standing against the back wall of the den behind the Old Man's rocker.

The detectives turned down the offer of drinks, and, with some reluctance, I followed their lead. After we were seated, Fats gulped down the remainder of his shawnee and set the empty glass on a coaster. He turned to Kalama and Blu, pointedly ignoring me. "Pops will be down later, but I've got a few things I want to say. You know why you're here. We want to know what happened to Benning's man, Bronzetooth. Your department has been investigating, but we haven't heard jack shit out of you. Bronzetooth was a good man. We want some fuckin' answers." He nodded at me with his chin without taking his eyes off the detectives. "If this ugly lug bumped him off, I want to know about it."

Kalama stared at Fats with a blank expression. "You think Southerland murdered him?" she asked after a beat.

"He looks like someone who might have tangled with a troll," Fats noted.

My right foot was covered in tape that extended above my shoe, and both my arms were in slings. Turns out that Cougar did nearly as much damage to me as he and I did to Bronzetooth, and even with my augmented powers of healing, my recovery was taking longer than I'd hoped it would.

The hint of a smile appeared on Kalama's lips. "Does he look like someone who won?"

Fats raised his voice a notch. "Never mind what I think! You mugs investigated the scene, right? I assume you've got a few people on your force who can find their ass with both hands—so what the fuck did you find out?"

Kalama shrugged. "Nothing. On of our witches got us through the dimensional barrier, but the place was clean. We figure he got away."

From across the room, Benning scoffed. "That's ridiculous. If he got away, then why hasn't he contacted me?"

Kalama turned to him with the same blank stare she'd given Fats. "I don't know, Mr. Benning. Sounds like an employee relations problem to me."

Benning's eyes narrowed, but he took a sip of his whiskey rather than respond to the taunt.

Kalama resumed speaking. "Mr. Southerland claims he was kidnapped by Bronzetooth and four Yerba City policemen. He further claims that these policemen are on your pad, Mr. Benning, and that you directed their actions. My captain is disturbed by this accusation. He wants to know if it's true."

Benning snorted. "Of course it's not true. He's lying."

I assumed Benning meant me. "Then why were those cops taking their orders from your man Bronzetooth?" I asked.

Benning looked at me down his nose. "We only have your word that Bronzetooth was there."

I raised my eyebrows. "Oh? Then why does Fats think I murdered him?"

Benning dismissed me with his eyes. "Mr. Hatfield is just blustering. Isn't that right, Fats?"

Fats turned from Benning to me and back again. "I have no idea what's going on. But somebody around here better start making sense, and fast!"

"Sounds like I got here just in time."

We all turned to see Bowman Hatfield standing at the open doorway, Slaywood at his back. The old patriarch's face was pale, and a cigarette dangled from his scowling lips. "Seems like Ferrell jumped the gun and started this meeting without me. And now he's confused. Wants someone to start making sense."

Fats wiped his mouth with the back of his sleeve. "Pops, I..."

The Old Man held up the palm of his hand to cut him off. "Not another word until I get a drink." He shuffled across the room to his overstuffed rocker while Slaywood poured him a glass of shawnee from a fresh bottle. After he'd had a sip, he scanned the room, making eye contact with everyone in it. "I see the city's finest are here. Good afternoon, Detective Kalama. Detective Blu. You've brought Mr. Southerland, the man I hired to investigate the death of my late daughter-in-law." He turned to speak directly to me. "Mr. Southerland, Anton assured me that you finished our job to everyone's satisfaction, but that apparently isn't true. Now Anton's bodyguard is missing. My son Ferrell believes that you murdered him for some reason. Anton isn't convinced that he's dead. Everyone is very upset. It would please me if you could, in the presence of these two fine homicide detectives, shed some light on this situation."

That sounded like my cue. "It's simple, Mr. Hatfield. Benning here is working for Lord Ketz. His contact is a man named Alejandro Ochoa, a member of the Dragon Lord's Sovereign Court, which isn't so much a court as Lord Ketz's private tribunal. The tribunal's job is to eliminate threats to the Realm, and they have a lot of latitude in how they define those threats. Benning has been feeding Counselor Ochoa a steady stream of information about the project you've been working on with the elf."

Bowman's eyes narrowed at me as he lifted his cigarette to his lips and dragged on it, hard, reducing the tip to an inch-long column of ash.

It took a second or two longer for Fats to process what I'd said. When he did, he jumped to his feet so suddenly that he nearly toppled his chair. "Alkwat's flaming pecker! Th'fuck you trying to pull, Southerland!" He winced and rubbed the back of his upper thigh.

Bowman turned to him, visibly annoyed. "Sit down, Ferrell, before you hurt yourself." Fats glared briefly at his father before lowering himself carefully into his seat.

Benning played it cool, I'll give him that. I had no doubt he was anticipating my revelation. He waved his glass in a dismissive gesture and spoke in an even tone. "That's an outrageous accusation. I have no idea what you're talking about."

I went on as if I hadn't been interrupted, speaking directly to the Old Man. "The elf's project is part of a conspiracy to overthrow the Dragon Lord. I'm sure you already know that. Benning has been working to undermine your operation."

Fats waved me off with a sneer. "That's bullshit. Anton has been running our side of that operation from the beginning and giving the elf his complete cooperation."

I spared Fats a sidelong glance. "I'm not saying otherwise. But he's been letting Counselor Ochoa know all about the operation's progress. I don't know if it started that way." I turned to the fixer. "How about it, Benning? Were you betraying the project from the beginning, or did the Counselor recruit you after it was underway?"

Benning fingered the carnation in his lapel and did his best to look bored. It was a look he'd perfected, and I might have been convinced by it if I hadn't known better. "It's your story, Southerland. Go ahead and tell it."

I turned back to Bowman, who was slowly sipping his drink and listening intently. I leaned forward in my seat and rested my elbows on the arms of the chair to take the pressure off my shoulders. "One of the engineers in your operation, a young man named Petros Papadopouli was having an affair with Alu's wife. He was quite smitten with her. She thought of him as a pet. She called him her 'Puppy.'" I glanced at Alu, whose eyes were fixed on the floor in front of his feet, his masked face unreadable. Turning back to Bowman, I said, "Sometime before the fire that burned down your warehouse, Papadopouli filmed an elf woman giving birth to triplets. It was the first elf birth in five thousand years. That's been the goal of the elf's project, to increase the fertility of elf women so that the elves could repopulate. That's a necessary prelude to any kind of action against the Dragon Lord, and the project was created to facilitate that end."

Bowman kept his eyes locked with mine but didn't speak.

I went on. "It bothered me that Papadopouli was able to find out where the birth was taking place, and that he was able to plant a surveillance device, a device that escaped the attention of all the elves in the room. A smart engineer like Papadopouli might have been able to come up with the device, but how did he know where to plant it, and when? I think someone fed him that information, someone high enough up in the operation to know when and where the birth would take place. It wasn't the elf. It certainly wasn't you. It wasn't Coleridge. I don't believe for a second that it was Fats, and Alu wasn't part of the operation. That only leaves one person. Benning."

Fats waved an arm in dismissal. "Alkwat's balls. That's bullshit," he declared, but the Old Man took another drag from his cigarette and said nothing.

Benning lifted his glass in my direction. "Cheers, Mr. Southerland. You have quite the imagination. But we have smart people working on our project. While we kept the goals of our operation as quiet as we could, they all knew from the very beginning that we were working with material associated with birth and fertility. Many of them deduced that the basic genetic material they were working with came from elves, even though elves are 'officially' extinct. The fact that we were working with an actual living elf was an open secret. The elf visited the facility on occasion, hooded, to be sure, but a hood isn't much of a disguise. As for Papadopouli, he wasn't just some engineer; he headed up all of our data processing operations. He, therefore, had access to an enormous amount of information. It wouldn't have been hard for him to deduce when and where the birth of the elf triplets was to take place. He didn't need me or anyone else to provide him with this information. Your conclusions are quite flawed, my dear boy, and you're wasting our time."

"Mr. Hatfield seems interested." I turned back to the Old Man. "Shall I continue?"

He blew smoke in my direction, and I took it as an affirmative.

"Benning wanted the video for Counselor Ochoa. I'm not sure how he convinced Papadopouli to get it for him. Maybe he paid him. Papadopouli would have wanted the money to make himself more attractive to Mrs. Hatfield. Maybe he threatened him or intimidated him. Maybe he simply told him to do it. After all, Benning was his boss. Maybe it was something Papadopouli wanted to do. In the end, it doesn't really matter. The important point is that Papadopouli made the video and gave it to Benning, who passed it on to Ochoa. But he also made a copy for himself, and I don't think Benning knew about that. Maybe he used it to impress Mrs. Hatfield. Maybe he had doubts about what he had done. In any case, Coleridge found out that Papadopouli was in possession of something he shouldn't've had, and she told Benning about it. Benning was there when Coleridge had Papadopouli brought to her office, and she released him to Benning at his request. That was the last she or anyone at the lab saw of Papadopouli until he showed up at the warehouse the night of the fire."

Fats sniffed and scowled. "How much longer are we going to sit here and listen to this crap?"

Bowman stopped him with a glare. "Mouth closed, Ferrell. Ears open. How many times I gotta tell you?"

Fats slumped in his chair, his face flushed. He gave me a look that told me I was a dead man as soon as he thought he could get away with it.

I turned away from him and spoke directly to his father. "After Ochoa saw the video, he told Benning to stop the operation at all costs. Either Ochoa or Benning made the decision that the elf had to go, and Benning needed to do it in a way that wouldn't draw attention to the fact that he was working against your family's interests. So he decided to use Papadopouli to eliminate the elf. The two of them had some talks, and Benning convinced him that the elf needed to be killed. I don't think it took much persuading. My guess is that Papadopouli was already horrified by the idea of a living elf. Most people would be. So Papadopouli built a bomb." I was speculating now, but I knew what I was saying had to be close to the truth. "Killing an elf isn't easy," I continued, "but a grease bomb would do the job. A clever engineer like Papadopouli would have no problem making one out of easy-to-acquire materials. The trick would be to get the elf within range."

I paused to make sure I had everyone's attention. Even Fats was listening. Seated apart from everyone else, Alu was leaning forward in his chair, his full glass clutched in his hand.

I turned to Benning. "I had a talk with the elf last night. He came to me in my dreams. It's... well, let's just say it's a thing he does with certain people. He told me that on the night of the fire, he was on his way to the warehouse to deactivate the hidden door to the lab. The lab had been moved and was empty, but the door was still enchanted, and the elf didn't think leaving loose magical energy floating around in a working warehouse was a good idea."

Everyone was now staring at Benning. He saw us all looking and shrugged. "I assume there's some point to this story?"

"I'm getting there," I told him. "It's important that I properly set the scene in order to avoid a lot of unnecessary questions. Now, where was I.... Right." I turned to speak directly to Benning. "When the lab was being moved, the elf was busy with his own affairs. He didn't supervise the move himself; he left that to you. Then, when he had the chance, he contacted you to find out whether the move was complete. When you told him it was, and that the lab was abandoned, he told you that he was going to go to the warehouse and lift the enchantment from the hidden door. That was the opportunity you'd been waiting for."

I kept my eyes locked on Benning's, reading his face. I was about seventy-five percent sure I knew what I was talking about, and I knew I needed to proceed carefully. "You made sure the elf knew that the back entrance to the lab, the one accessible from the tunnel, was locked from the inside, and that he'd have to go through the warehouse to get to the door. You suggested that he wait until the warehouse workers had cleared out for the day to avoid being seen by anyone and having to answer inconvenient questions. He agreed and told you he'd go the next evening when everything in the warehouse was supposed to be moved out. You called Papadopouli and arranged for him to set up the bomb in the warehouse and ambush the elf when he showed up. Papadopouli didn't have a key to the warehouse. I'm guessing you must have given him one at some point, probably when you were convincing him that elves were an abomination, and that he should build a bomb to take one out."

I cast my eyes about the den, checking the expressions and listening to the breathing of everyone in the room, before focusing on Bowman. "Everything went wrong when your son's wife found out what Papadopouli was up to and went to the warehouse to try to stop him. Benning didn't know that Coleridge was going to be in the abandoned lab that night doing some last-minute cleanup. Coleridge spotted Mrs. Hatfield in the warehouse on her security monitor and had her brought into the lab. For some reason, Papadopouli's bomb went off before it was supposed to, and Papadopouli was caught in the blast. The engineer was strictly an amateur when it came to making bombs, and he must have triggered it somehow without intending to. At any rate, Mrs. Hatfield saw Papadopouli on the floor, helpless, in the middle of the fire. He'd probably been killed instantly, but Mrs. Hatfield didn't know that, and she was out of her mind. She ran past Coleridge and her security team into the warehouse to try to save her Puppy." I shook my head. "She ran straight into the heart of an inferno. Poor dame never had a chance."

Benning chuckled and shook his head. "Oh, Mr. Southerland. Really. Your mind really does work in strange ways. But your story is pure fantasy. There was no bomb, and Papadopouli didn't die in the fire. As I explained to you before, Mrs. Hatfield came to the warehouse and accidentally caused the fire herself. This story you say you heard from Coleridge is pure nonsense. Where is she? Can you produce her to verify your version of what happened? No? I didn't think so." He grinned a satisfied grin and raised his glass to his lips for a delicate sip.

I, of course, couldn't produce Coleridge, and I wondered if anyone would ever be able to. But I had something else up my sleeve, or, to be more precise, in my sling. I produced a strip of melted plastic and stepped carefully out of my chair to place it on the table next to Bowman's rocker.

Bowman glanced up at me. "What's this?"

I limped back to my chair before replying to the Old Man. "It's what's left of a pocket protector. I took it from the rubble in the warehouse near the spot where the grease bomb went off. The strip was melted in the fire, but if you look carefully, you can see the monogrammed 'PP' for Petros Papadopouli. It matches an intact pocket protector that I found in his office when I searched the abandoned lab a few days ago."

Bowman looked up from the strip. "What's it supposed to mean?"

I pointed at the strip. "That proves that Papadopouli died in the fire."

I sat back and waited for a reaction, and for several moments I was met by nothing but silence. But I felt something in the room that I couldn't fully describe. It was as if a faint, chill mist had descended into the den, cooling and thickening the air. On impulse, I turned to glance at Alu, who was staring at the glass in his hand with narrowed eyes.

Finally, Bowman crushed out his cigarette in an ashtray and broke the silence. "That's a fascinating story, Mr. Southerland, and it appears that our detectives are already familiar with it. I'm thinking they came here with the intention of taking Anton into custody and charging him with conspiracy to commit murder. Although if you're thinking of using this piece of trash as evidence..." he indicated the plastic strip, "I don't think your case has a chance of standing up in a court of law. This thing tells us nothing. For all I know, you picked it out of a garbage can on your way here."

Kalama jumped in. "We're not convinced of anything yet, and we didn't come here to arrest anybody, Mr. Hatfield. We wanted to be here when Southerland told his story and then maybe ask a question or two. It's all part of our investigation."

Bowman whirled on her. "And now he's had his say. He's accused Anton, a man I love like a son, of betraying my family and of being responsible for the death of my youngest son's wife. He offers up a crazy story and a piece of plastic as proof. This might be the flimsiest attempt at a frame-up I've ever heard in my life."

He lifted a hand, and his aide handed him a fresh cigarette. We all waited in silence while he took his time lighting it and puffing it to life. After placing the pill in a slot on his ashtray to smolder, he turned in my direction. "Young man, you need to quit wasting my time. What I want to know is what Alu's wife's death has to do with the disappearance of Anton's bodyguard. Is he still alive? If he isn't, how did he die? Did you kill him? These are the answers I'm looking for. This is why I allowed you and the detectives to come to me today. But instead of giving me what I want, you've chosen to distract me with a lot of fancy yappin' and a big, steaming pile of bullshit. I find it insulting. I find it disrespectful."

He pounded the arm of his rocker with the flat of his hand and leaned forward, fixing me with a stare. "So I'll tell you what I'm going to do, you lying son of a bitch. I'm going to give you thirty seconds to tell me why I shouldn't have these detectives carry you out of my office on a fuckin' stretcher with a sheet pulled over your face, and the clock starts now."

Chapter Thirty-Three

Bowman had given me thirty seconds, and I let ten of them pass in silence before giving the Old Man a reply. "Mr. Hatfield, you say I have treated you disrespectfully, and I ask your pardon. I felt it was necessary to put things in their proper context. I'm afraid you aren't going to like what I tell you next, and I apologize in advance." I paused for a second, aware of a growing chill filling the room, before resuming. "One of the cops who helped Bronzetooth take me to Counselor Ochoa's compound is dead. The other three have spent the past couple of days with Madame Cuapa, enjoying her hospitality and singing like canaries."

Bowman's eyes widened, and Benning gulped down the remainder of his whiskey. I suppressed a grin and pressed forward. "It seems that Benning couldn't help talking about himself and his plans to Bronzetooth, and, from time to time, Bronzetooth liked to have a few drinks and share stories about Benning with his cop friends. The Madame will be more than happy to confirm that Benning is firmly in the Counselor's pocket, and that he's been betraying your family for some time now. He doesn't much like this partnership you negotiated with the elf. I can't blame him for that. Like most people, he was raised to believe that elves had been horrible bloodsucking monsters, and that they'd been hunted to extinction after the Great Rebellion. It was quite a shock for him when he discovered that, not only were they still around, but that the family had entered into a deal with one."

The air in the room continued to cool. Other people in the room were beginning to glance at the spinning blades of the ceiling fan, and as I was making my case to Bowman, Slaywood crossed the room to the bank of switches on the wall and turned the fan off. I edged forward in my seat to get closer to Bowman before continuing. "Benning allowed himself to be persuaded by Ochoa because he thinks you're a sick man, and that you don't have a lot of time left. He believes that Fats is an imbecile, and that Alu is worthless. It's only a matter of time, he thinks, before he gets them out of the way, and he'll be the one in the driver's seat. Counselor Ochoa has assured him that once he's in control of the syndicate, he won't have to worry about elves, and he can run things as he sees fit. His attempt to use Papadopouli to kill the elf with a grease bomb failed, and it resulted in the deaths of not only Papadopouli, but

Mrs. Hatfield, as well. He's desperate now. Counselor Ochoa is in the city, watching him. Helping him, too, I would think. I think you can expect Benning to make his next move soon."

Benning shook his head and turned to the Old Man. "He's lying. This is nothing but a transparent and, quite frankly, pathetic attempt to turn us against each other in order to save his own skin."

"I'm just telling you what those cops on your payroll told Madame Cuapa, and drawing a few logical conclusions," I said. "You can bet the farm that those cops gave the Madame the straight scoop. She has ways of getting people to tell her the truth. Of course, we only have her word for what they told her. The cops themselves seem to have disappeared. But if you think I'm lying, you can always ask the Madame herself for verification."

Old Man Bowman's hand shook as he lifted his cigarette to his lips, but Benning leaned back in his chair and crossed his ankle over his knee. "I'm not afraid of Madame Cuapa," he declared, a defiant smile on his face.

Bowman turned to face Benning. "Why not, Anton? Why aren't you afraid of the Barbary Coast Bruja? I certainly am. Any man with sense would be. The Madame is a most fearsome individual. And yet you claim that you do not fear her. Why is that, Anton? Is it because you believe that you are protected from her? And who is it that would be capable of offering you such protection?"

Benning's smile cracked. "Bowman, no. I..."

I cut him off. "He thinks Counselor Ochoa will protect him. And not just from Madame Cuapa, but from you and your sons, too."

Bowman dropped his cigarette into the ashtray. "Is this true, Anton? Has he been telling the truth after all? Will the Madame confirm his story? Have you been betraying the family? Did you put that engineer up to making a clumsy attempt on the elf's life, an attempt that resulted in the death of Alu's wife?"

The temperature in the den had dropped at least twenty degrees, but I'm not sure anyone had noticed. Benning turned and scanned the eyes in the room before returning his attention to Bowman. "Turned my back on the family?" His urbane face twisted into an expression of pure hatred, and he spat on the floor at his feet. "You betrayed your family when you sold yourself out to that prehistoric demon! You used to be a great man, Bowman, but that was long ago. You're past it, 'Old Man.' You should have done your family a favor and died years ago. It's too bad the heirs to your legacy are unworthy louts. Fortunately, that's a problem we can take care of right now."

Everything happened at once. Before I could blink, Benning's young troll pulled an automatic rifle out of his coat and opened fire on Fats and Dreadshadow. I sensed movement from beside me and heard the crack of gunfire. I turned to see Detective Blu dishing out lead in the direction of Benning and his troll. A burst of magical energy punched me in the face, loosening my teeth. Benning slammed back into his chair, and the troll staggered backwards a step, bumping into the wardrobe with a thud, before turning his rifle in Blu's direction. As he fired, Blu disappeared. Bullets shredded the chair where he'd been sitting, and four bulldogs sprang away from it in all directions. The detective's pistol fell to the floor.

Old Man Bowman rose to his feet. He opened his mouth to say something, but Benning, still alive, calmly took a gat from the inside of his coat and shot the astonished patriarch in the chest. The Old Man collapsed to the floor in front of his rocker. Benning turned and shot Slaywood through both eyes. The old troll was dead before he'd realized what was happening.

Kalama was on the floor, pistol in hand. I tore off my slings and scooped up Blu's heater. I tried to stand... and promptly found myself flat on my face, pain shooting from my taped foot all the way up the length of my leg. Three wild dogs launched themselves at the troll from three sides, while one sank his teeth into Benning's forearm, causing the duplicitous fixer to scream and drop his gun. Blood streamed down his arm.

I happened to catch a quick glance at Alu, still seated in the back of the room, his glass—now covered with frost—clutched in his hand. He was staring at the glass, wide-eyed, and I thought I knew what he was seeing on the surface of his untouched drink. I also thought I knew what he might be hearing.

My attention was ripped away from Alu as Kalama fired off a round, whether at the troll or at Benning I couldn't tell. The burst of magic I'd felt earlier slapped me upside the head again, and Kalama's shot either missed or had no effect. The troll's rifle went off as he struggled with three fighting dogs, all hanging from him by jaws powerful enough to snap two-by-fours, and I pushed myself away across the hardwood floor, trying to at least make myself a moving target.

A bright light caught my attention, and I looked up to see a flare shoot from the tip of Bowman's cigarette. In the next instant, the mahogany wardrobe at the back of the room was engulfed by orange and red flames. A bulldog leaped from the floor and crashed into Benning's chest, sending him tumbling into the blaze. Benning screamed and fell to his knees, flames racing up the back of his suit.

Benning's henchman had succeeded in freeing himself from the other three dogs and was raising his rifle. I drew a bead with Blu's pistol and sent a lead pill flying at the troll. His head snapped back, and magical energy once again kicked me in the face. As the barrel of his rifle swung in my direction, four snarling dogs launched a savage attack on the troll, causing his shots to go wild.

I rolled away until I'd bumped into the wall. A monotone robotic voice sounded from the other side of the room: "Get back!"

I turned and saw Alu—Al the Torch—striding purposefully across the room. He pointed at the troll, and with the electrolarynx pressed against his throat, he forced out a single word: "Burn!" He dropped the device to the floor and continued stepping toward the troll.

Fire shot from the blazing wardrobe and latched onto the troll's suit jacket. As the dogs leaped away, flames covered the troll from head to foot.

"Southerland?"

I turned to see Kalama lying in a pool of blood.

"Laurel! Are you okay?" I crawled toward her, my foot and shoulders throbbing with pain.

Blu appeared, wearing nothing except his bullet-riddled trench coat. I shouted, "Blu! Kalama's been hit!" But Blu was already scooping his partner up from the floor and heading for the door. With flames springing up throughout the room, I rose to my feet and staggered after the detectives, wincing with every step on my bad foot. At the doorway, I turned and called, "Alu!"

Across the room, Alu was locked into an embrace with the troll, fire raging all around them. Floating over their heads, barely visible in the billowing smoke, a familiar face gazed down at Alu, her strawberry-blond hair blowing free in a wind that didn't touch the room we were in, her eyes nothing but empty wells of darkness. "Alu!" I shouted again. A wall of fire rose in front of me, cutting off my view of the room, and I either saw or imagined scowling faces in the flickering flames. Heat raked at my face, and tears flooded my eyes, blurring my vision.

Blu called back to me, "Time to go, Suddalund!"

"Alu!" I shouted again. But Blu was right. The room was obscured by fire, and I felt my face blistering in the heat escaping through the door. I turned and fled from the flames.

***

"She's going to be okay," said the paramedic, closing the ambulance door. "She caught a bullet in the spleen, causing it to rupture. There was some internal bleeding. But the doctor sealed the rupture with a spell that will hold until we can get her to the operating table. She didn't lose more blood than she can handle, and we're pumping more into her now. We're about ready to move, but we'll keep the department informed of her condition."

After the ambulance had carried Kalama off, Blu and I watched Old Man Hatfield's three-story mansion finish burning to the ground. Firefighters had been helpless in the face of the inferno. One of them told me that all fires have a personality, and this one had sent a clear message: "Back off, motherfuckers, and let me burn."

The firefighters took credit for preventing the spread of the flames beyond the structure of the house itself, although the fireman I spoke with was forced to admit how odd it had been that none of the dry foliage surrounding the mansion had been so much as scorched. "It's like the fire set its own boundaries," he said.

While the house was burning, Blu, still wearing nothing but a trench coat and a gun, handed me two black stones, each affixed to silver chains with torn fasteners. "Found these around their necks," he said in a voice like gravel.

"Benning and the troll?" I asked, and he nodded.

I examined the necklaces, clenching my jaw against the vibration rising from the stones to rattle my teeth. The stones reminded me of the crystal Cody had worn around his neck at the Counselor's compound, except these were black, heavy, and smooth. "What is this, lead?" I mused out loud.

"Tastes like iron," Blu said. He took the necklaces from my hands. "Evidence."

I gazed back at the dying flames. "Think you'll be able to recover any bodies from there?"

Blu sniffed loudly, hawked phlegm from his throat, and sent it splattering to the street.

Two days later, Blu and I visited Kalama in the hospital.

"Doc says you'll be out of here in a week," I told her.

"I'll be out of here tomorrow," she corrected me. "Kai has arranged for an intern to teach his classes for a while, and he can fuss over me until I'm ready to go back to work. Nalani wanted to come up from Aztlan, but I convinced her to stay put. She's in a competitive program at the university there, and she can't afford to fall behind. Besides, she's got a new boyfriend who wanted to come with her, and I'm not going to let him meet her mother for the first time while I'm laid up like this. I told her it was just a flesh wound, and that I'd be fine."

"A flesh wound in the spleen," I said.

"Spleens are flesh," she countered.

I opened my mouth, closed it, and shook my head.

"Oh, relax," Kalama said. "They told me the operation was a success. They had to remove the spleen, but I can live without it. I just have to take a bunch of antibiotics and regular doses of a potion that tastes like citrus-flavored shit. Anyway, I'm on a waiting list for a new one, and they're threatening to fast-track me because I'm in law enforcement. I told them not to, but they insisted, so I might be getting it soon. Hell, it will probably be an improvement."

We shared an uncomfortable silence for a few moments before Kalama looked up at me. "Was it my imagination, or did the temperature in that room drop to near freezing before everyone started shooting each other?"

I suppressed a smile. "I wasn't sure anyone had noticed."

The detective continued to stare at me. "That plastic strip you say you found in the warehouse…. Even if belonged to Papadopouli, it was useless as evidence. Bowman was right. It was nothing but garbage."

"Maybe so, but it really did belong to Papadopouli, and he was wearing it when his bomb went off."

Kalama nodded slowly. "I've heard that ghosts are attracted to personal possessions that meant something to them when they were alive."

I allowed myself to smile. "I've heard that, too. When Madame Cuapa was filling me in on what she'd learned from those rogue cops, I showed her that piece of plastic. She whipped something up and smeared it over the strip. According to her, objects contain…, I'm not sure how to explain it…, let's call it pieces of the personality of individuals that own them. Clothing you wear a lot soaks up bits of your essence. Or something like that. The Madame explained it to me a lot better than that. Anyway, the stuff she smeared on the plastic enhanced the essence of Papadopouli that it had soaked up and kind of broadcast it."

"Making it a beacon for Cindy Hatfield's ghost to follow."

I removed my hat and scratched my head. "I wasn't sure it would work. But then the room started to get cold."

Kalama shot a glance at Blu before turning back to me. "Wow. I figured you were up to something, but that sounds like a real longshot. You walked into a nest of dangerous vipers with a ghost bomb?"

"I figured it would be more effective than a gun, given my condition."

Kalama closed her eyes and shook her head. "How are you still alive, gumshoe?"

"Good clean living, I guess. Anyway, I wasn't planning on using the pocket protector as a weapon. I needed Cindy to understand who was behind her death."

Kalama opened her eyes. "Benning."

"Right. But things got interesting when she showed herself to Alu. She appeared in his drink, of all things. I don't know what she said to him, but it brought him to his feet."

"And nearly got us all killed! You think Alu got out of there?"

I nodded toward Blu. "You want to tell her?"

Blu shrugged and stared out the window. I let out a chuckle. "Your loquacious partner gave me the summary earlier, and I think he's all talked out. Anyway, they found the toasted remains of five people in the ruins: three humans and two trolls, all burned beyond recognition."

Kalama looked up at me. "Three humans and two trolls? That's all?"

"Right. I'm thinking Old Man Bowman, Fats, Benning, Dreadshadow, and Slaywood, the Old Man's aide."

"But not Alu?"

"He knows his way around a fire. Especially one he set and controlled with elementals."

Kalama gave that some thought. "And Benning's troll?"

I scowled. "I saw him go up in flames. But there was more to him than it appears. I think he was one of Counselor Ochoa's men, and that he had some extra protection. Blu pulled charms off both him and Benning, and your lab analysts say they obliterate flying bullets. Pretty handy. I'm thinking of getting one for myself. Unfortunately, they cost more than I make in a year."

"Hmm. That explains why bullets didn't stop them. But Benning died in the fire, right?"

"Yep. His charm only stopped bullets, not flames. And your partner drew plenty of blood with his teeth. I think his troll must have been armored with other forms of protection besides the one Blu ripped off his neck."

"Lord's balls! You think he got away?" Kalama asked.

"Looks like a good bet," I said. "Like I said, they only found the bodies of two trolls, and there's no chance that Dreadshadow or Slaywood survived."

I heard a snort and turned to look at Blu. "What?" I asked.

"Work."

I frowned. "Huh?"

Kalama started to laugh and then stopped, reaching for her side. "Blu's had enough of this sewing circle. When Kai was here earlier, he told me that gang wars are breaking out around the city. Some of the nurses are afraid to go home. Blu wants to get back on the street and shoot some bad guys."

I gave Kalama a tight smile. "The Hatfields are done, and a lot of mugs are out there trying to fill the vacuum. Those streets are going to be busy for a good while until things settle down."

"All the more reason for me to get out of this hospital and back on the job," Kalama said, grimacing as she clutched her side.

"You all right?" I asked. "You need a nurse?"

"Shut up. All I need is my husband and a decent cup of coffee. The swill they serve here tastes like horse piss."

Chapter Thirty-Four

"... in the latest episode of gang violence sweeping through Yerba City in the aftermath of the fire at the Hatfield estate, which took the lives of family patriarch Bowman Hatfield, his son Ferrell "Fats" Hatfield, and family attorney Anton Benning, who also represents Yerba City Mayor Montavious Harvey. Mayor Harvey could not be reached for comment, but a spokesperson for the mayor indicated that Harvey would deliver a statement condemning the violence on Saturday during the funeral of his good friend, Mr. Benning.

"In other news—and hang on to your hats, folks, because this is a wild one—a video claiming to show a female elf—that's right, I said '*elf!*'— giving birth to *triplets* is gaining traction throughout the Inter-Realm Web. Government officials have been quick to denounce the video as a hoax, but that hasn't stopped it from trending on all of the most popular social media sites. And get this, folks: many are claiming that this alleged birth of the three 'elf kittens,' as they are being called, took place at an unknown location in our own Yerba City! Lord Ketz-Alkwat's public media office released a statement today saying, in part, quote: 'While elves certainly dominated this planet prior to the advent of the Dragon Lords, they were rendered extinct in the aftermath of the Great Rebellion more than six thousand years ago. Let's be clear: all responsible authorities agree that no elves are alive today. They are as dead as dinosaurs and dodo birds.' Unquote. The Bureau of Internet Safety is urging all users of the internet to report appearances of this video to site managers to facilitate its removal. So there you have it, folks. Whatever you do, don't go searching the Inter-Realm Web for this video. That would be against the policy of your government. Although... I'm told the 'elf kittens' are cute as the dickens.

"This has been Chet Sugarman for KYRB News. It's seven o'clock."

I clicked the radio off. I'd seen the video earlier that morning, and it was the same one I'd seen in Walks in Cloud's shop. I called Lubank as soon as the video was finished. He denied having anything to do with leaking it.

"Lord's balls, peeper!" he exclaimed when I asked him about it. "Of course I didn't release that video. Th'fuck you saying? I never even saw it before this morning when it hit the web. And neither did you."

***

The elf entered my dreams during the night.

"I see you haven't closed communications with me," he said in his spellbinding voice. "That is very good, very good indeed."

"I still don't know how," I said, either out loud or in my mind. I wasn't sure, and I didn't think it mattered.

"It's not hard to do. Have you tried?"

"Not really," I admitted.

The elf smiled, and all at once we were standing on the old Placid Point Pier, watching the gentle swell of the waves as they passed beneath the pier to the shore.

After a while, he spoke. "I have been forced to end my activities in Yerba City. Without the aid of the Hatfield Syndicate, I cannot operate there with sufficient security. Your actions have set me back a bit."

"Are you expecting an apology?"

The elf laughed. "Of course not. You acted according to your nature. I find no fault in your actions. In fact, I anticipated them. I've relocated the center of my operation to Angel City, where I've entered into an arrangement with an organization of considerable sway. You're familiar with them, I believe—the Claymore Cartel?"

I snorted. "You're kidding. First the Hatfield Syndicate, and now the biggest outlaw gang on the West Coast? What is it with you and criminal gangs?"

"I find that groups on the fringes of human society are best suited for my purposes. It is, after all, a criminal activity that I am engaged in, is it not? What could be more criminal in a world ruled by Dragon Lords than a conspiracy to dethrone them?"

"You've got a point," I conceded.

"I've engaged a member of my Yerba City operation to smooth the transition, one already adept at working with the substances that are essential to my immediate goals."

I turned my head and stared into his hood, searching for his eyes. "Wait. You aren't talking about Tom Kintay, are you?"

The elf chuckled. "Indeed I am. He is a most interesting human."

"He thinks you're an alien from outer space!"

"He may believe what he wishes. His mind is quite clever. Much of the progress I have made is due in no small part to his creative approach to alchemy."

I stared at the elf. "You know he's using those cloned stem cells to manufacture recreational drugs, don't you?"

"Of course! Those efforts have led him to devise ingenious solutions to the problems I've given him to solve. I daresay he knows more about the potential effects of cloned stem cells than anyone currently alive in this world."

I shook my head. Unbelievable.

"That reminds me," I said. "If you're looking for a couple of experienced heavies to help keep Kintay and the other thugs in your operation in line, Coleridge's old security goons, Blazearrow and Quarrelmace are looking for work, and they're already familiar with your project. You might want to give them a call. Just make sure Coleridge isn't part of the package. If she's still alive, that is. The two trolls are done with her."

"Thank you," the elf said. "I will take you up on your suggestion."

After a time, during which I almost lost myself in the rhythm of the rolling waves, the elf asked. "Did you get the justice you were seeking?"

"I think I did," I said. "The man behind Cindy's death paid for his crimes."

"Ah, I see. Anton Benning, you mean. But what about the man at his back, pulling his strings?"

"You mean Counselor Ochoa?"

"Indeed. You have held Anton Benning responsible for Mrs. Hatfield's death. But wouldn't she still be alive if Counselor Ochoa hadn't recruited Mr. Benning and pushed him to put an end to my plans by having me killed? Mr. Benning is dead, but isn't Counselor Ochoa the man who initiated the chain of events that led to poor Mrs. Hatfield's untimely death? And yet, he remains free from the consequences of his actions."

I had no answer for that.

But the elf wasn't done. "And yet, it doesn't end there, does it. Counselor Ochoa was acting on behalf of Lord Ketz-Alkwat, which means that the Dragon Lord himself stands at the beginning of that lethal chain. Surely, justice is not achieved until the Dragon Lord has been made to pay."

I watched the waves and pulled my coat close around me as a cool gust of wind blew in from over the water.

"One could even argue," the elf continued, "that I myself am to blame. It is because I conspire against Lord Ketz-Alkwat that the Dragon Lord sent Counselor Ochoa to Yerba City in the first place. If it weren't for me, it's very possible that Mrs. Hatfield would be living still. Would justice not be served if, in addition to Anton Benning, Counselor Ochoa, and Lord Ketz-Alkwat, I should also be held accountable for the chain of circumstances that led to Mrs. Hatfield's death? Where does it truly end, Alexander? If we were to trace back the causes and effects of every unjust act, wouldn't we be faced with an endless continuation of causes? Or would we at long last and after many acts of retribution finally be faced with an ultimate cause of injustice? I don't know the answer to this question, but I find it difficult to believe that we would. And if we did, I'm not sure the reality we live in would survive that final act of justice."

I turned from the waves to face the elf. "Once again, you seek to overwhelm the small world I live in with a bigger picture, one so big that it exceeds my limited imagination." I shook my head. "None of that matters to me. Cindy got the justice she was looking for, and I helped her get it. That's what's important, and that's *all* that's important."

"What do you think happens to her now that she's free from her attachment to this world, if she is indeed free? It may surprise you to learn that elves have an insatiable curiosity about death, perhaps because death is an incomprehensible and utterly final act. And yet after debating the subject for millennia, we know little about it. I once encouraged you to think of yourself as a drop of water in the ocean, to be both the drop of water and the ocean. Perhaps that's what death is. What about Mrs. Hatfield? Do you suppose that she is now free to immerse herself into a larger world? To be simultaneously the individual drop of water and the entirety of the infinite and eternal ocean? To cease being the questioner and to instead be the answer to the final question? Perhaps that is the true justice you have helped bring to her."

I turned back to the waves. "I don't know. Does death have any answers for a joe like me? All I know is there's no coming back from it, not really. Cindy didn't beat death. Her ghost isn't really her, and it has no place in the world of the living. I hope that I helped send her on her way. As for my own death, it will happen soon enough, and all I can do is put it off as long as possible. I can wait a long time to find out if death has any meaning for me."

"Is it meaning you're looking for? Are you hoping to find meaning in your life while you yet live? Do you think such a thing is possible?"

I thought about that. "I'm not looking for anything. But while I'm alive, I've got all the meaning I need right here amongst the living. Life is full of little mysteries, and I've made it my purpose to solve the mysteries that are presented to me. These big questions you talk about? The answers might not even exist. I deal in small questions, like, 'How did Cindy die?' That's enough for me. Well, almost enough. No one paid me for answering that question, and I've still gotta figure out a way to pay my next month's rent."

I continued to watch the waves until the world faded into nothingness, my consciousness fading with it.

***

tap tap tap tap tap

I woke with a groan, the scent of Mrs. Shipper's perfume in my head.

tap tap tap tap tap

I opened my eyes and stared in the direction of my window. The blinds were drawn, and the darkness in my bedroom was nearly absolute. I didn't want to open those blinds.

tap tap tap tap

I let out a long breath and sat up. It didn't look like I was going to get anymore sleep that night.

tap tap tap tap tap tap tap tap tap tap—

"All right!" I shouted. "Keep your shirt on, sister."

I slipped on a robe on my way to the window. When I opened the blinds, Cindy's disembodied face was staring at me through the glass. Or through me. She gave no indication that she knew I was there. Thinking I might be dreaming, I tried to will the rest of her into view, but to no avail. I blinked and continued to see nothing but a clear face framed by strawberry-blond curls. It was disconcerting, to say the least.

"Cindy?" I breathed. "Is that you?"

Her eyes focused on mine, looking frightened. The blackness outside the window shimmered, and I could just make out the softly glowing outline of Cindy's body behind a veil of darkness. It was as if she had poked her head through the surface of a still pond, or through a rip in the night sky.

"Cindy?" I repeated.

A hint of a smile appeared on her face, and her nostrils flared. "Alex? Is that you?" Although her lips were moving, I heard her voice in my head. "Why am I here?"

"I don't know. Where do you think you should be?"

The specter's eyes looked this way and that. "I was going somewhere. But I stopped. Here. I don't know why." Her eyes focused on mine. "You are holding me back."

"Me? I helped you find out why you died. Do you remember?"

Cindy's jaw set. "Benning. He told Puppy to kill the elf. Puppy built a bomb. But the bomb killed Puppy. And I... I..."

I sighed. "You tried to save him. We got you all wrong, Cindy. All of us, me included. We thought you were just using Papadopouli. We thought he was nothing to you but a plaything. A toy. But you ran into a fire to save him. You cared for him."

Cindy smiled, remembering. "I loved him."

I didn't want to say what I had to say next, but I knew I had to for Cindy's sake. I knew why she was trapped outside my bedroom window.

I opened the window, and a breeze came in from the night, cool, but pleasant.

"Cindy," I began. "Do you remember coming to the warehouse looking for Papadopouli? For Puppy?"

Cindy's smile widened. "Puppy came for me."

I looked into the eyes of the specter, seeing Cindy. "No. You're wrong, Cindy. He didn't come for you. He came to the warehouse to kill the elf."

Cindy shook her head. "Puppy came for me. He..."

"You got to the warehouse before he did, and you were taken through the wall, remember?"

Cindy's smile disappeared, and her face grew hard. A cold gust of wind chilled the air.

"You were in the lab when Papadopouli showed up. They were holding you in the bathroom. You couldn't get out, but you could hear them talking. You heard them say that Papadopouli—Puppy—was in the warehouse."

"Puppy came for me. He..."

"You shouted for him. You called out to him."

Cindy's eyes widened in panic. "I'm in here, Puppy! Puppy! I'm in here! Puppy? What are you doing? Come and get me! Puppy!"

"You called for him, but he didn't hear you. But you knew how to make him hear you, didn't you."

Her face hardened with determination. "Our secret line. No one knows."

"That's right, Cindy. The two of you had a secret way to talk to each other. You had cell phones with secret numbers. Burner phones. Only the two of you knew about them. You called each other on these secret phones so that no one would know you were talking with each other."

"I called him so he would know where I was. So he would come for me." She frowned. "But he didn't answer. He didn't come."

"He used his burner phone as a detonator to trigger the bomb." I bit my lip. "I'm sorry, Cindy. But when you called him to tell him where you were, your call caused his phone to detonate the bomb. He died in the blast."

"I.... He...."

I expected Cindy to deny it. I expected rage, accompanied by freezing winds and deadly curses. What I didn't expect was for the confusion and anger to leave Cindy's face and be replaced by an expression of calm acceptance.

"Yes," she said aloud, her voice sounding pleasant and gentle. "I see." She looked at me and smiled. "I see it now. It is as you say."

"Are you okay, Cindy?"

She turned her soft brown eyes on me. "I think I can go now. Thank you."

"Uh... sure. You're welcome. I guess."

I'd been wrong. I'd thought it was Cindy's desire to solve the mystery of her own death that was keeping her from proceeding on her journey. But all along it had been her desire to find out why Papadopouli had been killed that had kept her here. She knew now, and no longer had a reason to stay.

She looked past me then, and her eyes lost their focus. When she looked back at me, there was no recognition in her expression. "Hello," she said, her lips moving, and her voice sounding in my head. "Do I know you?"

A chill formed in the pit of my stomach. "It's me, Alex. Don't you recognize me?"

She stared at my face for a few moments before her lips again moved. "You look familiar, but.... Have we met?"

"We knew each other, briefly. You don't remember?"

Her eyes narrowed. "I'm sorry. I don't seem to be able to remember much of anything." She looked past me into my room. "I'm not sure why I'm here."

"Were you going somewhere?" I asked.

A hand appeared, and she rested a finger on her chin. "I think so. I don't know where, but it's somewhere I need to be."

I fought down a lump that had risen in my throat. "Do you want to go there?"

She thought for a moment before answering. "Yes. Yes, I think I do. Something was stopping me from going, but, whatever it was, it's gone now." Her lips stretched into an easy smile.

"You're okay then?" I asked. "Are you happy?"

Her nose crinkled. "Happy? I'm not sure. I don't know what happy feels like. I'm not sad, though. I feel like when I get to where I'm going, I'll belong. In the place I'm going to, I mean. Wherever that is. I feel like it's where I'm meant to be. Maybe I'll be happy when I get there."

"Maybe you will," I said.

"Maybe. Maybe it won't matter."

"Maybe Puppy will be there."

Her face lit up for a moment. "Puppy," she said, and she smiled.

"If he is, he'll forgive you. You ran into the fire to help him."

She looked at me with a puzzled expression. "Do I know you? It seems like I should. What did you say your name was?"

"Alex. Alexander Southerland."

"My name is... Huh. I can't remember." She frowned.

"Do you remember Alu? Or Puppy?"

She thought about it. "I don't think so, no."

"Anton Benning?"

She shook her head. "No, sorry."

"Do you remember anything?" I asked.

A soft smile came to the specter's face. "No, I don't. It seems like that should bother me, but it doesn't. Somehow it seems all right that I don't remember. That I leave it behind." She looked around her, as if getting her bearings. "I think I should go now." Her face lit up with a smile I'd seen often in my waking dreams and would never forget. "It was nice meeting you, Alex."

"It was nice meeting you, too. I hope you find happiness in the place you're going."

Her face went blank, and I wasn't sure she was still aware of me. She looked beyond me, and as she did, her lips moved, and I heard her voice clearly in my head: "Elves," she said. "Elves, and elves, and elves. So many elves." And though her lips continued to move for another few moments, I could no longer hear what she was saying.

"What was that? What did you say about elves?"

But the specter had turned away from me and was staring into the distance at something I couldn't see, not even with my elf-enhanced awareness. I called for her again, but she didn't seem to hear. I called one last time. "Hello? Can you hear me?" The specter drifted away from me into the swirling darkness, and as it did, the darkness slowly consumed the spectral image.

"The elves!" I called after her through the open window. "What were you saying about the elves!"

Cindy's specter faded into the night, and my words followed her down the dark, dark road she had taken. I wondered where it would lead her. Leiti La'aka had told me that there was only one destination for the dead, but it was different for everyone. Or something like that. I didn't understand what that meant. Maybe these different lands of the dead are simply stopping points on the way to complete oblivion and utter non-existence. Who knows. But as I looked into the darkness that had taken Cindy, I told myself that if there was justice in death, Cindy and Papadopouli would find happiness someplace far away, perhaps with each other. It was a pleasing thought, and it gave me hope.

And yet, standing there in the window extending my elf-enhanced vision far into the night, extending my gaze as far as it could go, searching for a glimpse of that world beyond all other worlds, all I could see was the never-ending darkness.

When light began to glow on the horizon, I stopped searching, closed the window, and went back to bed. The rent would be due in a couple of days, and I didn't know how I was going to be able to pay it.

Epilogue: Benedict Shade

The ebony cat called Void leaped from the balcony railing to the roof of the harbormaster's shack and stood still as a statue under the star-filled sky. Sensing no threats, Void padded noiselessly to the front of the shack, where she lowered himself to her stomach and listened to the voices coming from within. Some five minutes later, the small, thin human man with the checkered hat emerged from the shack and peddled away on a bicycle. Immediately after he left, a go-fast rig belonging to a known smuggler fired up its engine and pushed its way out of the harbor. Void transmitted this information to another cat, who was crouched beneath a bush across the parking lot some thirty yards away.

The second cat, a larger one called Lucky, was as black as the first, but had only a nub for a tail and was not a good climber. He was, however, fast on his feet, and when the little man passed by on his bike, Lucky chased after him.

Void climbed down from the roof of the shack and made her way toward a nearby café. When she was in range, she opened her mind to the remainder of the collective clowder: ten cats merged into the shape of a human man dressed in black from the stocking cap on his head to the rubber-soled sneakers on his feet. His long-sleeved buttonless shirt fitted him loosely, a size too large for his frame. The man was tucked into a corner booth in an all-night café, sitting by himself and pouring cream into a cup of black chai. He absently stirred the milky chai with a spoon, pondering the information he had received from the cat, wondering what to do about it. He scratched at the stubble on his chin with a four-fingered left hand and picked up his teacup with his five-fingered right one.

Presently, Void leaped into the café through an open window, walked up to the man, and merged into the collective. The man's chest swelled, and his shirt no longer seemed quite as loose as it had before.

A while later, one of the other café patrons decided he had consumed enough strong coffee to counteract the rum he'd spent most of the night imbibing and, after paying his bill, stumbled toward the front door. Lucky slipped through the door when the man opened it. He made his way to the man in the booth and disappeared up his pant leg. The twelve-cat collective was now complete in body and mind, and the shapeshifting man's shirt stretched tight across his chest.

The shapeshifter took a sip of chai and added more cream until the chai once again filled the teacup to the brim. He knew now that the man on the bicycle had disappeared into the labyrinthine slum that sprawled off the harbor, pedaling at a pace too fast for even the swift-footed Lucky to follow. That was okay. The man in the café booth didn't need the little man anymore. The item he'd possessed—an ancient dagger with a strangely carved ivory hilt—was on a smuggler's boat, making its way to a faraway destination.

Unfortunately, the man idly sipping chai in the booth wasn't the only one seeking the dagger. Extremely powerful people were desperate to retrieve it, desperate to contain the secrets that the dagger could reveal. As the man stared out the window, he saw a car speeding down the street outside the café toward the harbor. In a few minutes, men—dangerous men—a human and a troll, would emerge from the car and take the harbormaster into custody. The harbormaster would reveal everything he knew, hoping the dangerous men would spare his life if he talked. The man in the booth knew the harbormaster's chances of surviving were slim.

After finishing his chai in three gulps, the man slapped a few bills on the table and slipped out of the booth.

The dwarf behind the counter called out to him. "Calling it a night, Bennie?"

Benedict Shade nodded. "I'm going to be gone for a while, Ranbir. In fact, I think this is goodbye. I'll miss your chai. And maybe I'll miss you, too, you little bastard. Just a little."

The dwarf grunted. "I'll miss your business. And watch who you're calling a 'little bastard.' I don't mind the bastard part; that much is true enough. But 'little'? Call me that again and I'll bust your kneecap!" He flashed Shade a smile through his beard that bunched his cheeks into two ruddy lumps. "Where ya goin', anyway, if you don't mind me asking. And what's your fuckin' hurry?"

"Tolanica," Shade said. "But don't spread that around."

The dwarf shook his head. "So, the harbor patrol finally caught you with the goods, eh? What do you want me to tell them if they stop by for a visit?"

"Tell them to kiss your fat ass. No, don't do that. It's not the harbor patrol that's after me. Not this time. I'm on to something big. No, this time it's the Dragon Lord's hatchet men."

The dwarf's eyes widened, and he stopped wiping down his counter. "Lord Agni's flaming pecker—not the LIA!"

"I'm afraid so. And not only agents from Lord Agni's investigation agency, but from the Tolanican LIA, too. This one's big, Ranbir. Forget what I said earlier. If they come by, don't get cute. Tell them everything you know. Everything. They'll already know where I'm going, so don't even try to hide that from them. Tell them I'm the slimiest, rottenest son of a bitch you ever had the misfortune to know, and that you hope they catch me and string me up by my balls."

"Lord's flaming pecker! Whatever you say, Bennie. Good luck to you. Sounds like you're gonna need it."

"You're right about that. And best of luck to you and your sons, too. I've enjoyed drinking your tea and hearing your stories these past months." Shade gave the dwarf a brief salute and hurried out the door.

Shade knew this day was coming, and he was prepared for it. Everything he needed was packed in a duffel, and he had enough dough to get by. He'd hoped to get his hands on the dagger before it was shipped off, but he'd been too late—the artifact was already on its way to Tolanica. To Yerba City. Shade smiled. Yerba City wasn't far from his home in New Helvetia, a home he'd left months ago when he'd discovered the precious artifact he wanted to collect was in Sindhu. It would be good to get back.

But he'd have to use every resource he had to catch up to the dagger before it reached the man whose name and address Void had discovered that evening, and he'd be dogged by the LIA every step of the way. Their involvement was unfortunate, but inevitable.

The man the dagger had been shipped to was an unknown, a wild card, probably some crook with no idea what he was in for, or how much danger he'd be in if the dagger got to him before Shade could intercept it. Shade wondered why the little man—the notorious thief known as the Rat—had sent the dagger off to him. Lord's balls—if this man was a friend of the Rat's, the thief certainly wasn't doing him any favors!

Shade's eyes darted this way and that as he made his way down the street, hugging the shadows and moving just fast enough to avoid attracting the wrong kind of attention. It was a habit ingrained in him by long years of practice until it had become second nature: covering a surprising amount of distance in a remarkably short amount of time, practically invisible to anyone not specifically watching for him. It took him only minutes to reach the docks and find his skiff.

After sending a couple of cats through the boat to ensure no unwanted visitors were aboard, he cast off and steered for the open sea.

Once out of range of the harbor lights, he gunned the engine and leaned back in his skipper's seat as the skiff glided over the waves in the clear night. The shipment he sought was ahead of him, and he wouldn't be flying out of Sindhu until morning. The artifact would doubtless reach Yerba City before he did, but he hoped he could get to the package before it was delivered to the intended recipient.

From the rooftop of the harbormaster's shack, the sharp-eared Void had overheard the Rat pass the name and address of the recipient to the harbormaster before the package was added to the bag the smuggler's ship was carrying off the continent, and she'd brought that information back to the shapeshifter's collective mind. Shade turned the recipient's name over in his head, planting it in his memory: Southerland, he repeated to himself. Alexander Southerland. Apparently, the mug was a small-time private investigator.

THE END

Keep your eyes peeled for the first book of a new series featuring Shade the Collector

Thank You!

Thank you for reading *A Specter Raps on My Windowpane*. If you enjoyed it, I hope that you will consider writing a review—even a short one—on Amazon, Goodreads, BookBub, or your favorite book site.

All of my books, including this one, are self-published, and I'm proud to be an indie author. But without a traditional publishing company to market my books, I am dependent on the good will of my readers. Publishing is still driven by word of mouth, and every single voice helps. I owe a big debt of thanks to anyone and everyone who has read my books and taken the time to review them. Every review—good or bad—helps me in the end. Readers have an abundance of choices, and I appreciate every one of you who chose to read something I wrote. It's been a great ride, and I can't wait for you to see what's coming next!

Acknowledgements

First and foremost, as always, I want to thank Rita, my co-creator, co-editor, sounding board, best friend, wife, partner, inspiration, and hero. It wouldn't be nearly as much fun without her!

A big thank you to my parents, Bill and Carolyn, to my sisters, Teri and Karen, and to my cousin Juliana. I can't overstate how much support I get from my family, and I appreciate every bit of it.

I want to thank Elaine for her enthusiastic and thorough beta-reading.

My thanks once again to Assaph Mehr, author of the fantastic *Stories of Togas, Daggers, and Magic* series. He has beta-read all of my books except the first one, and I am a better writer because of it.

Another big thank you to Duffy Weber, the most talented and congenial audiobook producer/narrator in the world. Check out his Drachen audiobooks and prepare to be dazzled!

I've been supported by a number of readers and reviewers on Twitter and other social media—too many to mention—but I want to issue a special shoutout to Charlie Cavendish of FanFiAddict who has gone out of his way to spread the word about my books. Thanks, man—I appreciate you!

I thank anyone who ever gave me the slightest bit of encouragement or support. I've received a lot of great advice, and, if I didn't take it, that's my fault, not yours.

About the Author

My parents raised me right. Any mistakes I made were my own. Hopefully, I learned from them.

I earned a doctorate in medieval European history at the University of California Santa Barbara. Go Gauchos! I taught world history at a couple of colleges before settling into a private college prep high school in Monterey. After I retired, I began to write an urban fantasy series featuring hardboiled private eye Alexander Southerland as he cruises through the mean streets of Yerba City and interacts with trolls, femme fatales, shapeshifters, witches, and corrupt city officials.

I am happily married to my wife, Rita. The two of us can be found most days pounding the pavement in our running shoes. We both love living in Monterey, California, with its foggy mornings, ocean breezes, and year-round mild temperatures. Rita listens to all of my ideas and reads all of my work. Her advice is beyond value. In return, I make her coffee and tea whenever she wants it. It's a pretty sweet deal. We have two cats now, Cinderella and her new pal Prince. Both of them are happy to stay indoors. Cinderella continues to demand that we tell her how pretty she is, especially since we brought an interloper into the fold. Prince is excitable and loves to play for hours at a time until he drops from exhaustion.